"THANK YOU FOR LETTING ME COME."

Michael did not look in the least humiliated as he entered the luxurious library where Starr had chosen to receive him. He came forward to greet her just as if she had not cut him dead the very last time they met.

"Oh, that is all right," she said graciously; "won't you sit down? I am always glad to do a favor for a friend of my childhood."

It was a sentence that she had rehearsed many times in her mind, but somehow she felt that her voice was trembling and she had miserably failed in what she had meant to do. She felt strangely ashamed of her attitude, with those two clear soulful eyes looking straight at her. It reminded her of the way he had looked when he told her in the Florida chapel long ago that nobody but herself had ever kissed him—and she kissed him then. The thought made her cheeks rosy, and her society air deserted her entirely. It was a crazy thought. What was the matter with her anyway, and why did she feel so unnerved?

Bantam Books by Grace Livingston Hill
Ask your bookseller for the books you have missed

LO, MICHAEL

Grace Livingston Hill

BANTAM BOOKS
TORONTO • NEW YORK • LONDON • SYDNEY • AUCKLAND

LO, MICHAEL

*A Bantam Book / published by arrangement with
Harper & Row, Publishers Inc.*

PRINTING HISTORY
*First published in 1913
Bantam edition / July 1986*

ISBN 0-553-25806-0

Published simultaneously in the United States and Canada

PRINTED IN THE UNITED STATES OF AMERICA

KR   0 9 8 7 6 5 4 3 2

Chapter 1

"Hi, there! Mikky! Look out!"

It was an alert voice that called from a huddled group of urchins in the forefront of the crowd, but the child flashed past without heeding, straight up the stone steps where stood a beautiful baby smiling on the crowd. With his bundle of papers held high, and the late morning sunlight catching his tangle of golden hair, Mikky flung himself toward the little one. The sharp crack of a revolver from the opposite curbstone was simultaneous with their fall. Then all was confusion.

It was a great stone house on Madison Avenue where the crowd had gathered. An automobile stood before the door, having but just come quietly up, and the baby girl, three years old, in white velvet and ermines, with her dark curls framed by an ermine-trimmed hood, and a bunch of silk rosebuds poised coquettishly over the brow vying with the soft roses of her cheeks, came out the door with her nurse for her afternoon ride. Just an instant the nurse stepped back to the hall for the wrap she had dropped, leaving the baby alone, her dark eyes shining like stars under the straight dark brows, as she looked gleefully out on the world. It was just at that instant, as if by magic, that the crowd assembled.

Perhaps it would be better to say that it was just at that minute that the crowd focused itself upon the particular house where the baby daughter of the president of a great defaulting bank lived. More or less all the morning, men had been gathering, passing the house, looking up with troubled or threatening faces toward the richly laced windows, shaking menacing heads, muttering imprecations,

1

but there had been no disturbance, and no concerted crowd until the instant the baby appeared.

The police had been more or less vigilant all the morning but had seen nothing to disturb them. The inevitable small boy had also been in evidence, with his natural instinct for excitement. Mikky with his papers often found himself in that quarter of a bright morning, and the starry eyes and dark curls of the little child were a vision for which he often searched the great windows as he passed this particular house; but the man with the evil face on the other side of the street, resting a shaking hand against the lamppost, and sighting the baby with a vindictive eye, had never been seen there before. It was Mikky who noticed him first; Mikky, who circling around him innocently had heard his imprecations against the rich, who caught the low-breathed oath as the baby appeared, and saw the ugly look on the man's face. With instant alarm he had gone to the other side of the street, his eye upon the offender, and had been the first to see the covert motion, the flash of the hidden weapon and to fear the worst.

But a second behind him his street companions saw his danger and cried out, too late. Mikky had flung himself in front of the beautiful baby, covering her with his great bundle of papers, and his own ragged, neglected little body, and receiving the bullet intended for her, went down with her as she fell.

Instantly all was confusion.

A child's cry—a woman's scream—the whistle of the police—the angry roar of the crowd who were like a pack of wild animals that had tasted blood. Stones flew, flung by men whose wrongs had smothered in their breasts and bred a fury of hate and murder. Women were trampled upon. Two of the great plate-glass windows crashed as the flying missiles entered the magnificent home, regardless of the costly lace and velvet hangings.

The chauffeur attempted to run his car around the corner but was held up at once, and discreetly took himself out of the way, leaving the car in the hands of the mob who swarmed into it and over it, ruthlessly disfiguring it in their wrath. There was the loud report of exploding tires, the ripping of costly leather cushions, the groaning of fine machinery put to torture as the fury of the mob took vengeance on the car to show what they would like to do to its owner.

Gone into bankruptcy! He! With a great electric car like that, and servants to serve him! With his baby attired in the trappings of a queen and his house swathed in lace that had taken the eyesight from many a poor lace-maker! He! Gone into bankruptcy, and slipping away scot-free, while the men he had robbed stood helpless on his sidewalk, hungry and shabby and hopeless because the pittances they had put away in his bank, the result of slavery and sacrifice, were gone—hopelessly gone! And they were too old, or too tired, or too filled with hate, to earn it again.

The crowd surged and seethed madly, now snarling like beasts, now rumbling portentously like a storm, now babbling like an infant; a great emotional frenzy, throbbing with passion, goaded beyond fear, desperate with need; leaderless, and therefore the more dangerous.

The very sight of the luxurious baby with her dancing eyes and happy smiles "rolling in luxury," called to mind their own little puny darling, grimy with neglect, lean with want, and hollow-eyed with knowledge aforetime. Why should one baby be pampered and another starved? Why did the bank president's daughter have any better right to those wonderful furs and the exultant smile than their own babies? A glimpse into the depths of the rooms beyond the sheltering plate glass and drapery showed greater contrast even than they had dreamed between this home and the bare tenements they had left that morning, where the children were crying for bread and the wife shivering with cold. Because they loved their own their anger burned the fiercer, and for love of their pitiful scrawny babies that flowerlike child in the doorway was hated with all the vehemence of their untamed natures. Their every breath cried out for vengeance, and with the brute instinct they sought to hurt the man through his child, because they had been hurt by the wrong done to their children.

The policeman's whistle had done its work, however. The startled inmates of the house had drawn the beautiful baby and her small preserver within the heavy carven doors, and borne them back to safety before the unorganized mob.

had time to force their way in. Amid the outcry and the disorder no one had noticed that Mikky had disappeared until his small band of companions set up an outcry, but even then no one heard.

The mounted police had arrived, and orders were being given. The man who had fired the shot was arrested, handcuffed and marched away. The people were ordered right and left, and the officer's horses rode ruthlessly through the masses. Law and order had arrived and there was nothing for the downtrodden but to flee.

In a very short time the square was cleared and guarded by a large force. Only the newspapermen came and went without challenge. The threatening groups of men who still hovered about withdrew further and further. The wrecked automobile was patched up and taken away to the garage. The street became quiet, and by and by some workmen came hurriedly, importantly, and put in temporary protections where the window glass had been broken.

Yet through it all a little knot of ragged newsboys stood their ground in front of the house. Until quiet was restored they had evaded each renewed command of officer or passerby, and stayed there, whispering now and again in excited groups and pointing up to the house. Finally a tall policeman approached them:

"Clear out of this, kids!" he said not unkindly. "Here's no place for you. Clear out. Do you hear me? You can't stay here no longer."

Then one of them wheeled upon him. He was the tallest of them all, with fierce little freckled face and flashing black eyes in which all the evil passions of four generations back looked out upon a world that had always been harsh. He was commonly known as Fighting Buck.

"Mikky's in dare. He's hurted. We kids can't leave Mick alone. He might be dead."

Just at that moment a physician's runabout drew up to the door, and the policeman fell back to let him pass into the house. Hard upon him followed the bank president in a closed carriage attended by several men in uniform who escorted him to the door and touched their hats politely as he vanished within. Around the corners scowling faces haunted the shadows, and murmured imprecations were scarcely withheld in spite of the mounted officers. A shot was fired down the street, and several policemen hurried away. But through it all the boys stood their ground.

"Mikky's in dare. He's hurted. I seen him fall. Maybe he's deaded. We kids want to take him away. Mikky didn't do nothin', Mikky jes' tried to save der little kid. Mikky's a good'un. You get the folks to put Mikky out here. We kids'll take him away."

The policeman finally attended to the fierce pleading of the ragamuffins. Two or three newspapermen joined the knot around them and the story was presently written up with all the racy touches that the writers of the hour know how to use. Before night Buck, with his fierce black brows drawn in helpless defiance was adorning the evening papers in various attitudes as the different snapshots portrayed him, and the little group of newsboys and bootblacks and good-for-nothings that stood around him figured for once in the eyes of the whole city.

The small band held their place until forcibly removed. Some of them were barefoot, and stood shivering on the cold stones, their little sickly, grimy faces blue with anxiety and chill.

The doctor came out of the house just as the last one, Buck, was being marched off with loud-voiced protest. He eyed the boy, and quickly understood the situation.

"Look here!" he called to the officer. "Let me speak to the youngster. He's a friend, I suppose, of the boy that was shot?"

The officer nodded.

"Well, boy, what's all this fuss about?" He looked kindly, keenly into the defiant black eyes of Buck.

"Mikky's hurted—mebbe deaded. I wants to take him away from dare," he burst forth sullenly. "We kids can't go off 'n' leave Mikky in dare wid de rich guys. Mikky didn't do no harm. He's jes tryin' to save de kid."

"Mikky. Is that the boy that took the shot in place of the little girl?

The boy nodded and looked anxiously into the kindly face of the doctor.

"Yep. Hev you been in dare? Did youse see Mikky? He's got yaller hair. Is Mikky deaded?"

"No, he isn't dead," said the physician kindly, "but he's pretty badly hurt. The ball went through his shoulder and arm, and came mighty near some vital places. I've just been fixing him up comfortably, and he'll be all right after a bit, but he's got to lie very still right where he is and be taken care of."

"We kids'll take care o' Mikky!" said Buck proudly. "He tooked care of Jinney when she was sick, an' we'll take care o' Mikky, all right, all right. You jes' brang him out an' we'll fetch a wheelbarry an' cart him off'n yer han's. Mikky wouldn't want to be in dare wid de rich guys."

"My dear fellow," said the doctor, quite touched by the earnestness in Buck's eyes, "that's very good of you, I'm sure, and Mikky ought to appreciate his friends, but he's being taken care of perfectly right where he is, and he couldn't be moved. It might kill him to move him, and if he stays where he is he will get well. I'll tell you what I'll do," he added as he saw the lowering distress in the dumb eyes before him, "I'll give you a bulletin every day. You be here tonight at five o'clock when I come out of the house and I'll tell you just how he is. Then you needn't worry about him. He's in a beautiful room lying on a great big white bed and he has everything nice around him, and when I came away he was sleeping. I can take him a message for you when I go in tonight, if you like."

Half doubtfully the boy looked at him.

"Will you tell Mikky to drop us down word ef he wants anythin'? Will you ask him ef he don't want us to get him out?"

"Sure!" said the doctor in kindly amusement. "You trust me and I'll make good. Be here at five o'clock sharp and again tomorrow at quarter to eleven."

"He's only a slum kid!" grumbled the officer. "'Tain't worthwhile to take so much trouble. 'Sides, the folks won't want um botherin' 'round."

"Oh, he's all right!" said the doctor. "He's a friend worth having. You might need one yourself someday, you know. What's your name, boy? Who shall I tell Mikky sent the message?"

"Buck," said the child gravely, "Fightin' Buck, they calls me."

"Very appropriate name, I should think," said the doctor smiling. "Well, run along, Buck, and be here at five o'clock."

Reluctantly the boy moved off. The officer again took up his stand in front of the house and quiet was restored to the street.

Meantime, in the great house consternation reigned for a time.

The nursemaid had reached the door in time to hear the shot and see the children fall. She barely escaped the bullet herself. She was an old servant of the family and therefore more frightened for her charge than for herself. She had the presence of mind to drag both children inside the house and shut and lock the door immediately, before the seething mob could break in.

The mistress of the house fell in a dead faint as they carried her little laughing daughter up the stairs and a man and a maid followed with the boy who was unconscious. The servants rushed hither and thither; the housekeeper had the coolness to telepone the bank president what had happened, and to send for the family physician. No one knew yet just who was hurt or how much. Mikky had been brought inside because he blocked the doorway, and there was need for instantly shutting the door. If it had been easier to shove him out the nursemaid would probably have done that. But once inside common humanity bade them look after the unconscious boy's needs, and besides, no one knew as yet just exactly what part Mikky had played in the small tragedy of the morning.

"Where shall we take him?" said the man to the maid as they reached the second floor with their unconscious burden.

"Not here, Thomas. Here's no place for him. He's as dirty as a pig. I can't think what come over Morton to pull him inside, anyway. His own could have tended to him. Besides, such is better dead!"

They hurried on past the luxurious rooms belonging to the lady of the mansion; up the next flight of stairs, and Norah passed by the bathroom door where the full light of the hall windows fell upon the grimy little figure of the child they carried.

Norah the maid uttered an exclamation.

"He's not fit fer any place in this house. Look at his clothes. They'll have to be cut off 'n him, and he needs to go in the bathtub before he can be laid anywheres. Let's put him in the bathroom, and do you go an' call Morton. She got him in here and she'll have to bathe him. And bring me a pair of scissors. I'll mebbe have to cut the cloes off'n him, they're so filthy. Ach! The little beast!"

Thomas, glad to be rid of his burden, dropped the boy on the bathroom floor and made off to call Morton.

Norah, with little knowledge and less care, took no thought for the life of her patient. She was intent on making him fit to put between her clean sheets. She found the tattered garments none too tenacious in their hold to the little, half-naked body. One or two buttons and a string were their only attachments. Norah pulled them off with gingerly fingers, and holding them at arm's length took them to the bathroom window whence she pitched them down into the paved court below, that led to the kitchen regions. Thomas could burn them, or put them on the ash pile by and by. She was certain they would never go on again, and wondered how they had been made to hold together this last time.

Morton had not come yet, but Norah discovering a pool of blood under the little bare shoulder, lifted him quickly into the great white bathtub and turned on the warm water. There was no use wasting time, and getting blood on white tiles that she would have to scrub. She was not unkind but she hated dirt, and partly supporting the child with one arm she applied herself to scrubbing him as vigorously as possible with the other hand. The shock of the water not being very warm at first, brought returning consciousness to the boy for a moment, in one long shuddering sigh. The eyelashes trembled for an instant on the white cheeks, and his eyes opened; gazed dazedly, then wildly, on the strange surroundings, the water, and the vigorous Irishwoman who had him in her power. He threw his arms up with a struggling motion, gasped as if with suddenly pain and lost consciousness again, relaxing once more into the strong red arm that held him. It was just at this critical moment that Morton entered the bathroom.

Morton was a trim, apple-cheeked Scotswoman of about thirty years, with neat yellow-brown hair coiled on the top of her head, a cheerful tilt to her freckled nose, and eyes so blue that in company with her rosy cheeks one thought at once of a flag. Heather and integrity exhalted from her very being, flamed from her cheeks, spoke from her loyal, stubborn chin, and looked from her trustworthy eyes. She had been with the bank president's baby ever since the little star-eyed creature came into the world.

"Och! Look ye at the poor wee'un!" she exclaimed. "Ye're hurtin' him, Norah! Ye shouldn't have bathed him the noo! Ye should've waited the docther's comin'. Ye'll mebbe kin kill him."

"Ach! Get out with yer soft talk!" said Norah, scrubbing the more vigorously. "Did yez suppose I'll be afther havin' all this filth in the nice clean sheets? Get ye to work an' he'p me. Do ye hold 'im while I schrub!"

She shifted the boy into the gentler arms of the nurse, and went to splashing all the harder. Then suddenly, before the nurse could protest, she had dashed a lot of foamy suds on the golden head and was scrubbing that with all her might.

"Och, Norah!" cried the nurse in alarm. "You shouldn't a done that! Ye'll surely kill the bairn. Look at his poor wee shoulder a bleedin', and his little face so white an' still. Have ye no mercy at all, Norah? Rinse off that suds at once, an' dry him softly. What'll the docther be sayin' to ye fer all this I can't think. There, my poor bairnie," she crooned to the child, softly drawing him closer as though he was conscious.

"There, there my bairnie, it'll soon be over. It'll be all right in just a minute, poor wee b'y! Poor wee b'y! There! There—"

But Norah did her perfect work, and made the little lean body glistening white as polished marble, while the heavy hair hung limp like pale golden silk.

The two women carried him to a bed in a large room at the back of the house, not far from the nursery, and laid him on a blanket, with his shoulder stanched with soft linen rags. Morton was softly drying his hair and cooning to the child—although he was unconscious—begging Norah to put the blanket over him lest he catch cold, and Norah was still vigorously drying his feet unmindful of Morton's pleading, when the doctor entered with a trained nurse. The boy lay white and still upon the blanket as the two women, startled, drew back from their task. The body, clean now, and beautifully shaped, might have been marble except for the delicate blue veins in wrists and temples. In spite of signs of privation and lack of nutrition there was about the boy a showing of strength in well developed muscles, and it went to the heart to see him lying helpless so, with his drenched gold hair and his closed eyes. The white limbs did not quiver, the lifeless fingers drooped limply, the white chest did not stir with any sign of breath, and yet the tender lips that curved in a cupid's bow, were not altogether gone white.

"What a beautiful child!" exclaimed the nurse involuntarily as she came near the bed. "He looks like a young god!"

"He's far more likely to be a young devil," said the doctor grimly, leaning over him with practiced eyes, and laying a listening ear to the quiet breast. Then he started back.

"He's cold as ice! What have you been doing to him? It wasn't a case of drowning, was it? You haven't been giving him a bath at such a time as this, have you? Did you want to kill the kid outright?"

"Oauch, the poor wee b'y!" sobbed Morton under her breath, her blue eyes drenched with tears that made them like blue lakes. "He's like to my own we b'y that I lost when he was a baby," she explained in apology to the trained nurse who was not, however, regarding her in the least.

Norah had vanished frightened to consult with Thomas. It was Morton who brought the things the doctor called for, and showed the nurse where to put her belongings; and after everything was done and the boy was comfortable and brought back to consciousness, it was she who stood at the foot of the bed and smiled upon him first in this new world to which he opened his eyes.

His eyes were blue, heavenly blue and dark, but they were great with a brave fear as he glanced about on the strange faces. He looked like a wild bird, caught in a kindly hand—a bird whose instincts held him still because he saw no way of flight, but whose heart was beating frightfully against his captor's fingers. He looked from side to side of the room, and made a motion to rise from the pillow. It was a wild, furtive motion, as of one who has often been obliged to fly for safety, yet still has unlimited courage. There was also in his glance the gentle harmlessness and appeal of the winged thing that has been caught.

"Well, youngster, you had a pretty close shave," said the doctor jovially, "but you'll pull through all right! You feel comfortable now?"

The nurse was professionally quiet.

"Poor wee b'y!" murmured Morton, her eyes drenched again.

The boy looked from one to another doubtfully. Suddenly remembrance dawned upon him and comprehension entered his glance. He looked about the room and toward the door. There was question in his eyes that turned on the doctor but his lips fromed no words. He looked at Morton, and knew her for the nurse of his baby. Suddenly he smiled, and that smile seemed to light up the whole room, and filled the heart of Morton with joy unspeakable. It seemed to her it was the smile of her own lost baby come back to shine upon her. The tears welled up and the blue lakes ran over. The boy's face was most lovely when he smiled.

"Where is—de little kid?" It was Morton whose face he searched anxiously as he framed the eager question, and the woman's intuition taught her how to answer.

"She's safe in her own wee crib takin' her morning nap. She's just new over," answered the woman reassuringly.

Still the eyes were not satisfied.

"Did she," he began slowly, "get—hurted?"

"No, my bairnie, she's all safe and sound as ever. It was your own self that saved her life."

The boy's face lit up and he turned from one to another contentedly. His smile said: "Then I'm glad." But not a word spoke his shy lips.

"You're a hero, kid!" said the doctor huskily. But the boy knew little about heroes and did not comprehend.

The nurse by this time had donned her uniform and rattled up starchily to take her place at the bedside, and

Morton and the doctor went away, the doctor to step once
more into the lady's room below to see if she was feeling
quite herself again after her faint.

The nurse leaned over the boy with a glass and spoon.
He looked at it curiously, unknowingly. It was a situation
entirely outside his experience.

"Why don't you take your medicine?" asked the nurse.

The boy looked at the spoon again as it approached his
lips and opened them to speak.

"Is—"

In went the medicine and the boy nearly choked, but
he understood and smiled.

"A hospital?" he finished.

The nurse laughed.

"No, it's only a house. They brought you in, you know,
when you were hurt out on the steps. You saved the little
girl's life. Didn't you know it?" she said kindly, her heart
won by his smile.

A beautiful look rewarded her.

"Is de little kid—in this house?" he asked slowly, wonderingly. It was as if he had asked if he were in heaven,
there was so much awe in his tone.

"Oh, yes, she's here," answered the nurse lightly.
"Perhaps they'll bring her in to see you sometime. Her father's very grateful. He thinks it showed wonderful courage
in you to risk your life for her sake."

But Mikky comprehended nothing about gratitude.
He only took in the fact that the beautiful baby was in the
house and might come there to see him. He settled to sleep
quite happily with an occasional glad wistful glance toward
the door, as the long lashes sank on the white cheeks, for
the first sleep the boy had ever taken in a clean, white, soft
bed. The prim nurse, softened for once from her precise
attention to duties, stood and looked upon the lovely face of
the sleeping child, wondered what his life had been, and
how the future would be for him. She half pitied him that
the ball had not gone nearer to the vital spot and taken him
to heaven ere he missed the way, so angellike this face appeared in the soft light of the sick room, with the shining
gold hair fluffed back upon the pillow now, like a halo.

Chapter 2

Little Starr Endicott, sleeping in her costly lace-draped crib on her downy embroidered pillow, knew nothing of the sin and hate and murder that rolled in a great wave on the streets outside, and had almost touched her own little life and blotted it out. She knew not the three notable families whose names were interwoven in her own, and whose blood flowed in her tiny veins represented the great hated class of the rich, and that those upon whom they had climbed to this height looked upon them as an evil to be destroyed, nor did she know that she, being the last of the race, and in her name representing them all, was hated most of all.

Starr Delevan Endicott! It was graven upon her tiny pins and locket, upon the circlet of gold that jewelled her finger, upon her brushes and combs; it was broidered upon her dainty garments, and coverlets and cushions, and crooned to her by the adoring Scottish nurse who came of a line that knew and loved an aristocracy. The pride of the house of Starr, the wealth of the house of Delevan, the glory of the house of Endicott, were they not all hers, this one beautiful baby who lay in her arms to tend and to love. So mused Morton as she hummed:

O hush thee, my babie, thy sire was a knight,
Thy mother a ladie, both gentle and bright—

And what cared Morton that the mother in this case was neither gentle nor bright, but only beautiful and self-ish? It did but make the child the dearer that she had her love to herself.

And so the little Starr lay sleeping in her crib, and the boy, her preserver, from nobody knew where, and of nobody knew what name or fame lay sleeping also. And presently Delevan Endicott himself came to look at them both.

He came from the swirl of the sinful turbulent world outside, and from his fretting, petted wife's beside. She had been fretting at him for allowing a bank in which he happened to be president to do anything which should cause such a disturbance outside her home, when he knew she was so nervous. Not one word about the little step that had stood for an instant between her baby and eternity. Her husband reminded her gently how near the baby had come to death, and how she should rejoice that she was safe, but her reply had been a rush of tears, and "Oh, yes, you always think of the baby, never of me, your wife!"

With a sigh the man had turned from his fruitless effort to calm her troubled mind and gone to his little daughter. He had hoped that his wife would go with him, but he saw the hopelessness of that idea.

The little girl lay with one plump white arm thrown over her head, the curling baby fingers just touching the rosy cheek, flushed with sleep. She looked like a rosebud herself, so beautiful among the rose and lacey draperies of her couch. Her dark curls, so fine and soft and wonderful, with their hidden purple shadows, and the long dark curling lashes, to match the finely penciled brows, brought out each delicate feature of the lovely little face. The father, as he looked down upon her, wondered how it could have been in the heart of any creature, no matter how wicked, to put out this vivid little life. His little Starr, his one treasure!

The man that had tried to do it, could he have intended it really, or was it only a random shot? The testimony of those who saw judged it intention. The father's quickened heartbeats told him it was, and he felt that the thrust had gone deep. How they had meant to hurt him! How they must have hated him to have wished to hurt him so! How they would have hurt his life irretrievably if the shot had done its work. If that other little atom of human life had not intervened!

Where was the boy who had saved his child? He must go and see him at once. The gratitude of a lifetime should be his.

Morton divined his thought, as he stepped from the

sacred crib softly after bending low to sweep his lips over
the rosy velvet of little Starr's cheek. With silent tread she
followed her master to the door.

"The poor wee b'y's in the far room yon," she said in a
soft whisper, and her tone implied that his duty lay next in
that direction. The banker had often noticed this gentle
suggestion in the nurse's voice, it reminded him of something in his childhood and he invariably obeyed it. He
might have resented it if it had been less humble, less trustfully certain that of course that was the thing that he meant
to do next. He followed her direction now without a word.

The boy had just fallen asleep when he entered, and
lay as sweetly beautiful as the little vivid beauty he had left
in the other room. The man of the world paused and instinctively exclaimed in wonder. He had been told that it
was a little gamin who had saved his daughter from the assassin's bullet, but the features of this child were as delicately chiseled, his form as finely modeled, his hair as soft
and fine as any scion of a noble house might boast. He, like
the nurse, had the feeling that a young god lay before him.
It was so that Mikky always had impressed a stranger even
when his face was dirty and his feet were bare.

The man stood with bowed head and looked upon the
boy to whom he felt he owned a debt which he could never
repay.

He recognized the child as a representative of that
great unwashed throng of humanity who were his natural
enemies, because by their oppression and by stepping upon
their rights when it suited his convenience, he had risen to
where he now stood, and was able to maintain his position.
He had no special feeling for them, any of them, more than
if they had been a pack of wolves whose fangs he must keep
clear of, and whose hides he must get as soon as convenient,
but this boy was different! This spirit-child with the form of
Apollo, the beauty of Adonis, and the courage of a hero!
Could he have come from the hotbeds of sin and corrupt-
ion? It could not be! Sure there must be some mistake. He
must be of good birth. Inquiry must be made. Had anyone
asked the child's name and where he lived?

Then, as if in answer to his thought, the dark blue eyes
suddenly opened. He found them looking at him, and

started as he realized it, as if a picture on which he gazed
had suddenly turned out to be alive. And yet, for the instant, he could not summon words, but stood meeting that
steady searching gaze of the child, penetrating, questioning, as if the eyes would see and understand the very foundation principles on which the man's life rested. The man
felt it, and had the sensation of hastily looking at his own
motives in the light of this child's look. Would his life bear
that burning appealing glance?

Then, unexpectedly, the child's face lit up with his wonderful smile. He had decided to trust the man.

Never before in all his proud and varied experience
had Delevan Endicott encountered a challenge like that. It
beat through him like a mighty army and took his heart by
storm, it flashed into his eyes and dazzled him. It was the
challenge of childhood to the fatherhood of the man. With
a strange new impulse the man accepted it, and struggling
to find words, could only answer with a smile.

A good deal passed between them before any words
were spoken at all, a good deal that the boy never forgot,
and that the man liked to turn back to in his moments of
self-reproach, for somehow that boy's eyes called forth the
best that was in him, and made him ashamed of other
things.

"Boy, who is your father?" at last asked the man huskily. He almost dreaded to find another father owning a noble boy like this—and such a father as he would be if it were
true that he was only a street gamin.

The boy still smiled, but a wistfulness came into his
eyes. He slowly shook his head.

"Dead, is he?" asked the man more as if thinking
aloud. But the boy shook his head again.

"No, no father," he answered simply.

"Oh," said the man, and a lump gathered in his throat.
"Your mother?"

"No mother, never!" came the solemn answer. It
seemed that he scarcely felt that either of these were deep
lacks in his assets. Very likely fathers and mothers were not
on the average desirable kindred in the neighborhood from
which he came. The man reflected and tried again.

"Who are your folks? They'll be worried about you. We ought to send them word you're doing well."

The boy looked amazed, then a laugh rippled out.

"No folks," he gurgled, "on'y jest de kids."

"Your brothers and sisters?" asked Endicott puzzled.

"None o' dem," said Mikky. "Buck an' me're pards. We fights fer de other kids."

"Don't you know it's wrong to fight?"

Mikky stared.

Edicott tried to think of something to add to his little moral homily, but somehow could not.

"It's very wrong to fight," he reiterated lamely.

The boy's cherub mouth settled into firm lines.

"It's wronger not to, when de little kids is gettin' hurt, an' de big fellers what ought ter work is stole away they bread, an' they's hungry."

It was an entirely new proposition. It was the challenge of the poor against the rich, of the weak against the strong, and from the lips of a mere babe. The man wondered and answered not.

"I'd fight fer your little kid!" declared the young logician. He seemed to know by instinct that this was the father of his baby.

Ah, now he had touched the responsive chord. The father's face lit up. He understood. Yes, it was right to fight for his baby girl, his little Starr, his one treasure, and this boy had done it, given his life freely. Was that like fighting for those other unloved, uncared-for, hungry darlings? Were they then dear children, too, of somebody, of God, if nobody else? The boy's eyes were telling him plainly in one long deep look, that all the world of little children at least was kin, and the grateful heart of the father felt that in mere decency of gratitude he must acknowledge so much. Poor little hungry babies. What if his darling were hungry! A sudden longing seized his soul to give them bread at once to eat. But at least he would shower his gratitude upon this one stray defender of their rights.

He struggled to find words to let the child know of this feeling but only the tears gathering quickly in his eyes spoke for him.

"Yes, yes, my boy! You did fight for my little girl. I know. I'll never forget it of you as long as I live. You saved her life, and that's worth everything to me. Everything, do you understand?"

At last the words rushed forth, but his voice was husky, and those who knew him would have declared him more moved than they had ever seen him.

The boy understood. A slender brown hand stole out from the white coverlet and touched his. Its outline, long and supple and graceful, spoke of patrician origin. It was hard for the man of wealth and pride to realize that it was the hand of the child of the common people, the people who were his enemies.

"Is there anything you would like to have done for you, boy?" he asked at last because the depth of emotion was more than he could bear.

The boy looked troubled.

"I was thinkin', ef Buck an' them could see me, they'd know 'twas all right. I'd like 'em to know how 'tis in here."

"You want me to bring them up to see you?"

Mikky nodded.

"Where can I find them, do you think?"

"Buck, he won't go fur, till he knows what's comed o' me," said the boy with shining confidence in his friend. "He'd know I'd do that fur him."

Then it seemed there was such a thing as honor and loyalty among the lower ranks of men—at least among the boys. The man of the world was learning a great many things. Meekly he descended the two flights of stairs and went out to his own front doorsteps.

There were no crowds anymore. The police were still on duty, but curious passersby dared not linger long. The workmen had finished the windows and gone. The man felt little hope of finding the boys, but somehow he had a strange desire to do so. He wanted to see that face light up once more. Also, he had a curious desire to see these youngsters from the street who could provoke such loving anxiety from the hero upstairs.

Mikky was right, Buck would not go far away until he knew how it was with his comrade. He had indeed moved off at the officer's word when the doctor promised to bring him word later, but in his heart he did not intend to let a soul pass in or out of that house all day that he did not see, and so he set his young pickets here and there about the block, each with his bunch of papers, and arranged a judicious change occasionally, to avoid trouble with the officers.

Buck was standing across the street on the corner by the church steps, making a lively show of business now and then and keeping one eye on the house that had swallowed up his partner. He was not slow to perceive that he was being summoned by a man upon the steps, and ran eagerly up with his papers, expecting to receive his coin, and maybe a glimpse inside the door.

"All about der shootin' of der bank millionaire's baby!" he yelled in his most finished voice of trade, and the father, thinking of what might have been, felt a pang of horror at the careless words from the gruff little voice.

"Do you know a boy named Buck?" he questioned as he deliberately paid for the paper that was held up to him, and searched the unpromising little face before him. Then marveled at the sullen, sly change upon the dirty face.

The black brows drew down forebodingly, the dark eyes reminded him of a caged lion ready to spring if an opportunity offered. The child had become a man with a criminal's face. There was something frightful about the defiant look with which the boy drew himself up.

"What if i does?"

"Only that there's a boy in here," motioning toward the door, "would like very much to see him for a few minutes. If you know where he is, I wish you'd tell him."

Then there came a change more marvelous than before. It was as if the divine in the soul had suddenly been revealed through a rift in the sinful humanity. The whole defiant face became eager, the black eyes danced with question, the brows settled into straight pleasant lines, and the mouth sweetened as with pleasant thoughts.

"Is't Mikky?" he asked in earnest voice. "Kin we get in? I'll call de kids. He'll want 'em. He allus wants der kids." He plaes his fingers in his mouth, stretching it into a curious shape, and there issued forth a shriek that might have come from the mouth of an exulting fiend, so long and shrill and sharp it was. The man on the steps, his nerves already wrought to the snapping point, started angrily. Then suddenly around the corner at a swift trot emerged three ragged youngsters who came at their leader's command swiftly and eagerly.

"Mikky wants us!" explained Buck. "Now youse foller me, 'n don't you say nothin' 'less I tell you."

They fell in line, behind the bank president, and followed awed within the portal that unlocked a palace more wonderful than Aladin's to their astonished gaze.

Up the stairs they slunk, single file, the bare feet and the illy shod alike going silently and sleuthlike over the polished stairs. They skulked past open doors with frightened defiant glances, the defiance of the very poor for the very rich, the defiance that is born and bred in the soul from a face-to-face existence with hunger and cold and need of every kind. They were defiant but they took it all in, and for many a day gave details highly embellished of the palace where Mikky lay. It seemed to them that heaven itself could show no grander sights.

In a stricken row against the wall, with sudden consciousness of their own delinquencies of attire, ragged caps in hands, grimy hands behind them, they stood and gazed upon their fallen hero-comrade.

Clean, they had never perhaps seen his face before. The white robe that was upon him seemed a robe of unearthly whiteness. It dazzled their gaze. The shining of his newly washed hair was a glory crown upon his head. They saw him gathered into another world than any they knew. It could have seemed no worse to them if the far heaven above the narrow city streets had opened its grim clouds and received their comrade from their sight. They were appalled. How could he ever be theirs again? How could it all have happened in the few short hours since Mikky flashed past them and fell a martyr to his kindly heart and saved the wicked rich man his child? The brows of Buck drew together in his densest frown. He felt that Mikky, their Mikky was having some terrible change come upon him.

Then Mikky turned and smiled upon them all, and in his dear familiar voice shouted, "Say, kids, ain't this grand? Say, I jes' wish you was all in it! Ef you, Buck, an' the kids was here in this yer grand bed I'd be havin' the time o' me life!"

That turned the tide. Buck swallowed hard and smiled his darker smile, and the rest grinned sheepishly. Grandeur and riches had not spoiled their prince. He was theirs still and he had wanted them. He had sent for them. They gained courage to look around on the spotlessly clean room, on the nurse in her crackling dignity; on the dish of oranges which she promptly handed to them and of which each in awe partook a golden sphere; on the handful of bright flowers that Morton had brought but a few minutes before and placed on a little stand by the bed; on the pictures that hung upon the walls, the like of which they had never seen before, and then back to the white white bed that held their companion. They could not get used to the whiteness and the cleanness of his clean, clean face and hands, and bright gold hair. It burned like a flame against the pillow, and Mikky's blue eyes seemed darker and deeper than ever before. To Buck they had given their obedient following, and looked to him for protection, but after all he was one like themselves, only a little more fearless. To Mikky they all gave a kind of far-seeing adoration. He was fearless and brave like Buck, but he was something more. In their superstitious fear and ignorance he seemed to them almost supernatural.

They skulked silently down the stairs like frightened rabbits when the interview was over, each clutching his precious orange, and not until the great doors had closed upon them did they utter a word. They had said very little. Mikky had done all the talking.

When they had filed down the street behind their leader, and rounded the corner out of sight of the house, Buck gathered them into a little knot and said solemnly: "Kids, I bet cher Mik don't be comin' out o' this no more. Didn't you take notice how he looked jes' like the angel o' the monnemunt down at the cemetery?"

The little group took on a solemnity that was deep and real.

"Anyhow, he wanted us!" spoke up a curly-headed boy with old eyes and a thin face. He was one whom Mikky had always defended. He bore a hump upon his ragged back.

"Aw! he's all right fer us, is Mik," said Buck, "but he's different nor us. Old Aunt Sal she said one day he were named fer an 'n'angel, an' like as not he'll go back where he b'longs someday, but he won't never fergit us. He ain't like rich folks what don't care. He's our pard allus. Come on, fellers."

Down the back alley went the solemn little procession, single file, till they reached the rear of the Endicott house, where they stood silent as before a shrine, till at a signal from their leader, each grimy right hand was raised, and gravely each ragged cap was taken off and held high in the air toward the upper window, where they knew their hero-comrade lay. Then they turned and marched silently away.

They were all in place before the door whenever the doctor came thereafter, and always went around by the way of the alley afterward for their ceremonial good night, sometimes standing solemnly beneath the cold stars while the shrill wind blew through their thin garments, but always as long as the doctor brought them word, or as long as the light burned in the upper window, they felt their comrade had not gone yet.

Chapter 3

Heaven opened for Mikky on the day when Morton, with the doctor's permission, brought baby Starr to see him.

The baby, in her nurse's arms, gazed down upon her rescuer with the unprejudiced eyes of childhood. Mikky's smile flashed upon her and forthwith she answered with a joyous laugh of glee. The beautiful boy pleased her ladyship. She reached out her roseleaf hands to greet him.

The nurse held her down to the bed:

"Kiss the wee b'y, that's a good baby. Kiss the wee b'y. He took care of baby and saved her life when the bad man

tried to hurt her. Kiss the wee b'y and say 'I thank you,'"
commanded Morton.

The saving of her life meant nothing to little Starr, but
she obediently murmured "I'ee tank oo!" as the nurse had
drilled her to do before she brought her, and then laid her
moist pink lips on cheeks, forehead, eyes, and mouth in
turn, and Mikky, in ecstasy, lay trembling with the pleasure
of it. No one had ever kissed him before. Kissing was not in
vogue in the street where he existed.

Thereafter, every day until he was convalescent, Starr
came to visit him.

By degrees he grew accustomed to her gay presence
enough to talk with her freely as child with child. Her
words were few and her tongue as yet quite unacquainted
with the language of this world, but perhaps that was all the
better, for their conversations were more of the spirit than
of the tongue, Mikky's language, of circumstance, being
quite unlike that of Madison Avenue.

Starr brought her wonderful electric toys and dolls,
and Mikky looked at them with wonder, yet always with a
kind of rare indifference, because the child herself was to
him the wonder of all wonders, an angel spirit stooped to
earth. And every day, when the nurse carried her small
charge away after her frolic with the boy, she would always
lift her up to the bed and say:

"Now kiss the wee b'y, baby Starr, and thank him again
fer savin' yer life."

And Starr would lay her soft sweet mouth on his as
tenderly and gravely as if she understood the full import of
her obligation. At such times Mikky would watch her bright
face as it came close to his, and when her lips touched his he
would close his eyes as if to shut out all things else from this
sacred ceremony. After Starr and Morton were gone the
nurse was wont to look furtively toward the bed and note
the still, lovely face of the boy whose eyes were closed as if to
hold the vision and memory the longer. At such times her
heart would draw her strangely from her wonted formality
and she would touch the boy with a tenderness that was not
natural to her.

There were other times when Mr. Endicott would come
and talk briefly with the boy, just to see his eyes light and his

face glow with that wonderful smile, and to think what it would be if the boy were his own. Always Mikky enjoyed these little talks, and when his visitor was gone he would think with satisfaction that this was just the right kind of a father for his little lovely Starr. He was glad the baby Starr had a father. He had often wondered what it would be like to have a father, and now he thought he saw what the height of desire in a father might be. Not that he felt a great need for himself in the way of fathers. He had taken care of himself since he could remember and felt quite grown-up and fathers usually drank, but a baby like that needed a father, and he liked Starr's father.

But the dearest thing now in life for him was little Starr's kisses.

To the father, drawn first by gratitude to the boy who had saved his child's life, and afterwards by the boy's own irresistible smile, these frequent visits had become a pleasure. There had been a little boy before Starr came to their home, but he had only lived a few weeks. The memory of that golden, fuzzy head, the little appealing fingers, the great blue eyes of his son still lingered bitterly in the father's heart. When he first looked upon this waif the fancy seized him that perhaps his own boy would have been like this had he lived, and a strange and unexpected tenderness entered his heart for Mikky. He kept going to the little invalid's room night after night, pleasing himself with the thought that the boy was his own.

So strong a hold did this fancy take upon the man's heart that he actally began to consider the feasibility of adopting the child and bringing him up as his own—this, after he had by the aid of detectives, thoroughly searched out all that was known of him and found that no one owned Mikky nor seemed to care what became of him except Buck and his small following. And all the time the child, well fed, well cared for, happier than he had ever dreamed of being in all his little hard life, rapidly convalesced.

Endicott came home one afternoon to find Mikky down in the reception room dressed in black velvet and rare old lace, with his glorious sheaf of golden hair which had grown during his illness tortured into ringlets, and an adoring group of ladies gathered about him, as he stood with troubled, almost haughty mein, and gravely regarded their maudlin sentimentalities.

Mrs. Endicott had paid no attention to the boy heretofore, and her sudden interest in him came from a chance view of him as he sat up in a big chair for the first time, playing a game with little Starr. His big eyes and beautiful hair attracted her at once, and she lost no time in dressing him up like a doll and making him a show at one of her receptions.

When her husband remonstrated with her, declaring that such treatment would ruin the spirit of any real boy, and spoil him for life, she shrugged her shoulders, indifferently, and answered:

"Well, what if it does? He's nothing but a foundling. He ought to be glad we were willing to dress him up prettily and play with him for a while."

"And what would you do with him after you were done using him for a toy? Cast him aside?"

"Well, why not?" with another shrug for her handsome shoulders. "Or, perhaps we might teach him to be a butler or footman if you want to be benevolent. He would be charming in a dark blue uniform!"

The woman raised her delicate eyebrows, humming a light tune, and her husband turned from her in despair. Was it nothing at all to her that this child had saved the life of her baby?

That settled the question of adoption. His wife would never be the one to bring up the boy into anything like manhood. It was different with a girl—she must of necessity be frivolous, he supposed.

The next morning an old college friend came into his office, a plain man with a pleasant face, who had not gone from college days to a bank presidency. He was only a plain teacher in a little struggling college in Florida, and he came soliciting aid for the college.

Endicott turned from puzzling over the question of Mikky, to greet his old friend whom he had not seen for twenty years. He was glad to see him. He had always liked him. He looked him over critically, however, with his successful-businessman-of-New-York point of view. He noticed the plain cheap business suit, worn shiny in places, the shoes well polished but beginning to break at the side, the plentiful sprinkling of gray hairs, and then his eyes traveled to the kind, worn face of his friend. In spite of himself he could not but feel that the man was happier than himself.

He asked many questions, and found a keen pleasure in hearing all about the little family of the other, and their happy united efforts to laugh off poverty and have a good time anyway. Then the visitor told of the college, its struggles, its great needs and small funds, how its orange crop, which was a large part of its regular income, had failed that year on account of the frost, and they were in actual need of funds to carry on the work of the immediate school year. Endicott found his heart touched, though he was not as a rule a large giver to anything.

"I'd be glad to help you, Harkness," he said at last, "but I've got a private benevolence on my hands just now that is going to take a good deal of money, I'm afraid. You see we've narrowly escaped a tragedy at our house—" and he launched into the story of the shooting, and his own indebtedness to Mikky.

"I see," said the professor, "you feel that you owe it to that lad to put him in the way of a better life, seeing that he freely gave his life for your child's."

"Exactly!" said Endicott, "and I'd like to adopt him and bring him up as my own, but it doesn't seem feasible. I don't think my wife would feel just as I do about it, and I'm not sure I'd be doing the best after all for the boy. To be taken from one extreme to another might ruin him."

"Well, Endicott, why don't you combine your debt to the child with benevolence and send him down to us for a few years to educate?"

Endicott sat up interestedly.

"Could I do that? Would they take so young a child? He can't be over seven."

"Yes, we would take him, I think. He'd be well cared for, and his tuition in the prep department would help the institution along. Every little helps, you know."

Endicott suddenly saw before him the solution of his difficulties. He entered eagerly into the matter, talking over rates, plans, and so on. An hour later it was all settled.

Mikky was to take a full course with his expenses all pre-paid, and a goodly sum placed in the bank for his clothing and spending money. He was to have the best room the school afforded, at the highest price, and was to take music and art and everything else that was offered, for Endicott meant to do the handsome thing by the institution. The failure of the bank of which he was president had in no wise affected his own private fortune.

"If the boy doesn't seem to develop an interest in some of these branches, put some deserving one in his place, and put him at something else," he said. "I want him to have his try at everything, develop the best that is in him. So we'll pay for everything you've got there, and that will help out some other poor boy perhaps, for, of course one boy can't do everything. I'll arrange it with my lawyer that the payments shall be made regularly for the next twelve years, so that if anythings happens to me, or if this boy runs away or doesn't turn out worthy, you will keep on getting the money just the same, and someone else can come in on it."

Professor Harkness went away from the office with a smile on his face and in his pocket three letters of introduction to wealthy benevolent businessmen of New York. Mikky was to go south with him the middle of the next week.

Endicott went home that afternoon with relief of mind, but he found in his heart a most surprising reluctance to part with the beautiful boy.

When the banker told Mikky that he was going to send him to college, and explained to him that an education would enable him to become a good man and perhaps a great one, the boy's face was very grave. Mikky had never felt the need of an education, and the thought of going away from New York gave him a sensation as if the earth were tottering under his feet. He shook his head doubtfully.

"Kin I take Buck an' de kids?" he asked after a thoughtful pause, and with a lifting of the cloud in his eyes.

"No," said Endicott. "It costs a good deal to go away to school, and there wouldn't be anyone to send them."

Mikky's eyes grew wide with something like indignation, and he shook his head.

"Nen I couldn't go," he said decidedly. "I couldn't take nothin' great like that and not give de kids any. We'll stick together. I'll stay wid de kids. They needs me."

"But Mikky—" the man looked into the large determined eyes and settled down for combat—"you don't understand, boy. It would be impossible for them to go. I couldn't send them all, but I *can* send you, and I'm going to, because you risked your life to save little Starr."

"That wasn't nothin' t'all!" declared Mikky with fine scorn.

"It was everything to me," said the man, "and I want to do this for you. And, boy, it's your duty to take this. It's everybody's duty to take the opportunities for advancement that come to them."

Mikky looked at him thoughtfully. He did not understand the large words, and duty meant to him a fine sense of loyalty to those who had been loyal to him.

"I got to stay wid de kids," he said. "Dey needs ne."

With an exasperated feeling that it was useless to argue against this calmly stated fact, Endicott began again gently:

"But, Mikky, you can help them a lot more by going to college than by staying at home."

The boy's eyes looked unconvinced but he waited for reasons.

"If you get to be an educated man you will be able to earn money and help them. You can lift them up to better things; build good houses for them to live in; give them work to do that will pay good wages, and help them to be good men."

"Are you educated?"

Thinking he was making progress Endicott nodded eagerly.

"Is that wot you does fer folks?" The bright eyes searched his face eagerly, keenly, doubtfully.

The color flooded the bank president's cheeks and forehead uncomfortably.

"Well—I might—" he answered. "Yes, I might do a good deal for people, I suppose. I don't know as I do much, but I could if I had been interested in them."

He paused. He realized that the argument was weakened. Mikky studied his face.

"But dey needs me now, de kids does," he said gravely.

"Jimmie, he don't have no supper most nights less'n I share, and Bobs is so little he can't fight dem alley kids; n' sometimes I gets a flower off'n the florist's back door fer little sick Jane. Her's got a crutch, and can't walk much anyhow; and cold nights me an' Buck we sleeps close. We got a box hid away where we sleeps close an' keeps warm."

The moisture gathered in the eyes of the banker as he listened to the innocent story. It touched his heart as nothing ever had before. He resolved that after this his education and wealth should at least help these little slum friends of Mikky to an occasional meal, or a flower, or a warm bed.

"Suppose you get Buck to take your place with the kids while you go to school and get an education and learn how to help them better."

Mikky's golden head negatived this slowly.

"Buck, he's got all he kin do to git grub for hisse'f an' his sister Jane. His father is bad, and kicks Jane, and don't get her nothin' to eat. Buck he has to see after Janie."

"How would it be for you to pay Buck something so that he could take your place? I will give you some money that you may do as you like with, and you can pay Buck as much as you think he needs every week. You can send it to him in a letter."

"Would it be as much as a quarter?" Mikky held his breath in wonder and suspense.

"Two quarters if you like."

"Oh! Could I do that?" The boy's face fairly shone, and he came and threw his arms about Endicott's neck and laid his face against his. The man clasped him close and would fain have kept him there, for his well-ordered heart was deeply stirred.

Thus it was arranged.

Buck was invited to an interview, but when the silver half-dollar was laid in his grimy palm, and he was made to understand that others were to follow, and that he was to step up into Mikky's place in the community of the children while that luminary went to college to be educated, his face wore a heavy frown. He held out the silver sphere as if it burned him. What! Take money in exchange for Mikky's bright presence? Never!

It took a great deal of explanation to convince Buck
that anything could be better "fer de kids" than Mikky,
their own Mikky, now and forever. He was quick, however,
to see where the good lay for Mikky, and after a few plain
statements from Mr. Endicott there was no further demur
on the part of the boy. Buck was willing to give up Mikky
for Mikky's good but not for his own. But it was a terrible
sacrifice. The hard little face knotted itself into a fierce expression when he came to say good-bye. The long scrawny
throat worked convulsively, the hands gripped each other
savagely. It was like handing Mikky over to another world
than theirs, and though he confidently promised to return
to them as soon as the college should have completed the
mysterious process of education, and to live with them as of
yore, sleeping in Buck's box alongside, and taking care of
the others when the big alley kids grew troublesome, somehow an instinct taught them that he would never return
again. They had had him, and they would never forget him,
but he would grow into a being far above them. They
looked vindictively at the great rich man who had perpe-
trated this evil device of a college life for their comrade. It
was the old story of the helpless poor against the powerful
rich. Even heartbeats counted not against such power.
Mikky must go.

They went to the great station on the morning when
Mikky was to depart and stood shivering and forlorn until
the train was called. They listened sullenly while Professor
Harkness told them that if they wished to be fit to associate
with their friend when he came out of college they must
begin at once to improve all their opportunities. First of all
they must go to school, and study hard, and then their
friend in college would be proud to call them friends. They
did not think it worthwhile to tell the kindly but ignorant
professor that they had no time for school, and no clothes
to wear if they had the time or the inclination to go. Schools
were everywhere, free, of course, but it did not touch them.
They lived in dark places and casual crannies, like weeds or
vermin. No one cared whether they went to school. No one
suggested it. They would have as soon thought of entering
a great mansion and insisting on their right live there as to

present themselves at school. Why, they had to hustle for a
mere existence. They were the water rats, the bad boys, the
embryo criminals for the next generation. The problem
with any who thought of them was how to get rid of them.
But of course this man from another world did not understand. They merely looked at him dully and wished he
would walk away and leave Mikky to them while he stayed.
His presence made it seem as if their companion were already gone from them.

It was hard, too, to see Mikky dressed like the fine boys
on Fifth Avenue, handsome trousers and coat, and a great
thick overcoat, a hat on his shining crown of hair that had
always been guiltless of cap, thick stockings and shining
shoes on his feet that had always been bare and soiled with
the grime of the streets—gloves on his hands. This was a
new Mikky. "The kids" did not know him. In spite of their
best efforts they could not be natural. Great lumps arose in
their throats, lumps that never dared arise for hunger or
cold or curses at home.

They stood helpless before their own consciousness,
and Mikky, divining the touble with that exquisite keeness
of a spirit sent from heaven to make earth brighter, con-
ceived the bright idea of giving each of his comrades some
article of his apparel as a remembrance. Mr. Endicott came
upon the scene just in time to keep Mikky from taking off
his overcoat and enveloping Buck in its elegant folds. He
was eagerly telling them that Bobs should have his under-
coat, Jimmie his hat; they must take his gloves to Jane, and
there was nothing left for Sam but his stockings and shoes,
but he gave them all willingly. He seemed to see no reason
why he could not travel hatless and coatless, bare of foot
and hand, for had he not gone that way through all the
years of his existence? It was a small thing to do, for his
friends whom he was leaving for a long time.

The bright face clouded when he was told he could not
give these things away, that it would not be fair to the kind
professor to ask him to carry with him a boy not properly
dressed. But he smiled again trustfully when Endicott
promised to take the whole group to a clothing house and
fit them out.

They bade Mikky good-bye, pressing their grimy noses against the bars of the station gate to watch their friend disappear from their bare little lives.

Endicott himself felt like crying as he came back from seeing the boy aboard the train. Somehow it went hard for him to feel he should not meet the bright smile that night when he went home.

But it was not the way of "the kids" to cry when tragedy fell among them. They did not cry now—when he came back to them they regarded the banker with lowering brows as the originator of their bereavement. They had no faith in the promised clothing.

"Aw, what's he givin' us!" Buck had breathed under his breath. But to do Buck credit he had not wanted to take Mikky's coat from him. When their comrade went from them into another walk in life he must go proudly appareled.

Endicott led the huddled group away from the station, to a clothing house, and amused himself by fitting them out. The garments were not of as fine material, nor elegant a cut as those he had pleased himself by purchasing for Mikky's outfit, but they were warm and strong and wonderful to their eyes, and one by one the grimy urchins went into a little dressing room, presently emerging with awe upon their faces to stand before a tall mirror surveying themselves.

Endicott presently bade the little company farewell and with a conscience at ease with himself and all mankind left them.

They issued from the clothing house with scared expressions and walked solemnly a few blocks. Then Buck called them to a halt before a large plate glass show window.

"Take a good look at yersel's, kids," he ordered, "an' we'll go up to the park an' shine around, an' see how ther swells feels, then we'll go down to Sheeny's an' sell 'em."

"Sell 'em! Can't we keep 'em?" pitifully demanded Bobs who had never felt warm in winter in all his small life before.

"You wouldn't hev 'em long," sneered Buck. "That father o' yourn would hev 'em pawned 'afore night. You better enjoy 'em a while, an' then git the money. It's safer!"

The children with wisdom born of their unhappy circumstances recognized this truth. They surveyed themselves gravely in their fleeting grandeur and then turned to walk up to the aristocratic part of town, a curious little procession. They finished by rounding the Madison Avenue block, marched up the alley, and gave the salute with new hats toward the window where their prince and leader used to be. He was no longer there, but his memory was about them, and the ceremony did their bursting little hearts good. Their love for Mikky was the noblest thing that had so far entered their lives.

Jimmie suggested that they must let Jane see them before they disposed forever of their elegant garments, so Bobs, minus coat, hat, stockings and shoes was sent to bid her to a secluded retreat at the far end of the alley. Bobs hurried back ahead of her little tapping crutch to don his fine attire once more before she arrived.

Little Jane, sallow of face, unkempt of hair, tattered of clothing and shivering in cold twilight stood and watched the procession of pride as it passed and repassed before her delighted eyes. The festivity might have been prolonged but that the maudlin voice of Bobs' father reeling into the alley struck terror to their hearts, and with small ceremony they scuttled away to the pawnshop, leaving little Jane to hobble back alone to her cellar and wonder how it would feel to wear a warm coat like one of those.

"Gee!" said Jimmy as they paused with one consent before the shop door, and looked reluctantly down at their brief glory. "Gee! I wisht we could keep jest one coat fer little Jane!"

"Couldn't we hide it some'ere's?" asked Sam, and they all looked at Buck.

Buck, deeply touched for his sister's sake, nodded.

"Keep Jim's," he said huskily, "it'll do her best."

Then the little procession filed proudly in and gave up their garments to the human parasite who lived on the souls of other men, and came away bearing the one coat they had saved for Janie, each treasuring a pitiful bit of money which seemed a fortune in their eyes.

Little Jane received her gift with true spirit when it was presented, skillfully hid it from her inhuman father, and declared that each boy should have a turn at wearing the coat every Sunday at some safe hour, whereat deep satisfaction reigned among them. Their grandeur was not all departed after all.

Meantime, Mikky, in his luxurious berth in a sleeper, smiled drowsily to think of the fine new clothes that his friends must be wearing, and then fell asleep to dream of little Starr's kisses on his closed eyelids.

Chapter 4

Into a new world came Mikky, a world of blue skies, songbirds, and high tall pines with waving moss and dreamy atmosphere; a world of plenty to eat and wear, and light and joy and ease.

Yet it was a most bewildering world to the boy, and for the first week he stood off and looked at it questioningly, suspiciously. True, there were no dark cellars or freezing streets, no drunken fathers or frightened children, or blows, or hunger or privation; but this education he had come to seek that he might go back to his own world and better it, was not a garment one put on and exercised in so many times a day; it was not a cup from which one drank, nor an atmosphere that one absorbed. It was a strange, imperceptible thing got at in some mysterious way by a series of vague struggles followed by sudden and almost alarming perceptions. For a time it seemed to the boy, keen though his mind, and quick, that knowledge was a thing only granted to the few, and his was a mind that would never grasp it. How, for instance, did one know how to make just the right figures under a line when one added a long perplexity of numbers? Mikky the newsboy could tell like a flash how much change he needed to return to the fat gentleman who occasionally gave him a five-dollar bill to change on Broadway; but Mikky the scholar, though he knew figures, and was able to study out with labor easy words in his papers, had never heard of adding up figures in the way they did here, long rows of them on the blackboard. It became necessary that this boy should have some private instruction before he would be able to enter classes. Profession Harkness himself undertook the task, and gradually revealed to the child's neglected understanding some of the simple rudiments that would make his further progress possible. The sum that was paid for his tuition made it quite necessary that the boy advance reasonably, for his benefactor had made it understood that he might someday visit the institution and see how he was getting on. Some great pains were taken to enlighten Mikky's darkness.

There was another thing that the boy could not understand, and that was the discipline that ruled everywhere. He had always been a law unto himself, his only care being to keep out of the way of those who would interfere with this. Now he must rise with a bell, stay in his room until another bell, eat at a bell, go to the hard bench in the schoolroom with another bell, and even play ball when the recreation bell rang. It was hard on an independent spirit to get used to all this, and while he had no mind to be disorderly, he often broke forth into direct disobedience of the law from sheer misunderstanding of the whole regime.

The boys' dormitory was presided over by a woman who, while thorough in all housekeeping arrangements, had certainly mistaken her calling as a substitute mother for boys. She kept their clothes in order, saw to it that their rooms were aired, their stockings darned and their lights out at exactly half-past nine, but the grimness of her countenance forbade any familiarity, and she never thought of gaining the confidence of her rough, but affectionate charges. There was no tenderness in her, and Mikky never felt like smiling in her presence. He came and went with a sort of high, unconscious superiority that almost irritated the woman, because she was not great enough to see the unusual spirit of the child, and as a consequence she did not win his heart.

But he did not miss the lack of motherliness in her, for he had never known a mother and was not expecting it.

The professors he grew to like, some more, some less,

always admiring most those who seemed to him to deal in a fair and righteous manner with their classes—fairness being judged by the code in use among "the kids" in New York. But that was before he grew to know the president. After that his code changed.

His first interview with that dignitary was on an afternoon when he had been overheard by the matron to use vile language among the boys at the noon hour. She hauled him up with her most severe manner, and gave him to understand that he must answer to the president for his conduct.

As Mikky had no conception of his offense he went serenely to his fate walking affably beside her, only wishing she would not look so sour. As they crossed the campus to the president's house a blue jay flew overhead, and a mockingbird trilled in a live oak nearby. The boy's face lighted with joy and he laughed out gleefully, but the matron only looked the more severe, for she thought him a hardened little sinner who was defying her authority and laughing her to scorn. After that it was two years before she could really believe anything good of Mikky.

The president was a noble-faced, white-haired scholar, with a firm tender mouth, a brow of wisdom, and eyes of understanding. He was not the kind who win by great athletic prowess, he was an old-fashioned gentleman, well along in years, but young in heart. He looked at the child of the slums and saw the angel in the clay.

He dismissed the matron with a pleasant assurance and took Mikky to an inner office where he let the boy sit quietly waiting a few minutes till he had finished writing a letter. If the pen halted and the kind eyes furtively studied the beautiful face of the child, Mikky never knew it.

The president asked the boy to tell him what he had said, and Mikky, with sweet assurance repeated innocently the terrible phrases he had used, phrases which had been familiar to him since boyhood, conveying statements of facts that were horrible, but nevertheless daily happenings in the corner of the world where he had brought himself up.

With rare tact the president questioned the boy, until he made sure there was no inherent rottenness in him; and then gently and kindly, but firmly laid down the law and explained why it was right and necessary that there should be a law. He spoke of the purity of God. Mikky knew nothing of God and listened with quiet interest. The president talked of education and culture and made matters very plain indeed. Then when the interview was concluded and the man asked the boy for a pledge of good faith and clean language from that time forth, Mikky's smile of approval blazed forth and he laid his hand in that of the president readily enough, and went forth from the room with a great secret admiration of the man with whom he had just talked. The whole conversation had appealed to him deeply.

Mikky sought his room and laboriously spelled out with lately acquired clumsiness a letter to Buck:

> Dear Buck we mussent yuz endecent langwidg enny moor ner swar. God donte lyk it an' it ain't educated. I want you an' me to be educate. I ain't gone to, donte yoo ner let de kids.—Mikky.

In due time, according to previous arrangement about the monthly allowance, this letter reached Buck, and he tracked the doctor for two whole days before he located him and lay in wait till he came out to his carriage, when he got up his nerve to hand over the letter to be read.

The doctor, deeply touched, translated as best he could. Buck's education had been pitifully neglected. He watched the mystic paper in awe as the doctor read.

"Wot's indecent langwidge?" he asked with his heavy frown.

The doctor took the opportunity to deliver a brief sermon on purity, and Buck, without so much as an audible thank you, but with a thoughtful air that pleased the doctor, took back his letter, stuffed it into his ragged pocket and went on his way. The man watched him wistfully, wondering whether Mikky's appeal could reach the hardened little sinner, and, sighing at the wickedness of the world, went on his way grimly trying to make a few things better.

That night "the kids" were gathered in front of little Janie's window, for she was too weak to go out with them, and Buck delivered a lesson in ethical culture. Whatever Mikky, their prince, ordered, that must be done, and Buck was doing his level best, although for the life of him he couldn't see the sense in it. But thereafter none of "the kids" were allowed to use certain words and phrases, and swearing gradually became eliminated from their conversation. It would have been a curious study for a linguist to observe just what words and phrases were cut out, and what were allowed to flourish unrebuked, but nevertheless it was a reform, and Buck was doing his best.

With his schoolmates Mikky had a curiously high position even from the first. His clothes were good and he had always a little money to spend. That had been one of Endicott's wishes that the boy should be like other boys. It meant something among a group of boys, most of whom were the sons of rich fathers, sent down to Florida on account of weak lungs or throats. Moreover, he was brave beyond anything they had ever seen before, could fight like a demon in defense of a smaller boy, and did not shrink from pitching into a fellow twice his size. He could tell all about the great baseball and football games of New York City, knew the pitchers by name and yet did not boast uncomfortably. He could swim like a duck and dive fearlessly. He could outrun them all, by his lightness of foot, and was an expert in gliding away from any hand that sought to hold him back. They admired him from the first.

His peculiar street slang did not trouble them in the least, nor his lack of class standing, though that presently began to be a thing of the past, for Mikky, as soon as he understood the way, marched steadily, rapidly, up the hill of knowledge, taking in everything that was handed out to him and assimilating it. It began to look as if there would not be any leftover courses in the curriculum that might be given to some other deserving youth. Mikky would need them all. The president and the professors began presently to be deeply interested in this boy without a past; and everywhere, with everyone, Mikky's smile won his way, except with the matron who had not forgiven him that her recommendation of his instant dismissal from the college had not been accepted.

The boys had not asked many questions about him,

nor been told much. They knew his father and mother were dead. They thought he had a rich guardian, perhaps a fortune someday coming, but they did not care. Mikky never spoke about any of these things and there was a strange reticence about him that made them dislike to ask him questions, even when they came to know him well. He was entered under the name of Endicott, because, on questioning him Professor Harkness found he could lay no greater claim to any other surname, and called him that until he could write to Mr. Endicott for advice. He neglected to write at once and then, the name having become fastened upon the boy, he thought it best to let the matter alone as there was little likelihood of Mr. Endicott's coming down to the college, and it could do no harm. He never stopped to think out possible future complications and the boy became known as Michael Endicott.

But his companions, as boys will, thought the matter over, and rechristened him "Angel"; and Angel, or Angel Endy he became, down to the end of his college course.

One great delight of his new life was the out-of-door freedom he enjoyed. A beautiful lake spread its silver sheet at the foot of the campus slope and here the boy reveled in swimming and rowing. The whole country round was filled with wonder to his city-bred eyes. He attached himself to the teacher of natural sciences, and took long silent tramps for miles about. They penetrated dense hammocks, gathering specimens of rare orchids and exquisite flowers; they stood motionless and breathless for hours watching and listening to some strange wild bird; they became the familiar of slimy coiling serpents in dark bogs, and of green lizards and great black velvet spiders; they brought home ravishing butterflies and moths of pale green and gold and crimson. Mikky's room became a museum of curious and wonderful things, and himself an authority on a wide and varied range of topics.

The new life with plenty of wholesome plain food, plenty of fresh air, long nights of good sleep, and happy exercise was developing the young body into strength and beauty, even as the study and contact with life were developing the mind. Mikky grew up tall and straight and strong. In all the school, even among the older boys, there was

none suppler, none so perfectly developed. His face and
form were beautiful as Adonis, and yet it was no pink and
white feminine beauty. There was strength, simplicity,
and character in his face. With the acceptance of his new
code of morals according to the president, had grown gradually a certain look of high moral purpose. No boy in his
presence dared to use language not up to the standard. No
boy with his knowledge dared do a mean or wrong thing.
And yet, in spite of this, not a boy in the school but admired
him and was more or less led by him. If he had been one
whit less brave, one shade more conscious of self and self's
interests, one tiny bit conceited, this would not have been.
But from being a dangerous experiment in their midst
Mikky became known as a great influence for good. The
teachers saw it and marveled. The matron saw it and finally,
though grudgingly, accepted it. The president saw it and
rejoiced. The students saw it not, but acknowledged it in
their lives.

Mikky's flame of gold hair had grown more golden and
flaming with the years, so that when their ball team went to
a nearby town to play, Mikky was sighted by the crowd and
pointed out conspicuously at once.

"Who is that boy with the hair?" someone would ask
one of the team.

"That? Oh, that's the Angel! Wait till you see him play,"
would be the reply. And he became known among outsiders
as the Angel with the golden hair. At a game a listener
would hear:

"Oh, see! see! There'll be something doing now. The
Angel's at the bat!"

Yet in spite of all this the boy lived a lonely life. Giving
of himself continually to those about him, receiving in return their love and devotion, he yet felt in a great sense set
apart from them all. Every now and again some boy's father
or mother, or both, would come down for a trip through the
South, or a sister or a little brother. Then that boy would be
excused from classes and go off with his parents for perhaps a whole week; or they would come to visit him every
day, and Michael would look on and see the love-light
beaming in their eyes. That would never be for him. No one
had ever loved him in that way.

Sometimes he would close his eyes and try to get back in memory to the time when he was shot, and the wonder of the soft bed, the sweet room, and little Starr's kisses. But the years were multiplying now and room and nurse and all were growing very dim. Only little Starr's kisses remained, a delicate fragrance of baby love, the only kisses that the boy had ever known. One day, when a classmate had been telling of the coming of his father and what it would mean to him, Michael went into his room and locking his door sat down and wrote a stiff schoolboy letter to his benefactor, thanking him for all that he had done for him. It told briefly, shyly of a faint realization of that from which he had been saved; it showed a proper respect, and desire to make good, and it touched the heart of the busy man who had almost forgotten about the boy, but it gave no hint of the heart hunger which had prompted its writing.

The next winter, when Michael was seventeen, Delevan Endicott and his daughter Starr took a flying trip through the South, and stopped for a night and a day at the college.

The president told Michael of his expected coming. Professor Harkness had gone north on some school business.

The boy received the news quietly enough, with one of his brilliant smiles, but went to his room with a tumult of wonder, joy, and almost fear in his heart. Would Mr. Endicott be like what he remembered, kind and interested and helpful? Would he be pleased with the progress his protégé had made, or would he be disappointed? Would there be any chance to ask after little Starr? She was a baby still in the thoughts of the boy, yet of course she must have grown. And so many things might have happened—she might not be living now. No one would think or care to tell him.

Baby Starr! His beautiful baby! He exulted in the thought that he had flung his little useless life, once, between her lovely presence and death! He would do it again gladly now if that would repay all that her father had done for him. Michael the youth was beginning to understand all that that meant.

Those other friends of his, Buck, Jimmie, Bobs, and the rest, were still enshrined in his faithful heart, though their memory had grown dimmer with the full passing years. Faithfully every month the boy had sent Buck two dollars from his pocket money, his heart swelling with pleasure that he was helping those he loved, but only twice had any word come back from that far city where he had left them. In answer to the letter which the doctor had translated to them, there had come a brief laborious epistle, terse and to the point, written with a stub of pencil on the corner of a piece of wrapping paper, and addressed by a kindly clerk at the post office where Buck bought the stamped envelope. It was the same clerk who usually paid to the urchin his monthly money order, so he knew the address. For the inditing of the letter Buck went to night school two whole weeks before he could master enough letters and words to finish it to his satisfaction. It read:

> Deer Mik WE WunT
>
> > Buck.

The significant words filled the boy's heart with pride over his friend whenever he thought of it, even after some time had passed. He had faith in Buck. Somehow in his mind it seemed that Buck was growing and keeping pace with him, and he never dreamed that if Buck should see him now he would not recognize him.

When Mikky had been in Florida several years another letter had come from Buck addressed in the same way, and little better written than the other. Night school had proved too strenuous for Buck; besides, he felt he knew enough for all practical purposes and it was not likely he would need to write many letters. This, however, was an occasion that called for one.

> Dear Mikky Jany is DEAD sHe sayd tell yo hur LUV beeryd hur in owr kote we give hur ther wuz a angle wit pink wins on top uv the wite hurs an a wite hors we got a lot uv flowers by yur money so yo needn sen no more money kuz we ken get long now til yo cum BUCK.

After that, though Michael had written as usual every month for some time no reply had come, and the money orders had been returned to him as not called for. Buck in his simplicity evidently took it for granted that Mikky would not send the money and so came no more to the office, at least that was the solution Michael put upon it, and deep down in his heart he registered a vow to go and hunt up Buck the minute he was through at college, and free to go back to New York and help his friends. Meantime, though the years had dimmed those memories of his old life, and the days went rapidly forward in study, he kept always in view his great intention of one day going back to better his native community.

But the coming of Mr. Endicott was a great event to the boy. He could scarcely sleep the night before the expected arrival.

It was just before the evening meal that the through train from New York reached the station. Michael had been given the privilege of going down to meet his benefactor.

Tall and straight and handsome he stood upon the platform as the train rushed into the town, his cheeks glowing from excitement, his eyes bright with anticipation, his cap in his hand, and the last rays of the setting sun glowing in his golden hair, giving a touch like a halo round his head. When Endicott saw him he exclaimed mentally over his strength and manly beauty, and more than one weary tourist leaned from the open car window and gazed, for there was ever something strange and strong and compelling about Michael that reminded one of the beauty of an angel.

Chapter 5

Michael met Mr. Endicott unembarrassed. His early life in New York had given him a self-poise that nothing seemed to disturb, but when the father turned to introduce his young daughter, the boy caught his breath and gazed at her with deepening color, and intense delight.

She was here then, his Starr! She had come to see him, and she looked just as he would have her look. He had not realized before that she would be grown up, but of course she would, and the change in her was not so great as to shock his memory. The clear white of her skin with its fresh coloring was the same. New York life had not made it sallow. The roses were in her cheeks as much as when she was a little child. Her eyes were the same, dark and merry and looked at him straightly, unabashed, with the ease of a girl trained by a society mother. The dark curls were there, only longer, hanging to the slender waist and crowned with a fine wide Panama hat. She gave him a little gloved hand and said: "I'm afraid I don't remember you very well, but Daddy has been telling me about you and I'm very glad to see you."

She was only a little over twelve, but she spoke with ease and simplicity, and for the first time in his life Michael felt conscious of himself. She was so perfect, so lovely, so finished in every expression and movement. She looked at him intelligently, politely curious, and no longer with the baby eyes that wondered at nothing. He himself could not help wondering what she must think of him, and for a few minutes he grew shy before her.

Mr. Endicott was surprised and pleased at the appearance of the boy. The passing of the years had easily erased the tender feelings that Mikky the little street urchin had stirred in his heart. This visit to the school and college was not so much on account of the boy, to whom he had come to feel he had discharged his full duty, but because of the repeated invitations on the part of Professor Harkness and the president. It went not against him to see the institution to which he had from time to time contributed, in addition to his liberal allowance for the education of the boy. It was perfectly convenient for him to stop, being on the regular route he had laid out for his southern trip. His wife he had left at Palm Beach with her fashionable friends, and with Starr as his companion, the father was going through the orange belt on a tour of investigation with a view to investments. It suited him perfectly to stop off and receive the thanks of the college, therefore he stopped. Not that he was a heartless man, but there were so many things in his world to make him forget, and a little pleasant adulation is grateful to the most of us.

But when Michael in all his striking beauty stood before him with the deference of a more than son, his heart suddenly gave a great leap back to the day when he had first looked down upon the little white face on the pillow; when the blue eyes had opened and Mikky had smiled. Michael smiled now, and Endicott became aware at once of the subtle fascination of that smile. And now the thought presented itself, *What if this were my son! How proud I should be of him!*

Michael was indeed good to look upon even to the eyes of the city critic. Endicott had taken care to leave orders with his tailor for a full outfit to be sent to the boy, spring and fall, of suitable plain clothing for a schoolboy, little realizing how unnecessary it would have been to have dressed him so well. The tailor, nothing loth, had taken the measurements which were sent to him from year to year in answer to the letter of the firm, and had kept Michael looking as well as any rich man's son need desire to look. Not that the boy knew nor realized. The clothes came to him, like his board and tuition, and he took them well pleased and wrote his best letter of thanks each year as Professor Harkness suggested, but he had no idea that a part at least of his power of leadership with all the boys of the school was due to his plain though stylishly cut garments. This fact would not have counted for anything with boys who had been living in Florida for years, for any plain decent clothes were thought fit, no matter how they were cut; but the patronage of the school was at least one-half made up of rich men's sons who were sent south for a few years to a milder climate for their health. These as a rule, when they came, had exaggerated ideas of the importance of clothes and prevailing modes.

And so it was that Michael did not look like a dowdy country boy to his benefactor, but on the contrary presented a remarkable contrast to many of the boys with whom Endicott was acquainted at home. There was something about Michael even when he was a small lad that commanded marked attention from all who saw him. This attention Endicott and his daughter gave now as they walked beside him in the glow of the sunset, and listened as he pointed out the various spots of interest in the little college town.

The institution boasted of no carriage, and the single horsecar that traveled to the station belonged to the hotel and its guests. However, the walk was not long, and gave the travelers an opportunity to breathe the clear air and feel the stillness of the evening which was only emphasized by each separate sound now and again.

Starr, as she walked on the inside of the board sidewalk, and looked down at the small pink and white and crimson pea blossoms growing everywhere, and then up at the tallness of the great pines, felt a kind of awe stealing upon her. The one day she had spent at Palm Beach had been so filled with hotels and people and automobiles that she had had no opportunity to realize the tropical nature of the land. But here in this quiet spot, where the tiny station, the post office, the grocery, and a few scattered dwellings with the lights of the great tourists' hotel gleaming in the distance, seemed all there was of human habitation, and where the sky was wide even to bewilderment, she seemed suddenly to realize the difference from New York.

Michael had recovered his poise as soon as she no longer faced him, though he was profoundly conscious of her presence there on the other side of her father. But he talked easily and well. Yes, there was the hotel. It held five hundred guests and was pretty well filled at this season of the year. There were some distinguished people stopping there. The railroad president's private car was on the track for a few hours last week. That car over on the siding belonged to a great steel magnate. The other one had brought the wife of a great inventor. Off there at the right toward the sunset were the school and college buildings. No, they could not be seen until one passed the orange grove. Too bad there was no conveyance, but the one little car turned off toward the hotel at this corner, and the one beast of burden belonging to the college, the college mule—Minus, by name, because there were so many things that he was not—was lame today and therefore could not be called into requisition to bring the guests from the station.

Mr. Endicott felt that he was drawing nearer to nature

in this quiet walk than he had been since he was a boy and visited his grandfather's farm. It rested and pleased him immensely, and he was charmed with the boy, his protégé. His frank, simple conversation was free from all affectation on the one hand, or from any hint of his low origin on the other hand. He felt already that he had done a good thing in sending this boy down here to be educated. It was worth the little money he had put into it.

Starr watched Michael shyly from the shelter of her father's side and listened to him. He was not like the boys she met in New York. To begin with he was remarkably fine looking, and added to that there was a mingled strength and kindliness in his face, and above all about his smile, that made her feel instinctively that he was nobler than most of them. She could not think of a boy of her acquaintance who had a firm chin like that. This boy had something about him that made the girl know instantly that he had a greater purpose in life than his own pleasure. Not that she thought this all out analytically. Starr had never learned to think. She only felt it as she looked at him, and liked him at once. Moreover there was a sort of glamour over the boy in her eyes, for her father had just been telling her the story of how he had saved her life when she was barely three years old. She felt a prideful proprietorship in him that made her shy in his presence.

At the college president's gate, just on the edge of the campus, the president came out with apologies. He had been detained on a bit of business at the county seat five miles away, and had driven home with a friend whose horse was very slow. He was sorry not to have done their honored guests the courtesy of being at the station on their arrival. Endicott walked with the president after the greetings, and Michael dropped behind with Starr eagerly pointing out to her the buildings.

"That's the chapel, and beyond are the study and recitation rooms. The next is the dining hall and servants' quarters, and over on that side of the campus is our dormitory. My window looks down on the lake. Every morning I go before breakfast for a swim."

"Oh, aren't you afraid of alligators?" exclaimed Starr shivering prettily.

Michael looked down at her fragile loveliness with a softened appreciation, as one looks at the tender precious things of life that need protection.

"No," he answered without laughing, as some of the other boys would have done at her girlish fears, "they never bother us here, and besides, I'm sort of acquainted with them. I'm not afraid of them. Nothing will hurt you if you understand it well enough to look out for its rights."

"Oh!" said Starr eyeing him in wonder. As if an alligator had rights! What a strange, interesting boy. The idea of understanding an alligator. She was about to ask how understanding the creature would keep one from being eaten up when Michael pointed to the crimsoning west.

"See!" he said eagerly as if he were pointing to a loved scene, "the sun is almost down. Don't you love to watch it? In a minute more it will be gone and then it will be dark. Hear that evening bird? 'Titwiloo! Tit-wiloo!' He sings sometimes late at night."

Starr followed his eager words, and saw the sun slipping, slipping like a great ruby disc behind the fringe of palm and pine and oak that bordered the little lake below the campus; saw the wild bird dart from the thicket into the clear amber of the sky above, utter its sweet weird call, and drop again into the fine brown shadows of the living picture; watched, fascinated as the sun slipped lower, lower, to the half now, and now less than half.

Breathless they both stood and let the two men go on ahead, while they watched the wonder of the day turn into night. The brilliant liquid crimson poured itself away to other lands, till only a rim of wonderful glowing garnet remained; then, like a living thing dying into another life, it too dropped away, and all was night.

"Why! How dark it is!" exclaimed Starr as she turned to her companion again and found she could scarcely see his face. "Why! How queer! Where is the twilight? Is anything the matter? I never saw it get dark all at once like this!" She peered around into the strange velvet darkness with troubled eyes.

Michael was all attention at once.

"No, that's all right," he assured her. "That's the way we do here. Almost everybody from the north speaks about it at first. They can't understand it. It's the difference in the position of the sun, nearer the equator, you know. I'll show you all about it on the chart in the astronomical room if you care to see. We haven't any twilight here. I should think twilight would be queer. You wouldn't just know when night began and day ended. I don't remember about it when I lived in New York. Look up there! That's the evening star! It's come out for you tonight—to welcome another—Starr!"

Oh, Michael, of unknown origin! Whence came the skill of delicate compliment, that grace of courtesy, that you, plucked from the slime of the gutter, set apart from all sweetening influences of loving contact with womankind, should be able so gallantly and respectfully to guide the young girl through the darkness, touching her little elbow distantly, tactfully, reverently, exactly as the college president helps his wife across the road on Sabbath to the church? Is it only instinct, come down from some patrician ancestor of gallant ways and kind, or have you watched and caught the knack from the noble scholar who is your ideal of all that is manly?

They walked silently through the warm darkness until they came within the circle of light from the open door, and matron and teachers came out to welcome the young stranger and bring her into the house.

Michael lingered for a moment by the door, watching her as she went with the matron, her sweet face wreathed in smiles, the matron's thin arm around her and a new and gentle look upon her severe countenance; watched until they mounted the stairs out of sight; then he went out of doors.

Taking off his cap he stood reverently looking up at the star, communing with it perhaps about the human Starr that had come back to him out of the shadows of the past.

And she was a star. No one who saw her but acknowledged it. He marveled as he recalled the change wrought in the face of the matron and because of her gentleness to the little girl forgave her all that she had not been to his motherless boyhood.

Starr came down to dinner in a few minutes radiant in a little rosy frock of soft eastern silk, girdled with a fringed scarf of the same and a knot of coral velvet in her hair.

From the string of pearls about her white neck to the dainty point of her slipper she was exquisite and Michael watched her with open admiration; whereat the long lashes drooped shyly over the girl's rosy cheeks and she was mightily pleased.

She sat at her father's side to the right of the president, with Michael across the table. Well he bore the scrutiny of Endicott's keen eyes which through all the conversation kept searching the intelligent face of the boy.

The evening passed like a dream, and Michael lay awake again that night thinking of all the pleasure in antic-ipation for the next day. At last, at last he had some people who in a way he might call his own. They had cared to come and see him after all the years! His heart swelled with joy and gratitude.

The guests attended chapel exercises with the students the next morning, and Michael saw with pride the eyes of his companions turn toward the beautiful young girl, and look at him almost with envy. The color mounted into his strong young face, but he sat quietly in his place and no one would have guessed to look at him, the tumult that was run-ning riot in his veins. He felt it was the very happiest day of his life.

After chapel the guests were shown about the college buildings and campus. The president and Endicott walked ahead, Michael behind with Starr, answering her interested questions.

They had been through all the classrooms, the gym-nasium, the dining hall servants' quarters, and dormitories. They had visited the athletic ground, the tennis courts, and gone down by the little lake, where Michael had taken them out for a short row. Returning they were met by one of the professors who suggested their going to hear some of the classes recite, and as Mr. Endicott seemed interested they turned their steps toward the recitation hall.

"I think," said Starr as they walked slowly across the campus together, "that you must be a very brave boy. To think of you saving my life that way when you were just a little fellow!"

She looked up, her pretty face full of childish feeling. Michael looked down silently and smiled. He was wondering if any eyes were ever as beautiful as those before him. He had never had even a little girl look at him like that. The president's daughter was fat and a romp. She never took time to look at the boys. The few other girls he knew, daughters of the professors, were quiet and studious. They paid little attention to the boys.

"I want to thank you for what you did," went on Starr, "only I can't think of any words great enough to tell you how I feel about it. I wish there was something I could do to show you how I thank you?"

She lifted her sweet eyes again to his. They were entering the large hall of the college now.

"This way," said Michael guiding her toward the chapel door which had just swung to behind the two men.

"Isn't there something you would like that I could do for you?" persisted Starr earnestly, following him into the empty chapel where Mr. Endicott and the president stood looking at a tablet on the wall by the further door.

"Your father has done everything for me," said Michael sunnily, with a characteristic sweep of his hand that seemed to include himself, his garments, and his mental outfit. He turned upon her his blazing smile that spoke more eloquently than words could have done.

"Yes, but that is Papa," said Starr half impatiently, softly stamping her daintily shod foot. "He did that because of what you did for *him* in saving my life. I should like to do something to thank you for what you did for *me*. I'm worth something to myself you know. Isn't there something I could do for you?"

She stood still, looking up into his face anxiously, her vivid childish beauty seeming to catch all the brightness of the place and focus it upon him. The two men had passed out of the further door and on to the recitation rooms. The girl and boy were alone for the moment.

"You have done something for me, you did a great deal," he said, his voice almost husky with boyish tenderness. "I think it was the greatest thing that anybody ever did for me."

"I did something for you! When? What?" questioned Starr curiously.

"Yes," he said, "you did a great thing for me. Maybe

you don't remember it, but I do. It was when I was getting
well from the shot there at your house, and your nurse used
to bring you up to play with me every day; and always before you went away, you used to kiss me. I've never forgotten that."

He said it quite simply as if it were a common thing for
a boy to say to a girl. His voice was low as though the depths
of his soul were stirred.

A flood of pretty color came into Starr's cheeks.

"Oh!" she said quite embarrassed at the turn of the
conversation, "but that was when I was a baby. I couldn't do
that now. Girls don't kiss boys, you know. It wouldn't be
considered proper."

"I know," said Michael his own color heightening now,
"I didn't mean that. I wanted you to know how much you
had done for me already. You don't know what it is never to
have been kissed by your mother, or any living soul. Nobody ever kissed me in all my life that I know of but you."

He looked down at the little girl with such a grave,
sweet expression, his eyes so expressive of the long lonely
years without woman's love, that child though she was Starr
seemed to understand, and her whole young soul went
forth in pity. Tears sprang to her eyes.

"Oh!" she said. "That is dreadful! Oh! I don't care if it
isn't proper—"

And before he knew what she was about to do the little
girl tilted to her tiptoes, put up her dainty hands, caught
him about the neck and pressed a warm eager kiss on his
lips. Then she sprang away frightened, sped across the
room, and through the opposite door.

Michael stood still in a bewilderment of joy for the instant. The compelling of her little hands, the pressure of
her fresh lips still lingered with him. A flood tide of glory
swept over his whole being. There were tears in his eyes, but
he did not know it. He stood with bowed head as though in
a holy place. Nothing so sacred, so beautiful, had ever come
into his life. Her baby kisses had been half unconscious.
This kiss was given of her own free will, because she wanted
to do something for him. He did not attempt to understand
the wonderful joy that surged through his heart and pulsed
in every fiber of his being. His lonely, unloved life was

enough to account for it, and he was only a boy with a brief
knowledge of life, but he knew enough to enshrine that kiss
in his heart of hearts as a holy thing, not even to be thought
about carelessly.

When he roused himself to follow her she had disappeared. Her father and the president were listening to a
recitation, but she was nowhere to be seen. She had gone to
her own room. Michael went down by himself in a thicket
by the lake.

She met him shyly at dinner, with averted gaze and a
glow on her cheeks, as if half afraid of what she had done,
but he reassured her with his eyes. His glance seemed to
promise he would never take advantage of what she had
done. His face wore an exalted look, as if he had been lifted
above earth, and Starr, looking at him wonderingly, was
glad she had followed her impulse.

They took a horseback ride to the college grove that
afternoon. Mr. Endicott, one of the professors, Starr, and
Michael. The president had borrowed the horses from
some friends.

Michael sat like a king upon his horse. He had ridden
the college mule bareback every summer, and riding
seemed to be as natural to him as any other sport. Starr had
been to a New York riding school, and was accustomed to
taking her morning exercise with her father in the park, or
accompanied by a footman, but she sat her Florida pony as
happily as though he had been a shiny, well-groomed steed
of priceless value. Somehow it seemed to her an unusually
delightful experience to ride with this nice boy through the
beautiful shaded road of arching live oaks richly draped
with old gray moss. Michael stopped by the roadside, where
the shade was dense, dismounted and plunged into the
thicket, returning in a moment with two or three beautiful
orchids and some long vines of the wonderful yellow
jessamine whose exquisite perfume filled all the air about.
He wreathed the jessamine about the pony's neck, and
Starr twined it about her hat and wore the orchids in her
belt.

Starr had never seen an orange grove before and took
great delight in the trees heavily loaded with fruit, green
and yellow and set about by blossoms. She tucked a spray of

blossoms in her dark hair under the edge of her hat, and Michael looked at her and smiled in admiration. Mr. Endicott, glancing toward his daughter, caught the look, and was reminded of the time when he had found the two children in his own drawing room being made a show for his wife's guests, and sighed half in pleasure, half in foreboding. What a beautiful pair they were to be sure, and what had the future in store for his little girl?

On the way back they skirted another lake and Michael dismounted again to bring an armful of great white magnolia blossoms, and dainty bay buds to the wondering Starr, and then they rode slowly on through the wooded road, the boy talling tales of adventures here and there; pointing out a blue jay or calling attention to the mockingbird's song.

"I wish you could be here next week," said the boy wistfully. "It will be full moon then. There is no time to ride through this place like a moonlight evening. It seems like fairyland then. The moonbeams make fairy ladders of the jessamine vines."

"It must be beautiful," said Starr dreamily. Then they rode for a few minutes in silence. They were coming to the end of the overarched avenue. Ahead of them the sunlight shone clearly like the opening of a great tunnel framed in living green. Suddenly Starr looked up gravely.

"I'm going to kiss you good-bye tonight when we go away," she said softly, and touching her pony lightly with the whip rode out into the bright road; the boy, his heart leaping with joy, not far behind her.

Before supper Mr. Endicott had a talk with Michael that went further toward making the fatherless boy feel that he had someone belonging to him than anything that had happened yet.

"I think you have done enough for me, sir," said Michael respectfully opening the conversation as Endicott came out to the porch where the boy was waiting for him. "I think I ought to begin to earn my own living. I'm old enough now—" and he held his head up proudly. "It's been very good of you all these years—I never can repay you. I hope you will let me pay the money back that you have spent on me, someday when I can earn enough."

Michael had been thinking this speech out ever since the president had told him of Endicott's expected visit, but somehow it did not sound as well to him when he said it as he had thought it would. It seemed the only right thing to do when he planned it, but in spite of him as he looked into Mr. Endicott's kind, keen eyes, his own fell in troubled silence. Had his words sounded ungrateful? Had he seen a hurt look in the man's eyes?

"Son," said Endicott after a pause, and the word stirred the boy's heart strangely, "son, I owe you a debt I never can repay. You gave me back my little girl, flinging your own life into the chance as freely as if you had another on hand for use any minute. I take it that I have at least a father's right in you at any rate, and I mean to exercise it until you are twenty-one. You must finish a college course first. When will that be? Three years? They tell me you are doing well. The doctor wants to keep you here to teach after you have graduated, but I had thought perhaps you would like to come up to New York and have your chance. I'll give you a year or two in business, whatever seems to be your bent when you are through, and then we'll see. Which would you rather do? Or, perhaps you'd prefer to let your decision rest until the time comes."

"I think I'm bound to go back to New York, sir," said Michael lifting his head with that peculiar motion all his own, so like a challenge. "You know, sir, you said I was to be educated so that I might help my friends. I have learned of course that you meant it in a broader sense than just those few boys, for one can help people anywhere, but still I feel as if it wouldn't be right for me not to go back. I'm sure they'll expect me."

Endicott shrugged his shoulders half admiringly.

"Loyal to your old friends still? Well, that's commendable, but still I fancy you'll scarcely find them congenial now. I wouldn't let them hang too closely about you. They might become a nuisance. You have your way to make in the world, you know."

Michael looked at his benefactor with troubled brows. Somehow the tone of the man disturbed him.

"I promised," he said simply. Because there had been

so little in his affections that promise had been cherished
through the years, and meant much to Michael. It stood for
principle and loyalty in general.

"Oh, well, keep your promise, of course," said the man
of the world easily. "I fancy you will find the discharge of it
a mere form."

A fellow student came across the campus.

"Lndicott," he called, "have you seen Hallowell go toward the village within a few minutes?"

"He just went out the gate," responded Michael pleasantly.

Mr. Endicott looked up surprised.

"Is that the name by which you are known?"

"Endicott? Yes, sir, Michael Endicott. Was it not by your
wish? I supposed they had asked you. I had no other name
that I knew."

"Ah! I didn't know," pondered Endicott.

There was silence for a moment.

"Would you—shall I—do you dislike my having it?"
asked the boy delicately sensitive at once.

But the man looked up with something like tenderness
in his smile.

"Keep it, son. I like it. I wish I had a boy like you. It is
an old name and a proud one. Be worthy of it."

"I will try, sir," said Michael, as if he were registering a
vow.

There was an early supper for the guests and then
Michael walked through another sunset to the station with
Starr. He carried a small box carefully prepared in which
reposed a tiny green and blue lizard for a parting gift. She
had watched the lizards scuttling away under the board
sidewalks at their approach, or coming suddenly to utter
stillness, changing their brilliant colors to gray like the
fence boards that they might not be observed. She was won-
derfully interested in them, and was charmed with her gift.
The particular lizard in question was one that Michael had
trained to eat crumbs from his hand, and was quite tame.

The two said little as they walked along together. Each
was feeling what a happy time they had spent in one another's company.

"I shall write and tell you how the lizard is," said Starr

laughing, "and you will tell me all about the funny and interesting things you are doing, won't you?"

"If—I may," said Michael wistfully.

At the station a New York acquaintance of the Endicotts' invited them to ride in his private car which was on the side track waiting for the train to pick it up. Michael helped Starr up the steps, and carried the lizard into the car as well as the great sheaf of flowers she insisted on taking with her.

There were some ladies inside who welcomed Starr effusively, and Michael, suddenly abashed, laid down the flowers, lifted his cap and withdrew. A sudden blank had come upon him. Starr was absorbed by people from another world than his. He would have no opportunity to say good-bye—and she had promised. But then of course he ought not to expect her to do that. She had been very kind to him.

He was going down the steps now. An instant more and he would be on the cinders of the track.

A sudden rush, a soft cry, caused him to pause on the second step of the vestibuled car. It was Starr, standing just above him, and her eyes were shining like her namesake the evening star.

"You were going without good-bye," she reproved, and her cheeks were rosy red, but she stood her ground courageously. Placing a soft hand gently on either cheek as he stood below her, his face almost on a level with hers, she tilted his head toward her and touched his lips with her own red ones, delicately as if a rose had swept them.

Simultaneously came the sound of the distant train.

"Good-bye, you nice, splendid boy!" breathed Starr, and waving her hand darted inside the car.

Mr. Endicott, out on the platform still talking to the president, heard the oncoming train and looked around for Michael. He saw him coming from the car with this exalted look upon his face, his cap off, and the golden beams of the sun again sending their halo like a nimbus over his hair.

Catching his hand heartily, he said:

"Son, I'm pleased with you. Keep it up, and come to me when you are ready. I'll give you a start."

Michael gripped his hand and blundered out some

words of thanks. Then the train was upon them, and Endicott had to go.

The two younger ladies in the car, meantime, were plying Starr with questions. "Who is that perfectly magnificent young man, Starr Endicott? Why didn't you introduce him to us? I declare I never saw such a beautiful face on any human being before."

A moment more and the private car was fastened to the train, and Starr leaning from the window waved her tiny handkerchief until the train had thundered away among the pines, and there was nothing left but the echo of its sound. The sun was going down but it mattered not. There was sunshine in the boy's heart. She was gone, his little Starr, but she had left the memory of her soft kiss and her bright eyes, and someday, someday, when he was done with college, he would see her again. Meantime he was content.

Chapter 6

The joy of loving-kindness in his life, and a sense that somebody cared, seemed to have the effect of stimulating Michael's mind to greater energies. He studied with all his powers. Whatever he did he did with his might, even his play.

The last year of his stay in Florida, a department of scientific farming was opened on a small scale. Michael presented himself as a student.

"What do you want of farming, Endicott?" asked the president, happening to pass through the room on the first day of the teacher's meeting with his students. "You can't use farming in New York."

There was perhaps in the kindly old president's mind a hope that the boy would linger with them, for he had become attached to him in a silent, undemonstrative sort of way.

"I might need it sometime," answered Michael, "and

anyway I'd like to understand it. You said the other day that no knowledge was ever wasted. I'd like to know enough at least to tell somebody else."

The president smiled, wondered, and passed on. Michael continued in the class, supplementing the study by a careful reading of all the agricultural magazines, and government literature on the subject that came in his way. Agriculture had had a strange fascination for him ever since a noted speaker from the North had come that way and in an address to the students told them that the new field for growth today lay in getting back to nature and cultivating the earth. It was characteristic of Michael that he desired to know if that statement was true, and if so, why. Therefore he studied.

The three years flew by as if by magic. Michael won honors not a few, and the day came when he had completed his course, and as valedictorian of his class, went up to the old chapel for his last commencement in the college.

He sat on the platform looking down on the kindly, uncritical audience that had assembled for the exercises, and saw not a single face that had come for his sake alone. Many were there who were interested in him because they had known him through the years, and because he bore the reputation of being the honor man of his class and the finest athlete in school. But that was not like having someone of his very own who cared whether he did well or not. He found himself wishing that even Buck might have been there; Buck, the nearest to a brother he had ever had. Would Buck have cared that he had won highest rank? Yes, he felt that Buck would have been proud of him.

Michael had sent out three invitations to commencement, one to Mr. Endicott, one to Starr, and one addressed to Buck, with the inner envelope bearing the words "For Buck and the kids," but no response had come to any of them. He had received back the one addressed to Buck with "Not Called For" in big pink letters stamped across the corner. It had reached him that morning, just before he came on the platform. He wished it had not come till night; it gave him a lonely, almost forsaken feeling. He was "educated" now, at least enough to know what he did not know; and there was no one to care.

When Michael sat down after his oration amid a storm of hearty applause, prolonged by his comrades into something like an ovation, someone handed him a letter and a package. There had been a mistake made at the post office in sorting the mail and these had not been put into the college box. One of the professors going down later found them and brought them up.

The letter was from Mr. Endicott containing a businesslike line of congratulations, a hope that the recipient would come to New York if he still felt of that mind, and a check for a hundred dollars.

Michael looked at the check awesomely, reread the letter carefully and put both in his pocket. The package was tiny and addressed in Starr's handwriting. Michael saved that till he should go to his room. He did not want to open it before any curious eyes.

Starr's letters had been few and far between, girlish little epistles, and the last year they had ceased altogether. Starr was busy with life; finishing school and dancing school and music lessons and good times. Michael was a dim and pleasant vision to her.

The package contained a scarfpin of exquisite workmanship. Starr had pleased herself by picking out the very prettiest thing she could find. She had her father's permission to spend as much as she liked on it. It was in the form of an orchid, with a tiny diamond like a drop of dew on one petal.

Michael looked on it with wonder, the first suggestion of personal adornment that had ever come to him. He saw the reminder of their day together in the form of the orchid; studied the beautiful name, "Starr Delevan Endicott," engraved upon the card; then put them carefully back into their box and locked it into his bureau drawer. He would wear it the first time he went to see Starr. He was very happy that day.

The week after college closed Michael drove the college mule to the county seat, ten miles away, and bought a small trunk. It was not much of a trunk but it was the best the town afforded. In this he packed all his wordly possessions, bade good-bye to the president, and such of the professors as had not already gone north for their vacations, took a long tramp to all his old haunts, and boarded the midnight train for New York.

The boy had a feeling of independence which kept him from letting his benefactor know of his intended arrival. He did not wish to make him any unnecessary trouble, and though he had now been away from New York for fourteen years, he felt a perfect assurance that he could find his way about. There are some things that one may learn even at seven, that will never be forgotten.

When Michael landed in New York he looked around him with vague bewilderment for a moment. Then he started out with assurance to find a new spot for himself in the world.

Suitcase he had not, nor any baggage but his trunk to hinder him. He had discovered that the trunk could remain in the station for a day without charge. The handsome rain-coat and umbrella which had been a part of the outfit the tailor had sent him that spring were all his encumbrances, so he picked his way unhampered across Liberty Street, eyeing his former enemies, the policemen, and every little urchin or newsboy with interest. Of course Buck and the rest would have grown up and changed some; they wouldn't likely be selling papers now—but—these were boys such as he had been. He bought a paper of a little ragged fellow with a pinched face, and a strange sensation came over him. When he left this city he was the newsboy, and now he had money enough to buy a paper—and the education to read it! What a difference! Not that he wanted the paper at present, though it might prove interesting later, but he wanted the experience of buying it. It marked the era of change in his life and made the contrast tremendous. Immediately his real purpose in having an education, the uplift of his fellow beings, which had been most vague during the years, took form and leapt into vivid interest, as he watched the little skinny legs of the newsboy nimbly scrambling across the muddy street under the feet of horses, and between auto-mobiles, in imminent danger of his life.

Michael had thought it all out, just what he would do, and he proceeded to carry out his purpose. He had no idea what a fine picture of well-groomed youth and manly beauty he presented as he marched down the street. He

walked like a king, and New York abashed him no more
now that he had come back than it did before he went away.
There are some spirits born that way. He walked like a gentleman, unafraid.

He had decided not to go to Mr. Endicott until he had
found lodging somewhere. An innate delicacy had brought
him to this decision. He would not put one voluntary burden upon his kind benefactor. Born and bred in the slums,
whence came this fineness of feeling? Who shall say?

Michael threaded his way through the maze of traffic,
instinct and vague stirrings of memory guiding him to a
quiet shabby street where he found a dingy little room for a
small price. The dangers that might have beset a strange
young man in the great city were materially lessened for
him on account of his wide reading. He had read up New
York always whenever he found an article or book or story
that touched upon it, and without realizing it he was well
versed in details. He had even pondered for hours over a
map of New York that he found in the back of an old magazine, comparing it with his faint memories, until he knew
the location of things with relation to one another pretty
well. A stranger less versed might have gotten into most
undesirable quarters.

The boy looked around his new home with a strange
sinking of heart, after he had been out to get something to
eat, and arranged for his trunk to be sent to his room. It
was very tiny and not overclean. The wallpaper was a dingy
flowered affair quite ancient in design, and having to all
appearances far outlived a useful life. The one window
looked out to brick walls, chimneys, and roofs. The noise of
the city clattered in; the smells and the heat made it almost
stifling to the boy who had lived for thirteen years in the
sunshine of the south, and the freedom of the open.

The narrow bed looked uninviting, the bureau-wash-
stand was of the cheapest, and the reflection Michael saw in
its warped mirror would have made any boy with a particle
of vanity actually suffer. Michael, however, was not vain. He
thought little about himself, but this room was depressing.
The floor was covered with a nondescript carpet faded and
soiled beyond redemption, and when his trunk was placed
between the bureau and the bed there would be scarcely

room for the one wooden chair. It was not a hopeful outlook. The boy took off his coat and sat down on the bed to
whistle.

Life, grim, appalling, specterlike, uprose before his
mental vision, and he spent a bad quarter of an hour trying
to adjust himself to his surrondings; his previous sunny
philosophy having a tough tussle with the sudden realities
of things as they were. Then his trunk arrived.

It was like Michael to unpack it at once and put all his
best philosophical resolves into practice.

As he opened the trunk a whiff of the south exhaled.
He caught his breath with a sudden keen homesickness. He
realized that his school days were over, and all the sweetness
and joy of that companionful life passed. He had often felt
alone in those days. He wondered at it now. He had never in
all his experience known such aloneness as now in this great
strange city.

The last thing he had put into his trunk had been a
branch of mammoth pine needles. The breath of the tree
brought back all that meant home to him. He caught it up
and buried his face in the plumy tassels.

The tray of the trunk was filled with flags, pennants,
photographs, and college paraphernalia. Eagerly he pulled
them all out and spread them over the humpy little bed.
Then he grabbed for his hat and rushed out. In a few minutes he returned with a paper of tacks, another of pins, and
a small tack hammer. In an hour's time he had changed the
atmosphere of the whole place. Not an available inch of
bare wall remained with its ugly, dirty wallpaper. College
colors, pennants, and flags were grouped about pictures,
and over the unwashed window was draped Florida moss.
Here and there, apparently fluttering on the moss or about
the room, were fastened beautiful specimens of semi-
tropical moths and butterflies in the gaudiest of colors. A
small stuffed alligator reposed above the window, gazing
apathetically down upon the scene. A large alligator skin
was tacked on one wall. One or two queer bird's nests fastened to small branches hung quite naturally here and
there.

Michael threw down the hammer and sat down to sur-
vey his work, drawing a breath of relief. He felt more at

home now with the photographs of his fellow students smiling down upon him. Opposite was the baseball team, frowning and sturdy; to the right the glee Club with himself as their leader; to the left a group of his classmates, with his special chum in the midst. As he gazed at that kindly face in the middle he could almost hear the friendly voice calling to him: "Come on Angel! You're sure to win out!"

Michael felt decidedly better, and fell to hanging up his clothes and arranging his effects on clean papers in the rheumatic bureau drawers. These were cramped quarters but would do for the present until he was sure of earning some money, for he would not spend his little savings more than he could help now and he would not longer be dependent upon the benefaction of Mr. Endicott.

When his box of books arrived he would ask permission to put some shelves over the window. Then he would feel quite cozy and at home.

So he cheered himself as he went about getting into his best garments, for he intended to arrive at Madison Avenue about the time that his benefactor reached home for the evening.

Michael knew little of New York ways, and less of the habits of society; the few novels that had happened in his way being his only instructors on the subject. He was going entirely on his dim memories of the habits of the Endicott home during his brief stay there. As it happened Mr. Endicott was at home when Michael arrived and the family were dining alone.

The boy was seated in the reception room gazing about him with the ease of his habitual unconsciousness of self, when Endicott came down bringing Starr with him. A second time the man of the world was deeply impressed with the fine presence of this boy from obscurity. He did not look out of place even in a New York drawing room. It was incredible, though of course a large part of it was due to his city-made clothing. Still, that would not by any means account for ease of manner, graceful courtesy, and an instinct for saying the right thing at the right time.

Endicott invited the lad to dine with them and Starr eagerly seconded the invitation. Michael accepted as eagerly, and a few moments later found himself seated at the elegantly appointed table by the side of a beautiful and haughty woman who stared at him coldly, almost insultingly, and made not one remark to him throughout the whole meal. The boy looked at her half wonderingly. It almost seemed as if she intended to resent his presence, yet of course that could not be. His idea of this whole family was the highest. No one belonging to Starr could of course be aught but lovely of spirit.

Starr herself seemed to feel the disapproval of her mother, and shrink into herself, saying very little, but smiling shyly at Michael now and then when her mother was not noticing her.

Starr was sixteen now, slender and lovely as she had given promise of being. Michael watched her satisfied. At last he turned to the mother sitting in her cold grandeur, and with the utmost earnestness and deference in his voice said, his glance still half toward Starr:

"She is like you, and yet not!"

He said it gravely, as if it were a discovery of the utmost importance to them both, and he felt sure it was the key to her heart, this admission of his admiration of the beautiful girl.

Mrs. Endicott froze him with her glance.

From the roots of his hair down to the tips of his toes and back again he felt it, that insulting resentment of his audacity in expressing any opinion about her daughter, or in fact in having any opinion. For an instant his self-possession deserted him, and his face flushed with mingled emotions. Then he saw a look of distress on Starr's face as she struggled to make reply for her silent mother:

"Yes, Mamma and I are often said to resemble one another strongly," and there was a tremble in Starr's voice that roused all the manliness in the boy. He flung off the oppression that was settling down upon him and listened attentively to what Endicott was saying, responding gracefully, intelligently, and trying to make himself think that it was his inexperience with ladies that had caused him to say something inappropriate. Henceforth during the evening he made no more personal remarks.

Endicott took the boy to his den after dinner, and later Starr slipped in and they talked a little about their beautiful

day in Florida together. Starr asked him if he still rode and
would like to ride with her in the park the next morning
when she took her exercise, and it was arranged in the presence of her father and with his full consent that Michael
should accompany her in place of the groom who usually
attended her rides.

Mrs. Endicott came in as they were making this arrangement, and immediately called Starr sharply out of the
room.

After their withdrawal Endicott questioned the boy
carefully about his college course and his habits of living.
He was pleased to hear that Michael had been independent
enough to secure lodgings before coming to his house. It
showed a spirit that was worth helping, though he told him
that he should have come straight to him.

As Endicott was going off on a business trip for a week
he told Michael to enjoy himself looking around the city
during his absence, and on his return present himself at the
office at an appointed hour when he would put him in the
way of something that would start him in life.

Michael thanked him and went back to his hot little
room on the fourth floor, happy in spite of heat and din-
giness and a certain homesick feeling. Was he not to ride
with Starr in the morning? He could hardly sleep for thinking of it, and of all he had to say to her.

Chapter 7

When Michael presented himself at the appointed hour the
next morning he was shown into a small reception room by
a maid, and there he waited for a full half hour. At the end
of that time he heard a discreet rustle of garments in the
distance, and a moment later, became aware of a cold stare
from the doorway. Mrs. Endicott in an elaborate morning
frock was surveying him fixedly through a jeweled

lorgnette, her chin tilted contemptuously, and an expression of supreme scorn upon her handsome features. Woman of the world that she was, she must have noted the grace of his every movement as he rose with his habitual courtesy to greet her. Yet for some reason this only seemed to increase her dislike.

There was no welcoming hand held out in response to his good morning, and no answering smile displaced the severity of the woman's expression as she stood confronting the boy, slowly paralyzing him with her glance. Not a word did she utter. She could convey her deepest meaning without words when she chose.

But Michael was a lad of great self-control, and keen logical mind. He saw no reason for the woman's attitude of rebuke, and concluded he must be mistaken. Rallying his smile once more he asked:

"Is Miss Starr ready to ride, or have I come too early?"

Again the silence became impressive as the cold eyes looked him through, before the thin lips opened.

"My daughter is not ready to ride—with YOU, this morning or at any other time!"

"I beg your pardon, ma'am," said Michael now deeply astonished, and utterly unable to fathom the woman's strange manner. "Have I misunderstood? I thought she asked me to ride with her this morning. May I see her, please?"

"No, you may not see Miss Endicott!" said the cold voice. "And I have come down to tell you that I consider your coming here at all a great impertinence. Certainly my husband has fully discharged any obligations for the slight service he is pleased to assume that you rendered a good many years ago. I have always had my doubts as to whether you did not do more harm than good at that time. Of course you were only a child and it was impossible that you should have done any very heroic thing at that age. In all probability if you had kept out of things the trouble never would have happened, and your meddling simply gave you a wound and a soft bed for a while. In my opinion you have had far more done for you than you deserved, and I want you to understand that so far as my daughter is concerned the obligation is discharged."

Michael had stood immovable while the cruel woman uttered her harangue, his eyes growing wide with wonder and dark with a kind of manly shame for her as she went on. When she paused for a moment she saw his face was white and still like a statue, but there was something in the depth of his eyes that held her in check.

With utmost calm, and deference, although his voice rang with honest indignation, Michael spoke:

"I beg your pardon, Mrs. Endicott," he said, his tone clear and attention-demanding, "I have never felt that there was the slightest obligation resting upon any of this family for the trifling matter that occurred when, as you say, I was child. I feel that the obligation is entirely the other way, of course, but I cannot understand what you mean. How is my coming here at Mr. Endicott's invitation an impertinence?"

The woman looked at him contemptuously as though it were scarcely worth the trouble to answer him, yet there was something about him that demanded an answer.

"I suppose you are ignorant then," she answered cuttingly, "as you seem to be honest. I will explain. You are not fit company for my daughter. It is strange that you do not see that for yourself! A child of the slums, with nothing but shame and disgrace for an inheritance, and brought up a pauper! How could you expect to associate on a level with a gentleman's daughter? If you have any respect for her whatever you should understand that it is not for such as you to presume to call upon her and take her out riding. It is commendable in you of course to have improved what opportunities have been given you, but it is the height of ingratitude in a dependent to presume upon kindness and take on the airs of an equal, and you might as well understand first as last that you cannot do it. I simply will not have you here. Do you understand?"

Michael stood as if rooted to the floor, horror and dismay growing in his eyes, and stupor trickling through his veins. For a minute he stood after she had ceased speaking, as though the full meaning of her words had been slow to reach his consciousness. Yet outwardly his face was calm, and only his eyes had seemed to change and widen and suffer as she spoke. Finally his voice came to him:

"Madam, I did not know," he said in a stricken voice.

"As you say, I am ignorant." Then lifting his head with that fine motion of challenge to the world that was characteristic of him whenever he had to face a hard situation, his voice rang clear and undaunted:

"Madam, I beg your pardon. I shall not offend this way again. It was because I did not understand. I would not hurt your daughter in any way, for she has been the only beautiful thing that ever came into my life. But I will never trouble her again."

The bow with which he left her and marched past her into the hall and out of the great door where once his boy life had been freely laid down for her child, could have been no more gracefully or dramatically effected if he had been some great actor. It was natural, it was full of dignity and reproach, and it left the lady feeling smaller and meaner than she had ever felt in all of her rose-colored, velvet-lined existence. Somehow all the contempt she had purposely prepared for the crushing of the lad, he had suddenly flung from him as a hated garment and walked from her presence, leaving it wrapped about herself.

"Well, really!" she gasped at last when she realized that he was gone and her eloquence not half finished. "Well, really! What right had he to go away like that without my permission. Impertinent to the end! One would suppose he was a grand duke. Such airs! I always told Delevan it was a mistake to educate the masses. They simply don't know their place and will not keep it."

Nevertheless, the selfish woman was much shaken. Michael had made her feel somehow as if she had insulted a saint or a supernal being. She could not forget how the light had sifted through his wonderful hair and glinted through the depths of his great eyes, as he spoke those last words, and she resented the ease with which he had left her presence. It had been too much like the going of a victor, and not like one crushed back into his natural place. She was cross all day in consequence.

Starr meanwhile was lingering upstairs waiting for Michael. She had been purposely kept busy in a distant room at the back of the house by her mother, and was not told of his coming. As an hour went by beyond the appointed time she grew restless and disappointed, and then

annoyed and almost angry that he should have so easily forgotten her, but she did not tell her mother, and the old
Scottish nurse who would have been her confidante had
been sent on an errand to another part of the city.

Thus, as the days went by, and Michael came no more
to the house, the girl grew to think he did not want to come,
and her slight disappointment and mortification were succeeded by a haughty resentment, for her mother's teaching
had not been without some result in her character.

Michael had gone into the door of the Endicott mansion a boy with a light heart and a happy vision of the future. He came out from there an hour later, a man, with a
heavy burden on his heart, and a blank vision of the future.
So much had the woman wrought.

As he walked from the house his bright head drooped,
and his spirit was troubled within him. He went as one in a
terrible dream. His face had the look of an angel newly
turned out of paradise and for no fault of his own, an angel
who bowed to the supreme mandate, but whose life was
crushed within him. People looked at him strangely, and
wondered as they passed him. It was as if sorrow were em-
bodied suddenly, and looking through eyes intended for
love. For the first time Michael, beloved of all his companions for his royal unselfishness, was thinking of himself.

Yet even so there was no selfishness in his thought. It
was only as if that which had always given him life and the
breath of gladness had suddenly been withdrawn from him,
and left him panting, gasping in a wide and unexpected
emptiness.

Somehow he found his way to his room and locked the
door.

Then the great spirit gave way and he flung himself
upon the bed in supreme exhaustion. He seemed not to
have another atom of strength left wherewith to move or
think or even breathe consciously. All his physical powers
had oozed away and deserted him, now in this great crisis
when life's foundations were shaken to their depths and
nothing seemed to be anymore. He could not think it over
or find a way out of the horror, he could only lie and suffer
it, fact by fact, as it came and menaced him, slowly, cruelly
throughout that length of day.

Gradually it became distinct and separated itself into thoughts so that he could follow it, as if it were the separate parts of some great dragon come to twine its coils about him and claw and crush and strangle the soul of him.

First, there was the fact like a great knife which seemed to have severed soul from body, the fact that he might not see Starr, or have aught to do with her anymore. So deeply had this interdiction taken hold upon him that it seemed to him in his agitation he might no longer even think of her.

Next, following in stern and logical sequence, came the reason for this severing of soul from all it knew and loved: the fact of his lowly birth. Coming as it did, out of the blue of a trustful life that had never questioned much about his origin but had sunnily taken life as a gift, and thought little about self; with the bluntness and directness of an un-loving-kindness, it had seemed to cut and hack in every direction, all that was left of either soul or body, so that there came no hope of ever catching things together again.

That was the way it came over and over again as the boy without a friend in the whole wide world to whom he could turn in his first great trouble, lay and took it.

Gradually out of the blackness he began to think a little, think back to his own beginning. Who was he? What was he? For the first time in his life, though he knew life more than most of the boys with whom he had associated, the thought of shame in connection with his own birth came to him, and burrowed and scorched its way into his soul.

He might have thought of such a possibility before perhaps, had not his very youngest years been hedged about by a beautiful fancy that sprang from the brain of an old Irish-woman in the slums, whose heart was wide as her ways were devious, and who said one day when little Mikky had run her an errand, "Shure, an' then, Mikky, yer an angel sthraight frum hiven an' no misthake. Yer no jest humans like the rist av us; ye must av dhropped doon frum the skoy." And from that it had gone forth that Mikky was the child of the sky, and that was why no one knew who were his parents.

The bit of a fancy had guarded the boy's weird baby-hood, and influenced more than he knew his own thought of existence, until life grew too full to think much on it.

Out of the darkness and murk of the slums the soul of
Mikky had climbed high, and his ambitions reached up to
the limitless blue above him. It had never occurred to him
once that there might be an embargo put upon his upward
movements. He had taken all others to be as freehearted
and generous as himself. Heir of all things, he had breathed
the atmosphere of culture as though it were his right. Now,
he suddenly saw that he had no business climbing. He had
been seized just as he was about to mount a glorious height
from which he was sure other heights were visible, when a
rude hand had brushed him back and dropped him as
though he had been some crawling reptile, down, down,
down, at the very bottom of things. And the worst of all was
that he might not climb back. He might look up, he might
know the way up again, but the honor in him—the only bit
of the heights he had carried back to the foot with him—
forbade him to climb to the dizzy heights of glory, for they
belonged to others; those whom fortune favored, and on
whose escutcheon there was no taint of shame.

And why should it be that some souls should be more
favored than others? What had he, for instance, to do with
his birth? He would not have chosen shame, if shame there
was. Yet shame or not he was branded with it for life because his origin was enveloped in mystery. The natural con-
clusion was that sin had had its part.

Then through the boy's mind there tumbled a confusion of questions all more or less unanswerable, in midst
of which he slept.

He seemed to have wandered out into the open again
with the pines he loved above him, and underneath the
springy needles with their slippery resinous softness; and
he lay looking up into the changeless blue that covered all
the heights, asking all the tumultuous questions that throbbed through his heart, asking them of God.

Silently the noises of the city slunk away and dropped
into the ceaseless calm of the southland he had left. The
breeze fanned his cheek, the pines whispered, and a rippling bird song touched his soul with peace. A quietness
came down upon his troubled spirit, and he was satisfied to
take the burden that had been laid upon him and to bear it

greatly. The peace was upon him when he awoke, far into the next morning.

The hot June sun steamed into his stuffy room and fell aslant the bed. He was sodden and heavy with the heat and the oppression of his garments. His head ached, and he felt as nearly ill as he had ever felt in his life. The specter of the day before confronted him in all its torturing baldness, but he faced it now and looked it squarely in the eyes.. It was not conquered yet, not by any means. The sharp pain of its newness was just as great, and the deep conviction was still there that it was because of wrong that this burden was laid upon him, but there was an adjustment of his soul to the inevitable that there had not been at first.

The boy lay still for a few minutes looking out upon a new life in which everything had to be readjusted to the idea of himself and his new limitations. Heretofore in his mind there had been no height that was not his for the climbing. Now, the heights were his, but he would not climb because the heights themselves might be marred by his presence. It was wrong, it was unfair, that things should be so; but they were so, and as long as sin and wrong were in the world they would be so.

He must look upon life as he had looked upon every contest through his education. There were always things to be borne, hard things, but that only made the conquest greater. He must face this thing and win.

And what had he lost that had been his before? Not the beautiful girl who had been the idol of his heart all these years. She was still there, alive and well, and more beautiful than ever. His devotion might yet stand between her and harm if need arose. True, he had lost the hope of companionship with her, but that had been the growth of a day. He had never had much of it before, nor expected it when he came north. It would have been a glory and a joy beyond expression, but one could live without those things and be true. There was some reason for it all somewhere in the infinite he was sure.

It was not like the ordinary boy to philosophize in this way, but Michael had never been an ordinary boy. Ever his soul had been open to the greatness of the universe and optimistic in the most trying surroundings. He had come out of the hardest struggle his soul had yet met, but he had come out a man. There were lines about his pleasant mouth that had not been there the day before, which spoke of strength and self-control. There were new depths in his eyes as of one who had looked down, and seen things unspeakable, having to number himself with the lowly.

A new thought came to him while he lay there trying to take in the change that had come to him. The thought of his childhood companions, the little waifs like himself who came from the offscourings of the earth. They had loved him he knew. He recalled slowly, laboriously, little incidents from his early history. They were dim and uncertain, many of them, but little kindnesses stood out. A bad cut on his foot once and how Buck had bathed it and bound it up in dirty rags, doing double duty with the newspapers for several days to save his friend from stepping. There was a bitter cold night way back as far as he could remember when he had had bad luck, and came among the others supperless and almost freezing. Buck had shared a crust and found a warm boiler room where they crawled out of sight and slept. There were other incidents, still more blurred in his memory, but enough to recall how loyal the whole little gang had been to him. He saw once more their faces when they heard he was going away to college, blanched with horror at the separation, lighting with pleasure when he promised to return!

The years, how they had changed and separated! Where were they, these who really belonged to him, who were his rightful companions? What had the years done to them? And he had a duty toward them unperformed. How was it that he had been in the city all these hours and not even thought of going to look for those loyal souls who had stood by him so faithfully when they were all mere babies? He must go at once. He had lost his head over attempting to reach things that were not for him, and this shock had come to set him straight.

Gravely he rose at last, these thoughts surging through his brain.

The heat, the stifling air of the room, his recent struggling and the exhausting stupor made him reel dizzily as he got up, but his mettle was up now and he set his lips and went about making himself neat. He longed for a dip in the crystal waters of the little lake at college. The tiny washbowl in his room proved a poor substitute with its tepid water and diminutive towel.

He went out and breakfasted carefully as if it were a duty, and then, with his map in his pocket, started out to find his old haunts.

Chapter 8

Thirteen years in New York had brought many changes. Some of the well-remembered landmarks were gone and new buildings in their places. A prosperous looking soloon quite palatial in its entrance marked the corner where he used to sell papers. It used to be a corner grocery store. Saloons! Always and everywhere there were saloons! Michael looked at them wonderingly. He had quite forgotten them in his exile, for the college influence had barred them out from its vicinity.

The boy Mikky had been familiar enough with saloons, looking upon them as a necessary evil, where drinking fathers spent the money that ought to have bought their children food. He had been in and out of them commonly enough selling his papers, warming his feet, and getting a crust now and then from an uneaten bit on the lunch counter. Sometimes there had been glasses to drain, but Mikky with his observing eyes had early decided that he would have none of the stuff that sent men home to curse their little children.

College influence, while there had been little said on the subject, had filled the boy with horror for saloons and drunkards. He stood appalled now as he turned at last into an alley where familiar objects, doorsteps, turnings, cellars, met his gaze, with grog shops all along the way and taking command of every corner.

A strange feeling came over him as memory stirred by long-forgotten sights awoke. Was this really the place, and was that opening beyond the third steps the very blind alley where Janie used to live? Things were so much dirtier, so much worse in every way than he remembered them.

He hurried on, not noticing the attention he was attracting from the wretched little children in the gutters, though he scanned them all eagerly, hurriedly, with the wild idea that Buck and the rest might be among them.

Yes, the alley was there, dark and ill smelling as ever, and in its dim recesses on a dirty step a woman's figure hunched; a figure he knew at once that he had seen before and in that very spot. Who was she? What had they called her? Sally? Aunt Sal?

He hurried up to where she sat looking curiously, apathetically at him; her gray hair straggling down on her dirty cotton frock open at the neck over shriveled yellow skin; soiled old hands hanging carelessly over slatternly garments; stockingless feet stuck into a great tattered pair of men's shoes. Nothing seemed changed since he saw her last save that the hair had been black then, and the skin not so wrinkled. Aunt Sally had been good-natured always, even when she was drunk; her husband, when he came home was always drunk also, but never good-natured. These things came back to the boy as he stook looking down at the wreck of a woman before him.

The bleary eyes looked up unknowning, half resentful of his intrusion.

"Aunt Sally!" impulsively cried the boyish voice. "Aren't you Aunt Sally?"

The woman looked stupidly surprised.

"I be," she said thickly, "but wot's that to youse? I beant no hant o' yourn."

"Don't you remember Mikky?" he asked almost anxiously, for now the feeling had seized him that he must make her remember. He must find out if he could whether anything was known of his origin. Perhaps she could help him. Perhaps, after all, he might be able to trace his family, and find at least no disgrace upon him.

"Mikky!" the woman repeated dully. She shook her head.

"Mikky!" she said again stolidly. "Wot's Mikky?"

"Don't you remember Mikky the little boy that sold papers and brought you water sometimes? Once you gave me a drink of soup from your kettle. Think!"

A dim perception came into the sodden eyes.

"Thur was a Mikky long ago," she mused. "He had hair like a h'angel, bless the sweet chile; but he got shot an' never come back. That war long ago."

Michael took off his hat and the little light in the dark alley seemed to catch and tangle in the gleam of his hair.

The old woman started as though she had seen a vision.

"The saints preserve us!" she cried aghast, shrinking back into her doorway with raised hands, "an' who be yez? Yeh looks enough like the b'y to be the father of 'im. He'd hair loike the verra sunshine itself. Who be Yez? Spake quick. Be ye man, b'y, er angel?"

There was something in the woman's tone that went to the heart of the lonely boy, even while he recoiled from the repulsive creature before him.

"I am just Mikky, the boy, grown a little older," he said gently, "and I've come back to see the place where I used to live, and find the people I used to know."

"Y've lost yer way thin fer shure!" said the woman slightly recovering her equilibrium. "The loikes uv youse nivver lived in dis place; fer ef yous ain't angel you's gintulmun; an' no gintulmun ivver cum from the loikes o' this. An' besoides, the b'y Mikky. I tel'd yez, was shot an' nivver comed back no more. He's loikely up wid de angels where he b'longs."

"Yes, I was shot," said Michael, "but I wasn't killed. A good man sent me to college, and I've just graduated and come back to look up my friends."

"Frinds, is it, ye'll be afther a findin'? Thin ye'd bist look ilsewhar, fer thur's no one in this alley fit to be frinds with the loikes uv you. Ef that's wot they does with b'sy at co-lidge a pity 'tis more uv um can't git shot an' go there. But ef all youse tell is thrue, moi advice to yez is, juist bate it as hoird as ivver yez kin out'n yere, an' don't yez nivver set oies on this alley agin. Ye'd better stay to co-lidge all the days uv yer loife that set fut here agin, fer juist let 'em got holt uv yez an' they'll spile the pretty face uv ye. Look thar!" she pointed tragically toward a wreck of humanity that reeled into the alley just then. "Would yez loike to be loike that? My mon come home loike that ivvery day of his loife, rist his bones, an' he nivver knowed whin he died."

Maudlin tears rolled down the poor creature's cheeks, for they could be no tears of affection. Her man's departure from this life could have been but a relief. Michael recoiled from the sight with a sickening sadness. Nevertheless he meant to find out if this woman knew aught of his old friends, or of his origin. He rallied his forces to answer her.

"I don't have to be like that," he said. "I've come down to look up my friends I tell you, and I want you to tell me if you know anything about my parents. Did you ever hear anything about me? Did anybody know who I was or how I came to be here?"

The old woman looked at him only half comprehending, and tried to gather her scattered faculties, but she shook her grizzled head hopelessly.

"I ain't niver laid oies on yez before, an' how cud I know whar yez cum from, ner how yez cam to be here?" she answered.

He perceived that it would require patience to extract information from this source.

"Try to think," he said more gently. "Can you remember if anyone ever belonged to the little boy they called Mikky? Was there ever any mother or father, or—anybody that belonged to him at all."

Again she shook her head.

"Nivver as Oi knows on. They said he just comed a wee babby to the coourt a wanderin' with the other childer, with scarce a rag to his back, an' a smile on him like the arch-angel, and some said as how he niver had no father ner mother, but dthrapped sthraight frum the place where de angels live."

"But did no one take care of him or ever try to find out about him?" questioned Michael wistfully.

"Foind out, is it? Whist! An' who would tak toime to foind out whin ther's so miny uv their own. Mikky was allus welcome to a bite an' a sup ef any uv us had it by. There wuz old Granny Bane with the rheumatiks. She gave him a bed an' a bite now an' agin, till she died, an' afther that he made out to shift fer hisse'f. He was a moighty indepindint babby."

"But had he no other name? Mikky what? What was his whole name?" pursued Michael with an eagerness that could not give up the sought-for information.

The old woman only stared stupidly.

"Didn't he have any other name?" There was almost despair in his tone.

Another shake of the head.

"Just Mikky!" she said and her eyes grew dull once more.

"Can you tell me if there are any other people living here now that used to know Mikky? Are there any other men or women who might remember?"

"How kin Oi tell?" snarled the woman impatiently. "Oi can't be bothered."

Michael stood in troubled silence and the woman turned her head to watch a neighbor coming down the street with a basket in her hand. It would seem that her visitor interested her no longer. She called out some rough ribaldry to the woman who glanced up fiercely and deigned no further reply. Then Michael tried again.

"Could you tell me of the boys who used to go with Mikky?"

"No, Oi can't," she answered crossly, "Oi can't be bothered. Oi don't know who they was."

"There was Jimmie and Sam and Bobs and Buck. Surely you remember Buck, and little Janie. Janie who died after Mikky went away?"

The bleared eyes turned full upon him again.

"Janie? Fine Oi remimber Janie. They had a white hurse to her, foiner'n any iver cum to the coourt before. The b'ys stayed up two noights selling to git the money fur it, an' Buck he stayed stiddy while she was aloive. Pity she doied."

"Where is Buck?" demanded Michael with a sudden twinging of his heartstrings that seemed to bring back the old love and loyalty to his friend. Buck had needed him perhaps all these years and he had not known.

"That's whot the *po*lice would like fer yez to answer, I'm thinkin'!" laughed old Sal. "They wanted him bad fer breakin' into a house an' mos' killin' the lady an' gittin' aff wid de jewl'ry. He beat it dat noight an' ain't none o' us seen him these two year. He were a slick one, he were awful smart at breakin' an' stealin'. Mebbe Jimmie knows, but Jimmie, he's in jail, serving his time fer shootin' a man in the hand durin' a dhrunken fight. Jimmie, he's no good. Never wuz. He's jest like his foither. Bobs, he got both legs cut aff, bein' runned over by a big truck, and he doied in the horspittle. Bobbs he were better dead. He'd uv gone loike the rist. Sam, he's round these parts mostly nights. Ye'll hev to come at noight ef yez want to see him. Mebbe he knows more 'bout Buck'n he'll tell."

Sick at heart Michael put question after question but no more information was forthcoming and the old woman showed signs of impatience again. Carefully noting what she said about Sam and getting a few facts as to the best time and place to find him Michael turned and walked sadly out of the alley. He did not see the alert eyes of old Sal following him, nor the keen expression of her face as she stretched her neck to see which way he turned as he left the alley. As soon as he was out of sight she shuffled down from her doorstep to the corner and peered after him through the morning sunshine. Then she went slowly, thoughtfully back to her doorstep.

"Now whut in the divil could he be a wantin' wid Buck an' Sammie?" she muttered to herself. "All that story 'bout his bein' Mikky was puttin' it on my eye. I'll giv warnin' to Sammie this night, an' ef Buck's in those pairts he better git out west some'res. The *po*lice uv got onto 'im. But hoiwiver did they know he knowed Mikky? Poor little angel Mikky! I guv him the shtaight about Bobs an' Jimmie, fer they wuz beyant his troublin' but he'll niver foind Sammie from the directin' I sayed."

Michael, sorrowing, horror-filled, conscience-stricken, took his way to a restaurant and ate his dinner, thinking meanwhile what he could do for the boys. Could he perhaps visit Jimmie in prison and makes his life more comfortable in little ways? Could he plan something for him when he should come out? Could he help Sam? The old woman had said little about Sam's condition. Michael thought he might likely by this time have built up a nice little business for himself. Perhaps he had a prosperous newsstand in some frequented place. He looked forward eagerly to meeting him again. Sam had always been a silent child dependent on the rest, but he was one of the little gang and Michael's heart warmed toward his former comrade. It could not be that he would find him so loathsome and repulsive as the old woman Sal. She made him heartsick. Just to think of drinking soup from her dirty kettle! How could he have done it? And yet, he knew no better life then, and he was hungry, and a little child.

So Michael mused, and all the time with a great heart-hunger to know what had become of Buck. Could he and Sam together plan some way to find Buck and help him out of his trouble? How could Buck have done anything so dreadful? And yet even as he thought it he remembered that "pinching" had not been a crime in his childhood days, not unless one was found out. How had these principles, or lack of principles been replaced gradually in his own life without his realizing it at all? It was all strange and wonderful. Practically now he, Michael, had been made into a new creature since he left New York, and so gradually, and pleasantly that he had not at all realized the change that was going on in him.

Yet as he thought and marveled there shot through him a thought like a pang, that perhaps after all it had not been a good thing, this making him into a new creature, with new desires and aims and hopes that could never be fulfilled. Perhaps he would have been happier, better off, if he had never been taken out of that environment and brought to appreciate so keenly another one where he did not belong, and could never stay, since that old environment was the one where he must stay whether he would or no. He put the thought from him as unworthy at once, yet

the sharpness of the pang lingered and with it a vision of
Starr's vivid face as he had seen her two nights before in her
father's home, before he knew that the door of that home
was shut upon him forever.

Michael passed the day in idly wandering about the city
trying to piece together his old knowledge, and the new,
and know the city in which he had come to dwell.

It was nearing midnight, when Michael, by the advice
of old Sal, and utterly fearless in his ignorance, entered the
court where his babyhood had been spent.

The alley was dark and murky with the humidity of the
summer night; but unlike the morning hours it was alive
with a writhing, chattering, fighting mass of humanity.
Doorways were overflowing. The narrow alley itself seemed
fairly thronging with noisy, unhappy men and women.
Hoarse laughs mingled with rough cursing, shot through
with an occasional scream. Stifling odors lurked in cellar
doorways and struck one full in the face unawares. Curses
seemed to be the setting for all conversation whether angry
or jolly. Babies tumbled in the gutter and older children
fought over some scrap of garbage.

Appalled, Michael halted and almost turned back.
Then, remembering that this was where he had come
from—where he belonged—and that his duty, his obligation, was to find his friends, he went steadily forward.

There sat old Sal, a belligerent gleam in her small sodden eyes. Four men on a step opposite, with a candle stood
between them, were playing cards. Sal muttered a word as
Michael approached and the candle was suddenly ex-
tinguished. It looked as if one had carelessly knocked it
down to the pavement, but the glare flickered into darkness
and Michael could no longer see the men's faces. He had
wondered if one of them was Sam. But when he rubbed his
eyes and looked again in the darkness the four men were
gone and the step was occupied by two children holding a
sleeping baby between them and staring at him in open-
mouthed admiration.

The flickering weird light of the distant street lamps,
the noise and confusion, the odors and curses filled him
anew with a desire to flee, but he would not let himself turn

back. Never had Michael turned from anything that was his duty from fear or dislike of anything.

He tried to enter into conversation with old Sal again, but she would have none of him. She had taken "a wee drapth" and was alert and suspicious. In fact, the whole alley was on the alert for this elegant stranger who was none of theirs, and who of course could have come but to spy on someone. He wanted Sam, therefore Sam was hidden well and at that moment playing a crafty game in the back of a cellar on the top of an old beer barrel, by the light of a wavering candle, well guarded by sentinels all along the difficult way. Michael could have no more found him under those circumstances than he could have hoped to find a needle in a haystack the size of the whole city of New York.

He wandered for two hours back and forth through the alley seeing sights long since forgotten, hearing words unspeakable; following out this and that suggestion of the interested bystanders, always coming back without finding Sam. He had not yet comprehended the fact that he was not intended to find Sam. He had taken these people into his confidence just as he had always taken everyone into his confidence, and they were playing him false. If they had been the dwellers on Fifth Avenue he would not have expected them to be interested in him and his plans and desires; but these were his very own people, at least the "ownest" he had in the world, and among them he had once gone freely, confidently. He saw no reason why they should have changed toward him, though he felt the antagonism in the atmosphere as the night wore on, even as he had felt it in the Endicott house the day before.

Heartsick and baffled at last he took his way slowly, looking back many times, and leaving many messages for Sam. He felt as if he simply could not go back to even so uncomfortable a bed as he called his own in his new lodgings without having found some clue to his old comrades.

Standing at the corner of the alley opposite the flaunting lights of the saloon he looked back upon the swarming darkness of the alley and his heart filled with a great surging wave of pity, love, and sorrow. Almost at his feet in a dark shadow of a doorway a tiny white-faced boy crouched

fast asleep on the stone threshold. It made him think of
little Bobs, and his own barren childhood, and a mist came
before his eyes as he looked up, up at the sky where the very
stars seemed small and far away as if the sky had nothing to
do with this part of the earth.

"Oh, God!" he said under his breath. "Oh, God! I must
do something for them!"

And then as if the opportunity came with the prayer
there reeled into view a little group of people, three or four
men and a woman.

The woman was talking in a high frightened voice and
protesting. The men caught hold of her roughly, laughing
and flinging out coarse jests. Then another man came stealing from the darkness of the alley and joined the group,
seizing the woman by the shoulders and speaking words to
her too vile for repetition. In terrible fear the girl turned,
for Michael could see, now that she was nearer, that she was
but a young girl, and that she was pretty. Instantly he
thought of Starr and his whole soul rose in mighty wrath
that any man should dare treat any girl as he had seen these
do. Then the girl screamed and struggled to get away, crying: "It ain't true, it ain't true! Lem'me go! I won't go with
you—"

Instantly Michael was upon them, his powerful arms
and supple body dashing the men right and left. And because of the suddenness of the attack coming from this
most unexpected quarter—for Michael had stood somewhat in the shadow—and because of the cowardliness of all
bullies, for the moment he was able to prevail against all
four, just long enough for the girl to slip like a wraith from
their grasp and disappear into the shadows.

Then when the men, dazed from surprise, though not
seriously hurt, discovered that their prey was gone and that
a stranger from the higher walks of life had frustrated their
plans they fell upon him in their wrath.

Michael brave always, and well trained in athletics, par-
ried their blows for an instant, but the man, the one who
had come from the shadows of the alley, whose face was evil,
stole up behind and stabbed him in the shoulder. The sudden faintness that followed made him less capable of
defending himself. He felt he was losing his senses, and the

next blow from one of the men sent him reeling into the street where he fell heavily, striking his head against the curbing. There was a loud cry of murder from a woman's shrill voice, the padded rush of the villains into their holes, the distant ring of a policeman's whistle, and then all was quiet as a city night could be. Michael lay white and still with his face looking up to the faint pitying moon so far away and his beautiful hair wet with the blood that was flowing out on the pavement. There he lay on the edge of the world that was his own and would not own him. He had come to his own and his own received him not.

Chapter 9

Michael awoke in the hospital with a bandage around his head and a stinging pain in his shoulder whenever he tried to move.

Back in his inner consciousness there sounded the last words he heard before he fell, but he could not connect them with anything at first:

"Hit him again, Sam!"

Those were the words. What did they mean? Had he heard them or merely dreamed them? And where was he?

A glance about the long room with its rows of white beds each with an occupant answered his question. He closed his eyes again to be away from all those other eyes and think.

Sam! He had been looking for Sam. Had Sam then come at last? Had Sam hit him? Had Sam recognized him? Or was it another Sam?

But there was something really wrong with his head, and he could not think. He put up his right arm to feel the bandage and the pain in his shoulder stung again. Somehow to his feverish fancy it seemed the sting of Mrs. Endicott's words to him. He dropped his hand feebly and the nurse gave him something in a spoon. Then half dreaming he fell asleep, with a vision of Starr's face as he had seen her last.

Three weeks he lay upon that narrow white bed, and learned to face the battalion of eyes from the other narrow beds around him; learned to distinguish the quiet sounds of the marble-lined room from the rumble of the unknown city without, and when the rumble was the loudest his head ached with the thought of the alley and all the horrible sights and sounds that seemed written in letters of fire across his spirit.

He learned to look upon the quiet monotonous world of ministrations as a haven from the world outside into which he must presently go, and in his weakened condition he shrank from the new life. It seemed to be so filled with disappointments and burdens of sorrow.

But one night a man in his ward died and was carried silent and covered from the room. Some of his last moaning utterances had reached the ears of his fellow sufferers with a swift vision of his life and his home, and his mortal agony for the past, now that he was leaving it all.

That night Michael could not sleep, for the court and the alley, and the whole sunken humanity were pressing upon his heart. It seemed to be his burden that he must give up all his life's hopes to bear. And there he had it out with himself and accepted whatever should come to be his duty.

Meantime the wound on his head was healed, the golden halo had covered the scar, and the cut in his shoulder, which had been only a flesh wound, was doing nicely. Michael was allowed to sit up, and then to be about the room for a day or two.

It was in those days of his sitting up when the sun which crept in for an hour a day reached and touched to flame his wonderful hair, that the other men of the ward began to notice him. He seemed to them all as somehow set apart from the rest; one who was lifted above what held them down to sin and earth. His countenance spoke of strength and self-control, the two things that many of those men lacked, either through constant sinning or through constant fighting with poverty and trouble, and so, as he began to get about they sent for him to come to their bed-sides, and as they talked one and another of them poured out his separate tale of sorrow and woe, till Michael felt he could bear no more. He longed for power, great power to help; power to put these wretched men on their feet again to lead a new life, power to crush some of the demons in human form who were grinding them down to earth. Oh! for money and knowledge and authority!

Here was a man who had lost both legs in a defective machine he was running in a factory. He was a skilled work-man and had a wife and three little ones. But he was useless now at his trade. No one wanted a man with no legs. He might better be dead. Damages? No, there was no hope of that. He had accepted three hundred dollars to sign a re-lease. He had to. His wife and children were starving and they must have the money then or perish. There was no other way. Besides, what hope had he in fighting a great corporation? He was a poor man, a stranger in this country, with no friends. The company had plenty who were willing to swear it was the man's own fault.

Yonder was another who had tried to asphyxiate him-self by turning on the gas in his wretched little boarding-house room because he had lost his position on account of ill health, and the firm wished to put a younger man in his place. He had almost succeeded in taking himself out of this life.

Next to him was one, horribly burned by molten metal which he had been compelled to carry wouthout adequate precautions, because it was a cheaper method of handling the stuff and men cost less than machinery. You could al-ways get more men.

The man across from him was wasted away from insuf-ficient food. He had been out of work for months, and what little money he could pick up in odd jobs had gone mostly to his wife and children.

And so it was throughout the ward. On almost every life sin—somebody's sin—had left its mark. There were one or two cheery souls who, though poor, were blest with friends and a home of some kind and were looking forward to a speedy restoration, but these were the exception. Nearly all the others blamed someone else for their unhappy condition and in nearly every case someone else was undoubtedly to blame, even though in most cases each individual had been somewhat responsible.

All this Michael gradually learned, as he began his practical study of sociology. As he learned story after story, and began to formulate the facts of each he came to three conclusions: First, that there was not room enough in the city for these people to have a fair chance at the great and beautiful things of life. Second, that the people of the cities who had the good things were getting them all for themselves and cared not a straw whether the others went without. Third, that somebody ought to be doing something about it, and why not he?

Of course is was absurd for a mere boy just out of college, with scarcely a cent to his name—and not a whole name to call his own—to think of attempting to attack the great problem of the people single-handed, but still he felt he was called to do it, and he meant to try.

He hadn't an idea at this time whether anybody else had seen it just this way or not. He had read a little of city missions, and charitable enterprises, but they had scarcely reached his inner consciousness. His impression gathered from such desultory reading had been that the effort in that direction was sporadic and ineffective. And so, in his gigantic ignorance and egotism, yet with his exquisite sensitiveness to the inward call, Michael henceforth set himself to espouse the cause of the people.

Was he not one of them? Had he not been born there that he might be one of them, and know what they had to suffer? Were they not his kindred so far as he had any kindred? Had he not been educated and brought into contact with higher things that he might know what these other human souls might be if they had the opportunity? If he had known a little more about the subject he would have added "and if they *would*." But he did not; he supposed all souls were as willing to be uplifted as he had been.

Michael went out from the hospital feeling that his life work was before him. The solemn pledge he had taken as a little child to return and help his former companions became a voluntary pledge of his young manhood. He knew very little indeed about the matter, but he felt much, and he was determined to do, wherever the way opened. He had no doubt but that the way would open.

"Now, young man, take care of yourself," said the doctor in parting from his patient a few days later, "and for the land's sake keep away from back alleys at night. When you know a little more about New York you'll learn that it's best to keep just as far away from such places as possible. Don't go fooling around under the impression that you can convert any of those blackguards. They need to be blown up, every one of them, and the place obliterated. Mind, I say, keep away from them."

Michael smiled and thanked the doctor, and walked unsteadily down the hospital steps on feet that were strangely wobbly for him. But Michael did not intend to obey the doctor. He had been turning the matter over in his mind and he had a plan. And that very night about ten o'clock he went back to the alley.

Old Sal was sitting on her doorstep a little more intoxicated than the last time, and the young man's sudden appearance by her side startled her into an Irish howl.

"The saints presarve us!" she cried tottering to her feet. "He's cum back to us agin, sure he has! There's no killin' him! He's an angel shure. B'ys rin! bate it! bate it! The angel's here again!"

There was a sound of scurrying feet and the place seemed to suddenly clear of the children that had been underfoot. One or two scowling men, or curiously apathetic women in whose eyes the light of life had died and been left unburied, peered from dark doorways.

Michael stood quietly until the howling of Sal had subsided, and then he spoke in a clear tone.

"Can you tell if Sam has been around here tonight? Is he anywhere near here now?"

There was no answer for a minute but someone growled out the information that he might and then he might not have been. Someone else said he had just gone away but they didn't know where. Michael perceived that it was a good deal as it had been before.

"I have brought a message for him, a letter," he said, and he spoke so that anyone nearby might hear. "Will you give it to him when he comes? He will want to see it, I am sure. It is important. I think he will be glad to get it. It contains good news about an old friend of his."

He held out the letter courteously to old Sal, and she looked down at its white crispness as though it had been a message from the lower regions sent to call her to judgment. A letter, white, square-cornered and clean, with clear, firm inscription, had never come within her gaze before. Old Sal had never learned to read. The writing meant nothing to her, but the whole letter represented a mystic communication from another world.

Instinctively the neighbors gathered nearer to look at the letter, and Sal, seeing herself the center of observation, reached forward a dirty hand wrapped in a corner of her apron, and took the envelope as though it had been hot, eyeing it all the while fearfully.

Then with his easy bow and touching his hat to her as though she had been a queen, Michael turned and walked away out of the alley.

Old Sal stood watching him, a kind of wistful wonder in her bleary eyes. No gentleman had ever tipped his hat to her, and no man had ever done her reverence. From her little childhood she had been brought up to forfeit the respect of men. Perhaps it had never entered her dull mind before that she might have been aught but what she was, and that men might have given her honor.

The neighbors too were awed for the moment and stood watching in silence, till when Michael turned the corner out of sight, Sal exclaimed:

"Now that's the angel, shure! No gintlemin would iver uv tipped his at to the loikes of Sal. Saints presarve us! That we should hev an angel in this alley!"

When Michael reached his lodging he found that he was trembling so from weakness and excitement that he could scarcely drag himself up the three flights to his room. So had his splendid strength been reduced by trouble and the fever that came with his wounds.

He lay down weakly and tried to think. Now he had done his best to find Sam. If Sam did not come in answer to his letter he must wait until he found him. He would not give up. So he fell asleep with the burden on his heart.

The letter was as follows:

Dear Sam:

You can't have forgotten Mikky who slept with you in the boiler room and with whom you shared your crusts. You remember I promised when I went away to college I would come back and try to make things better for you all? And now I have come and I am anxious to find the fellows and see what we can do together to make life better in the old alley and make up for some of the hard times when we were children. I have been down to the alley but can get no trace of you. I spent the best part of one night hunting you and then a slight accident put me in the hospital for a few days, but I am well now and am anxious to find you all. I want to talk over old times, and find out where Buck and Jim are, and hear all about Janie and little Bobs.

I am going to leave this letter with Aunt Sally, hoping she will give it to you. I have given my address below and should be glad to have you come and see me at my room, or if you would prefer I will meet you wherever you say, and we will go together and have something to eat to celebrate.

Hoping to hear from you very soon, I am as always,

Your brother and friend,

MIKKY

A few days later a begrimed envelope addressed in pencil was brought to the door by the postman. Michael with sinking heart opened it. It read:

MiKY ef yo be reely hym cum to KelLys karner at 10 tumoroW nite. Ef you are mIK youz thee old whissel an doante bring no une wit yer Ef yO du I wunt be thar.

SAM

Michael seated on his humpy bed puzzled this out, word by word, until he made fairly good sense of it. He was to go to Kelly's corner. How memory stirred at the words. Kelly's corner was beyond the first turn of the alley, it was at the extreme end of an alley within an alley, and had no outlet except through Kelly's saloon. Only the "gang" knew the name, "Kelly's Corner," for it was not really a corner at all only a sort of pocket or hiding place so entitled by Buck for his own and "de kids" private purpose. If Michael had been at all inclined to be a coward since his recent hard usage in the vicinity of the alley he would have kept away from Kelly's corner, for once in there with enemies, and alone, no policeman's club, nor hospital ambulance would ever come to help. The things that happened at Kelly's corner never got into the newspapers.

Memory and instinct combined to make this perfectly clear to Michael's mind, and if he needed no other warning those words of the letter, "Don't bring no one with you. If you do, I won't be there," were sufficient to make him wise.

Yet Michael never so much as thought of not keeping the appointment. His business was to find Sam, and it mattered as little to him now that danger stood in the way as it had the day when he flung his neglected little body in front of Starr Endicott and saved her from the assassin's bullet. He would go, of course, and go alone. Neither did it occur to him to take the ordinary precaution of leaving his name and whereabouts at the police station to be searched for in case he did not turn up in reasonable time. It was all in the day's work and Michael thought no more about the possible peril he was facing than he had thought of broken limbs and bloody noses the last hour before a football scrimmage.

There was something else in the letter that interested Michael and stirred the old memories. The old whistle! Of course he had not forgotten that, although he had not used it much among his college companions. It was a strange, weird, penetrating sound, between a call and whistle. He and Buck had made it up between them. It was their old signal. When Michael went to college he had held it sacred as belonging strictly to his old friends, and never, unless by himself in the woods where none but the birds and the trees could hear, had he let it echoes ring. Sometimes he had flung it forth and startled the mockingbirds, and once he had let it ring into the midst of his astonished comrades in Florida when he was hidden from their view and they knew not who had made the sound. He tried it now softly, and then louder and louder, until with sudden fear he stopped lest his landlady should happen to come up that way and think him insane. But undoubtedly he could give the old signal.

The next night at precisely ten o'clock Michael's ringing step sounded down the alley; firm, decisive, secure. Such assurance must Daniel have worn as he faced the den of lions, and so went the three Hebrew children into the fiery furnace.

"It's him! It's the angel!" whispered old Sal who was watching. "Oi tould yez he'd come fer shure!"

"He's got his nerve with him!" murmured a girl with bold eyes and a coarse kind of beauty, as she drew further back into the shadow of the doorway. "He ain't comin' out again so pretty I guess. Not if Sam don't like. Mebbe he ain't comin' out 'tall!"

"Angels has ways, me darlint!" chuckled Sal. "He'll come back al roight, ye'll see!"

On walked Michael, down the alley to the narrow opening that to the uninitiated was not an opening between the buildings at all, and slipped in the old way. He had thought it all out in the night. He was sure he knew just how far beyond Sal's house it was; on into the fetid air of the close dark place, the air struck him in the face like a hot, wet blanket as he kept on.

It was very still all about when he reached the point known as Kelly's corner. It had been so as he remembered it. It had been the place of plots, the hatching of murders and robberies. Had it so changed that it was still tonight? He stood for an instant hesitating. Should he wait a while, or knock on some door? Would it be any use to call?

But the instinct of the slums was upon him again, his birthright. It seemed to drop upon him from the atmosphere, a sort of stealthy patience. He would wait. Something would come. He must do as he had done with the birds of the forest when he wished to watch their habits. He must stand still unafraid and show that he was harmless.

So he stood three, perhaps five minutes, then softly at first and gradually growing clearer, he gave the call that he had given years before, a little barefoot, hungry child in that very spot many times.

The echo died away. There was nothing to make him

know that a group of curious alley dwellers huddled at the mouth of the trap in which he stood, watching with eyes accustomed to the darkness, to see what would happen; to block his escape if escape should be attempted.

Then out of silence a sigh seemed to come, and out of the shadows one shadow unfolded itself and came forward till it stood beside him. Still Michael did not stir, but softly, through half-open lips, breathed the signal once more.

Sibilant, rougher, with a hint of menace as it issued forth the signal was answered this time, and with a thrill of wonder the mantle of the old life fell upon Michael once more. He was Mikky—only grown more wise. Almost the old vernacular came to his tongue.

"Hi! Sam! That you?"

The figure in the darkness seemed to stiffen with sudden attention. The voice was like, and yet not like the Mikky of old.

"Wot youse want?" questioned a voice gruffly.

"I want you, Sam. I want to see if you look as you used to, and I want to know about the boys. Can't we go where there's light and talk a little? I've been days hunting you. I've come back because I promised, you know. You expected me to come back someday, didn't you, Sam?"

Michael was surprised to find how eager he was for the answer to this question.

"Aw, what ye givin' us?" responded the suspicious Sam. "D'youse s'pose I b'lieve all that gag about yer comin' here to he'p we'uns? Wot would a guy like youse wid all dem togs an' all dem fine looks want wid us? Youse has got above us. Youse ain't no good to us no more."

Sam scratched a match on his trousers and lit an old pipe that he held between his teeth, but as the match flared up and showed his own face, a lowering brow, shifty eyes, a swarthy, unkempt visage, sullen and sly, the shifty eyes were not looking at the pipe but up at the face above him which shone out white and fine with its gold halo in the little gleam in the dark court. The watchers crowding at the opening of the passage saw his face, and almost fancied there were soft shadowy wings behind him. It was thus with old Sal's help that Michael got the name again, "the Angel." It was thus he became the "angel of the alley."

"Sam!" he said, and his voice was very gentle, although he was perfectly conscious that behind him there were two more shadows of men and more might be lurking in the dark corners. "Sam, if you remember me you will know I couldn't forget, and I do care. I came back to find you. I've always meant to come, all the time I was in college. I've had it in mind to come back here and make some of the hard things easier for"—he hesitated, and—"for *us* all."

"How did youse figger youse was goin' to do that?" Sam asked, his little shifty eyes narrowing on Michael, as he purposely struck another match to watch the effect of his words.

Then Michael's wonderful smile lit up his face, and Sam, however much he may have pretended to doubt, knew in his deepest heart that this was the same Mikky of old. There was no mistaking that smile.

"I shall need you to help me in figuring that out, Sam. That's why I was so anxious to find you."

A curious grunt from behind Michael warned him that the audience was being amused at the expense of Sam. Sam's brows were lowering.

"Humph!" he said, ungraciously striking a third match just in time to watch Michael's face. "Where's yer pile?"

"What?"

"Got the dough?"

"Oh," said Michael comprehendingly, "no, I haven't got money, Sam. I've only my education."

"An' wot good's it, I'd like to know. Tell me those?"

"So much good that I can't tell it all in one short talk," answered Michael steadily. "We'll have to get better acquainted and then I hope I can make you understand how it has helped. Now tell me about the others. Where is Buck?"

There was a dead silence.

"It's hard to say!" at last muttered Sam irresponsibly.

"Don't you know? Haven't you any kind of an idea, Sam? I'd so like to hunt him up."

The question seemed to have produced a tensity in the very atmosphere. Michael felt it.

"I might, an' then agin' I might not," answered Sam in that tone of his that barred the way for further questions.

"Couldn't you and I find him and—and—help him, Sam? Aunt Sally said he was in trouble."

Another match was scratched and held close to his face while the narrow eyes of Sam seemed to pierce his very soul before Sam answered with an ugly laugh.

"Oh, he don't need none o' your help, you bet. He's lit out. You don't need to worry 'bout Buck, he kin take car' o' hisse'f every time."

"But won't he come back sometime?"

"Can't say. It's hard to tell," noncommittally.

"And Jim?" Michael's voice was sad.

"Jim, he's doin' time," sullenly.

"I'm sorry!" said Michael sadly, and a strange hush came about the dark group. Now why should this queer chap be sorry? No one else cared, unless it might be Jim, and Jim had got caught. It was nothing to them.

"Now tell me about Janie—and little Bobs—" The questioner paused. His voice was very low.

"Aw, cut it out!" snarled Sam irritably. "Don't come any high strikes on their account. They're dead an' you can't dig 'em up an' weep over 'em. Hustle up an' tell us wot yer wantin' to do."

"Well, Sam," said Michael trying to ignore the natural repulsion he felt at the last words of his onetime friend, "suppose you take lunch with me tomorrow at twelve. Then we can talk over old times. I will tell you all about my college life and you must tell me all you are doing."

Sam was silent from sheer astonishment. Take lunch! Never in his life had he been invited out to luncheon. Nor had he any desire for an invitation now.

"Where?" he asked after a silence so long that Michael began to fear he was not going to answer at all.

Michael named a place not far away. He had selected it that morning. It was clean, somewhat, yet not too clean. The fare was far from princely, but it would do, and the locality was none too respectable. Michael was enough of a slum child still to know that his guest would never go with him to a really respectable restaurant, moreover he would not have the wardrobe nor the manners. He waited Sam's answer breathlessly.

Sam gave a queer little laugh as if taken off his guard.

The place named was so entirely harmless, to his mind, and the whole matter of the invitation took on the form of a great joke.

"Well, I might," he drawled indifferently. "I won't make no promises, but I might, an' then again I might not. It's jes' as it happens. Ef I ain't there by twelve sharp you needn't wait. Jes' go ahead an' eat. I wouldn't want to spoil your digestion fer my movements."

"I shall wait!" said Michael decidedly with his pleasant voice ringing clear with satisfaction. "You will come, Sam, I know you will. Good night!"

And then he did a most extraordinary thing. He put out his hand, his clean, strong hand, warm and healthy and groping with the keenness of love, found the hardened grimy hand of his onetime companion, and gripped it in a hearty grasp.

Sam started back with the instant suspicion of attack, and then stood shamedly still for an instant. The grip of that firm, strong hand, the touch of brotherhood, a touch such as had never come to his life before since he was a little child, completed the work that the smile had begun, and Sam knew that Mikky, the real Mikky was before him.

Then Michael walked swiftly down that narrow passage, at the opening of which the human shadows scattered silently and fled, to watch from other furtive doorways, down through the alley unmolested, and out into the street once more.

"The saints presarve us! Wot did I tell yez?" whispered Sal. "It's the angel all right fer shure."

"I wonder wot he done to Sam," murmured the girl. "He's got his nerve all right, he sure has. Ain't he beautiful!"

Chapter 10

Michael went early to his lunch party. He was divided between wondering if his strange guest would put in an appearance at all; if he did, what he should talk about; and how he would pilot him through the embarrassing experience of the meal. One thing he was determined upon. He meant to find out if possible whether Sam knew anything about his, Michael's origin. It was scarcely likely, and yet, Sam might have heard some talk by older people in the neighborhood. His one great longing was to find out and clear his name of shame if possible.

There was another thing that troubled Michael. He was not sure that he would know Sam even supposing that he came. The glimpse he had caught the night before when the matches were struck was not particularly illuminating. He had a dim idea that Sam was below the medium height; with thin, sallow face, small, narrow eyes, and slouching gait, and a head that was not wide enough from front to back. He had a feeling that Sam had not room enough in his brain for seeing all that ought to be seen. Sam did not understand about education. Would he ever be able to make him understand?

Sam came shuffling along ten minutes after twelve. His sense of dignity would not have allowed him to be on time. Besides, he wanted to see if Michael would wait as he had said. It was a part of the testing of Michael; not to prove if he were really Mikky, but to see what stuff he was made of, and how much he really had meant of what he said.

Michael was there, standing anxiously outside the eating house. He did not enjoy the surroundings nor the attention he was attracting. He was too well dressed for that locality, but these were the oldest clothes he had. He would have considered them quite shabby at college. He was getting worried lest after all his plan had failed. Then Sam slouched along, his hat drawn down, his hands in his pockets, and wearing an air of indifference that almost amounted to effrontery. He greeted Michael as if there had been no previous arrangement and this were a chance meeting. There was nothing about his manner to show that he had purposely come late to put him to the test, but Michael knew intuitively it was so.

"Shall we go in now?" said Michael smiling happily. He found he was really glad that Sam had come, repulsive in appearance though he was, hard of countenance and unfriendly in manner. He felt that he was getting on just a little in his great object of finding out and helping his old friends, and perhaps learning something more of his own history.

"Aw, I donno's I care 'bout it!" drawled Sam, just as if he had not intended going in all the time, nor had been thinking of the "feed" all the morning in anticipation.

"Yes, you better," said Michael putting a friendly hand on the other's shoulder. If he felt a repugnance to touching the tattered, greasy coat of his onetime friend, he controlled it, remembering how he had once worn garments far more tattered and filthy. The greatness of his desire to uplift made him forget everything else. It was the absorption of a supreme task that had come upon the boy to the exclusion of his own personal tastes.

It was not that Michael was so filled with love for this miserable creature who used to be his friend, nor so desired to renew old associations after those long years of separation; it was the terrible need, the conditions of which had been called vividly to his experience, that appealed to his spirit like a call of authority to which he answered proudly because of what had once been done for him. It had come upon him without his knowledge, suddenly, with the revival of old scenes and memories, but as with all workers for humanity it had gone so deeply into his soul as to make him forget even that there was such a thing as sacrifice.

They passed into the restaurant. Michael in his well-made clothing and with his strikingly handsome face and gold hair attracting at once every eye in the place; Sam with an insolent air of assurance to cover a sudden embarrassment of pride at the company he was in.

Michael gave a generous order, and talked pleasantly as they waited. Sam sat in low-browed silence watching him furtively, almost disconcertingly.

It was when they had reached the course of three kinds of pie and a dab of dirty looking, pink ice cream professing to be fresh strawberry, that Michael suddenly looked keenly at his guest and asked:

"What are you doing now, Sam? In business for yourself?"

Sam's eyes narrowed until they were almost eclipsed, though a keen steel glitter could be seen beneath the colorless lashes. A kind of mask, impenetrable as lead, seemed to have settled over his face, which had been gradually relaxing during the meal into a half-indulgent grin of interest in his queer host.

"Yas, I'm in business fer myself," he drawled at last after carefully scrutinizing the other's face to be sure there was no underlying motive for the question.

"Newsstand?" asked Michael.

"Not eggs-act-ly!"

"What line?"

Sam finished his mince pie and began on the pumpkin before he answered.

"Wal, there's sev'ral!"

"Is that so? Got more than one string to your bow? That's a good thing. You're better off than I am. I haven't looked around for a job yet. I thought I'd get at it tomorrow. You see I wanted to look you fellows up first before I got tied down to anything where I couldn't get off when I wanted to. Perhaps you can put me onto something. How about it?"

It was characteristic of Michael that he had not once thought of going to Endicott for the position and help offered him, since the setting down he had received from Mrs. Endicott. The time appointed for his going to Endicott's office was long since passed. He had not even turned the matter over in his mind once since that awful night of agony and renunciation. Mrs. Endicott had told him that her husband "had done enough for him" and he realized that this was true. He would trouble him no more. Sometime perhaps the world would turn around so that he would have opportunity to repay Endicott's kindness that he might not repay in money, but until then Michael would keep out of his way. It was the one poor little rag of pride he allowed himself from the shattering of all his hopes.

Sam narrowed his eyes and looked Michael through, then slowly widened them again, an expression of real interest coming into them.

"Say! Do you mean it?" he asked doubtfully. "Be you straight goods? Would you come back into de gang an not snitch on us ner nothin'?"

"I'm straight goods, Sam, and I won't snitch!" said Michael quickly. He knew that he could hope for no fellow's confidence if he "snitched."

"Wal, say, I've a notion to tell yeh!"

Sam attacked his ice cream contemplatively.

"How would a bluff game strike you?" he asked suddenly as the last delectable mouthful of cream disappeared and he pulled the fresh cup of coffee toward him that the waiter had just set down.

"What sort?" said Michael wondering what he was coming on in the way of revelation, but resolving not to be horrified at anything. Sam must not suspect until he could understand what a difference education had made in the way of looking at things.

"Wal, there's diffrunt ways. Cripple's purty good. Foot all tied up in bloody rags, arm an' hand tied up, a couple o' old crutches. I could lend the clo'es. They'd be short fer yeh, but that'd be all the better gag. We cud swap an' I'd do the gen'lman act a while." He looked covetously at Michael's handsome brown tweeds—"Den you goes fom house to house, er you stands on de corner—"

"Begging!" said Michael aghast. His eyes were on his plate and he was trying to control his voice, but something of his horror crept into his tones. Sam felt it and hastened on apologetically—

"Er ef you want to go it one better, keep on yer good cloes an' have the asthma bad. I know a feller what'll teach you how, an' sell you the whistles to put in yer mouth. You've no notion how it works. You just go around in the subbubs tellin' thet you've only been out of the 'orspittal two days an' you walked all this way to get work an' couldn't get it, an' you want five cents to get back—see? Why, I know a feller—course he's been at it fer years an' he has his regular beats—folks don't seem to remember—and he can work the ground over 'bout once in six months er so, and he's made high's thirty-eight dollars in a day at asthma work."

Sam paused triumphant to see what effect the statement had on his friend, but Michael's face was toward his coffee cup.

"Seems sort of small business for a man!" he said at last, his voice steady with control. "Don't believe I'd be good at that. Haven't you got something that's real *work?*"

Sam's eyes narrowed.

"Ef I thought you was up to it," he murmured. "You'd be great with that angel face o' yourn. Nobody'd ever suspect you. You could wear them clo'es too. But it's work all right, an' mighty resky. Ef I thought you was up to it—" He continued to look keenly at Michael, and Michael, with innate instinct felt his heart beat in discouraged thumps. What new deviltry was Sam about to propose?

"You used to be game all right!" murmured Sam interrogatively. "You never used to scare easy."

"Wal, I'll tell you," in answer to Michael's questioning eyes which searched his little sharp wizened face—Michael was wondering if there was anything in that face to redeem it from utter repulsiveness.

"You see it's a reg'ler business, an' you hev to learn, but I'd give you pinters, all you'd need to know. I'm pretty slick myself. There's tools to open things, an' you hev to be ready to 'xplain how you come thur an' jolly up a parlor maid per'aps. It's easy to hev made a mistake in the house, er be a gas man er a plumber wot the boss sent up to look at the pipes. But night work's best pay after you get onto things. Thur's houses where you ken lay your han's on things goin' into the thousands an' lots ov um easy to get rid of without anybody findin' out. There's Buck, he used to be great at it. He taught all the gang. The day he lit out he bagged a bit o' glass wuth tree tousand dollars, 'sides a whole handful of fivers an' tens wot he found lying' on a dressin' table pretty as you please. Buck he were a slick one at it. He'd be pleased to know you'd took up the work—"

Sam paused and eyed Michael with the first friendly gleam he had shown in his eyes, and Michael, with his heart in a tumult of varied emotions, and the quick color flooding brow and cheek, tried to hold himself in check. He must not speak too hastily. Perhaps he had not understood Sam's meaning.

"Where is Buck?" Michael looked Sam straight in the eye. The small pupils seemed to contract and shut out even his gaze.

"They ain't never got a trace of Buck," he said evasively.

"But don't you know?" There was something in Michael's look that demanded an answer.

"I might an' I might not," responded Sam sullenly.

Michael was still for several seconds watching Sam; each trying to understand the other.

"Do you think he will come back where I can see him?" he asked at length.

"He might, an' he might not. 't depends. Ef you was in th' bizness he might. It's hard to say. 'T depends."

Michael watched Sam again thoughtfully.

"Tell me more about the business," he said at last, his lips compressed, his brows drawn down into a frown of intensity.

"Thur ain't much more t' tell," said Sam, still sullen. "I ain't sure you're up to it."

"What do you mean by that?"

"Ain't sure you got de sand. You might turn faint and snitch." Sam leaned forward and spoke in low rapid sentences. "Wen we'd got a big haul, 'sposen you'd got into de house an' done de pinchin', and we got the stuff safe hid, an' you got tuk up? Would you snitch? Er would you take your pill like a man? That's what I'd want to be sure. Mikky would a' stood by the gang, but you—you've had a edicashun! They might go soft at college. I ain't much use fer edicated persons myself. But I'll give you a show ef you promise stiff not to snitch. We've gota big game on tonight up on Madison Avenue, an' we're a man short. Dere's

dough in it if we make it go all right. Rich man. Girl goin'
out to a party tonight. She's goin' to wear some dimons
wurth a penny. Hed it in de paper. Brung 'em home fom de
bank this mornin'. One o' de gang watched de feller come
out o' de bank. It's all straight so fur. It's a pretty big haul to
let you in de first try, an' you'll hev to run all de risks; but ef
you show you're game we'll make it a bargain."

Michael held himself tensely and fought the desire to
choke the fellow before him; tried to remember that he was
the same Sam who had once divided a crust with him, and
whom he had come to help; reflected that he might have
been as bad himself if he had never been taken from the
terrible environment of the slums and shown a better way;
knew that if he for one fraction of a second showed his horror at the evil plot, or made any attempt to stop it all hope
of reaching Sam, or Buck, or any of the others was at an
end; and with it all hope of finding any stray links of his
own past history. Besides, though honor was strong in him
and he would never "snitch" on his companions, it would
certainly be better to find out as much as possible about the
scheme. There might be other ways besides "snitching" of
stopping such things. Then suddenly his heart almost
stopped beating. Madison Avenue! Sam had said Madison
Avenue, and a girl! What if it were Starr's jewels they were
planning to take? He knew very little about such matters
save what he had read. It did not occur to him tht Starr was
not yet "out" in society; that she would be too young to wear
costly jewels and have her costume put in the paper. He
only knew that his heart was throbbing again painfully, and
that the fellow before him seemed too vile to live longer on
the same earth with Starr, little, beautiful, exquisite Starr.

He was quite still when Sam had finished; his face was
white with emotion and his eyes were blazing blue flames
when he raised them to look at Sam. Then he became aware
that his answer was awaited.

"Sam, do you mean *burglary*?" He tried to keep his
voice low and steady as he spoke but he felt as if he had
shouted the last word. The restaurant was almost empty
now, and the waiters had retired behind the scenes amid a
clatter of dishes.

"That's about as pretty a word as you can call it, I guess," said Sam, drawing back with a snarl as he saw the light in Michael's eyes.

Michael looked him through for an instant, and if a glance can burn then surely Sam's little soul shrank scorching into itself, but it was so brief that the brain which was only keen to things of the earth had not analyzed it. Michael dropped his glance to the table again, and began playing with his spoon and trying to get calm with a deep breath as he used to when he knew a hard spot in a ball game was coming.

"Well, why don't you speak? You 'fraid?" It was said with a sneer that a devil from the pit might have given.

Then Michael sat up calmly. His heart was beating steadily now and he was facing his adversary.

"No! I'm not afraid, Sam, if there were any good reason for going, but you know I never could feel comfortable in getting my living off somebody else. It doesn't seem fair to the other fellow. You see they've got a right to the things they own and I haven't, and because I might be smart enough to catch them napping and sneak away with what they prize doesn't make it right either. Now that girl probably thinks a lot of her diamonds, you see, and it doesn't seem quite the manly thing for a big strong fellow like me to get them away from her, does it? Of course you may think differently, but I believe I'd rather do some good hard work that would keep my muscles in trim, than to live off someone else. There's a kind of pretty gray moss that grows where I went to college. It floats along a little seed blown in the air first and lodges on the limb of a tree and begins to fasten itself into the bark, and grow and grow and suck life from the big tree. It doesn't seem much at first, and it seems as if the big tree might spare enough juice to the little moss. But wait a few years and see what happens. The moss grows and drapes itself in great long festoons all over that tree and by and by the first thing you know that tree has lost all its green leaves and stands up here stark and dead with nothing on its bare branches but that old gray moss which has to die too because it has nothing to live on any longer. It never learned to gather any juice for itself. They call the moss a parasite. I couldn't be a human parasite. Sam. You may feel differently about it, but I couldn't. I really couldn't."

Michael's eyes had grown dreamy and lost their fire as he remembered the dear Southland, and dead sentinel pines with their waving gray festoons against the every blue sky. As he talked he saw the whole great out-of-doors again where he had wandered now so many years free and happy, free from burdens of humanity which were pressing him now so sorely. A great longing to fly back to it all, to get away from the sorrow and the degradation and the shame which seemed pressing so hard upon him, filled his heart, leaped into his eyes, caught and fascinated the attention of the listening Sam, who understood very little of the peroration. He had never heard of a parasite. He did not know he had always been a human parasite. He was merely astonished and a trifle fascinated by the passion and appeal in Michael's face as he spoke.

"Gosh!" he said in a tone almost of admiration. "Gosh! Is that wot edicashun done fer you?"

"Perhaps," said Michael pleasantly, "though I rather think, Sam, that I always felt a bit that way, I just didn't know how to say it."

"Wal, you allus was queer!" muttered Sam half apologetically. "I couldn't see it that way myself, as you say, but o' course it's your fun'ral! Ef you kin scratch up enough grub bein' a tree, why that's your own lookout. Moss is good 'nough fer me fer de present."

Michael beamed his wonderful smile on Sam and answered: "Perhaps you'll see it my way someday, Sam, and then we can get a job together!"

There was so much comradery in the tone, and so much dazzling brilliancy in the smile that Sam forgot to be sullen.

"Wal, mebbe," he chuckled, "but I don't see no edicashun comin' my way dis late day, so I guess I'll git along de way I be."

"It isn't too late yet, Sam. There's more than one way of getting an education. It doesn't always come through college."

After a little more talk in which Sam promised to find

out if there was any way for Michael to visit Jim in his temporary retirement from the law-abiding world, and Michael promised to visit Sam in the alley again at an appointed time, the two separated.

Then Michael went forth to reconnoiter and to guard the house of Endicott.

With no thought of any personal danger, Michael laid his plans. Before sundown he was on hand, having considered all visible and invisible means of ingress to the house. He watched from a suitable distance all who came and went. He saw Mr. Endicott come home. He waited till the evening drew near when a luxurious limousine stopped before the door, assured himself that only Mrs. Endicott had gone out. A little later Mr. Endicott also left the house. Starr had not gone out. He felt that he had double need to watch now as she was there alone with only the servants.

Up and down he walked. No one passed the Endicott house unwatched by him. None came forth or went in of whom he did not take careful notice.

The evening passed, and the master and mistress of the house returned. One by one the lights went out. Even in the servants' rooms all was dark at last. The night deepened and the stars thickened overhead.

The policeman's whistle sounded through the quiet streets and the city seemed at last to be sinking into a brief repose. It was long past midnight, and still Michael kept up his patrol. Up this side of the street, down that, around the corner, through the alley at the back where "de kids" had stood in silent respect uncovered toward his window years ago, back to the avenue again, and on around. With his cheery whistle and his steady ringing step he awakened no suspicion even when he came near to a policeman; and besides, no lurkers of the dark would steal out while he was so noisily in the neighborhood.

And so he watched the night through, till the morning broke and sunshine flooded the window of the room where Starr, unconscious of his vigil, lay sleeping.

Busy milk wagons were making their rounds, and sleepy workmen with dinner pails slung over their arms were striding to their day's work through the cool of the morning, as Michael turned his steps toward his lodging.

Broad morning was upon them and deeds of darkness
could be no more. The night was passed. Nothing had happened. Starr was safe. He went home and to sleep well
pleased. He might not companion with her, but it was his
privilege to guard her from unsuspected evils. That was
one joy that could not be taken from him by the taint that
was upon him. Perhaps his being a child of the slums might
yet prove to be a help to guard her life from harm.

Chapter 11

It was the first week in September that Michael, passing
through a crowded thoroughfare, came face to face with
Mr. Endicott.

The days had passed into weeks and Michael had not
gone near his benefactor. He had felt that he must drop out
of his old friend's life until a time came that he could show
his gratitude for the past. Meantime he had not been idle.
His winning smile and clear eyes had been his passport, and
after a few preliminary experiences he had secured a position as salesman in a large department store. His college
diploma and a letter from the college president were his
references. He was not earning much, but enough to pay
his absolute expenses and a triffle over. Meantime he was
gaining experience.

This Saturday morning of the first week of September
he had come to the store as usual, but had found that on
account of the sudden death of a member of the firm the
store would be closed for the day.

He was wondering how he should spend his holiday
and wishing that he might get out into the open and
breathe once more the free air under waving trees, and listen to the birds, and the waters and the winds. He was half
tempted to squander a few cents and go to Coney Island or
up the Hudson, somewhere, anywhere to get out of the

grinding noisy tempestuous city, whose sin and burden pressed upon his heart night and day because of that from which he had been saved, and of that from which he had not the power to save others.

Then out of an open doorway rushed a man, going toward a waiting automobile, and almost knocking Michael over in his progress.

"Oh! It is you, young man! At last! Well, I should like to know what you have done with yourself all these weeks and why you didn't keep your appointment with me?"

"Oh!" said Michael, pleasure and shame striving together in his face. He could see that the other man was not angry, and was really relieved to have found him.

"Where are you going, son?" Endicott's tone had already changed from gruffness to kindly welcome. "Jump in and run down to the wharf with me while you give an account of yourself. I'm going down to see Mrs. Endicott off to Europe. She is taking Starr over to school this winter. I'm late already, so jump in."

Michael seemed to have no choice and stepped into the car, which was whirled through the intricate maze of humanity and machinery down toward the regions where the oceangoing steamers harbor.

His heart was in a tumult at once, both of embarrassed joy to be in the presence of the man who had done so much for him, and of eager anticipation. Starr! Would he see Starr again? That was the thought uppermost in his mind. He had not as yet realized that she was going away for a long time.

All the springtime he had kept guard over the house in Madison Avenue. Not all night of course, but hovering about there now and then, and for two weeks after he had talked with Sam, nightly. Always he had walked that way before retiring and looked toward the window where burned a soft light. Then they had gone to the seashore and the mountains and the house had put on solemn shutters and lain asleep.

Michael knew all about it from a stray paragraph in the society column of the daily paper which he happened to read.

Toward the end of August he had made a round

through Madison Avenue every night to see if they had returned home, and for a week the shutters had been down
and the lights burning as of old. It had been good to know
that his charge was back there safely. And now he was to see
her.

"Well! Give an account of yourself. Were you trying to
keep out of my sight? Why didn't you come to my office?"

Michael looked him straight in the eye with his honest,
clear gaze that showed no sowing of wild oats, no dissipation or desire to get away from friendly espionage. He decided in a flash of a thought that this man should never
know the blow his beautiful, haughty wife had dealt him. It
was true, all she had said, and he, Michael, would give the
real reason why he had not come.

"Because I thought you had done for me far more than
I deserved already, and I did not wish to be any further
burden to you."

"The dickens you did!" exclaimed Endicott. "You
good-for-nothing rascal, didn't you know you would be far
more of a burden running off in that style without leaving
trace of yourself behind so I could hunt you up, than if you
had behaved yourself and done as I told you? Here I have
been doing a lot of unnecessary worrying about you. I
thought you had fallen among thieves or something, or else
gone to the dogs. Don't you know that is a most unpardona-
ble thing to do, run off from a man who has told you he
wants to see you? I thought I made you understand that I
had more than a passing interest in your welfare!"

The color came into the fine, strong face and a pained
expression in his eyes.

"I'm sorry, sir! I didn't think of it that way. I thought
you felt some kind of an obligation; I never felt so, but you
said you did, and I thought if I got out of your way I would
trouble you no more."

"Trouble me! Trouble me! Why, son, I like to be troubled once in a while by something besides getting money
and spending it. You never gave me a shadow of trouble,
except these last weeks when you've disappeared and I
couldn't do anything for you. You've somehow crept into
my life and I can't get you out. In fact, I don't want to. But,
boy, if you felt that way, what made you come to New York

at all? You didn't feel that way the night you came to my house to dinner."

Michael's eyes owned that this was true, but his firm lips showed that he would never betray the real reason for the change.

"I—didn't—realize—sir!"

"Realize? Realize what?"

"I didn't realize the difference between my station and yours, sir. There had never been anything during my years in school to make me know. I am a 'child of the slums'"— unconsciously he drifted into quotations form Mrs. Endicott's speech to him—"and you belong to a fine old family. I don't know what terrible things are in my blood. You have riches and a name beyond reproach." He had seen the words in an article he had read the evening before, and felt that they fitted the man and the occasion. He did not know that he was quoting. They had become a part of his thoughts.

"I might make the riches if I tried hard," he held up his head proudly, "but I could never make the name. I will always be a child of the slums, no matter what I do!"

"Child of the fiddlesticks!" interrupted Endicott. "Wherever did you get all that rot? It sounds as if you had been attending society functions and listening to their twaddle. It doesn't matter what you are the child of, if you're a mind to be a man. This is a free country, son, and you can be and climb where you please. Tell me, where you get all these ideas?"

Michael looked down. He did not wish to answer.

"In a number of places," he answered evasively.

"Where?"

"For one thing, I've been down to the alley where I used to live." The eyes were looking into his now, and Endicott felt a strange swelling of pride that he had had a hand in the making of this young man.

"Well?"

"I know from what you've taken me—I can never be what you are!"

"Therefore you won't try to be anything? Is that it?"

"Oh, no! I'll try to be all that I can, but—I don't belong with you. I'm of another class—"

"Oh, bosh! Cut that out, son! Real men don't talk like that. You're a better man now than any of the pedigreed dudes I know of, and as for taints in the blood, I could tell you of some of the sons of great men who have taints as bad as any child of the slums. Young man, you can be whatever you set out to be in this world! Remember that."

"Everyone does not feel that way," said Michael with conviction, though he was conscious of great pleasure in Endicott's hearty words.

"Who, for instance?" said Endicott looking at him sharply.

Michael was silent. He could not tell him.

"Who?" asked the insistent voice once more.

"The world!" evaded Michael.

"The world is brainless. You can make the world think what you like, son, remember that! Here we are. Would you like to come aboard?"

But Michael stood back.

"I think I will wait here," he said gravely. It had come to him that Mrs. Endicott would be there. He must not intrude, not even to see Starr once more. Besides, she had made it a point of honor for him to keep away from her daughter. He had no choice but to obey.

"Very well," said Endicott, "but see you don't lose yourself again. I want to see you about something. I'll not be long. It must be nearly time for starting." He hurried away and Michael stood on the edge of the throng looking up at the great floating village.

It was his first view of an ocean-going steamer at close range and everything about it interested him. He wished he might have gone aboard and looked the vessel over. He would like to know about the engines and see the cabins, and especially the steerage about which he had read so much. But perhaps there would be an opportunity again. Surely there would be. He would go to Ellis Island, too, and see the emigrants as they came into the country, seeking a new home where they had been led to expect to find comfort and plenty of work, and finding none; landing most of them, inevitably, in the slums of the cities where the population was already congested and where vice and disease stood ready to prey upon them. Michael had been spending enough time in the alleys of the metropolis to be already deeply interested in the problem of the city, and deeply pained by its sorrows.

But his thoughts were not altogether of the masses and the classes as he stood in the bright sunlight and gazed at the great vessel about to plow its way over the bright waters. He was realizing that somewhere within those many little windowed cabins was a bright-faced girl, the only one of womankind in all the earth about whom his tender thoughts had ever hovered. Would he catch a glimpse of her face once more before she went away for the winter? She was going to school, her father had said. How could they bear to send her across the water from them? A whole winter was a long time, and yet, it would pass. Thirteen years had passed since he went away from New York, and he was back. It would not be so long as that. She would return, and need him perhaps. He would be there and be ready when he was needed.

The fine lips set in a strong line that was good to see. There were the patient, fearless lines of a soldier in the boy's face, and rugged strength in spite of his unusual beauty of countenance. It is not often one sees a face like Michael's. There was nothing womanish in his looks. It was rather the completeness of strength and courage combined with mighty modeling and perfection of coloring, that made men turn and look after him and look again, as though they had seen a god, and made women exclaim over him. If he had been born in the circles of aristocracy he would have been the idol of society, the spoiled of all who knew him. He was even now being stared at by everyone in sight, and more than one pair of marine glasses from the first cabin deck were pointed at him, but he stood deep in his thoughts and utterly unconscious of his own attraction.

It was only a moment before the first warning came, and people crowded on the wharf side of the decks, while others hurried down the gangplank. Michael watched the confusion with eagerness, his eyes searching the decks for all possible chance of seeing Starr.

When the last warning was given, and just as the gangplank was about to be hauled up, Mr. Endicott came hurrying down, and Michael suddenly saw her face in the crowd on the deck above, her mother's haughtily pretty face just behind her.

Without in the least realizing what he was doing Michael moved through the crowd until he stood close behind Starr's father, and then all at once be became aware that her starry eyes were upon him, and she recognized him.

He lifted his hat and stood in reverent attitude as though in the presence of a queen, his eyes glowing eloquently, his speaking face paying her tribute as plainly as words could have done. The noonday sun burnished his hair with its aureole flame, and more than one of the passengers called attention to the sight.

"See that man down there!" exclaimed a woman of the world close behind Mrs. Endicott. "Isn't he magnificent! He has a head and shoulders like a young god!" She spoke as if her acquaintance with gods was wide, and her neighbors turned to look.

"See, Mamma," whispered Starr glowing rosily with pleasure, "they are speaking of Michael!"

Then the haughty eyes turned sharply and recognized him.

"You don't mean to tell me that upstart has dared to come down and see us off. The impudence of him! I am glad your father had enough sense not to bring him on board. He would probably have come if he had let him. Come away, Starr. He simply shall not look at you in that way!"

"What! Come away while Papa is standing there watching us out of sight. I simply couldn't. What would Papa think? And besides, I don't see why Michael shouldn't come if he likes. I think it was nice of him. I wonder why he hasn't been to the house to explain why he never came for that horseback ride."

"You're a very silly ignorant little girl, or you would understand that he has no business presuming to come to our house, and he knows it perfectly well. I want you to stop looking in that direction at once. I simply will not have him devouring you with his eyes in that way. I declare I would like to go back and tell him what I think of him. Starr, stop I tell you, Starr!"

But the noise of the starting drowned her words, and Starr, her cheeks like roses and her eyes like two stars, was waving a bit of a handkerchief and smiling and throwing kisses. The kisses were for her father, but the smiles and the starry glances, and the waving bit of cambric were for Michael, and they all traveled through the air quite promiscuously, drenching the bright uncovered head of the boy with sweetness. His eyes gave her greeting and thanks and parting all in one in that brief moment of her passing; and her graceful form and dainty vivid face were graven on his memory in quick sweet blows of pain, as he realized that she was going from him.

Slowly the great vessel glided out upon the bright waters and grew smaller and smaller. The crowd on the wharf were beginning to break away and hurry back to business or home or society. Still Michael stood with bared head gazing, and that illumined expression upon his face.

Endicott, a mist upon his own glasses at parting from his beloved baby, saw the boy's face as it were the face of an angel, and was half startled, turning away embarrassedly as though he had intruded upon a soul at prayer; then looked again.

"Come, son!" he said almost huskily. "It's over! We better be getting back. Step in."

The ride back to the office was a silent one. Somehow Endicott did not feel like talking. There had been some differences between himself and his wife that were annoying, and a strange belated regret that he had let Starr go away for a foreign education was eating into his heart. Michael, on his part, was living over again the passing of the vessel and the blessing of the parting.

Back in the office, however, all was different. Among the familiar walls and gloomy desks and chairs Endicott was himself, and talked business. He put questions, short, sharp and in quick succession.

"What are you doing with yourself? Working? What at? H'm! How'd you get there? Like it? Satisfied to do that all your life? You're not? Well, what's your line? Any ambitions? You ought to have got some notion in college of what you're fit for. Have you thought what you'd like to do in the world?"

Michael hesitated, then looked up with his clear, direct, challenging gaze.

"There are two things," he said, "I want to earn money and buy some land in the country, and I want to know about laws."

"Do you mean you want to be a lawyer?"

"Yes."

"What makes you think you'd be a success as a lawyer?"

"Oh, I might not be a success, but I need to know law. I want to try to stop some things that ought not to be."

"H'm!" grunted Endicott disapprovingly. "Don't try the reform game, it doesn't pay. However, if you feel that way you'll probably be all right to start. That'll work itself off and be a good foundation. There's no reason why you shouldn't be a lawyer if you choose, but you can't study law selling calico. You might get there someday, if you stick to your ambition, but you'd be pretty old before you were ready to practice if you started at the calico counter and worked your way up through everything you came to. Well, I can get you into a law office right away. How soon can you honorably get away from where you are? Two weeks? Well, just wait a minute."

Endicott called up a number on the telephone by his side, and there followed a conversation, brief, pointed, but in terms that Michael could barely follow. He gathered that a lawyer named Holt, a friend of Mr. Endicott's, was being asked to take him into his office to read law.

"It's all right, son," said Endicott as he hung up the receiver and whirled around from the phone. "You're to present yourself at the office as soon as you are free. This is the address"—hurriedly scribbling something on a card and handing it to him.

"Oh, thank you!" said Michael, "but I didn't mean to have you take any more trouble for me. I can't be dependent on you any longer. You have done so much for me."

"Bosh!" said Endicott. "I'm not taking any trouble. And you're not dependent on me. Be as independent as you like. You're not quite twenty-one yet, are you? Well, I told you you were my boy until you were of age, and I suppose there's nothing to hinder me doing as I will with my own. It's paid well all I've done for you so far, and I feel the investment was a good one. You'll get a small salary for some office work while you're studying, so after you are twenty-one you can be on your own if you like. Till then I claim the privilege of giving you a few orders. Now that's settled. Where are you stopping? I don't intend to lose sight of you again."

Michael gave him the street and number. Endicott frowned.

"That's not a good place. I don't like the neighborhood. If you're going to be a lawyer, you must start in right. Here, try this place. Tell the woman I sent you. One of my clerks used to board there."

He handed Michael another address.

"Won't that cost a lot?" asked Michael studying the card. "Not any more than you can afford," said Endicott, "and remember, I'm giving orders until your majority."

Michael beamed his brilliant smile at his benefactor.

"It is like a real father!" said the boy deeply moved. "I can never repay you. I can never forget it."

"Well, don't!" said Endicott. "Let's turn to the other thing. What do you want land for?"

Michael's face sobered instantly.

"For an experiment I want to try," he said without hesitation, and then, his eyes lighting up, "I'll be able to do it now, soon, perhaps, if I work hard. You see I studied agriculture in college—"

"The dickens you did!" exclaimed Endicott. "What did you do that for?"

"Well, it was there and I could, and I wanted to know about it."

"H'm!" said Endicott. "I wonder what some of my pedigreed million-dollar friends' sons would think of that? Well, go on."

"Why, that's all," laughed Michael happily. "I studied it and I want to try it and see what I can do with it. I want to buy a farm."

"How would you manage to be a farmer and a lawyer both?"

"Well, I thought there might be a little time after hours to work, and I could tell others how—"

"Oh, I see you want to be a gentleman farmer,"

laughed Endicott. "I understand that's expensive business."

"I think I could make it pay, sir," said Michael shutting his lips with that firm challenge of his. "I'd like to try."

Endicott looked at him quizzically for a minute and then whirling around in his office chair he reached out his hand to a pigeonhole and took out a deed.

"I've a mind to let you have your try," said Endicott, chuckling as if it were a good joke. "Here's a little farm down in Jersey. It's swampy and thick with mosquitoes. I understand it won't grow a beanstalk. There are twelve acres and a tumbledown house on it. I've had to take it in settlement of a mortgage. The man's dead and there's nothing but the farm to lay hands on. He hasn't even left a chick or child to leave his debt to. I don't want the farm and I can't sell it without a lot of trouble. I'll give it to you. You may consider it a birthday present. If you'll pay the taxes I'll be glad to get it off my hands. That'll be something for you to be independent about."

He touched a bell and a boy appeared.

"Take this to Jowett and tell him to have a deed made out to Michael Endicott, and to attend to the transfer of the property, nominal sum. Understand?"

The boy said, "Yes, sir," and disappeared with the paper.

"But I can't take a present like that from you after all you have done for me," gasped Michael, a granite determination showing in his blue eyes. "Nonsense," said Endicott. "Other men give their sons automobiles when they come of age. Mayn't I give you a farm if I like? Besides, I tell you it's of no account. I want to get rid of it, and I want to see what you'll make of it. I'd like to amuse myself seeing you try your experiment."

"If you'll let me pay you for it little by little."

"Suit yourself after you have become a great lawyer," laughed Endicott, "but not till then, remember. There, cut it out, son! I don't want to be thanked. Here's the description of the place and directions how to get there. It isn't many miles away. If you've got a half holiday run down and look it over. It'll keep you out of mischief. There's nothing like an ambition to keep people out of mischief. Run along now, I haven't another minute to spare, but mind you turn up at Holt's office this day two weeks, and report to me afterwards how you like it. I don't want to lose sight of you again."

Then entrance of another man on business cut short the interview, and Michael, bestowing an agonizingly happy grip on Endicott's hand and a brilliant smile like a benediction, took his directions and hurried out into the street.

Chapter 12

With the precious paper in his hand Michael took himself with all swiftness to the DesBrosses Ferry. Would there be a train? It was almost two o'clock. He had had no lunch, but what of that? He had that in his heart which made mere eating seem unnecessary. The experiences of the past two hours had lifted him above earth and its necessities for the time. And a farm, a real farm! Could it be true? Had his wish come true so soon? He could scarcely wait for the car to carry him or the boat to puff its way across the water. He felt as if he must fly to see his new possession. And Mr. Endicott had said he might pay for it sometime when he got to be a great lawyer. He had not doubt but that he would get there if such a thing were possible, and anyhow he meant to pay for that ground. Meantime it was his. He was not a poor nobody after all. He owned land, and a house.

His face was a mingling of delightful emotions as he stood by the rail of the ferryboat and let his imagination leap on ahead of him. The day was perfect. It had rained the night before and everything, even the air seemed newly washed for a fresh trail at living. Every little wavelet sparkled like a jewel, and the sunlight shimmered on the water in a most alluring way. Michael forgot for the moment the sorrow and misery of the crowded city he was leaving behind him. For this afternoon at least he was a boy again wandering off into the open.

His train was being called as he stepped from the fer-

ryboat. The next boat would have missed it. He hurried
aboard and was soon speeding through the open country,
with now and again a glimpse of the sea, as the train came
closer to the beach. They passed almost continuously beautiful resorts, private villas, great hotels, miles of cottages set
in green terrace with glowing autumn flowers in boxes or
bordering the paths.

Michael watched everything with deep interest. This
was the land of his new possession. Whatever was growing
here would be likely to grow on his place if it were properly
planted and cared for. Before this flowers had had little part
in his farming scheme, but so soon as he saw the brilliant
display he resolved that he must have some of those also.
And flowers would sell as well if not better than vegetables
if properly marketed.

That vivid hedge of scarlet and gold, great heavy-
headed dahlias they were. He did not know the name, but
he would find it out somehow. They would take up little
room and would make his new place a thing of beauty. Farther on, one great white cottage spread its veranda wings
on either side to a tall fringe of pink and white and crimson
cosmos; and again a rambling gray stone piece of quaint
architecture with low sloping roofs of mossy green, and velvet lawn creeping down even to the white beach sands, was
set about with flaming scarlet sage. It was a revelation to the
boy whose eyes had never looked upon the like before.
Nature in its wildness and original beauty had been in Florida; New York was all pavements and buildings with a window box here and there. He as yet knew nothing of country
homes in their luxury and perfection, save from magazine
pictures. All the way along he was picking out features that
he meant someday to transfer to his own little farm.

It was after three when he reached the station, and a
good fifteen minutes' walk to the farm, but every step of it
was a delight.

Pearl Beach, they called the station. The beach was half
a mile from the railroad, and a queer little straggling town
mostly cottages and a few stores hovered between railroad
and beach. A river, broad and shallow, wound its silver way
about the village and lost itself in the wideness of the ocean.
Here and there a white sail flew across its gleaming center,

and fishermen in little boats sat at their idle task. What if his
land should touch somewhere this bonny stream!

Too eager to wait for investigation he stopped a passing stranger and questioned him. Yes, the river was salt. It
had tides with the sea, too. There was great fishing and
sailing, and some preferred bathing there to the ocean. Yes,
Old Orchard farm was on its bank. It had a river frontage
of several hundred feet but it was over a mile back from the
beach.

The stranger was disposed to delay and gossip about
the death of the former owner of Old Orchard and its probable fate now that the mortgage had been foreclosed, but
Michael with a happy light in his eyes thanked him courteously and hurried on. Wings were upon his feet, and his
heart was light and happy. He felt like a bird set free. He
breathed in the strong salt air with delight.

And the the burden of the city came to him again, the
city with all its noise and folly and sin; with its smells and
heat, and lack of air; with its crowded, suffering, awful humanity, herded together like cattle, and living in conditions
worse than the beasts of the fields. If he could but bring
them out here, bring some of them at least, and show them
what God's earth was like! Ah!

His heart beat wildly at the thought! It was not new. He
had harbored it ever since his first visit to the alley. It was
his great secret, his much hoped for experiment. If he
might be able to do it sometime. This bit of a farm would
open the way. There would be money needed of course,
and where was it to come from? But he could work. He was
strong. He would give his young life for his people—save
them from their ignorance and despair. At least he could
save some; even one would be worthwhile.

So he mused as he hurried on, eyes and mind open to
all he saw.

There was no fence in front of Old Orchard farm. A
white road bordered with goldenrod and wild asters met
the scraggly grass that matted and tangled itself beneath
the gnarled apple trees. A grassy rutted wagon track
curved itself in vistas between the trees up to the house
which was set far back from the road. A man passing identi-
fed the place for Michael, and looked him over apprizingly,

wondering as did all who saw him, at the power and
strength of his beauty.

The house was weather-beaten unpainted clapboards,
its roof of curled and mossy shingles possessing undoubted
leakable qualities, patched here and there. A crazy veranda
ambled across the front. It contained a long low room with
a queer old-fashioned chimney place wide enough to sit in,
a square south room that must have been a dining room
because of the painted cupboard whose empty shelves
gazed ghastly between half-open doors, and a small
kitchen, not much more than a shed. In the long low room
a staircase twisted itself up oddly to the four rooms under
the leaky roof. It was all empty and desolate, save for an old
cot bed and a broken chair. The floors had a sagged, shaky
appearance. The doors quaked when they were opened.
The windows were cobwebby and dreary, yet it looked to
the eyes of the new householder like a palace. He saw it in
the light of future possibilities and gloried in it. That
chimney place now. How would it look with a great log
burning in it, and a rug and rocking chair before it. What
would—Aunt Sally—perhaps—say to it when he got it fixed
up? Could he ever coax her to leave her dirty doorstep and
her drink and come out her to live? And how would he
manage it all if he could? There would have to be something to feed her with, and to buy the rug and the rocking
chair. And first of all there would have to be a bathtub.
Aunt Sally would need to be purified before she could enter
the portals of this ideal cottage, when he had made it as he
wanted it to be. Paint and paper would make wonderful
transformations he knew, for he had often helped at re-
modeling the rooms at college during summer vacations.
He had watched and been with the workmen and finally
taken a hand. This habit of watching and helping had
taught him many things. But where were paper and paint
and time to use it coming from? Ah, well, leave that to the
future. He would find a way. Yesterday he did not have the
house nor the land for it to stand upon. It had come and
the rest would follow in their time.

He went happily about planning for a bathroom.
There would have to be water power. He had seen windmills on other places as he passed. That was perhaps the

solution of this problem, but windmills cost money of course. Still—all in good time.

There was a tumbledown barn and chicken house, and a frowzy attempt at a garden. A strawberry bed overgrown with weeds, a sickly cabbage lifting its head bravely; a gaunt row of currant bushes; another wandering, outreaching row of raspberries; a broken fence; a stretch of soppy bog land to the right, and the farm trailed off into desolate neglect ending in a charming grove of thick trees that stood close down to the river's bank.

Michael went over it all carefully, noted the exposure of the land, kicked the sandy soil to examine its unpromising state, walked all around the bog and tried to remember what he had read about cranberry bogs; wondered if the salt water came up here, and if it were good or bad for cranberries; wondered if cowpeas grew in Jersey and if they would do for a fertilizing crop as they did in Florida. Then he walked through the lovely woods, scenting the breath of pines and drawing in long whiffs of life as he looked up to the green roof over his head. They were not like the giant pines of the Southland, but they were sweeter and more beautiful in their form.

He went down to the brink of the river and stood looking across.

Not a soul was in sight and nothing moved save a distant sail fleeing across the silver sheen to the sea. He remembered what the man had said about bathing and yielding to an irresistible impulse was soon swimming out across the water. It was like a new lease on life to feel the water brimming to his neck again, and to propel himself with strong, graceful strokes through the element where he could. A bird shot up into the air with a wild sweet note, and he felt like answering to its melody. He whistled softly in imitation of its voice, and the bird answered, and again and again they called across the water.

But a look toward the west where the water was crimsoning already with the setting sun warned him that his time was short, so he swam back to the sheltered nook where he had left his clothes, and improvising a towel from his handkerchief he dressed rapidly. The last train back left at seven. If he did not wish to spend the night in his new

and uninhabitable abode he must make good time. It was
later than he supposed, and he wished to go back to the
station by way of the beach if possible, though it was out of
his way. As he drew on his coat and ran his fingers through
his hair in lieu of a brush, he looked wistfully at the bright
water, dimpling now with hues of violet, pink, and gold and
promising a rare treat in the way of a sunset. He would like
to stay and watch it. But there was the ocean waiting for
him. He must stand on the shore once and look out across
it, and know just how it looked near his own house.

He hurried through the grove and across the farm to
the eastern edge, and looking beyond the broken fence that
marked the bounds of the bog and over the waste of salt
grass he could see the white waves dimly tumbling, hurrying ever, to get past one another. He took the fence at a
bound, made good time over the uncertain footing of the
marsh grass and was soon standing on the broad smooth
beach with the open stretch of ocean before him.

It was the first time he had ever stood on the seashore
and the feeling of awe that filled him was very great. But
beyond any other sensation, came the thought that Starr,
his beautiful Starr, was out there on that wide vast ocean,
tossing in a tiny boat. For now the great steamer that had
seemed so large and palatial, had dwindled in his mind to a
frail toy, and he was filled with a nameless fear for her. His
little Starr out there on that fearful deep, with only that
cold-eyed mother to take care of her. A wild desire to fly to
her and bring her back possessed him, a thrilling, awesome
something, he had never known before. He stood
speechless before it; then raised his eyes to the roseate already purpling in streaks for the sunset and looking solemnly up he said, aloud:

"Oh, God, I love her!"

He stood facing the thought with solemn joy and pain
for an instant, then turned and fled from it down the purpling sands, fleeing yet carrying his secret with him.

And when he came opposite the little village he trod its
shabby, straggling, ill-paved streets with glory in his face;
and walking thus with hat in hand, and face illumined toward the setting sun, folks looked at him strangely and
wondered who and what he was, and turned to look again.

In that half-light of sunset, he seemed a being from another world.

A native watching, dropped his whip, and climbing down from his rough wagon spoke the thought that all the bystanders felt in common:

"Gosh hang it! I thought he was one o' them glass angels stepped out of a church winder over to 'Lizabethtown. We don't see them kind much. I wonder now how he'd be to live with. Think I'd feel kinder creepy hevin' him 'round all time, wouldn't you?"

All the way home the new thought came surging over him, he loved her and she could never be his. It was deluging, it was beautiful, but it was agonizing. He recalled how beautiful she had been as she waved farewell. And some of her smiles had been for him, he was sure. He had known of course that the kisses were for her father, and yet, they had been blown freely his way, and she had looked her pleasure at his presence. There had been a look in her eyes such as she had worn that day in the college chapel when she had thrown precautions to the winds and put her arms about his neck and kissed him. His young heart thrilled with a deep joy over the memory of it. It had been wonderful that she had done it; wonderful! when he was what he was, a *child of the slums!* The words seemed burned upon his soul now, a part of his very life. He was not worthy of her, not worthy to receive her favor.

Yet he closed his eyes, leaning his hand against the window frame as the train hurried along through the gathering darkness, and saw again the bright lovely face, the dainty fingers blowing kisses, the lips wreathed in smiles, and knew some of the farewell had been surely meant for him. He forgot the beautiful villas along the way, forgot to watch for the twinkling lights, or to care how the cottages looked at evening. Whenever the track veered toward the sea and gave a glimpse of gray sky and yawning ocean with here and there a point of light to make the darkness blacker, he seemed to know instinctively, and opening his eyes strained them to look across it. Out there in the blackness somewhere was his Starr and he might not go to her, nor she come to him. There was a wide stretch of unfathomable sea between them. There would always be that gray, impassable sky and sea of impossibility between them.

As he neared New York, however, these thoughts dropped from him; and standing on the ferryboat with the million twinkling lights of the city; and the looming blackness of the huddled mass of towering buildings against the illuminated sky, the call of the people came to him. Over there in the darkness, swarming in the fetid atmosphere of a crowded court were thousands like himself, yes, *like himself,* for he was one of them. He belonged there. They were his kind and he must help them!

Then his mind went to the farm and his plans, and he entered back into the grind of life and assumed its burden with the sweet pain of his secret locked in his inmost heart.

Chapter 13

"Sam, have you ever been in the country?"

It was Michael who asked the question. They were sitting in a small dismal room that Michael had found he could afford to rent in a house on the edge of the alley. Not that he had moved there, oh, no! He could not have endured life if all of it that he could call his own had to be spent in that atmosphere. He still kept his little fourth floor back in the dismally respectable street. He had not gone to the place recommended by Endicott, because he found that the difference he would have to pay would make it possible for him to rent this sad little room near the alley; and for his purposes this seemed to him an absolute necessity at present.

The weather was growing too cold for him to meet with his new old acquaintances of the alley out of doors, and it was little better indoors even if he could have endured the dirt and squalor of those apartments that would have been open to him. Besides, he had a great longing to show them something brighter than their own forlorn houses.

There was a settlement house three or four blocks away, but it had not drawn the dwellers in this particular alley. They were sunken too low, perhaps, or there were so many more hopeful quarters in which to work; and the city was so wide and deep and dark. Michael knew little about the settlement house. He had read of such things. He had looked shyly toward its workers now and then, but as yet knew none of them, though they had heard now and again of the "angel-man of the alley," and were curious to find him out.

But Michael's enterprise was all his own, and his ways of working were his own. He had gone back into the years of his childhood and found out from his inner consciousness what it was he had needed, and now he was going to try to give it to some other little "kids" who were as forlorn and friendless as he had been. It wasn't much that he could do, but what he could he would do, and more as soon as possible.

And so he had rented this speck of a room, and purified it. He had literally compelled Sam to help him. That compelling was almost a modern miracle, and wrought by radiant smiles, and a firm grip on Sam's shoulder when he told him what he wanted done.

Together they had swept and scrubbed and literally scraped the dirt from that room.

"I don't see what you're making sech a darned fuss about dirt fer!" grumbled Sam as he arose from his knees after scrubbing the floor for the fourth time. "It's what we're all made of, dey say, an' nobuddy'll know de diffrunce."

"Just see if they won't, Sam," encouraged Michael as he polished off the door he had been cleaning. "See there, how nice that looks! You didn't know that paint was gray, did you? It looked brown before, it was so thick with dirt. Now we're ready for paint and paper!"

And so, in an atmosphere of soap and water they had worked night after night till very late, and Sam had actually let a well-planned and promising raid go by because he was so interested in what he was doing and he was ashamed to tell Michael of his engagement.

Sam had never assisted at the papering of a room before; in fact, it is doubtful if he ever saw a room with clean fresh paper on its walls in all his life, unless in some house he had entered unlawfully. When this one stood arrayed at last in its delicate newness, he stood back and surveyed it in awed silence.

Michael had chosen paper of the color of the sunshine, for the court was dark and the alley was dark and the room was dark. The souls of the people too were dark. They must have light and brightness if he would win them to better things. Besides, the paper was only five cents a roll, the cheapest he could find in the city. Michael had learned at college during vacations how to put it on. He made Sam wash and wash and wash his hands before he was allowed to handle any of the delicate paper.

"De paper'll jest git dirty right away," grumbled Sam sullenly, albeit he washed his hands, and his eyes glowed as they used to when a child at a rare "find" in the gutter.

"Wot'll you do when it gits dirty?" demanded Sam belligerently.

"Put on some clean," said Michael sunnily. "Besides, we must learn to have clean hands and keep it clean."

"I wish we had some curtains," said Michael wistfully. "They had thin white curtains at college."

"Are you makin' a college fer we?" asked Sam looking at him sharply.

"Well, in a way, perhaps," said Michael smiling. "You know I want you to have all the advantages I had as far as I can get them."

Sam only whistled and looked perplexed but he was doing more serious thinking than he had ever done in his life before.

And so the two had worked, and planned, and now tonight, the work was about finished.

The walls reflected the yellow of the sunshine, the woodwork was painted white enamel. Michael had just put on the last gleaming coat.

"We can give it another coat when it looks a little soiled," he had remarked to Sam, and Sam, frowning, had replied: "Dey better hev dere han's clean."

The floor was painted gray. There was no rug. Michael

felt its lack and meant to remedy it as soon as possible, but rugs cost money. There was a small coal stove set up and polished till it shone, and a fire was laid ready to start. They had not needed it while they were working hard. The furniture was a wooden table painted gray with a cover of bright cretonne, two wooden chairs, and three boxes. Michael had collected these furnishings carefully and economically, for he had to sacrifice many little comforts that he might get them.

On the walls were two or three good pictures fastened by brass tacks; and some of the gray moss and pine branches from Michael's own room. In the central wall appeared one of Michael's beloved college pennants. It was understood by all who had yet entered the sacred precincts of the room to be the symbol of what made the difference between them and "the angel," and they looked at it with awe, and mentally crossed themselves in its presence.

At the windows were two lengths of snowy cheesecloth crudely hemmed by Michael, and tacked up in pleats with brass-headed tacks. They were tied back with narrow yellow ribbons. This had been the last touch and Sam sat looking thoughtfully at the stiff angular bows when Michael asked the question:

"Have you ever been in the country?"

"Sure!" said Sam scornfully. "Went wid de Fresh Air folks wen I were a kid."

"What did you think of it?"

"Don't tink much!" shrugged Sam. "Too empty. Nothin' doin'! Good 'nough fer kids. Never again fer *me*."

It was three months since Michael had made his memorable first visit down to Old Orchard Farm. For weeks he had worked shoulder to shoulder every evening with Sam and as yet no word of that plan which was nearest his heart had been spoken. This was his first attempt to open the subject.

That Sam had come to have a certain kind of respect and fondness for him he was sure, though it was never expressed in words. Always he either objected to any plan Michael suggested, or else he was extremely indifferent and would not promise to be on hand. He was almost always there, however, and Michael had come to know that Sam was proud of his friendship, and at least to a degree interested in his plans for the betterment of the court.

"There are things in the country, other things, that make up for the stir of the city," said Michael thoughtfully. This was the first unpractical conversation he had tried to hold with Sam. He had been leading him up, through the various stages from dirt and degradation, by means of soap and water, then paper and paint, and now they had reached the doorway of nature's school. Michael wanted to introduce Sam to the great world of out-of-doors. For, though Sam had lived all his life out-of-doors, it had been a world of brick walls and stone pavements, with little sky and almost no water. Not a green thing in sight, not a bird, nor a beast except of burden. The first lesson was waiting in a paper bundle that stood under the table. Would Sam take it, Michael wondered, as he rose and brought it out, unwrapping the papers carefully, while Sam silently watched and pretended to whistle, not to show too much curiosity. "What tings?" at last asked Sam.

"Things like this," answered Michael eagerly setting out on the table an earthen pot containing a scarlet geranium in bloom. It glowed forth its brilliant torch at once and gave just the touch to the little empty clean room that Michael had hoped it would do. He stood back and looked at it proudly, and then looked at Sam to see if the lesson had been understood. He half expected to see an expression of scorn on the hardened sallow face of the slum boy, but instead Sam was gazing open-mouthed, with unmitigated admiration.

"Say! Dat's all right!" he ejaculated. "Where'd you make de raise? Say! Dat makes de paper an' de paint show up fine!" taking in the general effect of the room.

Then he rose from the box on which he had been sitting and went and stood before the blossom.

"Say! I wisht Jim cud see dat dere!" he ejaculated after a long silence, and there was that in the expression of his face that brought the quick moisture to Michael's eyes.

It was only a common red geranium bought for fifteen cents, but it had touched with its miracle of bright life the hardened soul of the young burglar, and opened his vision to higher things than he had known. It was in that moment of open vision that his heart turned to his old companion who was uncomplainingly taking the punishment which rightfully belonged to the whole gang.

"We will take him one tomorrow," said Michael in a low voice husky with feeling. It was the first time Sam had voluntarily mentioned Jim and he had seemed so loth to take Michael to see him in jail that Michael had ceased to speak of the matter.

"There's another one just like this where I bought this one. I couldn't tell which to take, they were both so pretty. We'll get it the first thing in the morning before anybody else snaps it up, and then, when could we get in to see Jim? Would they let us in after my office hours or would we have to wait till Sunday? You look after that will you? I might get off at four o'clock if that's not too late."

"Dey'll let us in on Sunday ef *you* ask, I reckon," said Sam much moved. "But it's awful dark in prison. It won't live, will it? Dere's only one streak o' sun shines in Jim's cell a few minutes every day."

"Oh, I think it'll live," said Michael hastily, a strange choking sensation in his throat at thought of his onetime companion shut into a dark prison. Of course, he deserved to be there. He had broken the laws, but then no one had ever made him understand how wrong it was. If someone had only tried perhaps Jim would never have done the thing that put him in prison.

"I'm sure it will live," he said again cheerfully. "I've heard that geraniums are very hardy. The man told me they would live all winter in the cellar if you brought them up again in the spring."

"Jim will be out again in de spring," said Sam softly. It was the first sign of anything like emotion in Sam.

"Isn't that good!" said Michael heartily. "I wonder what we can do to make it pleasant for him when he comes back to the world. We'll bring him to this room, of course, but in the spring this will be getting warm. And that makes me think of what I was talking about a minute ago. There's so much more in the country than in the city!"

"More?" questioned Sam uncomprehendingly.

"Yes, things like this to look at. Growing things that you

get to love and understand. Wonderful things. There's a river that sparkles and talks as it runs. There are trees that laugh and whisper when the wind plays in their branches. And there are wonderful birds, little live breaths of air with music inside that make splendid friends when you're lonely. I know, for I made lots of bird friends when I went away from you all to college. You know I was pretty lonely at first."

Sam looked at him with quick, keen wonder, and a lighting of his face that made him almost attractive and sent the cunning in his eyes slinking out of sight. Had this fine greathearted creature really missed his old friends when he went away? Had he really need of them yet with all his education—and—difference? It was food for thought.

"Then there's the sky, so much of it," went on Michael, "and so wide and blue, and sometimes soft white clouds. They make you feel rested when you look at them floating lazily through the blue, and never seeming to be tired; not even when there's a storm and they have to hurry. And there's the sunset. Sam, I don't believe you ever saw the sunset, not right anyway. You don't have sunsets here in the city, it just gets dark. You ought to see one I saw not long ago. I mean to take you there someday and we'll watch it together. I want to see if it will do the same thing to you that it did to me."

Sam looked at him in awe, for he wore his exalted look, and when he spoke like that Sam had a superstitious fear that perhaps after all he was as old Sal said, more of angel than of man.

"And then, there's the earth, all covered with green, plenty of it to lie in if you want to, and it smells so good, and there's so much air—enough to breathe your lungs full, and with nothing disagreeable in it, no ugly smells nor sounds. And there are growing things everywhere. Oh, Sam! Wouldn't you like to make things like this grow?"

Sam nodded and put forth his rough forefinger shamedly to touch the velvet of a green leaf, as one unaccustomed might touch a baby's cheek.

"You'll go with me, Sam, to the country sometime, won't you? I've got a plan and I'll need you to help me carry it out. Will you go?"

"Sure!" said Sam in quite a different voice from any reluctant assent he had ever given before. "Sure, I'll go!"

"Thank you, Sam," said Michael more moved than he dared show. "And now that's settled I want to talk about this room. I'm going to have five little kids here tomorrow early in the evening. I told them I'd show them how to whittle boats and we're going to sail them in the scrub bucket. They're about the age you and I were when I went away to college. Perhaps I'll teach them a letter or two of the alphabet if they seem interested. They ought to know how to read, Sam."

"I never learned to read—" muttered Sam half belligerently. "That so?" said Michael as if it were a matter of small moment. "Well, what if you were to come in and help me with the boats. Then you could pick it up when I teach them. You might want to use it someday. It's well to know how, and a man learns things quickly you know."

Sam nodded.

"I don't know's I care 'bout it," he said indifferently, but Michael saw that he intended to come.

"Well, after the kids have gone, I won't keep them late you know, I wonder if you'd like to bring some of the fellows in to see this?"

Michael glanced around the room.

"I've some pictures of alligators I have a fancy they might like to see. I'll bring them down if you say so."

"Sure!" said Sam trying to hide his pleasure.

"Then tomorrow morning I'm going to let that little woman that lives in the cellar under Aunt Sally's room, bring her sewing here and work all day. She makes buttonholes in vests. It's so dark in her room she can't see and she's almost ruined her eyes working by candlelight."

"She'll mess it all up!" grumbled Sam, "an' she might let other folks in an' they'd pinch the picters an' the posy."

"No, she won't do that. I've talked to her about it. The room is to be hers for the day, and she's to keep it looking just as nice as it did when she found it. She'll only bring her work over, and go home for her dinner. She's to keep the fire going so it will be warm at night, and she's to try it for a day and see how it goes. I think she'll keep her promise. We'll try her anyway."

Sam nodded as to a superior officer who nevertheless was awfully foolish.

"Mebbe!" he said.

"Sam, do you think it would be nice to bring Aunt Sally over now a few minutes?"

"No," said Sam shortly, "she's too dirty. She'd put her fingers on de wall first thing—"

"But, Sam, I think she ought to come. And she ought to come first. She's the one that helped me find you—"

Sam looked sharply at Michael and wondered if he suspected how long that same Aunt Salley had frustrated his efforts to find his friends.

"We could tell her not to touch things, perhaps—"

"Wal, you lemme tell her. Here! I'll go fix her up an' bring her now?" And Sam hurried out of the room.

Michael waited, and in a few minutes Sam returned with Aunt Sally. But it was a transformed Aunt Sally. Her face had been painfully scrubbed in a circle out as far as her ears, and her scraggy gray hair was twisted in a tight knot at the back of her neck. Her hands were several shades cleaner than Michael had ever seen them before, and her shoes were tied. She wore a small three-cornered plaid shawl over her shoulders and entered cautiously as if half afraid to come. Her hands were clasped high across her breast. She had evidently been severely threatened against touching anything.

"The saints be praised!" she ejaculated warmly after she had looked around in silence for a moment. "To think I should ivver see the loikes uv this in de alley. It lukes loike a palace. Mikky, ye're a nangel, me b'y! An' a rale kurtin, to be sure! I ain't seen a kurtin in the alley since I cummed. An' will ye luke at the purty posy a blowin' as foine as ye plaze! Me mither had the loike in her cottage window when I was a leetle gal! Aw, me pure auld mither!"

And suddenly to Michael's amazement, and the disgust of Sam, old Sal sat down on the one chair and wept aloud, with the tears streaming down her seamed and sin-scarred face.

Sam was for putting her out at once, but Michael soothed her with his cheery voice, making her tell of her old home in Ireland, and the kind mother whom she had loved, though it was long years since she had thought of her now.

With rare skill he drew from her the picture of the little Irish cottage with its thatched roof, its peat fire, and well-swept hearth; the table with the white cloth, the cat in the rocking chair, the curtain starched stiffly at the window, the bright posy on the deep window ledge, and, lastly, the little girl with clean pinafore and curly hair who kissed her mother every morning and trotted off to school. But that was before the father died, and the potatoes failed. The school days were soon over, and the little girl with her mother came to America. The mother died on the way over, and the child fell into evil hands. That was the story, and as it was told Michael's face grew tender and wistful. Would that he knew even so much of his own history as that!

But Sam stood by struck dumb and trying to fancy that this old woman had ever been the bright rosy child she told about. Sam was passing through a sort of mental and moral earthquake.

"Perhaps someday we'll find another little house in the country where you can go and live," said Michael, "but meantime, suppose you go and see if you can't make your room look like this one. You scrub it all up and perhaps Sam and I will come over and put some pretty paper on the walls for you. Would you like that? How about it, Sam?"

"Sure!" said Sam rather grudgingly. He hadn't much faith in Aunt Sally and didn't see what Michael wanted with her anyway, but he was loyal to Michael.

Irish blessings mingled with tears and garnished with curses in the most extraordinary way were showered upon Michael and at last when he could stand no more, Sam said:

"Aw, cut it out, Sal. You go home an' scrub. Come on, now!" and he bundled her off in a hurry.

Late as it was, old Sal lit a fire, and by the light of a tallow candle got down on her stiff old knees and began to scrub. It seemed nothing short of a miracle that her room could ever look like that one she had just seen, but if scrubbing could do anything toward it, scrub she would. It was ten years since she had thought of scrubbing her room. She hadn't seemed to care, but tonight as she worked with her trembling old drink-shaken hands the memory of her

childhood's home was before her vision, and she worked
with all her might.

So the light and cheeriness of the little white room in
the dark alley began to work. "The angel's quarters" it was
named, and to be called to go within its charmed walls was
an honor that all coveted as time went on. And that was how
Michael began the salvation of his native alley.

Chapter 14

Michael had been three months with the new law firm and
was beginning to get accustomed to the violent contrast
between the day spent in the atmosphere of low-voiced,
quiet-stepping, earnest men who moved about in their environment of polished floors, oriental rugs, leather chairs
and walls with leather-covered law books, and the evening
down in the alley where his bare, little, white and gold room
made the only tolerable spot in the neighborhood.

He was still occupying the fourth floor back at his original boardinghouse, and had seen Mr. Endicott briefly
three or four times, but nothing had been said about his
lodgings.

One morning he came to the desk set apart for him in
the law office, and found a letter lying there for him.

"Son:" it said, "your board is paid at the address given
below, up to the day you are twenty-one. If you don't get the
benefit it will go to waste. Mrs. Semple will make you quite
comfortable and I desire you to move to her house at once.
If you feel any obligation toward me this is the way to discharge it. Hope you are well. Yours, Delevan Endicott."

Michael's heart beat faster with varied emotions. It was
pleasant to have someone care, and of course if Mr.
Endicott wished it so much he would manage it somehow—
perhaps he could get some night work or copying to do—

but he would never let him bear his expenses. That could not be.

He hurried off at the noon hour to find his benefactor and make this plain with due gratitude. He found, however, that it was not so easy to change this man's mind, once made up. Endicott would not hear to any change in arrangements. He had paid the board for the remaining months of Michael's minority and maintained his right to do so if he chose. Neither would he let Michael refund him any of the amount.

So Michael moved, bag and baggage, and found the change good. The regular, well-cooked meals gave zest to his appetite which had been going back on him for sometime under his own economical regime, and the larger room with better outlook and more air, to say nothing of a comfortable bed with adjoining bathroom, and plenty of heat and light, made life seem more worthwhile. Besides there were other boarders with whom he now came in pleasant contact, and there was a large pleasant parlor with easy chairs and an old-fashioned square piano which still retained much of its original sweetness of tone.

Mrs. Semple had a daughter Hester, an earnest, gray-eyed girl with soft brown hair and a firm little chin, who had taken an art course in Cooper Institute and painted very good pictures which, however, did not sell. Hester played the piano—not very well, it is true, but well enough to make it pleasant to a lonely boy who had known no music in his life except the birds or his own whistle. She played hymns on Sunday after church while they waited for the dinner to be ready, and evenings after supper she played other things; old ballads and tender, touching melodies from old masters simplified for such as she. Michael sometimes lingered a half hour before hurrying away to the alley, and joined his rich natural tenor with her light pretty soprano. Sometimes Will French, a young fellow who was in the same law office and also boarded at Mrs. Semple's, stayed awhile and sang bass. It was very pleasant and made it seem more as if he were living in a home.

All this time Michael was carrying on his quiet work in the alley, saying nothing about it to anybody. In the first

place he felt shy about it because of his personal connection
with the place. Not that he wished to hide his origin from
his employers, but he felt he owed it to Mr. Endicott who
had recommended him, to be as respectable in their sight as
possible; and so long as they neither knew nor cared it did
not matter. Then, it never occurred to Michael that he was
doing anything remarkable with his little white room in the
blackness of the stronghold of sin. Night after night he
gathered his newsboys and taught them whittling, basketry,
reading, arithmetic, and geography, with a little philosophy
and botany thrown in unawares. Night after night the older
fellows dropped in, one or two at a time, and listened to the
stories Michael told; sometimes of college life and games in
which they were of course interested; sometimes of nature
and his experiences in finding an alligator, or a serpent, or
watching some bird. It was wonderful how interesting he
managed to make those talks. He never realized that he was
preparing in the school of experience to be a magnificent
public speaker. With an audience as difficult as any he
could have found in the whole wide city, he managed to
hold them every time.

And the favorite theme often was agriculture. He
would begin by bringing a new little plant to the room, setting it up and showing it to them; talking about conditions
of soil and how plants were being improved. It was usually
the *résumé* of some article on agriculture that he had taken
time to read at noon and was reviewing for their benefit.

They heard all about Burbank and his wonderful ex-
periments in making plants grow and develop, and as they
listened they went and stood around the blossom that
Michael had just brought to them and looked with new
wonder at it. A flower was a strange enough sight in that
court, but when they heard these stories it became filled
with new interest. For a little while they forgot their evil
plotting and were lifted above themselves.

Another night the talk would be on fertilizers, and how
one crop would sometimes give out something that another
crop planted later, needed. Little by little, because he talked
about the things in which he himself was interested, he was
giving these sons of ignorance a dim knowledge of and interest in the culture of life, and the tilling of the ground,

getting them ready for what he had hardly as yet dared to put into words even to himself.

And one day he took Sam down to Old Orchard. It was the week before Christmas. They had made their second visit to Jim the week before and he had spoken of the spring and when he should get out into the world again. He seemed to be planning to get even with those who had confined him for his wrongdoing. Michael's heart was filled with anxiety for him.

There was something about Jim that appealed to Michael from the first.

He had seen him first standing behind the grating of his cell, a great unkempt hulk of a fellow with fiery red hair and brown eyes that roved restlessly, hungrily through the corridor. He would have been handsome but for his weak, girlish chin. Jim had melted almost to tears at sight of the scarlet geranium they had carried him on that first visit, and seemed to care more for the appearance of his old comrade "Mikky" than ever Sam had cared.

Jim was to get out in April. If only there were some place for him to go!

They talked of it on the way down. Sam seemed to think that Jim would find it pretty hard to leave New York. Sam himself wasn't much interested in the continued hints of Michael about going to the country.

"Nothin' doin'" was his constant refrain when Michael tried to tell him how much better it would be if some of the congested part of the city could be spread out into the wide country; especially for the poor people, how much greater opportunity for success in life there would be for them.

But Sam had been duly impressed with the wideness of the landscape, on this his first long trip out of the city, and as Michael unfolded to him the story of the gift of the farm, and his own hopes for it, Sam left off his scorn and began to give replies that showed he really was thinking about the matter.

"Say!" said he suddenly, "ef Buck was to come back would you let him live down to your place an' help do all them things you're plannin'?"

"I surely would," said Michael happily. "Say, Sam, do you, or do you *not* know where Buck is?"

Sam sat thoughtfully looking out of the window. At this point he turned his gaze down to his feet and slowly, cautiously nodded his head.

"I thought so!" said Michael eagerly. "Sam, is he in hiding for something he has done?"

Still more slowly, cautiously, Sam nodded his head once more.

"Sam, will you send him a message from me?"

Another nod.

"Tell him that I love him," Michael breathed the words eagerly. His heart remembered kindness from Buck more than any other lighting of his sad childhood. "Tell him that I want him—that I need him! Tell him that I want him to make an appointment to meet me somewhere and let us talk this plan of mine over. I want him to go in with me and help me make that farm into a fit place to take people who haven't the right kind of homes, where they can have honest work and good air and be happy! Will you tell him?"

And Sam nodded his head emphatically.

"An' Jim'll help too ef Buck goes. That's dead sure!" Sam volunteered.

"And, Sam, I'm counting on you!"

"Sure thing!" said Sam.

Michael tramped all over the place with Sam, showing him everything and telling all his plans. He was very familiar with his land now. He had planned the bog for a cranberry patch, and had already negotiated for the bushes. He had trimmed up the berry bushes in the garden himself during his various holiday trips, and had arranged with a fisherman to dump a few haulings of shellfish on one field where he thought that kind of fertilizer would be effective. He had determined to use his hundred-dollar graduation present in fertilizer and seed. It would not go far but it would be a beginning. The work he would have to get some other way. He would have but little time to put to it himself until late in the summer probably, and there was a great deal that ought to be done in the early spring. He would have to be contented to go slow of course, and must remember that unskilled labor is always expensive and wasteful; still it would likely be all he could get. Just how he would feed and house even unskilled labor was a problem yet to be solved.

It was a day of many revelations to Sam. For one thing even the bare snowy stretch of wide country had taken on a new interest to him since Michael had been telling all these wonderful things about the earth. Sam's dull brain which up to this time had never busied itself about anything except how to get other men's goods away from them, had suddenly awakened to the wonders of the world.

It was he that recognized a little colony of cocoons on the underside of leaves and twigs and called attention to them.

"Say, ain't dem some o' de critters you was showin' de fellers t'other night?"

And Michael fell upon them eagerly. They happened to be rare specimens, and he knew from college experience that such could be sold to advantage to the museums. He showed Sam how to remove them without injuring them. A little further on they came to a wild growth of holly, crazy with berries and burnished thorny foliage, and near at hand a mistletoe bough loaded with tiny white transparent berries.

"Ain't dem wot dey sell for Chris'sum greens?" Sam's city eyes picked them out at once.

Of course," said Michael delighted. "How stupid of me not to have found them before. We'll take a lot back with us and see if we can get any price for it. Whatever we get we'll devote to making the house liveable. Holly and mistletoe ought to have a good market about now. That's another idea! Why not cultivate a lot of this stuff right in this tract of land? It seems to grow without any trouble. See! There are lots of little bushes. We'll encourage them, Sam. And say, Sam, if you hadn't come along I might never have thought of that. You see I needed you."

Sam grunted in a pleased way.

When they came to the house it looked to Michael still more desolate in the snowy stretch of setting than it had when the grass was about it. His heart sank.

"I don't know as we can ever do anything with the old shack," he said, shaking his head wistfully. "It looks worse than I thought."

" 'Tain't so bad," said Sam cheerfully. "Guess it's water-tight." He placed a speculative eye at the dusty windowpane he had wiped off with his coat sleeve. "Looks dry inside. 'Twould be a heap better'n sleepin' on de pavement fer some. Dat dere fire hole would take in a bit lot o'wood an' I guess dere's a plenty round de place without robbin' de woods none."

Michael led him to the seashore and bade him look. He wanted to see what effect it would have upon him. The coast swept wild and bleak in the cold December day, and Sam shivered in his thin garments. A look of awe and fear came into his face. He turned his back upon it.

"Too big!" he said sullenly, and Michael understood that the sea in its vastness oppressed him.

"Yes, there's a good deal of it," he admitted, "but after all it's sort of like the geranium flower."

Sam turned back and looked.

"H'm! I don't see nothin' like!" he grunted despairingly.

"Why, it's wonderful! It's beyond us! We couldn't make it. Look at that motion! See the white tossing rim of the waves! See that soft green-gray! Isn't it just the color of the little down on the geranium leaf? See the silver light playing back and forth, and look how it reaches as far as you can see. Now, doesn't it make you feel a little as it did when you first looked at the geranium?"

Michael looked down at Sam from his greater height almost wistfully. He wanted him to understand, but Sam looked in vain.

"Not fer mine!" he shrugged. "Gimme the posy every time."

They walked in silence along the beach toward the flowing of the river, and Sam eyed the ocean furtively as if he feared it might run up and engulf them suddenly when they were not looking. He had seen the ocean from wharves of course; and once stole a ride in a pilot boat out into the deep a little way, but he had never been alone thus with the whole sea at once as this seemed. It was too vast for him to comprehend. Still, in a misty way he knew what Michael was trying to make him understand, and it stirred him uncomfortably.

They hired a little boat for a trifle and Michael with strong strokes rowed them back to the farm, straight into the sunset. The sky was purple and gold that night, and empurpled the golden river, whose ripples blended into pink and lavender and green. Sam sat huddled in the prow of the boat facing it all. Michael had planned it so. The oars dipped very quietly, and Sam's small eyes changed and widened and took it all in. The sun slipped lower in a crimson ball, and a flood of crimson light broke through the purple and gold for a moment and left a thin, clear line of flame behind.

"Dere!" exclaimed Sam pointing excitedly. "Dat's like de posy. I kin see *thet* all right!"

And Michael rested on his oars and looked back at the sunset, well pleased with this day's work.

They left the boat at a little landing where its owner had promised to get it, and went back through the wood, gathering a quantity of holly branches and mistletoe, and when they reached the city Michael found a good market for it, and received enough for what he had brought to more than cover the price of the trip. The best of it was that Sam was as pleased with the bargain as if it were for his personal benefit.

When they parted Sam wore a spring of mistletoe in his ragged buttonhole, and Michael carried several handsome branches of holly back to his boarding place.

Most of this he gave to Hester Semple to decorate the parlor with, but one fine branch he kept and carried to his room and fastened it over his mirror. Then after looking at it wistfully for a long time he selected a glossy spray containing several fine large berries, cut it off and packed it carefully in a tiny box. This without name or clue to sender, he addressed in printing letters to Starr. Mr. Endicott had asked him to mail a letter to her as he passed by the box the last time he had been in the office, and without his intention the address had been burned into his memory. He had not expected to use it ever, but there could be no harm surely in sending the girl this bit of Christmas greeting out of the nowhere of a world of possible people. She would never know he had sent it, and perhaps it would please her to get a piece of Christmas holly from home. She might think her father had sent it. It mattered not, he knew, and it helped him to think he might send this much of his thoughts over the water to her. He pleased himself with thinking how she would look when she opened the box. But whether she would be pleased or not he must only surmise, for she would never know to thank him. Ah, well, it was as near as he dared hope for touching life's happiness. He must be glad for what he might have, and try to work and forget the rest.

Chapter 15

Now about this time the law firm with whom Michael worked became deeply interested in their new boy. He studied hard, and seemed to know what he was about all day. They saw signs of extraordinary talent in him. Once or twice, thinking to make life pleasant for him, they had invited him to their club, or to some evening's entertainment, and always Michael had courteously declined, saying that he had an engagement for the evening. They casually questioned Will French, the other student, who was a happy-go-lucky and in the office because his father wished him to study something and not because he wanted to. Will said that Michael went out every evening and came in late. Mrs. Semple had remarked that she often didn't know whether he came in at all until she saw him come down to breakfast.

This report and a certain look of weariness about the eyes some mornings led the senior member of the firm to look into Michael's affairs. The natural inference was that Michael was getting into social life too deeply, perhaps wasting the hours in late revelry when he should have been sleeping. Mr. Holt liked Michael, and dreaded to see the signs of dissipation appear on that fine face. He asked Will French to make friends with him and find out if he could where he spent his evenings. Will readily agreed, and at once entered on his mission with a zeal which was beyond all baffling.

"Hello, Endicott!" called Will as Michael reached the front door on his way to his mission that same evening. "Where're you going? Wait, can't you, and I'll walk along with you? I was going to ask you if you wouldn't go to a show with me this evening. I haven't anything on for to-night and it's slow."

As he spoke he seized his coat and hat which he had purposely left in the hall near at hand, and put them on.

"Thank you," said Michael, as they went out together, "I'd be glad to go with you but I have something that can't be put off."

"Well, go tomorrow night with me, will you? I like you and I think we ought to be friends."

Will's idea was that they would get to talking at a show and he could find out a good deal in that way. He thought it must be a girl. He had told the senior Holt that it was a girl of course, and he wouldn't take long to spot her. It must be either a girl or revelry to take the fellow out every night in the week so late.

"Well, I'm sorry," said Michael again, "but I'm afraid I have an engagement every night. It's rather a permanent job I'm engaged in. What do you do with your evenings?

Will launched into a gay description of parties and en-tertainments to which he had been bidden, and nice girls he knew, hinting that he might introduce Michael if he was so inclined, and Michael talked on leading his unsuspecting companion further and further from the subject of his own evenings. Finally they came to a corner and Michael halted.

"I turn here," he said; "which way do you go?"

"Why, I turn too," laughed French. "That is, if you don't object. I'm out for a walk and I don't care much what I do. If I'm not welcome just tell me and I'll clear out."

"Of course you're quite welcome," said Michael; "I'm glad to have company, but the quarter I'm walking to is not a pleasant one for a walk, and indeed you mightn't like to return alone even so early in the evening if you walk far. I had an unpleasant encounter myself once, but I know the ways of the place now and it's different."

Will eyed him curiously.

"Is it allowable to ask where we're going?" he asked in a comical tone.

Michael laughed.

"Certainly. If you're bound to go I'll have to tell you all about it, but I strongly advise you to turn back now, for it isn't a very savory neighborhood, and I don't believe you'll care for it."

"Where thou goest I will go," mocked Will. "My curiosity is aroused. I shall certainly go. If it's safe for you, it is for me. My good looks are not nearly so valuable as yours, nor so noticeable. As I have no valuables in the world, I can't be knocked down for booty."

"You see they all know me," explained Michael.

"Oh, they do! And can't you introduce me? Or don't you like to?"

"I suppose I can," laughed Michael, "if you really want me to, but I'm afraid you'll turn and run when you see them. You see they're not very—handsome. They're not what you're used to. You wouldn't want to know them."

"But you do."

"I had to," said Michael desperately. "They needed something and I had to help them!"

Up to this point Will French had been sure that Michael had fallen into the hands of a set of sharpers, but something in his companion's tone made him turn and look, and he saw Michael's face uplifted in the light of the street lamp, glowing with a kind of intent earnestness that surprised and awed him.

"Look here, man," he said. "Tell me who they are, and what you are doing, anyway."

Michael told him a few words, saying little about himself, or his reason for being interested in the alley in the first place. There were a few neglected newsboys, mere kids. He was trying to teach them a few things, reading and figures and a little manual training. Something to make life more than a round of suffering and sin.

"Is it settlement work?" asked French. He was puzzled and interested.

"No," explained Michael, "there's a settlement, but it's too far away and got too big a district to reach this alley. It's just my own little work."

"Who pays you for it?"

"Who pays me?"

"Yes, who's behind the enterprise? Who forks over the funds and pays you for your job?"

Michael laughed long and loud.

"Well, now, I hadn't thought about pay, but I guess the kiddies themselves do. You can't think how they enjoy it all."

"H'm!" said French, "I think I'll go along and see how you do it. I won't scare 'em out, will I?"

"Well, now I hadn't thought of that," said Michael. "In fact, I didn't suppose you'd care to go all the way, but if you think you do, I guess it will be all right."

"Not a very warm welcome, I must say," laughed Will, "but I'm going just the same. You get me in and I'll guarantee not to scare the crowd. Have any time left over from your studies for amusement? If you do I might come in on that. I can do tricks."

"Can you?" said Michael looking at his unbidden guest doubtfully. "Well, we'll see. I'm afraid you'll be disappointed. It's very informal. Sometimes we don't get beyond the first step in a lesson. Sometimes I have to stop and tell stories."

"Good!" said Will. "I'd like to hear you."

"Oh, you wouldn't enjoy it, but there are a few books there. You might read if you get tired looking around the room."

And so Michael and his guest entered the yellow and white room together. Michael lit the gas, and Will looked about blinking in amazement.

Coming through the alley to the room had taken away Will's exclamatory powers and exhausted his vocabulary. The room in its white simplicity, immaculately kept, and constantly in touch with fresh paint to hide any stray finger marks, stood out in startling contrast with the regions round about it. Will took it all in, paint, paper, and pictures. The tiny stove glowing warmly, the improvised seats, the blackboard in the corner, and the bits of life as manifested in geranium, butterfly cocoons, and bird's nests; then he looked at Michael, tall and fine and embarrassed, in the center of it all.

"Great Scott!" he exclaimed. "Is this an enchanted island, or am I in my right mind?"

But before he could be answered there came the sound of chattering young feet and a tumult outside the door. Then eager, panting, but decorous, they entered, some with clean faces, most of them with clean hands, or moderately so, all with their caps off in homage to their prince; and Michael welcomed them as if he stood in a luxurious drawing room on Fifth Avenue and these were his guests.

He introduced them, and Will entered into the spirit of the affair and greeted them chummily. They stood shyly off from him at first with great eyes of suspicion, huddled together in a group near Michael, but later when the lesson on the blackboard was over and Michael was showing a set of pictures, Will sat down in a corner with a string from his pocket and began showing two of the boldest of the group some tricks. This took at once, and when he added a little sleight-of-hand pulling pennies from the hair and pockets and hands of the astonished youngsters and allowing them to keep them after the game was over, they were ready to take him into their inner circle at once.

When, however, Sam, who was most unaccountably late that night, sidled in alone, he looked at the stranger with eyes of belligerence, and when Michael introduced him as his friend, Sam's eyes glinted with a jealous light. Sam did not like Michael to have any friends of that sort. This new man had shiny boots, fine new clothes, wore his hair nicely brushed, and manipulated a smooth handkerchief with fingers as white as any gentleman. To be sure Michael was like that, but then Michael was Michael. He belonged to them, and his clothes made him no worse. But who was this intruder? A gentleman? All gentlemen were natural enemies to Sam.

"Come outside," said Sam to Michael gruffly, ignoring the white hand Will held out cordially. Michael saw there was something on his mind.

"Will, can you amuse these kids a minute or two while I step out? I'll not be long."

"Sure!" said Will heartily. He hadn't had such a good time in months and what a story he would have to tell the senior partner in the morning.

"Ever try to lift a fellow's hand off the top of his head?

Here, you kid, sit in that chair and put your right hand flat on the top of your head. Now, sonny, you lift it off. Pull with all your might. That's it—"

Michael's eyes shone, and even Sam grinned surreptitiously.

"He'll do," he said to Sam as they went ont. "He was lonesome this evening and wanted to come along with me."

Lonesome! A fellow like that! It gave Sam a new idea to think about. Did people who had money and education and were used to living in clothes like that get lonesome? Sam cast a kindlier eye back at Will as he closed the door.

Alone in the dark cold entry where the wind whistled up from the river and every crack seemed a conductor of a blast, Sam and Michael talked in low tones:

"Say, he's lit out!" Sam's tone conveyed dismay as well as apology.

It was a sign of Michael's real eagerness that he knew at once who was meant.

"Buck?"

Sam grunted assent.

"When?"

"Day er so ago. I tuk yer word to 'im but he'd gone. Lef' word he had a big deal on, an' ef if it came troo all right 'e'd send fer us. You see it wan't safe round ere no more. The *po*lice was onto his game. Thur wan't no more hidin' fer him. He was powerful sorry not to see you. He'd always thought a heap o' Mikky!"

"How long had he known I was here?" Michael's face was grave in the darkness. Why had Buck not sent him some word? Made some appointment?

"Since you first cum back."

"Why—oh, Sam, why didn't he let me come and see him?"

"It warn't safe," said Sam earnestly. "Sure thing, it warn't! 'Sides—"

"Besides what, Sam?" the question was eager.

"'Sides, he knowed you'd had edicashun, an' he knowed how you looked on his way o' livin'. He didn't know but—"

"You mean he didn't trust me, Sam?" Sam felt the keen eyes upon him even in the darkness.

"Naw, he didn't tink you'd snitch on him ner nothin',
but he didn't know but you might tink you had to do some
tings what might kick it all up wid him. You'd b'en out o'
tings fer years, an' you didn't know de ways o' de city. 'Sides,
he ain't seed you like I done—"

"I see," said Michael, "I understand. It's a long time
and of course he only knows what you have told him, and if
there was danger—but oh, Sam, I wish he could go down to Old
Orchard. Did you ever tell him about it, and about my plans?"

"Sure ting I did. Tole 'im all you tole me. He said 'twar
all right. Ef he comes out on dis deal he'll be back in a while,
an' he'll go down dere ef you want him. He said he'd bring a
little wad back to make things go ef dis deal went troo."

"Do you know what the deal is, Sam?"

"Sure!"

"Is it dis—is it"—he paused for a word that would convey his meaning and yet not offend—"is it—dangerous,
Sam?"

"Sure!" admitted Sam solemnly as though it hurt him
to pain his friend.

"Do you mean it will make more hiding for him?"

"Sure!" emphatically grave.

"I wish he hadn't gone!" There was sharp pain in
Michael's voice.

"I wisht so too!" said Sam with a queer little choke to
his voice. "Mebbe 'twon't come off after all. Mebbe it'll git
blocked. Mebbe he'll come back."

The anxiety in Sam's tone touched Michael, but another thought had struck him hard.

"Sam," said he plucking at the other's sleeve in the
darkness, "Sam, tell me, what was Buck doing—before he
went away. Was it all straight? Was he in the same business
with you?"

Sam breathed heavily but did not answer. At last with
difficulty he answered a gruff, "Nope!"

"What was it, Sam? Won't you tell me?"

"It would be snitchin'."

"Not to me, Sam. You know I belong to you all."

"But you've got new notions."

"Yes," admitted Michael, "I can't help that, but I don't
go back on you, do I?"

"No, you don't go back on we'uns, thet's so. But you don't like we's doin's."

"Never mind. Tell me, Sam. I think I must know."

"He kep a gamin' den—"

"Oh, Sam!" Michael's voice was stricken, and his great athletic hand gripped Sam's hard skinny one, and Sam in the darkness gripped back.

"I knowed you'd feel thet way," he mourned as if the fault were all in his telling. "I wisht I hadn't 'a tole yer."

"Never mind, Sam, you couldn't help it, and I suppose I wouldn't have known the difference myself if I hadn't gone away. We mustn't judge Buck harshly. He'll see it the other way by and by."

Sam straightened perceptibly. There was something in this speech that put him in the same class with Michael. He had never before had any qualms of conscience concerning gambling, but now he found himself almost unawares arrayed against it.

"I guess mebbe!" he said comfortingly, and then seeking to change the subject. "Say, is dat guy in dere goin' along to de farm?"

"Who?"

"Why, dat ike you lef' in de room. Is he goin' down 'long when wees go?"

"Oh, Will French! No, Sam. He doesn't know anything about it yet. I may tell him sometime, but he doesn't need that. He is studying to be a lawyer. Perhaps someday if he gets interested he'll help do what I want for the alley, and all the other alleys in the city; make better laws and see that they're enforced."

"Laws!" said Sam in a startled voice. "What laws?"

Laws were his natural enemies he thought.

"Laws for better tenement houses, more room and more windows, better air, cleaner streets, room for grass and flowers, pure milk and meat, and less crowding and dirt. Understand?"

It was the first time Michael had gone so deep into his plans with Sam, and he longed now to have his comradeship in this hope too.

"Oh, sure!" said Sam much relieved that Michael had not mentioned laws about gambling dens and pickpockets.

Sam might be willing to reform his own course in the brilliant wake of Michael but as yet he had not reached the point where he cared to see vice and dishonesty swept off the globe.

They went slowly back to the white room to find Will French leading a chorus of small urchins in the latest popular melody while they kept time with an awkward shuffle of their ill-shod feet.

Sam growled: "Cut it out, kids, you scratch de floor," and Will French subsided with apologies.

"I never thought of the floor, Endicott. Say, you ought to have a gymnasium and a swimming pool here."

Michael laughed.

"I wish we had," he declared, "but I'd begin on a bathroom. We need that first of all."

"Well, let's get one," said Will eagerly. "That wouldn't cost so much. We could get some people to contribute a little. I know a man that has a big plumbing establishment. He'd do a little something. I mean to tell him about it. Is there any place it could be put?"

Sam followed them wondering, listening, interested, as they went out into the hall to see the little dark hole which might with ingenuity be converted into a bathroom, and while he leaned back against the doorjamb, hands in his pockets, he studied the face of the newcomer.

"Guess dat guy's all right," he reassured Michael as he helped him turn the lights out a little later, while Will waited on the doorstep whistling a new tune to his admiring following. Will had caught "de kids."

"I say, Endicott," he said as they walked up the noisy midnight street and turned into the avenue, "why don't you get Hester to go down there and sing sometime? Sunday afternoon. She'd go. Ask her."

And that night was the beginning of outside help for Michael's mission.

Hester fell into the habit of going down Sunday afternoons, and soon she had an eager following of sad-eyed women, and eager little children, and Will French spent his leisure hours in hunting up tricks and games and puzzles, for the kids.

Meantime, the account he had given to Holt and Holt of the way Michael spent his evenings was not without fruit.

About a week after French's first visit to the alley, the senior Mr. Holt paused beside Michael's desk one afternoon just before going out of the office and laid a bit of paper in his hand.

"French tells me you're interested in work in the slums," he said in the same tone he used to give Michael an order for his daily routine. "I'd like to help a little if you can use that." He passed on out of the office before Michael had fully comprehended what had been said. The young man looked down at the paper and saw it was a check made out to himself for one hundred dollars!

With a quick exclamation of gratitude he was on his feet and out into the hall after his employer.

"That's all right, Endicott. I don't get as much time as I'd like to look after the charities, and when I see a good thing I like to give it a boost. Call on me if you need money for any special scheme. And I'll mention it to some of my clients occasionally," said the old lawyer, well pleased with Michael's gratitude.

He did, and right royally did the clients respond. Every little while a ten-dollar bill or a five, and now and then a check for fifty would find its way to Michael's desk, for Will French, thoroughly interested, kept Holt and Holt well supplied with information concerning what was needed.

Chapter 16

Before the winter was over Michael was able to put in the bathroom and had bought a plow and a number of necessary farm implements, and secured the services of a man who lived near Old Orchard to do some early plowing and planting. He was able to buy seeds and fertilizer, enough at least to start his experiment; and toward spring, he took advantage of a holiday, and with Sam and a carpenter went down to the farm and patched up the old house.

After that a few cots, some boxes for chairs and tables, some cheap comforters for cool nights, some dishes and cooking utensils from the ten-cent store, and the place would be ready for his alley-colony when he should dare to bring them down. A canvas cot and a wadded comforter would be luxury to any of them. The only question was, would they be contented out of the city?

Michael had read many articles about the feasibility of taking the poor of the cities into the country, and he knew that experience had shown they were in most cases miserable to get back again. He believed in his heart that this might be different if the conditions were made right. In the first place they must have an environment full of new interest to supply the place of the city's rush, and then they must have some great object which they would be eager to attain. He felt, too, that they should be prepared beforehand for their new life.

To this end he had been for six months spending two or three hours a week with five or six young fellows Sam had tolled in. He had brought the agricultural papers to the room, and made much of the illustrations. The boys as a rule could not read, so he read to them, or rather translated into their own slangful English. He told them what wonders had been attained by farming in the right way. As these fellows had little notion about farming in any way, or little knowledge of farm products save as they came to them through the markets in their very worst forms, it became necessary to bring cabbages and apples, and various other fruits and vegetables for their inspection.

One night he brought three or four gnarled, little green-skinned, sour, speckled apples, poorly flavored. He called attention to them very carefully, and then because an apple was a treat, however poor it might be, he asked them to notice the flavor as they ate. Then he produced three or four magnificent specimens of applehood, crimson and yellow, with polished skin and delicious flavor, and set them in a row on the table beside some more of the little speckled apples. They looked like a sunset beside a ditch. The young men drew around the beautiful apples admiringly, feeling of their shiny streaks as if they half thought them painted, and listening to the story of their development from the little sour ugly specimens they had just been eating. When it came to the cutting up of the perfect apples every man of them took an intelligent pleasure in the delicious fruit.

Other nights, with the help of Will and Hester, Michael gave demonstrations of potatoes, and other vegetables, with regular lessons on how to get the best results with these particular products. Hester managed in some skillful manner to serve a very tasty refreshment from roasted potatoes, cooked just right, at the same time showing the difference in the quality between the soggy potatoes full of dry rot, and those that were grown under the right conditions. Occasionally a cup of coffee or some delicate sandwiches helped out on a demonstration of lettuce or celery or cold cabbage in the form of slaw, and the light refreshments served with the agricultural lessons became a most attractive feature of Michael's evenings. More and more young fellows dropped in to listen to the lesson and enjoy the plentiful "eats" as they called them. When they reached the lessons on peas and beans the split pea soup and good rich bean soup were ably appreciated.

Not that all took the lessons with equal eagerness, but Michael began to feel toward spring that his original five with Sam as their leader would do comparatively intelligent work on the farm, the story of which had been gradually told them from night to night, until they were quite eager to know if they might be included in those who were to be pioneers in the work.

Will French faithfully reported the condition of the work, and more and more friends and clients of the office would stop at Michael's desk and chat with him for a moment about the work, and always leave something with him to help it along. Michael's eyes shone and his heart beat high with hopes in these days.

But there was still a further work for him to do before his crude apprentices should be ready to be sent down into the wilds of nature.

So Michael began one evening to tell them of the beauty and the wonder of the world. One night he used a

cocoon as illustration and for three evenings they all came
with bated breath and watched the strange little insignifi-
cant roll, almost doubting Michael's veracity, yet full of curiosity, until one night it burst its bonds and floated up into
the white ceiling, its pale green, gorgeously marked wings
working a spell upon their hearts, that no years could ever
make them quite forget. It was the miracle of life and they
had never seen it nor heard of it before.

Another night he brought a singing bird in a cage, and
pictures of other birds who were naturally wild. He began
to teach them the ways of the birds they would see in New
Jersey, how to tell their songs apart, where to look for their
nests; all the queer little wonderful things that a bird lover
knows, and that Michael because of his long habits of roam-
ing about the woods knew by heart. The little bird in its
cage stayed in the yellow and white room, and strange to say
thrived, becoming a joy and a wonder to all visitors, and a
marvel to those who lived in the court because of its contin-
uous volume of brilliant song, bursting from a heart that
seemed to be too full of happiness and must bubble over
into music. The kids and even the older fellows felt a proprietorship in it, and liked to come and stand beneath the
cage and call to it as it answered "peep" and peeked between the gilded bars to watch them.

One night, with the help of Will French who had some
wealthy friends, Michael borrowed a large picture of a sunset, and spoke to them about the sunlight and its effects on
growing things, and the wonder of its departure for the
night.

By this time they would listen in awed silence to anything Michael said, though the picture was perhaps one too
many for most of them. Sam, however, heard with approval,
and afterwards went up reverently and laid his finger on
the crimson and the purple and the gold of the picture.
Sam knew, and understood, for he had seen the real thing.
Then he turned to the others and said:

"Say, fellers, it's aw-right. You wait till yer see one. Fine
ez silk, an' twicet as nateral."

One big dark fellow who had lately taken to coming to
the gatherings, turned scornfully away, and replied: "Aw
shucks! I don't see nodding in it!" but loyalty to Michael

prevented others who might have secretly favored this view from expressing it, and the big dark fellow found himself in the minority.

And so the work went on. Spring was coming, and with it the end of Jim's "term," and the beginning of Michael's experiment on the farm.

Meantime Michael was working hard at his law, and studying half the night when he came back from the alley work. If he had not had an iron constitution, and thirteen years behind him of healthy outdoor life, with plenty of sleep and exercise and good food, he could not have stood it. As it was, the hard work was good for him, for it kept him from brooding over himself, and his own hopeless love of the little girl who was far across the water.

Some weeks after Christmas there had come a brief note from Starr, his name written in her hand, the address in her father's:

Dear Michael,

I am just almost sure that I am indebted to you for the lovely little sprig of holly that reached me on Christmas. I have tried and tried to think who the sender might be, for you see I didn't know the writing, or rather printing. But today it fell down from over the picture where I had fastened it on the wall, and I noticed what I had not seen before, 'A Happy Christmas' in the very tiny little letters of the message cut or scratched on the underside of the stem; and the letters reminded me of you and the charming little surprises you used to send me long ago from Florida when I was a little girl. Then all at once I was sure it was you who sent the holly, and I am sitting right down to write and thank you for it. You see, I was very lonesome and homesick that Christmas morning, for most of the girls in the school had gone home for Christmas, and Mamma, who had been intending to come and take me away to Paris for the holidays, had written that she was not well and couldn't come after all, so I knew I would have to be here all through the gay times by myself. I was feeling quite doleful even with the presents that Mamma sent me, until I opened the little box and saw the dear little bright holly berries; that cheered me up and made me think of home. I kept it on my desk all day so that the bright berries would make me feel Christmassy, and just before dinner that night what do you think happened? Why, my dear Daddy came to surprise me, and we took the loveliest trip together, to Venice and Florence and Rome. It was beautiful! I wish you could have been along and seen everything. I know you would have enjoyed it. I must not take the time to write about it because I ought to be studying. This is a very pleasant place and a good school but I would rather be at home, and I shall be glad when I am done and allowed to come back to my own country.

Thanking you ever so much for the pretty little Christmas reminder, for you see I am sure you sent it, and wishing you a belated Happy New Year, I am

Your friend,
STARR DELEVAN ENDICOTT

Michael read and reread the letter, treasured the thoughts and visions it brought him, pondered the question of whether he might answer it, and decided that he had no right. Then he put it away with his own heartache, plunging into his work with redoubled energy, and taking an antidote of so many pages of Blackstone when his thoughts lingered on forbidden subjects. So the winter fled away and spring came stealing on apace.

Chapter 17

As Michael had no definite knowledge of either his exact age, or what month his birthday came, there could be no day set for his coming of age. The little information that could be gathered from his own memory of how many summers and winters he had passed showed that he was approximately seven years old at the time of the shooting affray. If that were correct it would make him between nineteen and twenty at the time of his graduation.

On the first day of July following his first winter in New York Michael received a brief letter from Mr. Endicott, containing a check for a thousand dollars, with congratulations on his majority and request that he call at the office the next day.

Michael, eager, grateful, overwhelmed, was on hand to the minute appointed.

The wealthy businessman, whose banking affairs had long since righted themselves, turned from his multifarious duties, and rested his eyes upon the young fellow, listening half-amused to his eager thanks.

The young man in truth was a sight to rest weary eyes.

The winter in New York had put new lines on his face and deepened the wells of his blue eyes; they were the work of care and toil and suffering, but they had made a man's face out of a boy's fresh countenance. There was power in the fine brow, strength in the firm, well-molded chin, and both kindliness and unselfishness in the lovely curves of his pleasant lips. The city barber had been artist enough not to cut the glorious hair too short, while yet giving it the latest clean-cut curve behind the ears and in the neck. By instinct Michael's hands were well cared for. Endicott's tailor had looked out for the rest.

"That's all right, son," Endicott cut Michael's sentence short. "I'm pleased with the way you've been doing. Holt tells me he never had a more promising student in his office. He says you're cut out for the law, and you're going to be a success. But what's this they tell me about you spending your evenings in the slums? I don't like the sound of that. Better cut that out."

Michael began to tell in earnest protesting words of what he was trying to do, but Endicott put up an impatient hand:

"That's all very well, son, I've no doubt they appreciate your help and all that, and it's been very commendable in you to give your time, but now you owe yourself something, and you owe the world something. You've got to turn out a great lawyer and prove to the world that people from that

district are worth helping. That's the best way in the long
run to help those people. Give them into somebody else's
hands now. You've done your part. When you get to be a
rich man you can give them something now and then if you
like, but it's time to cut out the work now. That sort of thing
might be very popular in a political leader, but you've got
your way to make and it's time you gave your evenings to
culture, and to going out into society somewhat. Here's a list
of concerts and lectures for next winter. You ought to go to
them all. I'm sorry I didn't think of it this winter, but perhaps it was as well not to go too deep at the start. However,
you ought to waste no more time. I've put your application
in for season tickets for those things on that list, and you'll
receive tickets in due time. There's an art exhibition or two
where there are good things to be seen. You've got to see
and hear everything if you want to be a thoroughly educated man. I said a word or two about you here and there,
and I think you'll receive some invitations worth accepting
pretty soon. You'll need a dress suit, and I had word sent to
the tailor about it this morning when it occurred to me—"

"But," said Michael amazed and perturbed, "I do not
belong in society. People do not want one like me there. If
they knew they would not ask me."

"Bosh! All bosh! Didn't I tell you to cut that out? People don't know and you've no need to tell them. They think
you are a distant relative of mine if they think anything
about it, and you're not to tell them you are not. You owe it
to me to keep still about it. If I guarantee you're all right
that ought to suit anybody."

"I couldn't go where people thought I was more than I
was," said Michael, head up, eyes shining, his firmest expression on his mouth, but intense trouble in his eyes. It was
hard to go against his benefactor.

"You got all those foolish notions from working down
there in the slums. You've got a false idea of yourself and a
false notion of right and wrong. It's high time you stopped
going there. After you've been to a dance or two and a few
theater suppers, and got acquainted with some nice girls
who'll invite you to their house parties you'll forget you ever
had anything to do with the slums. I insist that you give that

work up at once. Promise me you will not go near the place again. Write them a letter—"

"I couldn't do that!" said Michael, his face expressive of anguish fighting with duty.

"Couldn't! Nonsense. There is no such word. I say I want you to do it. Haven't I proved my right to make that request?"

"You have," said Michael, dropping his sorrowing eyes slowly, and taking out the folded check from his pocket. "You have the right to ask it, but I have no right to do what you ask. I have begun the work, and it would not be right to stop it. Indeed, I couldn't. If you knew what it means to those fellows—but I cannot keep this if you feel that way! I was going to use it for the work—but now—"

Michael's pauses were eloquent. Endicott was deeply touched but he would not show it. He was used to having his own way, and it irritated, while it pleased him in a way, to have Michael so determined. As Michael stopped talking he laid the check sadly on the desk.

"Nonsense!" said Endicott irritably, "this has nothing to do with the check. That was your birthday present. Use it as you like. What I have given I have given and I won't take back even if I have nothing more to do with you from this time forth. I have no objection to your giving away as much money as you can spare to benevolent institutions, but I say that I do object to your wasting your time and your reputation in such low places. It will injure you eventually, it can't help it. I want you to take your evenings for society and for lectures and concerts—"

"I will go to the concerts and lectures gladly," said Michael gravely. "I can see they will be fine for me, and I thank you very much for the opportunity, but that will not hinder my work. It begins always rather late in the evening, and there are other times—"

"You've no business to be staying out in places like that after the hour of closing of decent places of amusement."

Michael refrained from saying that he had several times noticed society ladies returning from balls and entertainments when he was on his way home.

"I simply can't have it if I'm to stand back of you."

"I'm sorry," said Michael. "You won't ever know how sorry I am. It was so good to know that I had somebody who cared a little for me. I shall miss it very much. It has been almost like having a real father. Do you mean that you will have to give up the—fatherliness?"

Endicott's voice shook with mingled emotions. It couldn't be that this young upstart who professed to be so grateful and for whom he had done so much would actually for the sake of a few wretched beings and a sentimental feeling that he belonged in the slums and ought to do something for them, run the risk of angering him effectually. It could not be!"

"It means that I shall not do any of the things I had planned to do for you, if you persist in refusing my most reasonable request. Listen, young man—"

Michael noticed with keen pain that he had dropped the customary "son" from his conversation, and it gave him a queer choky sensation of having been cut off from the earth.

"I had planned—" the keen eyes searched the beautiful manly face before him and the man's voice took on an insinuating tone; the tone he used when he wished to buy up some political pull; the tone that never failed to buy his man. Yet even as he spoke he felt an intuition that here was a man whom he could not buy.

"I had planned to do a good many things for you. You will be through your studies pretty soon and be ready to set up for yourself. Had you thought ahead enough to know whether you would like a partnership in some old firm or whether you want to set up for yourself?"

Michael's voice was grave and troubled but he answered at once:

"I would like to set up for myself, sir. There are things I must do, and I do not know if a partner would feel as I do about them."

"Very well," said Endicott with satisfaction. He could not but be pleased with the straightforward, decided way in which the boy was going ahead and shaping his own life. It showed he had character. There was nothing Mr. Endicott prized more than character—or what he called character. "Very well, when you get ready to set up for yourself, and I don't think that is going to be so many years off from what I hear, I will provide you an office, fully furnished, in the most desirable quarter of the city, and start you off as you ought to be started in order to win. I will introduce you to some of my best friends, and put lucrative business in your way, business with great corporations that will bring you into immediate prominence; then I will propose your name for membership in two or three good clubs. Now those things I will do because I believe you have it in you to make good, but you'll need the boosting. Every man in this city does. Genius alone can't work you up to the top, but I can give you what you need and I mean to do it, only I feel that you on your part ought to be willing to comply with the conditions."

There was a deep silence in the room. Michael was struggling to master his voice, but when he spoke it was husky with suppressed feeling:

"It is a great plan," he said. "It is just like you. I thank you, sir, for the thought, with all my heart. It grieves me more than anything I ever had to do to say no to you, but I cannot do as you ask. I cannot give up what I am trying to do. I feel it would be wrong for me. I feel that it is imperative, sir!"

"Cannot! Hump! Cannot! You are like all the little up-start reformers, filled with conceit of course. You think there is no one can do the work but yourself! I will pay someone to do what you are doing! Will that satisfy you?"

Michael slowly shook his head.

"No one could do it for pay," he said with conviction. "It must be done from—perhaps it is love—I do not know. But anyway, no one was doing it, and I must, for THEY ARE MY PEOPLE!"

As he said this the young man lifted his head with that angel-proud look of his that defied a universe to set him from his purpose, and Endicott while he secretly reveled in the boy's firmness ad purpose, yet writhed that he could not control this strength as he would.

"Your people! Bosh! You don't even know that! You may be the son of the richest man in New York for all you know."

"The more shame mine, then, if he left me where you

found me! Mr. Endicott, have you ever been down in the alley where I used to live? Do you know the conditions down there?"

"No, nor do I want to go. And what's more I don't want you to go again. Whatever you were or are, you ought to see that you are mine now. Why, youngster, how do you know but you were kidnapped for a ransom, and the game went awry? There are a thousand explanations of your unknown presence there. You may have been lost—"

"Then have I not a debt to the people with whom I lived!"

"Oh, poppycock!" exclaimed the man angrily. "We'd better close the conversation. You understand how I feel. If you think it over and change your mind come back and tell me within the week. I sail Saturday for Europe. I may not be back in three or four months. If you don't make up your mind before I go you can write to me here at the office and my secretary will forward it. You have disappointed me beyond anything I could have dreamed. I am sure when you think it over you will see how wrong you are and change your mind. Until then, good-bye!"

Michael arose dismissed, but he could not go that way.

"I shall not change my mind," he said sadly, "but it is terrible not to have you understand. Won't you let me tell you all about it? Won't you let me explain?"

"No, I don't want to hear any explanations. There is only one thing for me to understand and that is that you think more of a set of vagabonds in an alley than you do of my request!"

"No! That is not true!" said Michael. "I think more of you than of any living man. I do not believe I could love you more if you were my own father. I would give my life for you this minute."

"There is an old word somewhere that says, 'To obey is better than sacrifice.' Most people think they would rather be great heroes than do simple everyday things demanded of them. The test does not always prove that they would."

Michael's head went up almost haughtily, but there were great tears in his eyes. Endicott dropped his own gaze from that sorrowful face. He knew his words were false and cruel. He knew that Michael would not hesitate a second to give his life. But the man could not bear to be withstood.

"If you feel that way I cannot take this!" Michael sadly, proudly held out the check.

"As you please!" said Endicott curtly. "There's the wastebasket. Put it in if you like. It isn't mine any longer. You may spend it as you please. My conditions have nothing to do with what is past. If you do not prize my gift to you by all means throw it away."

With a glance that would have broken Endicott's heart if he had not been too stubborn to look up, Michael slowly folded the check and put it back into his pocket.

"I do prize it," he said, "and I prize it because you gave it to me. It meant and always will mean a great deal to me."

"H'm!"

"There is one more thing perhaps I ought to tell you," hesitated Michael. "The farm. I am using it in my work for those people. Perhaps you will not approve of that."

"I have nothing further to do with the farm. You bought it, I believe. You desired to pay for it when you were earning enough money to be able to do so. That time has not yet come, therefore nothing further need be said. It is your farm and you may use it as a pleasure park for pigs if you like. I don't go back on my bargains. Good afternoon."

Endicott turned to the phone, took up the receiver and called up a number. Michael saw that the conversation was ended. Slowly, with heavy step and heavier heart, he went out of the office.

There were new lines of sadness on Michael's face that day, and when he went down to the alley that evening his gentleness with all the little kids, and with the older ones, was so great that they looked at him more than once with a new kind of awe and wonder. It was the gentleness of sacrifice, of sacrifice for them, that was bringing with it the pain of love.

Old Sal who came over to "look in" that evening, as she put it, shook her head as she stumped back to her rejuvenated room with its gaudy flowered wall, bit of white curtain and pot of flowers in the window, all the work of Michael and his follower Sam.

"I'm thinkin' he'll disuppeer one o' these days. Ye'll wake up an' he'll be gahn. He's not of this worrld. He'll sprid his wings an' away. He's a man-angel, thet's wot he is!"

Michael went home that night and wrote a letter to Mr. Endicott that would have broken a heart of stone, telling his inmost thought, showing his love and anguish in every sentence, and setting forth simply and unassumingly the wonderful work he was doing in the alley.

But though he waited in anxiety day after day he received not a word of reply. Endicott read the letter every word, and fairly gloated over the boy's strength, but he was too stubborn to let it be known. Also he rather enjoyed the test to which he was putting him.

Michael even watched the outgoing vessels on Saturday, looked up the passenger lists, went down to the wharf and tried to see him before he sailed, but for some reason was unable to get in touch with him.

Standing sadly on the wharf as the vessel sailed he caught sight of Endicott, but though he was sure he had been seen he received no sign of recognition, and he turned away sick at heart, and feeling as if he had for conscience sake stabbed one who loved him.

Chapter 18

Those were trying days for Michael.

The weather had turned suddenly very warm. The office was sometimes stifling. The daily routine got upon his nerves, he who had never before known that he had nerves. There was always the aching thought that Starr was gone from him—forever—and now he had by his own word cut loose from his father—forever! His literal heart saw no hope in the future.

About that time, too, another sorrow fell upon him. He was glancing over the paper one morning on his way to the office, and his eye fell on the following item:

LONE TRAIN BANDIT HURT IN FIGHT
AFTER GETTING LOOT

Captured by Conductor After He Had Rifled
Mail Bags on Union Pacific Express

Topeka, Kan., July 20. A daring bandit was captured last night after he robbed the mail car on Union Pacific train which left Kansas City for Denver at 10 o'clock.

The train, known as the Denver Express, carrying heavy mail, was just leaving Kansas City, when a man ran across the depot platform and leaped into the mail car through the open door. The clerk in charge faced the man, who aimed a revolver at him. He was commanded to bind and gag his five associates, and obeyed. The robber then went through all the registered pouches, stuffing the packages into his pockets. Then he commanded the clerk to untie his comrades.

At Bonner Springs where the train made a brief stop the bandit ordered the men to continue their work, so as not to attract the attention of persons at the station. When Lawrence was reached the robber dropped from the car and ran toward the rear of the train. The conductor summoned two Lawrence policemen and all three followed. After a quick race, and a struggle during which the bandit's arm was broken, he was captured. It appears that the prisoner is an old offender, for whom the police of New York have been searching in vain for the past ten months. He is known in the lower districts of New York City as "Fighting Buck," and has a list of offenses against him too numerous to mention.

Michael did not know why his eye had been attracted to the item nor why he had read the article through to the finish. It was not the kind of thing he cared to read, yet of late all crime and criminals had held a sort of sorrowful fascination for him. "It is what I might have done if I had stayed in the alley," he would say to himself when he heard of some terrible crime that had been committed.

But when he reached the end of the article and saw Buck's name his heart seemed to stand still.

Buck! The one of all his old comrades whom he had loved the most, who had loved him, and sacrificed for him; to whom he had written and sent money; whose brain was brighter and whose heart was bigger than any of the others; for whom he had searched in vain, and found only to lose before he had seen him; whom he had hoped yet to find and to save. Buck had done this, and was caught in the guilt. And a government offense, too, robbing the mail-bags! It would mean long, hard service. It would mean many years before Michael could help him to the right kind of life, even if ever.

He asked permission to leave the office that afternoon, and took the train down to the farm where Sam had been staying for some weeks. He read the article to him, hoping against hope that Sam would say there was some mistake, would know somehow that Buck was safe. But Sam listened with lowering countenance, and when the reading was finished he swore a great oath, such as he had not uttered before in Michael's presence, and Michael knew that the story must be true.

Nothing could be done now. The law must have its course, but Michael's heart was heavy with the weight of what might have been if he could but have found Buck sooner. The next day he secured permission to begin his vacation at once, and in spite of great need of his presence at Old Orchard he took the train for Kansas. He felt that he must see Buck at once.

All during the long dismal ride Michael's heart was beating over and over with the story of his own life. "I might have done this thing. I would have dared and thought it brave if I had not been taught better. I might be even now in jail with a broken arm and a useless life; the story of my crime might be bandied through the country in the newspapers if it had not been for Mr. Endicott—and little Starr! And yet I have hurt his feelings and alienated his great kindness by refusing his request. Was there no other way? Was there no other way?" And always his conscience answered, "There was no other way!"

Michael, armed with a letter from the senior Holt to a

powerful member of western municipal affairs, found entrance to Buck in his miserable confinement quite possible. He dawned upon his onetime friend, out of the darkness of the cell, as a veritable angel of light. Indeed, Buck, waking from a feverish sleep on his hard little cot, moaning and cursing with the pain his arm was giving him, started up and looked at him with awe and horror! The light from the corridor caught the gold in Michael's hair and made his halo perfect, and Buck thought for the moment that some new terror had befallen him, and he was in the hands of the angel of death sent to summon him to a final judgment for all his misdeeds.

But Michael met his old friend with tenderness, and a few phrases that had been wont to express their childish loyalty, and Buck, weakened by the fever and the pain, and more than all by his own defeat and capture, broke down and wept, and Michael wept with him.

"It might have been me instead of you, Buck. If I had stayed behind, I'd have done all those things. I see it clearly. I might have been living here and you out and free. Buck, if it could give you my chance in life, and help you see it all as I do I'd gladly lie here and take your place."

"Mikky! Mikky!" cried Buck. "It's me own Mikky! You was allus willin' to take de rubs! But, Mikky, ef you'd hed de trainin' you'd hev made de fine robber! You'd hev been a peach an' no mistake!"

Michael had found a soft spot in the warden's heart and succeeded in doing a number of little things for Buck's comfort. He hunted up the chaplain and secured a promise from him to teach Buck to read and write, and also to read to him all letters that Buck received, until such a time as he should be able to read them for himself. He sent a pot of roses with buds and full bloom to perfume the dark cell, and he promised to write often; while Buck on his part could only say over and over: "Oh, Mikky! Mikky! Ef we wos oney kids again! Oh, Mikky, I'll git out o'here yit an' find ye. Ye'll not be ashamed o' me. Ef I oney hadn't a bungled de job. It was a bum job! Mikky! A bum job!"

Michael saw that there was little use in talking to Buck about his sin. Buck had nothing whatever to build upon in the lines of morals. To be loyal to his friends, and to do his "work" so that he would not get caught were absolutely the only articles in his creed. To get ahead of the rich, to take from them that which was theirs if he could, regardless of life or consequences, that was virtue; the rich were enemies, and his daring code of honor gave them the credit of equal courage with himself. They must outwit him or lose. If they died it was "all in the day's work" and their loss. When his turn came he would take his medicine calmly. But the trouble with Buck now was that he had "bungled the job." It was a disgrace on his profession. Things had been going against him lately, and he was "down on his luck."

Michael went back from the West feeling that the brief time allowed him with Buck was all too short for what he wanted to do for him; yet he felt that it had been worth the journey. Buck appreciated his sympathy, if he did not have an adequate sense of his own sinfulness. Michael had talked and pitied and tried to make Buck see, but Buck saw not, and Michael went home to hope and write and try to educate Buck through sheer love. It was all he saw to do.

It was about this time that Michael began to receive money in small sums, anonymously, through the mail. "For your work" the first was labeled and the remittances that followed had no inscriptions. They were not always addressed in the same hand, and never did he know the writing. Sometimes there would be a ten-dollar bill, sometimes a twenty, and often more, and they came irregularly, enclosed in a thin, inner envelope of foreign looking paper. Michael wondered sometimes if Starr could have sent them, but that was impossible of course, for she knew nothing of his work, and they were always postmarked New York. He discovered that such thin foreign-looking envelopes could be had in New York, and after that he abandoned all idea of trying to solve the mystery. It was probably some eccentric, kind person who did not wish to be known. He accepted the help gladly and broadened his plans for the farm accordingly.

Sam and his five friends had gone down early in the spring, bunking in the old house, and enjoying the outing immensely. Under Sam's captaincy, and the tutelage of an old farmer whom Michael had found, who could not work much himself but could direct, the work had gone forward,

Michael himself coming down Saturdays, and such of the tail ends of the afternoons as he could get. It is true that many mistakes were made through ignorance, and more through stupidity. It is true that no less than five times the whole gang went on a strike until Michael should return to settle some dispute between the new scientific farming that he had taught them, and some old superstition, or clumsy practice of the farmer's. But on the whole they did tolerably good work.

The farm colony had been meantime increasing. Michael picked them up in the alley; they came to him and asked to be taken on for a trial. They had heard of the experiment through Sam, or one of the other boys who had come back to the city for a day on some errand for the farm.

One glorious summer morning Michael took ten small eager newsboys down to pick wild strawberries for the day, and they came back dirty, tired, strawberry streaked, and happy, and loudly sang the praises of Old Orchard as though it had been a heaven. After that Michael had no trouble in transplanting anyone he wished to take with him.

He found a poor wretch who had lately moved with his family to one of the crowded tenements in the alley. He was sodden in drink and going to pieces fast. Michael sobered him up, found that he used to be a master carpenter, and forthwith transplanted him to Old Orchard, family and all.

Under the hand of the skilled carpenter there sprang up immediately a colony of tents and later small one-roomed shacks or bungalows. Michael bought lumber and found apprentices to help, and the carpenter of the colony repaired barns and outhouses, fences, or built shacks, whenever the head of affairs saw fit to need another.

The only person in the whole alley whom Michael had invited in vain to the farm was old Sally. She had steadily refused to leave her gaily papered room, her curtained window and her geranium. It was a symbol of "ould Ireland" to her, and she felt afraid of this new place of Michael's. It seemed to her superstitious fancy like an immediate door to heaven, from which she felt herself barred by her life. It assumed a kind of terror in her thoughts. She was not ready to leave her little bit of life and take chances even for Michael. And so old Sal sat on her doorstep and watched the alley dwellers come and go, listening with interest to each new account of the farm, but never willing to see for herself. Perhaps the secret of her hesitation after all went deeper than superstition. She had received information that Old Orchard had no rum shop around the corner. Old Sally could not run any risks, so she stayed at home.

But the carpenter's wife was glad to cook for the men when the busy days of planting and weeding and harvesting came, and the colony grew and grew. Two or three other men came down with their families, and helped the carpenter to build them little houses, with a bit of garden back, and a bed of flowers in front. They could see the distant sea from their tiny porches, and the river wound its salty silver way on the other hand. It was a great change from the alley. Not all could stand it, but most of them bore the summer test well. It would be when winter set its white distance upon them, chilled the flowers to slumber, and stopped the labor that the testing time would come, and Michael was thinking about that.

He began hunting out helpers for his purposes.

He found a man skilled in agricultural arts and secured his services to hold a regular school of agriculture during the winter for the men. He found a poor student at Princeton who could run up on the train daily and give simple lessons in reading and arithmetic. He impressed it upon Sam and the other young men that unless they could read for themselves enough to keep up with the new discoveries in the science other farmers would get ahead of them and grow bigger potatoes and sweeter ears of corn than they did. He kept up a continual sunny stream of eager converse with them about what they were going to do, and how the place was going to grow, until he felt as if they owned the earth and meant to show the world how well they were running it. In short, he simply poured his own spirit of enthusiasm into them, and made the whole hard summer of unaccustomed labor one great game; and when the proceeds from their first simple crops came in from the sale of such products as they did not need for their own use in the colony, Michael carefully divided it among his various workmen and at his wish they went in a body and each started a bank account at the little National Bank of the town. It was a very little of course, absurdly little, but it made the workers feel like millionaires, and word of the successes went back to the city, and more and more the people were willing to come down, until by fall there were thirty-eight men, women and children, all told, living on the farm.

Of course that made little appreciable difference in the population of the alley, for as soon as one family moved out another was ready to move in, and there was plenty of room for Michael's work to go on. Nevertheless, there were thirty-eight souls on the way to a better knowledge of life, with clean and wholesome surroundings and a chance to learn how to read and how to work.

The carpenter was set to get ready more tiny houses for the next summer's campaign, the tents were folded away, the spring wheat was all in; the fall plowing and fertilizing completed and whatever else ought to be done to a farm for its winter sleep; half a dozen cows were introduced into the settlement and a roomy chicken house and run prepared. Sam set about studying incubators, and teaching his helpers. Then when the cranberries were picked the colony settled down to its study.

The Princeton student and the agricultural student grew deeply interested in their motley school, and finally produced a young woman who came down every afternoon for a consideration, and taught a kindergarten, to which many of the prematurely grown-up mothers came also with great delight and profit, and incidentally learned how to be better, cleaner, wiser mothers. The young woman of her own accord added a cooking school for the women and girls.

Once a week Michael brought down someone from New York to amuse these poor childish people. And so the winter passed.

Once a wealthy friend of Mr. Holt asked to be taken down to see the place, and after going the rounds of the farm and making himself quite friendly roasting chestnuts around the great open fire in the "big house," as the original cottage was called, returned to New York with many congratulations for Michael. A few days afterward he mailed to Michael the deed of the adjoining farm of one hundred acres, and Michael, radiant, wondering, began to know that his dreams for his poor downtrodden people were coming true. There would be room enough now for many a year to come for the people he needed to bring down.

Of course this had not all been done without discouragements. Some of the most helpful of the colonists had proved unmanageable, or unwilling to work; some had run away, or smuggled in some whiskey. There had been two or three incipient rows, and more than double that number of disappointing enterprises, but yet, the work was going on.

And still, there came no word from Mr. Endicott.

Michael was holding well with his employers, and they were beginning to talk to him of a partnership with them when he was done, for he had far outstripped French in his studies, and seemed to master everything he touched with an eagerness that showed great intellectual appetite.

He still kept up his work in the little white room in the alley, evenings, though he divided his labors somewhat with Will French, Miss Semple and others who had heard of the word and had gradually offered their services. It had almost become a little settlement or mission in itself. The one room had become two and a bath; then the whole first floor with a small gymnasium. French was the enthusiastic leader in this, and Hester Semple had done many things for the little children and women. The next set of colonists for Michael's farm were always being got ready and were spoken of as "eligibles" by the workers.

Hester Semple had proved to be a most valuable assistant, ever ready with suggestions, tireless and as enthusiastic as Michael himself. Night after night the three toiled, and came home happily together. The association with the two was very sweet to Michael, whose heart was famished for friends and relations who "belonged." But it never occurred to Michael to look on Miss Semple in any other light than friend and fellow worker.

Will French and Michael were coming home from the office one afternoon together, and talking eagerly of the progress at the farm.

"When you get married, Endicott," said Will, "you

must build a handsome bungalow or something for your summer home, down there on the knoll just overlooking the river where you can see the sea in the distance."

Michael grew sober at once.

"I don't expect ever to be married, Will," he said after a pause, with one of his faraway looks, and his chin up, showing that what he had said was an indisputable fact.

"The dickens!" said Will stopping in his walk and holding up Michael. "She hasn't refused you, has she?"

"Refused me? Who? What do you mean?" asked Michael looking puzzled.

"Why, Hester—Miss Semple. She hasn't turned you down, old chap?"

"Miss Semple! Why, Will, you never thought—you don't think she ever thought—?"

"Well, I didn't know," said Will embarrassedly, "it looked pretty much like it sometimes. There didn't seem much show for me. I've thought lately you had it all settled and were engaged sure."

"Oh, Will," said Michael in that tone that showed his soul was moved to its depth.

"I say, old chap!" said Will, "I'm fiercely sorry I've butted into your affairs. I never dreamed you'd feel like this. But seeing I have, would you mind telling me if you'll give me a good send-off with Hester? Sort of bless-you-my-son, you know, and tell me you don't mind if I go ahead and try my luck."

"With all my heart, Will. I never thought of it, but I believe it would be great for you both. You seem sort of made for each other."

"It's awfully good of you to say so," said Will, "but I'm afraid Hester doesn't think so. She's all taken up with you."

"Not at all!" said Michael eagerly. "Not in the least. I've never noticed it. I'm sure she likes you best."

And it was so from that night that Michael almost always had some excuse for staying later at the room, or for going somewhere else for a little while so that he would have to leave them halfway home, and Hester and Will from that time forth walked together more and more. Thus Michael took his lonely way, cut off from even this friendly group.

And the summer and the winter made the second year of the colony at Old Orchard.

Then, the following spring Starr Endicott and her mother came home and things began to happen.

Chapter 19

Starr was eighteen when she returned, and very beautiful. Society was made at once aware of her presence.

Michael, whose heart was ever on the alert to know of her, and to find out where Mr. Endicott was, saw the first notice in the paper.

Three times had Endicott crossed the water to visit his wife and daughter during their stay abroad, and every time Michael had known and anxiously awaited some sign of his return. He had read the society columns now for two years solely for the purpose of seeing whether anything would be said about the Endicott family, and he was growing wondrously wise in the ways of the society world.

Also, he had come to know society a little in another way.

Shortly after his last interview with Endicott, Miss Emily Holt, daughter of the senior member of the firm of Holt and Holt, had invited Michael to dine with her father and herself; and following this had come an invitation to a house party at the Holts' country seat. This came in the busy season of the farm work, but Michael, anxious to please his employers, took a couple of days off and went. And he certainly enjoyed the good times to the full. He had opportunity to renew his tennis in which he had been a master hand, and to row and ride, in both of which he excelled. Also, he met a number of pleasant people who accepted him for the splendid fellow he looked to be and asked not who he was. Men of his looks and bearing came

not in their way every day and Michael was good company
wherever he went.

However, when it came to the evenings, Michael was at
a loss. He could not dance nor talk small talk. He was too
intensely in earnest for society's ways, and they did not understand. He could talk about the books he had read, and
the things he had thought, but they were great thoughts
and not at all good form for a frivolous company to dwell
upon. One did not want a problem in economics or a deep
philosophical question thrust upon one at a dance. Michael
became a delightful but difficult proposition for the girls
present, each one undertaking to teach him how to talk in
society, but each in turn making a miserable failure. At last
Emily Holt herself set out to give him gentle hints on light
conversation and found herself deep in a discussion of
Wordsworth's poems about which she knew absolutely
nothing, and in which Michael's weary soul had been steep-
ing itself lately.

Miss Holt retired in laughing defeat at last, and advised
her protégé to take a course of modern novels. Michael,
always serious, took her at her word, and with grave earnestness proceeded to do so, but his course ended after two
or three weeks. He found them far from his taste, the most
of them too vividly portraying the sins of his alley in a setting of high life. Michael had enough of that sort of thing in
real life, and felt he could not stand the strain of modern
fiction, so turned back to his Wordsworth again and found
soothing and mental stimulus.

But there followed other invitations, some of which he
accepted and some of which he declined. Still, the handsome, independent young Adonis was in great demand in
spite of his peculiar habit of always being in earnest about
everything. Perhaps they liked him and ran after him but
the more because of his inaccessibility, and the fact that he
was really doing something in the world. For it began to be
whispered about among those who knew—and perhaps
Emily Holt was the originator—that Michael was going to
be something brilliant in the world of worthwhile things
one of these days.

The tickets that Endicott promised him had arrived in

due time, and anxious to please his benefactor, even in his alienation, Michael faithfully attended concerts and lectures, and enjoyed them to the full, borrowing from his hours of sleep to make up what he had thus spent, rather than from his work or his study. And thus he grew in knowledge of the arts, and in love of all things great, whether music, or pictures, or great minds.

Matters stood thus when Starr appeared on the scene.

The young girl made her debut that winter, and the papers were full of her pictures and the entertainments given in her honor. She dined and danced day after day and night after night, and no debutante had ever received higher praise of the critics for beauty, grace, and charm of manner.

Michael read them all, carefully cut out and preserved a few pleasant things that were written about her, looked at the pictures, and turned from the pomp and pride of her triumph to the little snapshot of herself on horseback in the park with her groom, which she had sent to him when she was a little girl. That was his, and his alone, but these others belonged to the world, the world in which he had no part.

For from all this gaiety of society Michael now held aloof. Invitations he received, not a few, for he was growing more popular every day, but he declined them all. A fine sense of honor kept him from going anywhere that Starr was sure to be. He had a right, of course, and it would have been pleasant in a way to have her see that he was welcome in her world, but always there was before his mental vision the memory of her mother's biting words as she put him down from the glorified presence of her world, into an existence of shame and sin and sorrow. He felt that Starr was so far above him that he must not hurt her by coming too near. And so, in deference to the vow that he had taken when the knowledge of his unworthiness had first been presented to him, he stayed away.

Starr, as she heard more and more of his conquests in her world, wondered and was piqued that he came not near her. And one day meeting him by chance on Fifth Avenue, she greeted him graciously and invited him to call.

Michael thanked her with his quiet manner, while his heart was in a tumult over her beauty, and her dimpled

smiles that blossomed out in the old childish ways, only still
more beautifully, it seemed to him. He went in the strength
of that smile many days, but he did not go to call upon her.

The days passed into weeks and months, and still he
did not appear, and Starr, hearing more of his growing inaccessibility, determined to show the others that she could
draw him out of his shell. She humbled her Endicott pride
and wrote him a charming little note asking him to call on
one of the afternoons when she and her mother held court.
But Michael, though he treasured the note, wrote a graceful, but decided refusal.

This angered the young woman exceedingly, and she
decided to cut him out of her good graces entirely. And
indeed the whirl of gaiety in which she was involved scarcely gave her time for remembering old friends. In occasional
odd moments when she thought of him at all, it was with a
vague kind of disappointment, that he too, with all the
other things of her childhood, had turned out to be not
what she had thought.

But she met him face to face one bright Sunday afternoon as she walked on the avenue with one of the many
couriers who eagerly attended her every step. He was a
slender, handsome young fellow, with dark eyes and hair
and reckless mouth. There were jaded lines already around
his youthful eyes and lips. His name was Stuyvesant Carter.
Michael recognized him at once. His picture had been in
the papers but the week before as leader with Starr of the
cotillion. His presence with her in the bright sunny afternoon was to Michael like a great cloud of trouble looming
out of a perfect day. He looked and looked again, his expressive eyes searching the man before him to the depths,
and then going to the other face, beautiful, innocent,
happy.

Michael was walking with Hester Semple.

Now Hester, in her broadcloth tailored suit, and big
black hat with plumes, was a pretty sight, and she looked
quite distinguished walking beside Michael, whose garments seemed somehow always to set him off as if they had
been especially designed for him, and after whom many
eyes were turned as he passed by.

Had it been but the moment later, or even three minutes before, Will French would have been with them and Michael would have been obviously a third member of the party, for he was most careful in these days to let them both know that he considered they belonged together. But Will had stopped a moment to speak to a business acquaintance, and Hester and Michael were walking slowly ahead until he should rejoin them.

"Look!" said Hester excitedly. "Isn't that the pretty Miss Endicott whose picture is in the papers so much? I'm sure it must be, though she's ten times prettier than any of her pictures."

But Michael needed not his attention called. He was already looking with all his soul in his eyes.

As they came opposite he lifted his hat with such marked deference to Starr that young Stuyvesant Carter turned and looked at him insolently, with a careless motion of his own hand toward his hat. But Starr, with brilliant cheeks, and eyes that looked straight at Michael, continued her conversation with her companion and never so much as by the flicker of an eyelash recognized her former friend.

It was but an instant in the passing, and Hester was so taken up with looking at the beauty of the idol of society that she never noticed Michael's lifted hat until they were passed. Then Will French joined them breezily.

"Gee whiz, but she's a peach, isn't she?" he breathed as he took his place beside Hester, and Michael dropped behind, "but I suppose it'll all rub off. They say most of those swells aren't real."

"I think she's real!" declared Hester. "Her eyes are sweet and her smile is charming. The color on her cheeks wasn't put on like paint. I just love her. I believe I'd like to know her. She certainly is beautiful, and she doesn't look a bit spoiled. Did you ever see such eyes?"

"They aren't half as nice as a pair of gray ones I know," said Will looking meaningfully at them as they were lifted smiling to his.

"Will, you mustn't say such things—on the street—anyway—and Michael just behind. Why, where is Michael? See! He has dropped away behind and is walking slowly. Will, does Michael know Miss Endicott? I never thought before about their names being the same. But he lifted his hat to her—and she simply stared blankly at him as if she had never seen him before."

"The little snob!" said Will indignantly. "I told you they were all artificial. I believe they are some kind of relation or other. Come to think of it I believe old Endicott introduced Michael into our office. Maybe she hasn't seen him in a long time and has forgotten him."

"No one who had once known Michael could ever forget him," said Hester with conviction.

"No, I suppose that's so," sighed Will, looking at her a trifle wistfully.

After the incident of this meeting Michael kept more and more aloof from even small entrances into society, and more and more he gave his time to study and to work among the poor.

So the winter passed in a round of gaieties, transplanted for a few weeks to Palm Beach, then back again to New York, then to Tuxedo for the summer, and Michael knew of it all, yet had no part anymore in it, for now she had cut him out of her life herself, and he might not even cherish her bright smiles and words of the past. She did not wish to know him. It was right, it was just; it was best, but it was agony!

Michael's fresh color grew white that year, and he looked more like the man-angel than ever as he came and went in the alley; old Sally from her doorstep, drawing nearer and nearer to her own end, saw it first, and called daily attention to the spirit look of Michael as he passed.

One evening early in spring, Michael was starting home weary and unusually discouraged. Sam had gone down to the farm with Jim to get ready for the spring work, and find out just how things were going and what was needed from the city. Jim was developing into a tolerably dependable fellow save for his hot temper, and Michael missed them from the alley work, for the rooms were crowded now every night. True Hester and Will were faithful, but they were so much taken up with one another in these days that he did not like to trouble them with unusual cases, and he had no one with whom to counsel. Several things had been going awry and he was sad.

Hester and Will were ahead walking slowly as usual.

Michael locked the door with a sigh and turned to follow them, when he saw in the heavy shadows on the other side of the court two figures steal from one of the openings between the houses and move along toward the end of the alley. Something in their demeanor made Michael watch them instinctively. As they neared the end of the alley toward the street they paused a moment and one of the figures stole back lingeringly. He thought he recognized her as a girl cursed with more than the usual amount of beauty. She disappeared into the darkness of the tenement, but the other after looking back a moment kept on toward the street. Michael, quickened his steps and came to the corner at about the same time, crossing over as the other man passed the light and looking full in his face.

To his surprise he saw that the man was Stuyvesant Carter!

With an exclamation of disgust and horror Michael stepped full in the pathway of the man and blocked his further passage.

"What are you doing here?" He asked in tones that would have made a brave man tremble.

Stuyvesant Carter glared at the vision that had suddenly stopped his way, drew his hat down over his evil eyes and snarled: "Get out of my way or you'll be sorry! I'm probably doing the same thing that you're doing here!"

"Probably not!" said Michael with meaning tone. "You know you can mean no good to a girl like that one you were just with. Come down here again at your peril! And if I hear of you having anything to do with that girl I'll take means to have the whole thing made public."

"Indeed!" said young Carter insolently. "Is she your girl? I think not! And who are you anyway?"

"You'll find out if you come down here again!" said Michael, his fingers fairly aching to grip the gentlemanly villain before him. "Now get out of here at once or you may not be able to walk out."

"I'll get out when I like!" sneered the other, nevertheless backing rapidly away through the opening given him. When he had reached a safe distance, he added tantalizingly: "And I'll come back when I like, too."

"Very well, I shall be ready for you, Mr. Carter!"

Michael's tones were clear and distinct and could be heard two blocks away in the comparative stillness of the city night. At sound of his real name spoken fearlessly in such environment, the leader of society slid away into the night as if he had suddenly been erased from the perspective; nor did sound of footsteps linger from this going.

"Who was dat guy?"

It was a small voice that spoke at Michael's elbow. Hester and Will were far down the street in the other direction and had forgotten Michael.

Michael turned and saw one of his smallest "kids" crouching in the shadow beside him.

"Why, Tony, are you here yet? You ought to have been asleep long ago."

"Was dat de guy wot comes to see Lizzie?"

"See here, Tony, what do you know about this?"

Whereupon Tony proceeded to unfold a tale that made Michael's heart sick. "Lizzie, she's got swell sence she went away to work to a res'trant at de sheeshole. She ain't leavin' her ma hev her wages, an' she wears fierce cloes, like de swells!" finished Tony solemnly as if these things were the worst of all that he had told.

So Michael sent Tony to his rest and went home with a heavy heart, to wake and think through the night long what he should do to save Starr, his bright beautiful Starr, from the clutches of this human vampire.

When morning dawned Michael knew what he was going to do. He had decided to go to Mr. Endicott and tell him the whole story. Starr's father could and would protect her better than he could.

As early as he could get away from the office he hurried to carry out his purpose, but on arriving at Mr. Endicott's office he was told that the gentleman had sailed for Austria and would be absent some weeks, even months, perhaps, if his business did not mature as rapidly as he hoped. Michael asked for the address, but when he reached his desk again and tried to frame a letter that would convey the truth convincingly to the absent father, who could not read it for more than a week at least, and would then be thousands of miles away from the scene of action, he gave it up as useless. Something more effectual must be done and done quickly.

In the first place he must have facts. He could not do anything until he knew beyond a shadow of doubt that what he feared was true absolutely. If he could have told Mr. Endicott all would have been different; he was a man and could do his own investigating if he saw fit. Michael might have left the matter in his hands. But he could not tell him.

If there was some other male member of the family to whom he could go with the warning, he must be very sure of his ground before he spoke. If there were no such man friend or relative of the family he must do something else—what? He shrank from thinking.

And so with the sources open to a keen lawyer, he went to work to ferret out the life and doings of Stuyvesant Carter, and it is needless to say that he unearthed a lot of information that was so sickening in its nature that he felt almost helpless before it. It was appalling—and the more so because of the rank and station of the man. If he had been brought up in the slums one might have expected—but this!

The second day, Michael, haggard and worn with the responsibility, started out to find that useful male relative of the Endicott family. There seemed to be no such person. The third morning he came to the office determined to tell the whole story to Mr. Holt, senior, and ask his advice and aid in protecting Starr, but to his dismay he found that Mr. Holt, senior, had been taken seriously ill with heart trouble, and it might be weeks before he was able to return to the office.

Deeply grieved and utterly baffled, the young man tried to think what to do next. The junior Mr. Holt had never encouraged confidences, and would not be likely to help in this matter. He must do something himself.

And now Michael faced two alternatives.

There were only two people to whom the story could be told, and they were Starr herself, and her mother!

Tell Starr all he knew he could not. To tell her anything of this story would be gall and wormwood! To have to drop a hint that would blacken another man's character would

place him in a most awkward position. To think of doing it
was like tearing out his heart for her to trample upon.

Yet on the other hand Michael would far go into battle
and face a thousand bristling cannon mouths than meet the
mother on her own ground and tell her what he had to tell,
while her steel-cold eyes looked him through and through
or burned him with scorn and unbelief. He had an in-
stinctive feeling that he should fail if he went to her.

At last he wrote a note to Starr:

Dear Miss Endicott:
    Can you let me have a brief interview at your con-
    venience and just as soon as possible? I have a favor to
    ask of you which I most earnestly hope you will be will-
    ing to grant.

                                        Sincerely yours,
                                        Michael

He sent the note off with fear and trembling. Every
word had been carefully considered and yet it haunted him
continually that he might have written differently. Would
she grant the interview? If she did not what then should he
do?

The next day he received a ceremonious little note on
creamy paper crested with a silver star monogrammed in
blue:

    Miss Endicott will receive Mr. Endicott tomorrow
    morning at eleven.

A shiver ran through him as he read, and consigned
the elegant communication to his wastebasket. It was not
from his Starr. It was from a stranger. And yet, the subtle
perfume that stole forth from the envelope reminded him
of her. On second thought he drew it forth again and put in
it in his pocket. After all she had granted the interview, and
this bit of paper was a part of her daily life; it had come
from her, she had written it, and sent it to him. It was therefore precious.

Starr had been more than usually thoughtful when she
read Michael's note. It pleased her that at last she had

brought him to her feet, though not for the world would she let him know it. Doubtless he wished her influence for some position or other that he would have asked her father instead if he had been at home. Starr knew nothing of the alienation between her father and Michael. But Michael should pay for his request, in humility at least. Therefore she sent her cool little stab of ceremony to call him to her.

But Michael did not look in the least humiliated as he entered the luxurious library where Starr had chosen to receive him. His manner was grave and assured, and he made no sign of the tumult it gave him to see her thus in her own home once more where all her womanliness and charm were but enhanced by the luxury about her.

He came forward to greet her just as if she had not cut him dead the very last time they met, and Starr as she regarded him was struck with wonder over the exalted beauty of manhood that was his unique inheritance.

"Thank you for letting me come," he said simply. "I will not intrude long upon your time—"

Starr had a strange sensation of fear lest he was going to slip away from her again before she was willing.

"Oh, that is all right," she said graciously; "won't you sit down? I am always glad to do a favor for a friend of my childhood."

It was a sentence she had rehearsed many times in her mind, and it was meant to convey reproach and indifference in the extreme, but somehow as she fluttered into a great leather chair she felt that her voice was trembling and she had miserably failed in what she had meant to do. She felt strangely ashamed of her attitude, with those two clear soulful eyes looking straight at her. It reminded her of the way he had looked when he told her in the Florida chapel long ago that nobody but herself had ever kissed him—and she had kissed him then. Suppose he should be going to ask her to do it again! The thought made her cheeks rosy, and her society air deserted her entirely. But of course he would not do that. It was a crazy thought. What was the matter with her anyway, and why did she feel so unnerved? Then Michael spoke.

"May I ask you if you know a man by the name of Stuyvesant Carter?"

Starr looked startled, and then stiffened slightly.

"I do!" she answered graciously. "He is one of my intimate friends. Is there anything he can do for you that you would like my intercession?"

Starr smiled graciously. She thought she understood the reason for Michael's call now, and she was pleased to think how easily she could grant his request. The idea of introducing the two was stimulating. She was pondering what a handsome pair of men they were, and so different from each other.

But Michael's clear voice startled her again out of her complacence.

"Thank God there is not!" he said, and his tone had that in it that made Starr sit up and put on all her dignity.

"Indeed!" she said with asperity, her eyes flashing.

"Pardon me, Miss Endicott," Michael said sadly. "You do not understand my feeling, of course!"

"I certainly do not." All Starr's icicle sentences were inherited from her mother.

"And I cannot well explain," he went on sadly. "I must ask you to take it on trust. The favor I have come to ask is this, that you will not have anything further to do with that young man until your father's return. I know this may seem very strange to you, but believe me if you understood you would not hesitate to do what I have asked."

Michael held her with his look and with his earnest tones. For a moment she could not speak from sheer astonishment at his audacity. Then she froze him with a look copied from her mother's haughty manner.

"And what reason can you possibly give for such an extraordinary request?" she asked at last, when his look compelled an answer.

"I cannot give you a reason," he said gravely. "You must trust me that this is best. Your father will explain to you when he comes."

Another pause and then Starr haughtily asked:

"And you really think that I would grant such a ridiculous request which in itself implies a lack of trust in the character of one of my warmest friends?"

"I most earnestly hope that you will," answered Michael.

In spite of her hauteur she could not but be impressed by Michael's manner. His grave tones and serious eyes told her heart that here was something out of the ordinary, at least she gave Michael credit for thinking there was.

"I certainly shall not do anything of the kind without a good reason for it." Starr's tone was determined and cold.

"And I can give you no reason beyond telling you that he is not such a man as a friend of yours should be."

"What do you mean?"

"Please do not ask me. Please trust me and give me your promise. At least wait until I can write to your father."

Starr rose with a look of her father's stubbornness now in her pretty face.

"I wish to be told," she demanded angrily.

"You would not wish to be told if you knew," he answered.

She stood looking at him steadily for a full moment, then with a graceful toss of her lovely head, she said haughtily:

"I must decline to accede to your request, Mr. Endicott. You will excuse me, I have a luncheon engagement now."

She stood aside for him to go out the door, but as he rose with pleading still in his eyes, he said:

"You will write to your father and tell him what I have said? You will wait until you hear from him?"

"It is impossible, Mr. Endicott." Starr's tone was freezing now, and he could see that she was very angry. "Mr. Carter is my friend!" she flung at him as he passed her and went out into the hall.

Another night of anguish brought Michael face to face with the necessity for an interview with Starr's mother.

Taking his cue from the hour Starr had set for his call, he went a little before eleven o'clock and sent up the card of the firm with his own name written below, for he had very serious doubts of obtaining an interview at all if the lady thought he might be there on his own business.

It is doubtful whether Mrs. Endicott recognized the former "Mikky" under the title written below his most respectable law firm's name. Any representative of Holt and Holt was to be recognized of course. She came down within a half hour, quite graciously with lorgnette in her hand, until she had reached the center of the reception room where he had been put to await her. Then Michael arose, almost from the same spot where she had addressed him nearly four years before, the halo of the morning shining through the high window on his hair, and with a start and stiffening of her whole form she recognized him.

"Oh, it is *you*!" There was that in her tone that argued ill for Michael's mission, but with grave and gentle bearing he began:

"Madam, I beg your pardon for the intrusion. I would not have come if there had been any other way. I tried to find Mr. Endicott but was told he had sailed—"

"You needn't waste your time, and mine. I shall do nothing for you. As I told you before, if I remember, I think far too much already has been done for you and I never felt that you had the slightest claim upon our bounty. I must refuse to hear any hard-luck stories."

Michael's face was a study. Indignation, shame, and pity struggled with a sudden sense of the ridiculousness of the situation.

What he did was to laugh, a rich, clear, musical laugh that stopped the lady's tirade better than he could have done it in any other way.

"Well! Really! Have you come to insult me?" she said angrily. "I will call a servant," and she stepped curtly toward the bell.

"Madam, I beg your pardon," said Michael quickly, grave at once. "I intended no insult and I have come to ask no favor of you. I came because of a serious matter, perhaps a grave danger to your home, which I thought you should be made acquainted with."

"Indeed! Well, make haste," said Mrs. Endicott, half mollified. "My time is valuable. Has someone been planning to rob the house?"

Michael looked straight in her face and told her briefly a few facts, delicately worded, forcefully put, which would have convinced the heart of any true mother that the man before her had none but pure motives.

Not so this mother. The more Michael talked the stiffer, haughtier, more hateful, grew her stare; and when he paused, thinking not to utterly overwhelm her with his facts, she remarked, superciliously:

"How could you possibly know all these things, unless you had been in the same places where you claim Mr. Carter has been? But, oh, of course I forgot! Your former home was there, and so of course you must have many friends among—ah—*those people*!" She drew her mental skirts away from contaminating contact as she spoke the last two words, and punctuated them with a contemptuous look through the lorgnette.

"But, my dear fellow," she went on adopting the most outrageously patronizing manner, "you should never trust those people. Of course you don't understand that, having been away from them so many years among respectable folks, but they really do not know what the truth is. I doubt very much whether there is a grain of foundation for all that you have been telling me."

"Madam, I have taken pains to look into the matter and I know that every word which I have been telling you is true. Two of the most noted detectives of the city have been making an investigation. I would not have ventured to come if I had not had indisputable facts to give you."

Mrs. Endicott arose still holding the lorgnette to her eyes, though she showed that the interview was drawing to a close:

"Then, young man," she said, "it will be necessary for me to tell you that the things you have been saying are not considered proper to speak of before ladies in respectable society. I remember of course your low origin and lack of breeding and forgive what otherwise I should consider an insult. Furthermore, let me tell you, that it is not considered honorable to investigate a gentleman's private life too closely. All young men sow their wild oats of course, and are probably none the worse for it. In fact, if a man has not seen life he really is not worth much. It is his own affair, and no business of yours. I must ask you to refrain from saying anything of this matter to anyone. Understand? Not a word of it! My husband would be deeply outraged to know that a young friend of his daughter's, a man of refinement and position, had been the object of scandal by one who should honor anyone whom he honors. I really cannot spare any more time this morning."

"But, madam! You certainly do not mean that you will

not investigate this matter for yourself? You would not let your daughter accept such a man as her friend?"

The lorgnette came into play again but its stare was quite ineffectual upon Michael's white earnest face. His deep eyes lit with horror at this monstrous woman who seemed devoid of mother love.

"The time has come for you to stop. It is none of your business what I mean. You have done what you thought was your duty by telling me, now put the matter entirely out of your mind. Desist at once!"

With a final stare she swept out of the room and up the broad staircase and Michael, watching her until she was out of sight, went out of the house with bowed head and burdened heart. Went out to write a letter to Starr's father, a letter which would certainly have performed its mission as his other efforts had failed, but which because of a sudden and unexpected change of address just missed him at every stopping place, as it traveled its silent unfruitful way about the world after him, never getting anywhere until too late.

Chapter 20

Starr was very angry with Michael when he left her. There was perhaps more hurt pride and pique in her anger than she would have cared to own. He had failed to succumb to her charms, he had not seemed to notice her as other men did; he had even lost the look of admiration he used to wear then they were boy and girl. He had refused utterly to tell her what she had a great curiosity to know.

She had been sure, was sure yet, that if Michael would tell her what he had against Stuyvesant Carter she could explain it satisfactorily. Her flattered little head was almost turned at this time with the adoration she had received. She thought she knew almost everything that Stuyvesant Carter had ever done. He was a fluent talker and had spent many hours detailing to her incidents and anecdotes of his eventful career. He had raced a good deal and still had several expensive racing cars. There wasn't anything very dreadful about that except, of course, it was dangerous. He used to gamble a great deal but he had promised her he would never do it anymore because she thought it unrefined. Of course it wasn't as though he hadn't plenty of money, and her mother had told her that all young men did those things. No, not her father of course, for he had been unusual, but times were different nowadays. Young men were expected to be a little wild. It was the influence of college life and a progressive age she supposed. It didn't do any harm. They always settled down and made good husbands after they were married. Michael of course did not understand these things. He had spent a great many years in Florida with a dear old professor and a lot of good little boys. Michael was unacquainted with the ways of the world.

Thus she reasoned, yet nevertheless Michael's warning troubled her and finally she decided to go to the best source of information and ask the young man himself.

Accordingly three days after Michael's visit when he dropped in to ask if she would go to the opera that evening with him instead of something else they had planned to do together, she laughingly questioned him.

"What in the world can you ever have done, Mr. Carter, that should make you unfit company for me?"

She asked the question lightly yet her eyes watched his face most closely as she waited for the answer.

The blood rolled in dark waves over his handsome face and his brows grew dark with anger which half hid the start of almost fear with which he regarded her.

"What do you mean, Starr?" He looked at her keenly and could not tell if she were in earnest or not.

"Just that," she mocked half gravely. "Tell me what you have been doing that should make you unfit company for me? Someone has been trying to make me promise to have nothing to do with you, and I want to know what it means."

"Who has been doing that?" There were dangerous lights in the dark eyes, lights that showed the brutality of the coward and the evildoer.

"Oh, a man!" Said Starr provokingly; "but if you look

like that I shant't tell you anything more about it. I don't like you now. You look as if you could eat me. You make me think there must be something in it all."

Quick to take the warning the young man brought his face under control and broke into a hoarse artificial laugh. A sudden vision of understanding had come to him and a fear was in his heart. There was nothing like being bold and taking the bull by the horns.

"I'll wager I can explain the riddle for you," he said airily. "I lost my way the other evening coming home late. You see there had been some mistake and my car didn't come to the club for me. I started on foot, leaving word for it to overtake me." He lied as he went along. He had had a short lifetime of practice and did it quite naturally and easily, "and I was thinking about you and how soon I dared ask you a certain question, when all at once I noticed that things seemed sort of unfamiliar. I turned to go back but couldn't for the life of me tell which way I had turned at the last corner—you see what a dangerous influence you have over me—and I wandered on and on, getting deeper and deeper into things. It wasn't exactly a savory neighborhood and I wanted to get out as soon as possible for I suspected that it wasn't even very safe down there alone at that hour of the night. I was hesitating under a streetlight close to a dark alley, trying to decide which would be the quickest way out, and meditating what I should do to find a policeman, when suddenly there loomed up beside me in the dark out of the depths of the alley a great tall brute of a fellow with the strangest looking yellow hair and a body that looked as if he could play football with the universe if he liked, and charged me with having come down there to visit his girl.

"Well, of course the situation wasn't very pleasant. I tried to explain that I was lost; that I had never been down in that quarter of the city before and didn't even know his girl. But he would listen to nothing. He began to threaten me. Then I took out my card and handed it to him, most unwisely of course, but then I am wholly unused to such situations, and I explained to him just who I was and that of course I wouldn't want to come to see *his* girl, even if I would be so mean, and all that. But do you believe me, that fellow wouldn't take a word of it. He threw the card on the sidewalk, ground his heel into it, and used all sorts of evil language that I can't repeat, and finally after I thought he was going to put me in the ditch and pummel me he let me go, shouting after me that if I ever came near his girl again he would publish it in the newspapers. Then of course I understood what a foolish thing I had done in giving him my card. But it was too late. I told him as politely as I knew how that if he would show me the way to get home I would never trouble him again, and he finally let me go."

Starr's eyes were all this time quizzically searching his face. "Was the man intoxicated?" she asked.

"Oh, I presume so, more or less. They all are down there, though he was not of the slums himself I should say. He was rather well dressed, and probably angry that I had discovered him in such haunts."

"When did this happen?"

"About a week ago."

"Why didn't you tell me about it before?"

"Oh I didn't want to distress you, and besides, I've had my mind too full of other things. Starr, darling, you must have seen all these weeks how much I love you, and how I have only been waiting the proper opportunity to ask you to be my wife."

Starr was in a measure prepared for this proposal. Her mother had instructed her that the alliance was one wholly acceptable, even desirable, and her own fancy was quite taken up with this handsome new admirer who flattered her hourly and showered attentions upon her until she felt quite content with herself, the world, and him. There was a spice of daring about Starr that liked what she thought was the wildness and gaiety of young Carter, and she had quite made up her mind to accept him.

One week later the society papers announced the engagement, and the world of gaiety was all in a flutter over the many functions that were immediately set agoing in their honor.

Michael, at his desk in the busy office, read, and bowed his head in anguish. Starr, his bright beautiful Starr, to be sacrificed to a beast like that! Would that he might once more save her to life and happiness!

For the next few days Michael went about in a state that

almost bordered on the frantic. His white face looked drawn, and his great eyes burned in their clear setting like live coals. People turned to look after him on the street and exclaimed: "Why, look at that man!" and yet he seemed more like an avenging angel dropped down for some terrible errand than like a plain ordinary man.

Mr. Holt noticed it and spoke to him about it.

"You ought to drop work and take a good vacation, Endicott," he said kindly. "You're in bad shape. You'll break down and be ill. If I were in your place I'd cancel the rent of that office and not try to start out for yourself until fall. It'll pay you in the end. You're taking things too seriously."

But Michael smiled and shook his head. He was to open his own office the following week. It was all ready, with its simple furnishings, in marked contrast to the rooms that would have been his if he had acceded to his benefactor's request. But Michael had lost interest in office and work alike, and the room seemed now to him only a refuge from the eyes of men where he might hide with his great sorrow and try to study out some way to save Starr. Surely, surely, her father would do something when he received his letter! It was long past time for an answer to have come. But then there was the hope that he was already doing something, though he was unwilling to afford Michael the satisfaction of knowing it.

He gave much thought to a possible cablegram that he might send, that would tell the story to the father while telling nothing to the world, but abandoned the idea again and again.

Sam came up from the farm and saw Michael's face and was worried.

"Say, pard, wot yer bin doin' t'yersef? Better come down t' th' farm an' git a bit o' fresh air."

The only two people who did not notice the change in Michael's appearance were Hester and Will. They were too much engrossed in each other by this time to notice even Michael.

They had fallen into the habit of leaving the rooms in the alley earlier than Michael and going home by themselves.

They left him thus one night about three weeks after

Starr's engagement had been announced. Michael stayed in the room for an hour after all the others had gone. He was expecting Sam to return. Sam had been up from the farm several times lately and this time without any apparent reason he had lingered in the city. He had not been to the room that night save for ten minutes early in the evening when he had mumbled something about a little business, and said he would be back before Michael left.

Michael sat for a long time, his elbow on the table, his head in his hands, trying to think. A way had occurred to him which might or might not do something to prevent Starr from throwing away her happiness. The morning paper had hinted that plans for a speedy wedding were on foot. It was rumored that Miss Endicott was to be married as soon as her father reached home. Michael was desperate. He feared that now the father would arrive too late for him to get speech with him. He had begun to know that it was hard to convince people of the evil of those they had chosen as friends. It would take time.

There was a way. He might have the whole story published in the papers. A public scandal would doubtless delay if not altogether put a stop to this alliance, but a public scandal that touched Mr. Carter would now also touch and bring into publicity the girl whose life was almost linked with his. Not until the very last resort would Michael bring about that publicity. That such a move on his part would beget him the eternal enmity of the entire Endicott family he did not doubt, but that factor figured not at all in Michael's calculations. He was not working for himself in this affair. Nothing that ever happened could make things right for him, he felt, and what was his life, or good name even, beside Starr's happiness?

Wearily, at last; his problem unsolved, he got up and turned out the lights. As he was locking the door his attention was arrested by two figures standing between himself and the streetlight at the end of the alley. It was a man and a woman, and the woman seemed to be clinging to the man and pleading with him.

Such sights were not uncommon in the alley; some poor woman often thus appealed to all that used to be good in the man she married, to make him stay away from the saloon, or to give her a little of his money to buy food for the children.

More than once in such instances Michael had been able successfully to add his influence to the wife's and get the man to go quietly home.

He put the key hastily in his pocket and hurried toward the two.

"You shan't! You shan't! You shan't never go back to her!" he heard the woman cry fiercely. "You promised me—"

"Shut up, will you? I don't care what I promised," said the man in a guarded voice that Michael felt sure he had heard before.

"I shan't shut up! I'll holler ef you go, so the police'll come. You've got a right to stay with me. You shan't do me no wrong ner you shan't go back to that stuck-up piece. You're mine, I say, and you promised!"

With a curse the man struck her a cruel blow across the mouth, and tried to tear her clinging hands away from his coat, but they only clung the more fiercely.

Michael sprang to the woman's side like a panther.

"Look out!" he said in clear tones. "You can't strike a woman!" His voice was low and calm, and sounded as it used to sound on the ball field when he was giving directions to his team at some crisis in the game.

"Who says I can't?" snarled the man, and now Michael was sure he knew the voice. Then the wretch struck the woman between her eyes and she fell heavily to the ground.

Like a flash Michael's great arm went out and felled the man, and in the same breath, from the shadows behind there sprang out the slender, wiry figure of Sam and flung itself upon the man on the ground who with angry imprecations was trying to struggle to his feet. His hand had gone to an inner pocket as he fell and in a moment more there was a flash of light and Michael felt a bullet whiz by his ear. Nothing but the swerving of the struggling figures had saved it from going through his brain. It occurred to Michael in that instant that that was what had been intended. The conviction that the man had also recognized him gave strength to his arm as he wrenched the revolver from the hand of the would-be assassin. Nobody knew better than Michael how easy it would be to plead "self-defense" if the fellow got into any trouble. A man in young Carter's position with wealth and friends galore need not fear to wipe an unknown fellow out of existence; a fellow whose friends with few exceptions were toughs and jailbirds and ex-criminals of all sorts.

It was just as he gave Carter's wrist the twist that sent the revolver clattering to the ground beside the unconscious woman that Michael heard the hurried footsteps of the officer of the law accompanied by a curious motley crowd who had heard the pistol shot and come to see what new excitement life offered for their delectation. He suddenly realized how bad matters would look for Sam if he should be found in the embrace of one of society's pets who would all too surely have a tale to tell that would clear himself regardless of others. Michael had no care for himself. The police all about that quarter knew him well, and were acquainted with his work. They looked upon him with almost more respect than they gave the priests and deaconesses who went about their errands of mercy; for Michael's spirit look of being more than man, and the stories that were attached to his name in the alley filled them with a worshipful awe. There was little likelihood of trouble for Michael with any of the officers he knew. But Sam was another proposition. His life had not all been strictly virtuous in the past; and of late he had been away in New Jersey so much that he was little known, and would be at once suspected of having been the cause of the trouble. Besides, the woman lay unconscious at their feet!

With a mighty effort Michael now reached forth and plucked Sam, struggling fiercely, from the arms of his antagonist and put him behind him in the doorway, standing firmly in front. Carter thus released, sprawled for an instant in the road, then taking advantage of the momentary release struggled to his feet and fled in the opposite direction from that in which the officers were approaching.

"Let me go! I must get him!" muttered Sam pushing fiercely to get by Michael.

"No, Sam, stay where you are and keep quiet. You'll gain nothing by running after him. You'll only get into trouble yourself."

"I don't care!" said Sam frantically. "I don't care what happens to me. I'll kill him. He stole my girl!"

But Michael stood before him like a wall, adamant in the strength that was his for the extremity.

"Yes, Sam, my poor fellow, I know," said Michael gently, sadly. "I know, Sam. He stole mine too!"

Sam subsided as if he had been struck, a low awful curse upon his lips, his face pale and baleful.

"You, too?" The yearning tenderness went to Michael's heart like sweet salve, even in the stress of the moment. They were brothers in sorrow, and their brotherhood saved Sam from committing a crime.

Then the police and crowds swept up breathless.

"What does all this mean?" panted a policeman touching his cap respectfully to Michael. "Someone been shooting?"

He stooped and peered into the white face of the still unconscious woman, and then looked suspiciously toward Sam who was standing sullenly behind Michael.

"He's all right," smiled Michael throwing an arm across Sam's shoulder. "He only came in to help me when he saw I was having a hard time of it. The fellow made off in that direction." Michael pointed after Carter whose form had disappeared in the darkness.

"Any of the gang?" asked the officer as he hurried away.

"No!" said Michael. "He doesn't belong here!"

One officer hurried away accompanied by a crowd, the other stayed to look after the woman. He touched the woman with his foot as he might have tapped a dying dog to see if there was still life there. A low growl like a fierce animal came from Sam's closed lips.

Michael put a warning hand upon his arm.

"Steady, Sam, steady!" he murmured, and went himself and lifted the poor pretty head of the girl from its stony pillow.

"I think you'd better send for the ambulance," he said to the officer. "She's had a heavy blow on her head. I arrived just in time to see the beginning of the trouble—"

"Ain't she dead?" said the officer indifferently. "Best get her into her house. Don't reckon they want to mess up the hospital with such cattle as this."

Michael caught the fierce gleam in Sam's eyes. A second more would have seen the officer lying beside the girl in the road and a double tragedy to the record of that night; for Sam was crouched and moving stealthily like a cat toward the officer's back, a look of almost insane fury upon his small thin face. It was Michael's steady voice that recalled him to sanity once more, just as many a time in the midst of a game he had put self-control and courage into the hearts of his team.

"Sam, could you come here and hold her head a minute, while I try to get some water? Yes, officer, I think she is living, and she should be got to the hospital as soon as possible. Please give the call at once."

The officer sauntered off to do his bidding. Michael and Sam began working over the unconscious girl, and the crowd stood idly round waiting until the ambulance rattled up. They watched with awe as the form of the woman was lifted in and Michael and Sam climbed up on the front seat with the driver and rode away; then they drifted away to their several beds and the street settled into the brief night respite.

The two young men waited at the hospital for an hour until a white-capped nurse came to tell them that Lizzie had recovered consciousness, and there was hope of her life. Then they went out into the late night together.

"Sam, you're coming home with me tonight!" Michael put his arm affectionately around Sam's shoulders. "You never would come before, but you must come tonight."

And Sam, looking into the other's face for an instant, saw that in Michael's suffering eyes that made him yield.

"I ain't fit!" Sam murmured as they walked along silently together. It was the first hint that Sam had ever given that he was not every whit as good as Michael, and Michael with rare tact had never by a glance let Sam know how much he wished to have him cleaner, and more suitably garbed.

"Oh, we'll make that all right!" said Michael fervently thankful that at last the time had come for the presentation of the neat and fitting garments which he had purchased some weeks before for a present for Sam, and which had been waiting for a suitable opportunity of presentation.

The dawn was hovering in the east when Michael led Sam up to his own room, and throwing wide the door of his own little private bathroom told Sam to take a hot bath, it would make him feel better.

While Sam was thus engaged Michael made a compact bundle of Sam's old garments, and stealing softly to the back hall window, landed them by a neat throw on the top of the ash barrel in the court below. Sam's clothes might see the alley again by way of the ash man, but never on Sam's back.

Quite late that very same morning, when Sam, clothed and in a new and righter mind than ever before in his life, walked down with Michael to breakfast, and was introduced as "my friend Mr. Casey" to the landlady, who was hovering about the now deserted breakfast table; he looked every inch of him a respectable citizen. Not handsome and distinguished like Michael, of course, but quite unnoticeable, and altogether proper as a guest at the respectable breakfast table of Mrs. Semple.

Michael explained that they had been detained out late the night before by an accident, and Mrs. Semple gave special orders for a nice breakfast to be served to Mr. Endicott and his friend, and said it wasn't any trouble at all.

People always thought it was no trouble to do things for Michael.

While they ate, Michael arranged with Sam to take a trip out to see Buck.

"I was expecting to go this morning," he said. "I had my plans all made. They write me that Buck is getting uneasy and they wish I'd come, but now"—he looked meaningly at Sam—"I think I ought to stay here for a little. Could you go in my place? There are things here I must attend to."

Sam looked, and his face grew dark with sympathy. He understood.

"I'll keep you informed about Lizzie," went on Michael with delicate intuition, "and anyway you couldn't see her for some time. I think if you try you could help Buck as much as I. He needs to understand that breaking laws is all wrong. That it doesn't pay in the end, and that there has got to be a penalty—you know. You can make him see things in a new way if you try. Are you willing to go, Sam?"

"I'll go," said Sam briefly, and Michael knew he would do his best. It might be that Sam's change of viewpoint would have more effect upon Buck than anything Michael could say. For it was an open secret between Sam and Michael now that Sam stood for a new order of things and that the old life, so far as he was concerned, he had put away.

And so Sam was got safely away from the danger spot, and Michael stayed to face his sorrow, and the problem of how to save Starr.

Chapter 21

The papers the next morning announced that Mr. Stuyvesant Carter while taking a shortcut through the lower quarter of the city, had been cruelly attacked, beaten and robbed, and had barely escaped with his life.

He was lying in his rooms under the care of a trained nurse, and was recovering as rapidly as could be expected from the shock.

Michael reading it next morning after seeing Sam off to Kansas, lifted his head with that quiet show of indignation. He knew that the message must have been telephoned to the paper by Carter himself shortly after he had escaped from the police. He saw just how easy it was for him to give out any report he chose. Money and influence would buy even the public press. It would be little use to try to refute anything he chose to tell about himself.

The days that followed were to Michael one long blur of trouble. He haunted Mr. Endicott's office in hopes of getting some news of his return but they told him the last letters had been very uncertain. He might come quickly, and he might be delayed a month yet, or even longer, and a cablegram might not reach him much sooner than a letter, as he was traveling from place to place.

After three days of this agony, knowing that the enemy would soon be recovering from his bruises and be about again, he reluctantly wrote a note to Starr:

My dear Miss Endicott:

At the risk of offending you I feel that I must make one more attempt to save you from what I feel cannot but be great misery. The young man of whom we were speaking has twice to my knowledge visited a young woman of the slums within the last month, and has even since your engagement been maintaining an intimacy with her which can be nothing but an insult to you. Though you may not believe me, it gives me greater pain to tell you this than anything I ever had to do before. I have tried in every way I know to communicate with your father, but have thus far failed. I am writing you thus plainly and painfully, hoping that though you will not take my word for it, you will at least be willing to find some trustworthy intimate friend of your family in whom you can confide, who will investigate this matter for you, and give you his candid opinion of the young man. I can furnish such a man with information as to where to go to get the facts. I know that what I have said is true. I beg for the sake of your future happiness that you will take means to discover for yourself.

Faithfully yours,

Michael

To this note, within two days, he received a condescending, patronizing reply:

Michael:

I am exceedingly sorry that you have lent yourself to means so low to accomplish your end, whatever that may be. It is beyond me to imagine what possible motive you can have for all this ridiculous calumny that you are trying to cast on the one who has shown a most noble spirit toward you.

Mr. Carter has fully explained to me his presence at the home of that girl, and because I do not like to have *anyone* think evil of the man whom I am soon to marry, I am taking the trouble to explain to you. The young woman is a former maid of Mr. Carter's mother, and she is deeply attached to her. She does up Mrs. Carter's fine laces exquisitely, and Mr. Carter has twice been the bearer of laces to be laundered, because his mother was afraid to trust such valuable pieces to a servant. I hope you will now understand that the terrible things you have tried to say against Mr. Carter are utterly false. Such things are called blackmail and bring terrible consequences in court I am told if they become known, so I must warn you never to do anything of this sort again. It is dangerous. If my father were at home he would explain it to you. Of course, having been in that out-of-the-way Florida place for so long you don't understand these things, but for Papa's sake I would not like you to get into trouble in any way.

There is one more thing I must say. Mr. Carter tells me that he saw you down in that questionable neighborhood, and that you are yourself interested in this girl. It seems strange when this is the case, that you should have thought so ill of him.

Trusting that you will cause me no further annoyance in this matter,

S. D. Endicott

When Michael had read this he bowed himself upon his desk as one who had been stricken unto death. To read such words from her whom he loved better than his own soul was terrible! And he might never let her know that these things that had been said of him were false. She would probably go always with the idea that his presence in that alley was a matter of shame to him. So far as his personal part in the danger to herself was concerned, he was from this time forth powerless to help her. If she thought such things of him—if she had really been made to believe them—then of course she could credit nothing he told her. Some higher power than his would have to save her if she was to be saved.

To do Starr justice she had been very much stirred by Michael's note, and after a night of wakefulness and meditation had taken the letter to her mother. Not that Starr turned naturally to her most unnatural mother for help in personal matters usually, but there seemed to be no one else to whom she could go. If only her father had been home! She thought of cabling him, but what could she say in a brief message? How could she make him understand? And then there was always the world standing by to peer curiously over one's shoulder when one sent a message. She could not hope to escape the public eye.

She considered showing Michael's note to Morton, her faithful nurse, but Morton, wise in many things, would not understand this matter, and would be powerless to help her. So Starr had gone to her mother.

Mrs. Endicott, shrewd to perfection, masked her indignation under a very proper show of horror, told Starr that of course it was not true, but equally of course it must be investigated; gave her word that she would do so immediatly and her daughter need have no further thought of the matter; sent at once for young Carter with whom she held a brief consultation at the end of which Starr was called and cheerfully given the version of the story which she had written to Michael.

Stuyvesant Carter could be very alluring when he tried, and he chose to try. The stakes were a fortune, a noble name, and a very pretty girl with whom he was as much in love at present as he ever had been in his checkered career, with any girl. Moreover he had a nature that held revenge long. He delighted to turn the story upon the man who pretended to be so righteous and who had dared to give him orders about a poor worthless girl of the slums. He set his cunning intellect to devise a scheme whereby his adversary should be caught in his own net and brought low. He found a powerful ally in the mother of the girl he was to marry.

For reasons of ambition Mrs. Endicott desired supremely an alliance with the house of Carter, and she was most determined that nothing should upset her plans for her only daughter's marriage.

She knew that if her husband should return and hear any hint of the story about Carter he would at once put an end to any relations between him and Starr. It would be mortifying beyond anything to have any balk in the arrangements after things had gone thus far, and there was that hateful Mrs. Waterman, setting her cap for him so odiously everywhere even since the engagement had been announced. Mrs. Endicott intended to risk nothing. Therefore she planned with the young people for an early marriage. She was anxious to have everything so thoroughly cut and dried, and matters gone so far that her husband could not possibly upset them when he returned. Finally she cabled him, asking him to set a positive date for his homecoming as the young people wished to arrange for an early wedding. He cabled back a date not so very far off, for in truth, though he had received none of Michael's warnings he was uneasy about this matter of his daughter's engagement. Young Carter had of course seemed all right, and he saw no reason to demur when his wife wrote that the two young people had come to an understanding, but somehow it had not occurred to him that the marriage would be soon. He was troubled at the thought of losing the one bright treasure of his home, when he had but just got her back again from her European education. He felt that it was unfortunate that imperative business had called him abroad almost as soon as she returned. He was in haste to be back.

But when his wife followed her cable message with a letter speaking of an immediate marriage and setting a date but four days after the time set for his arrival, he cabled to her to set no date until his return, which would be as soon as he could possibly come.

However, Mrs. Endicott had planned well. The invitations had been sent out that morning. She thought it unnecessary to cable again but wrote, "I'm sorry, but your message came too late. The invitations are all out now, and arrangements going forward. I knew you would not want to stop Starr's plans and she seems to have her heart set on being married at once. Dear Stuyvesant finds it imperative to take an ocean trip and he cannot bear the thought of going without his wife. I really do not see how things could possibly be held off now. We should be the laughingstock of society and I am sure you would not want me to endure that. And Starr, dear child, is quite childishly happy over her arrangements. She is only anxious to have you properly home in time, so do hurry and get an earlier boat if possible."

Over this letter Mr. Endicott frowned and looked troubled. His wife had ever taken things in her own hands where she would; but concerning Starr they had never quite agreed, though he had let her have her own way about everything else. It was like her to get this marriage all fixed up while he was away. Of course it must be all right, but it was so sudden! And his little Starr! His one little girl!

Then, with his usual abrupt action he put the letter in his inner pocket and proceeded to hurry his business as much as possible that he might take an earlier boat than the one he had set. And he finally succeeded by dint of working night as well as day, and leaving several important matters to go as they would.

The papers at last announced that Mr. Delevan Endicott who had been abroad for three months on business had sailed for home and would reach New York nearly a week before the date set for the wedding. The papers also were filled with elaborate foreshadowings of what that event was likely to mean to the world of society.

And Michael, knowing that he must drink every drop of his bitter cup, knowing that he must suffer and endure to the end of it, if perchance he might yet save her in some miraculous way, read every word, and knew the day and the hour of the boat's probable arrival. He had it all planned to meet the boat himself. If possible he would go out on the pilot and meet his man before he landed.

Then the silence of the great deep fell about the traveler, and the day went by with the waiting one in the city; the preparation hurried forward by trained and skillful workers. The Endicott home was filled with comers and goers. Silks and satins and costly fabrics, laces and jewels and rare trimmings from all over the world were brought together by hands experienced in costuming the great of the earth.

Over the busy machinery which she had set going, Mrs. Endicott presided with the calmness and positive determination of one who had a great purpose in view and meant to carry it out. Not a detail escaped her vigilant eye, not an item was forgotten of all the millions of little necessities that the world expected and she must have forthcoming. Nothing that could make the wedding unique, artistic, perfect, was too hard or too costly to be carried out. This was her pinnacle of opportunity to shine, and Mrs. Endicott intended to make the most of it. Not that she had not shone throughout her worldly career, but she knew that with the marriage of her daughter her life would reach its zenith point and must henceforth begin to decline. This event must be one to be remembered in the annals of the future so long as New York should continue to marry and be given in marriage. Starr's wedding must surpass all others in wonder and beauty and elegance.

So she planned, wrought, carried out, and day by day the gleam in her eyes told that she was nearing her triumph.

It did not disturb her when the steamer was overdue one whole day, and then two. Starr, even amid the round of gaieties in her young set, all given in her honor, found time to worry about her father, but the wife only found in this fact a cause for congratulations. She felt instinctively that her crucial time was coming when her husband reached home. If Michael had dared to carry out his threats, or if a breath of the stories concerning young Carter's life should reach him there would be trouble against which she had no power.

It was not until the third morning with still no news of the vessel that Mrs. Endicott began to feel uneasy. It would be most awkward to have put off the ceremony, and of course it would not do to have it without the bride's father when he was hurrying to be present. If he would arrive just in time so much the better, but late—ah—that would be dreadful! She tightened her determined lips, and looked like a Napoleon saying to herself, *There shall be no Alps!* In like manner she would have said if she could: *There shall be no sea if I wish it.*

But the anxiety she felt was only manifested by her closer vigilance over her helpers as swiftly and hourly the perfected preparations glided to their finish.

Starr grew nervous and restless and could not sleep, but hovered from room to room in the daytime looking out of the windows, or fitfully telephoning the steamship company for news. Her fiancé found her most unsatisfactory and none of the plans he proposed for her diversion pleased her. Dark rings appeared under her eyes, and she looked at him with a troubled expression sometimes when she should have been laughing in the midst of a round of pleasures.

Starr deeply loved her father, and some vague presentiment of coming trouble seemed to shadow all the brightness of life. Now and then Michael's face with its great, true eyes, and pleading expression came between her and Carter's face, and seemed to blur its handsome lines, and then indefinite questions haunted her. What if those terrible things Michael had said were true? Was she sure, *sure*? And at times like that she saw a weakness in the lines about Carter's eyes and mouth.

But she was most unused to studying character, poor child, and had no guide to help her in her lonely problem of choosing, for already she had learned that her mother's ways and hers were not the same, and her father did not come. When he came it would be all right. It had to be, for there was no turning back, of course, now. The wedding was but two days off.

Michael, in his new office, frankly acknowledged to himself these days that he could not work. He had done all that he could and now was waiting for a report of that vessel. When it landed he hoped to be the first man on board; in fact, he had made arrangements to go out to meet it before it landed. But it did not come! Was it going to be prevented until the day was put off? Would that make matters any better? Would he then have more time? And could he accomplish anything with Mr. Endicott, even supposing he had time? Was he not worse than foolish to try? Mr. Endicott was already angry with him for another reason. His wife and Starr, and that scoundrel of a Carter, would tell all sorts of stories. Of course he would believe them in preference to his! He groaned aloud sometimes, when he was alone in the office, and wished that there were but a way he could fling himself between Starr and all evil once for all; give his life for hers. Gladly, gladly would he do it if it would do any good. Yet there was no way.

And then there came news. The vessel had been heard

from still many miles out to sea, with one of her propellers broken, and laboring along at great disadvantage. But if all went well she would reach her dock at noon of the following day—eight hours before the time set for the wedding!

Starr heard and her face blossomed into smiles. All would go well after all. She telephoned again to the steamship company a little while later and her utmost fears were allayed by their assurances.

Mrs. Endicott heard the news with intense relief. Her husband would scarcely have time to find out anything. She must take pains that he had no opportunity to see Michael before the ceremony.

The young man heard and his heart beat wildly. Would the time be long enough to save her?

Noon of the next day came, but the steamer had not yet landed, though the news from her was good. She would be in before night, there was no doubt of it now. Mr. Endicott would be in time for the wedding, but just that and no more. He had sent reassurances to his family, and they were going forward happily in the whirl of the last things.

But Michael in his lonely office hung up the telephone receiver with a heavy heart. There would be no time now to save Starr. Everything was against him. Even if he could get speech with Mr. Endicott which was doubtful now, was it likely the man would listen at this the last minute? Of course his wife and daughter and her fiancé could easily persuade him all was well, and Michael a jealous fool!

As he sat thus with bowed head before his desk, he heard footsteps along the stone floor of the corridor outside. They halted at his door, and hesitating fingers fumbled with the knob. He looked up frowning and was about to send any chance client away, with the explanation that he was entirely too much occupied at present to be interrupted, when the face of the woman who opened the door caught his attention.

Chapter 22

It was Lizzy, with her baby in her arms; the girl he had defended in the alley, and whose face he had last seen lying white and unconscious in the moonlight, looking ghastly enough with the dark hair flung back against the harsh pillow of stone.

The face was white now, but softened with the beauty of motherhood. The bold, handsome features had somehow taken on a touch of gentleness, though there glowed and burned in her dark eyes a fever of passion and unrest.

She stood still for a moment looking at Michael after she had closed the door, and was holding the baby close as if fearing there might be someone there who was minded to take it from her.

As Michael watched her, fascinated, cut to the heart by the dumb suffering in her eyes, he was reminded of one of the exquisite Madonnas he had seen in an exhibition not long ago. The draperies had been dainty and cloudlike, and the face refined and wonderful in its beauty, but there had been the same sorrowful mother-anguish in the eyes. It passed through his mind that this girl and he were kin because of a mutual torture. His face softened, and he felt a great pity for her swelling in his heart.

His eyes wandered to the little upturned face of the baby wrapped close in the shabby shawl against its mother's breast. It was a very beautiful little sleeping face, with a look still of the spirit world from which it had been recently come. There was something almost unearthly in its loveliness, appealing even in its sleep, with its innocent baby curves and outlines. A little stranger soul, whose untried feet had wandered into unwelcome quarters where sorrows

211

and temptations were so thickly strewn that it could not hope to escape them.

What had the baby come for? To make one more of the swarming mass of sinful wretches who crowded the alley? Would those cherub lips half-parted now in a seraphic smile live to pour forth blasphemous curses as he had heard from even very small children in the alley? Would that tiny seashell hand, resting so trustingly against the coarse cloth of its mother's raiment, looking like a rosebud gone astray, live to break open safes and take their contents? Would the lovely little soft round body whose tender curves showed pitifully beneath the thin old shawl, grow up to lie in the gutter someday? The problem of the people had never come to Michael so forcibly, so terribly as in that moment before Lizzie spoke.

"Be you a real lawyer?" she asked. "Kin you tell what the law is 'bout folks and thin's?"

Michael smiled and rose to give her a chair as courteously as though she had been a lady born.

"Sit down," he said. "Yes, I am a lawyer. What can I do for you?"

"I s'pose you charge a lot," said the girl with a meaningful glance around the room. "You've got thin's fixed fine as silk here. But I'll pay anythin' you ast ef it takes me a lifetime to do it, ef you'll jest tell me how I kin git my rights."

"Your rights?" questioned Michael sadly. Poor child! *Had* she any rights in the universe that he could help her to get? The only rights he knew for such as she were room in a quiet graveyard and a chance to be forgotten.

"Say, ain't it against the law fer a man to marry a woman when he's already got one wife?"

"It is," said Michael, "unless he gets a divorce."

"Well, I ain't goin' to give him no divorce, you bet!" said the girl fiercely. "I worked hard enough to get a real marriage an' I ain't goin' to give up no fash'nable swell. I'm's good's she is, an' I've got my rights an I'll hev 'em. An' besides, there's baby!" Her face softened and took on a lovelight; and immediately Michael was reminded of the Madonna picture again. "I've got to think o' him!" Michael marveled to see that the girl was reveling in her possession of the little helpless burden who had been the cause of her sorrow.

"Tell me about it." His voice was very gentle. He recalled suddenly that this was Sam's girl. Poor Sam, too! The world was a terrible tangled mess of trouble.

"Well, there ain't much to tell that counts, only he kep' comp'ny with me, an' I wouldn't hev ennythin' else but a real marriage, an' so he giv in, an' we had a couple o' rooms in a real respectable house an' hed it fine till he had to go away on business, he said. I never b'leeved that. Why he was downright rich. He's a real swell, you know. What kind o' business cud he have?" Lizzie straightened herself proudly and held her head high.

"About whom are you talking?" asked Michael.

"Why, my husband, 'course, Mr. Sty-ve-zant Carter. You ken see his name in the paper real often. He didn't want me to know his real name. He hed me call him Dan Hunt fer two months, but I caught on, an' he was real mad fer awhile. He said his ma didn't like the match, an' he didn't want folks to know he'd got married, it might hurt him with some of his swell friends—"

"You don't mean to tell me that Mr. Stuyvesant Carter ever really married you!" said Michael incredulously.

"Sure!" said Lizzie proudly, "married me jest like enny. swell; got me a dimon ring an' a silk-lined suit an' a willer plume an' everythin'." Lizzie held up a grimy hand on which Michael saw a showy glitter of jewelry.

"Have you anything to show for it?" asked Michael, expecting her of course to say no. "Have you any certificate or paper to prove that you were married according to law?"

"Sure!" said Lizzie triumphantly, drawing forth a crumpled roll from the folds of her dress and smoothing it out before his astonished eyes.

There it was, a printed wedding certificate, done in blue and gold with a colored picture of two clasped hands under a white dove with a gold ring in its beak. Beneath was an idealized boat with silken sails bearing two people down a rose-lined river of life; and the whole was bordered with orange blossoms. It was one of those old-fashioned affairs that country ministers used to give their parishioners in the years gone by, and are still to be had in some dusty corners

of a forgotten drawer in country bookstores. But Michael
recognized at once that it was a real certificate. He read it
carefully. The blanks were all filled in, the date she gave of
the marriage was there, and the name of the bridegroom
though evidently written in a disguised hand could be de-
ciphered: "Sty. Carter." Michael did not recognize the
names of either the witnesses or the officiating minister.

"How do you happen to have Mr. Carter's real name
here when you say he married you under an assumed
name?" he asked, moving his finger thoughtfully over the
blurred name that had evidently been scratched out and
written over again.

"I made him put it in after I found out who he was,"
said Lizzie. "He couldn't come it over me thet-a-way. He was
awful gone on me then, an' I cud do most ennythin' with
him. It was 'fore she cum home from Europe! She jes' went
fer him an' turned his head. Ef I'd a-knowed in time I'd
gone an' tole her, but land sakes! I don't 'spose 'twould a
done much good. I would a-ben to her before, only I was
fool 'nough to promise him I wouldn't say nothin' to her ef
he'd keep away from her. You see I needed money awful
bad fer baby. He don't take to livin' awful good. He cries a
lot an' I hed to hev thin's fer 'im, so I threatened him ef he
didn't do sompin' I'd go tell her, an' he up an' forked over,
but not till I promised. But now they say the papers is tellin'
he's to marry her tonight, an' I gotta stop it somehow. I got
my rights an' baby's to look after, promise er no promise.
Ken I get him arrested?"

"I am not sure what you can do until I look into the
matter," Michael said gravely. Would the paper he held help
or would it not, in his mission to Starr's father? And would
it be too late? His heavy heart could not answer.

"Do you know these witnesses?"

"Sure," said Lizzie confidently. "They're all swells.
They come down with him when he come to be married. I
never seen 'em again, but they was real jolly an' nice. They
gave me a bokay of real roses an' a bracelet made like a
snake with green glass eyes."

"And The minister? Which is his church?"

"I'm sure I donno," said Lizzi. "I never ast. He come

along an' was ez jolly ez enny of 'em. He drank more'n all of
'em put together. He was awful game fer a preacher."

Michael's heart began to sink. Was this a genuine marriage after all? Could anything be proved? He questioned
the girl carefully, and after a few minutes sent her on her
way promising to do all in his power to help her and arranging to let her know as soon as possible if there was anything
she could do.

That was a busy afternoon for Michael. The arrival of
the steamer was forgotten. His telephone rang vainly on the
desk to a silent room. He was out tramping over the city in
search of the witnesses and the minister who had signed
Lizzie's marriage certificate.

Meantime the afternoon papers came out with a glowing account of the wedding that was to be, headed by the
pictures of Starr and Mr. Carter, for the wedding was a
great event in society circles.

Lizzie on her hopeful way back to the alley, confident
that Michael, the angel of the alley, would do something for
her, heard the boys crying the afternoon edition of the paper, and was seized with a desire to see if her husband's
picture would be in again. She could ill spare the penny
from her scanty store that she spent for it, but then, what
was money in a case like this? Michael would do something
for her and she would have more money. Besides, if worst
came to worst she would go to the fine lady and threaten to
make it all public, and she would give her money.

Lizzie had had more advantages than most of her class
in the alley. She had worked in a seashore restaurant several
summers and could read a little. From the newspaper account she gathered enough to rouse her half-soothed
frenzy. Her eyes flashed fire as she went about her dark
little tenement room making baby comfortable. His feeble
wail and his sweet eyes looking into hers only fanned the
fury of her flame. She determined not to wait for Michael,
but to go on her own account at once to that girl that was
stealing away her husband, her baby's father, and tell her
what she was doing.

With the cunning of her kind Lizzie dressed herself in
her best; a soiled pink silk shirtwaist with elbow sleeves, a

spotted and torn black skirt that showed a tattered orange silk petticoat beneath its ungainly length, a wide white hat with soiled and draggled willow plume of Alice blue, and high-heeled pumps run over on their uppers. If she had but known it she looked ten times better in the old Madonna shawl she had worn to Michael's office, but she took great satisfaction in being able to dress appropriately when she went to the swells.

The poor baby she wrapped in his soiled little best, and pinned a large untidy pink satin bow on the back of his dirty little blanket. Then she started on her mission.

Now Starr had just heard that her father's vessel would be at the dock in a trifle over an hour and her heart was light and happy. Somehow all her misgivings seemed to flee away, now that he was coming. She flew from one room to another like a wild bird, trilling snatches of song, and looking prettier than ever.

"Aw, the wee sweet bairnie!" murmured the old Scottish nurse. "If only her man will be gude to her!"

There was some special bit of Starr's attire for the evening that had not arrived. She was in a twitter of expectancy about it, to be sure it pleased her, and when she heard the bell she rushed to the head of the stairs and halfway down to see if it had come, when the servant opened the door to Lizzie and her baby.

One second more and the door would have closed hopelessly on poor Lizzie, for no servant in that house would have thought of admitting such a creature to the presence of their lady a few hours before her wedding; but Starr, poised halfway on the landing, called, "What is it, Graves, someone to see me?"

"But she's not the sort of person—Miss Starr!" protested Graves with the door only open a crack now.

"Never mind, Graves, I'll see her for a minute. I can't deny anyone on my wedding day you know, and father almost safely here. Show her into the little reception room." She smiled a ravishing smile on the devoted Graves, so with many qualms of conscience and misgivings as to what the mistress would say if she found out, Graves ushered Lizzie and her baby to the room indicated and Starr fluttered down to see her. So it was Starr's own doings that Lizzie came into her presence on that eventful afternoon.

"Oh, what a sweet baby!" exclaimed Starr eagerly. "Is he yours?" Lizzie's fierce eyes softened.

"Sit down and tell me who you are. Wait, I'll have some tea brought for you. You look tired. And won't you let me give that sweet baby a little white shawl of mine. I'm to be married tonight and I'd like to give him a wedding present," she laughed gaily, and Morton was sent for the shawl and another servant for the tea, while Starr amused herself by making the baby crow at her.

Lizzie sat in wonder. Almost for the moment she forgot her errand watching this sweet girl in her lovely attire making much of her baby. But when the tea had been brought and the soft white wool shawl wrapped around the smiling baby Starr said again:

"Now please tell me who you are and what you have come for. I can't give you but a minute or two more. This is a busy day, you know."

Lizzie's brow darkened.

"I'm Mrs. Carter!" she said drawing herself up with conscious pride.

"Carter?" said Starr politely.

"Yes, I'm the wife of the man you're goin' to marry tonight, an' this is his child. I thought I'd come an' tell you 'fore 'twas too late. I thought ef you had enny goodness in you you'd put a stop to this an' give me my rights, an' you seem to hev some heart. Can't you call it off? You wouldn't want to take my husband away from me, would you? You can get plenty others an' I'm jest a plain workin' girl, an' he's mine anyhow, an' this is his kid."

Starr had started to her feet, her eyes wide, her hand fluttering to her heart.

"Stop!" she cried. "You must be crazy to say such things. My poor girl, you have made a great mistake. Your husband is some other Mr. Carter I suppose. My Mr. Carter is not that kind of a man. He has never been married—"

"Yes, he has!" interposed Lizzie fiercely. "He's married all right, an' I got the c'tif'ct all right too, only I couldn't bring it this time cause I lef' it with my lawyer; but you can see if ef you want to, with his name all straight, Sty-Vee-Zant Carter, all writ out. I see to it that he writ it himself. I kin read meself, pretty good, so I knowed."

"I am very sorry for you," said Starr sweetly, though her heart was beating violently in spite of her efforts to be calm and to tell herself that she must get rid of this wretched imposter without making a scene for the servants to witness; "I am very sorry, but you have made some great mistake. There isn't anything I can do for you now, but later when I come back to New York if you care to look me up I will try to do something for baby."

Lizzie stood erect in the middle of the little room, her face slowly changing to a stony stare, her eyes fairly blazing with anger.

"De'yer mean ter tell me yer a goin' t'go on an' marry my husban' jes' ez ef nothin' had happened? Ain't yer goin' ter ast him ef it's true ner nothin'? Ain't yer goin' t' find out what's true 'bout him? 'R d'ye want 'im so bad ye don't care who yer hurt, or wot he is, so long's he makes a big splurge before folks? Ain't you a-goin' ter ast him 'bout it?"

"Oh, why certainly, of course," said Starr as if she were pacifying a frantic child, "I can ask him. I will ask him of course, but I *know* that you are mistaken. Now really, I shall have to say good afternoon. I haven't another minute to spare. You must go!"

"I shan't stir a step till you promise me thet you'll ast him right straight away. Ain't you all got no telyphone? Well, you kin call him up an' ast him. Jest ast him why he didn't never speak to you of his wife Lizzie, and where he was the evenin' of Augus' four. That's the date of the c'tif'ct! Tell him you seen me an' then see wot he says. Tell him my lawyer is a goin' to fix him ef he goes on. It'll be in all the papers tomorrer mornin' ef he goes on. An' you c'n say I shan't never consent to no *di*-vorce, they ain't respectable, an' I got to think o' that on baby's account."

"If you will go quietly away now and say nothing more about this to anyone I will tell Mr. Carter all about you," said Starr, her voice trembling with the effort at self-control.

"D'ye promus you will?"

"Certainly," said Starr with dignity.

"Will ye do it right off straight?"

"Yes, if you will go at once."

"Cross yer heart?"

"What?"

"Cross yer hert ye will? Thet's a sort o' oath t' make yer keep yer promus," explained Lizzie.

"A lady needs no such thing to make her keep her promise. Don't you know that ladies always keep their promises?"

"I wasn't so sure!" said Lizzie. "You can't most allus tell, 't's bes' to be on the safe side. Will yer promus me yer won't marry him ef ye find out he's my husband?"

"Most certainly I will not marry him if he is already married. Now go, please, at once. I haven't a minute to spare. If you don't go at once I cannot have time to call him up."

"You sure I kin trust you?"

Starr turned on the girl such a gaze of mingled dignity and indignation that her eye quailed before it.

"Well, I s'pose I gotta," she said, dropping her eyes before Starr's righteous wrath. "But no weddin' bells fer you tonight ef yeh keep yer promus. So long!"

Starr shuddered as the girl passed her. The whiff of unwashed garments, stale cooking, and undefinable tenement odor that reached her nostrils sickened her. Was it possible that she must let this creature have a hold even momentarily upon her last few hours? Yet she knew she must. She knew she would not rest until she had been reassured by Carter's voice and the explanation that he would surely give her. She rushed upstairs to her own private phone, locking the door on even her old nurse, and called up the phone in Carter's private apartments.

Without owning it to herself she had been a little troubled all the afternoon because she had not heard from Carter. Her flowers had come—magnificent in their costliness and arrangement, and everything he was to attend to was done, she knew, but no word had come from himself. It was unlike him.

She knew that he had given a dinner the evening before to his old friends who were to be his ushers, and that the festivities would have lasted late. He had not probably arisen very early, of course, but it was drawing on toward the hour of the wedding now. She intended to begin to dress at once after she had phoned him. It was strange she had not heard from him.

After much delay an unknown voice answered the phone, and told her Mr. Carter could not come now. She asked who it was but got no response, except that Mr. Carter couldn't come now. The voice had a muffled, thick sound. "Tell him to call me then as soon as possible," she said, and the voice answered, "Awright!"

Reluctantly she hung up the receiver and called Morton to help her dress. She would have liked to get the matter out of the way before she went about the pretty ceremony, and submitted herself to her nurse's hands with an ill grace and troubled thoughts. The coarse beauty of Lizzie's face haunted her. It reminded her of an actress that Carter had once openly admired, and she had secretly disliked. She found herself shuddering inwardly every time she recalled Lizzie's harsh voice, and uncouth sentences.

She paid little heed to the dressing process after all and let Morton have her way in everything, starting nervously when the phone bell rang, or anyone tapped at her door.

A message came from her father finally. He hoped to be with her in less than an hour now, and as yet no word had come from Carter! Why did he not know she would be anxious? What could have kept him from his usual greeting of her, and on their wedding day!

Suddenly, in the midst of Morton's careful draping of the wedding veil which she was trying in various ways to see just how it should be put on at the last minute, Starr started up from her chair.

"I cannot stand this Mortie. That will do for now. I must telephone Mr. Carter. I can't understand why he doesn't call me."

"Oh, but the poor man is that busy!" murmured Morton excusingly as she hurried obediently out of the room. "Now, mind you don't muss that beautiful veil."

But after a half hour of futile attempt to get into communication with Carter, Star suddenly appeared in her door calling for her faithful nurse again.

"Mortie!" she called excitedly. "Come here quick! I've

ordered the electric. It's at the door now. Put on your big cloak and come with me! I've got to see Mr. Carter at once and I can't get him on the phone."

"But, Miss Starr!" protested Morton. "You've no time to go anywhere now, and look at your pretty veil!"

"Never mind the veil, Mortie, I'm going. Hurry. I can't stop to explain. I'll tell you on the way. We'll be back before anyone has missed us."

"But your mamma, Miss Starr! She will be very angry with me!"

"Mamma must not know. And anyway I must go. Come, if you won't come with me I'm going alone."

Starr with these words grasped a great cloak of dark green velvet, soft and pliable as a skin of fur, threw it over her white bridal robes, and hurried down the stairs.

"Oh, Miss Starr, darlin'," moaned Morton looking hurriedly around for a cloak with which to follow. "You'll spoil yer veil sure! Wait till I take it off'n ye."

But Starr had opened the front door and was already getting into the great luxurious car that stood outside.

Chapter 23

Michael, as he went about on his search kept crying over and over again in his heart: "O, God! Do something to save her! Do something to save my little Starr!"

Over and over the prayer prayed itself without seeming thought or volition on his part, as he went from place to place, faithfully, keenly, step by step, searching out what he needed to know. At last toward six o'clock, his chain of evidence led him to the door of Stuyvesant Carter's apartments.

After some delay the door was opened reluctantly a little way by a servant with an immobile mask of a face who stared at him stupidly, but finally admitted that the three men whose names he mentioned were inside. He also said that Mr. Carter was in, but could not be seen.

He closed the door on the visitor and went inside again to see if any of the others would come out. There ensued an altercation in loud and somewhat unsteady tones, and at last the door opened against and a fast-looking young man who admitted himself to be Theodore Brooks slid out and closed it carefully behind him. The air that came with him was thick with tobacco smoke and heavy with liquor, and the one glimpse Michael got to the room showed a strange radiance of some peculiar light that glowed into the dusky hall weirdly.

The heavy-eyed youth who stood braced against the wall uncertainly looked into Michael's face with an impudent laugh.

"Well, parson, what's the grouch? Are you the devil or an angel sent to bring retribution?" He ended with a silly laugh that told the experienced ear of the young lawyer that the young man had been drinking heavily. And this was the man whose name was signed as Rev. Theodore Brooks, D.D., on the tawdry little marriage certificate that Michael held in his hand. His heart sank at the futility of the task before him.

"Are you a minister?" asked Michael briefly.

"Am I a minister?" drawled young Brooks. "M-my-m-m-m'nster! Well now that get's my goat! Say, boys, he wants t' know' 'f I'm a m-min'ster! Min-ster of what? Min-ster plen-p'ten'sherry?"

"Did you ever perform a marriage?" asked Michael sharply to stop to loud guffaw that was reechoing through the polished corridors of the apartment.

"P'form a m'riage, d'ye say? No, but I'm goin' perform 't a marriage tonight 'f the dead wakes up in time. Goin' t' be bes' man. Say, boys! Got 'im 'wake yet? Gettin' late!"

Michael in despair took hold of the other's arm and tried to explain what he wanted to know. Finally he succeeded in bringing the matter into the fellow's comprehension.

"Wedding, oh, yes, I 'member, peach of a girl! Stuyvy awfully fond of her. No harm meant. Good joke! Yes, I borr'wed Grand'f'ther Brooks's old gown'n ban's. Awf'lly good disguise! No harm meant—on'y good joke—girl awf'lly set on getting married. Stuyvy wanted t' please 'er—awfully good joke!"

"A ghastly joke, I should say, sir!" said Michael sternly and then the door was flung open by hands from inside, loud angry voices protesting while another hand sought unavailingly to close the door again, but Michael came and planted himself in the open door and stood like an avenging angel come to call to judgment. The scene that was revealed to him was too horrifying for words.

A long banquet table stood in the midst of the handsome room whose furnishings were of the costliest. Amid the scattered remains of the feast, napkins lying under the table, upset glasses still dripping their ruby contents down the damask of the tablecloth, broken china, scattered plates and silver, stood a handsome silver-bound coffin, within which, pallid and deathlike, lay the handsome form of the bridegroom of the evening. All about the casket in high sconces burned tall tapers casting their spectral light over the scene.

Distributed about the room lounging in chairs, fast asleep on the couches, lying under the table, fighting by the doorway, one standing on a velvet chair raising an unsteady glass of wine and making a flabby attempt at a drinking song, were ten young men, the flower of society, the expected ushers of the evening's wedding.

Michael with his white face, his golden hair aflame in the flickering candlelight, his eyes full of shocked indignation, stood for a moment surveying the scene, and all at once he knew that his prayer was answered. There would be no wedding that night.

"Is this another of your ghastly jokes?" he turned to Brooks who stood by as master of ceremonies, not in the least disturbed by the presence of the stranger.

"That's just what it is," stuttered Brooks, "a j-j-joke, a p-p-p-pract'cal joke. No harm meant, only Stuyvy's hard to wake up. Never did like gettin' up in the mornin'. Wake 'im up boys! Wake 'im up! Time to get dressed for the wedding!"

"'Has anyone sent word to Miss Endicott?"

"Sent word to Mish Endicott? No, I'd 'no's they have. Think she'd care to come? Say, boys, that's a good joke. This old fellow—don't know who he is—devil'n' all his angels p'raps—he s'gests we send word to Mish Endicott t' come' th' fun'ral."

"I said nothing of the kind," said Michael fiercely. "Have you no sense of decency? Go and wash your face and try to realize what you have been doing. Have someone telephone for a doctor. I will go and tell the family," and Michael strode out of the room to perform the hardest task that had ever yet fallen to his lot.

He did not wait for the elevator but ran down the flights of stairs trying to steady his thoughts and realize the horror through which he had just passed.

As he started down the last flight he heard the elevator door clang below, and as it shot past him he caught a glimpse of white garments and a face with eyes that he knew. He stopped short and looked upward. Was it—could it be? But no, of course not. He was foolish. He turned and compelled his feet to hurry down the rest of the stairs, but at the door his worst fears were confirmed, for there stood the great electric car, and the familiar face of the Endicot chauffeur assured him that someone of the family had just gone to the ghastly spectacle upstairs.

In sudden panic he turned and fled up the stairs. He could not wait for elevators now. He fain would have had wings, the wings of a protecting angel, that he might reach her ere she saw that sight of horror.

Yet even as he started he knew that he must be too late.

Starr stopped startled in the open doorway, with Morton, protesting, apprehensive, just behind her. The soft cloak slid away from her down the satin of her gown, and left her revealed in all her wedding whiteness, her eyes like stars, her beautiful face flushed excitedly. Then the eyes rested on the coffin and its deathlike occupant and her face went white as her dress, while a great horror grew in her eyes.

Brooks, more nearly sober than the rest, saw her first, and hastened to do the honors.

"Say, boys, she's come," he shouted. "Bride's come. Git up, Bobby Trascom. Don't yer know ye mustn't lie down when there's a lady present—Van—get out from under that table. Help me pick up these things. Place all in a mess. Glad to see you, Miss Endicott." He bowed low and staggered as he recovered himself.

Starr turned her white face toward him:

"Mr. Brooks," she said in a tone that sobered him somewhat, "what does it mean? Is he dead?"

"Not at all, not at all, Mish Endicott," he tried to say gravely. "Have him all right in plenty time. Just a little joke, Mish Endicott. He's merely shlightly intoxicated."

But Starr heard no more. With a little stifled cry and a groping motion of her white-clad arms, she crumpled into a white heap at the feet of her horrified nurse. It was just as she fell that Michael appeared at the door, like the rescuing angel that he was, and with one withering glance at the huddled group of men he gathered her in his arms and sped down the stairs, faithful Morton puffing after him. Neither of them noticed a man who got out of the elevator just before Starr fell and walking rapidly toward the open door saw the whole action. In a moment more Mr. Endicott stood in the door surveying the scene before him with stern, wrathful countenance.

Like a dash of cold water his appearance brought several of the participants in the disgraceful scene to their senses. A few questions and he was possessed of the whole shameful story; the stag dinner growing into a midnight orgy; the foolish dare, and the reckless acceptance of it by the already intoxicated bridegroom; the drugged drinks; and the practical joke carried out by brains long under the influence of liquor. Carter's men who had protested had been bound and gagged in the back room. The jokers had found no trouble in securing the necessary tools to carry out their joke. Money will buy anything, even an undertaker for a living man. The promise of secrecy and the generous fees brought all they needed. Then when the ghastly work was completed and the unconscious bridegroom lying in state in his coffin amid the debris of the table, they drowned the horror of their deed in deeper drinking.

Mr. Endicott turned from the scene, his soul filled with loathing and horror.

He had reached home to find the house in a tumult

and Starr gone. Morton, as she went out the door after her
young mistress, had whispered to the butler their destina-
tion, and that they would return at once. She had an innate
suspicion that it would be best for someone to know.

Mr. Endicott at once ordered the runabout and
hastened after them, arriving but a moment or two later.
Michael had just vanished up the apartment stairs as he
entered the lower hallway. The vague indefinite trouble that
had filled his mind concerning his daughter's marriage to a
man he little knew except by reputation, crystallized into
trouble, clear and distinct, as he hurried after his daughter.
Something terrible must have come to Starr or she would
never have hurried away practically alone at a time like this.

The electric car was gone by the time Mr. Endicott
reached the lower hall again, and he was forced to go back
alone as he came, without further explanation of the affair
than what he could see, but he had time in the rapid trip to
become profoundly thankful that the disgraceful scene he
had just left had occurred before and not after his daughter's marriage. Whatever alleviating circumstances there
were to excuse the reckless victim of his comrade's joke, the
fact remained that a man who could fall victim to a joke like
that was not the companion for his daughter's life; she who
had been shielded and guarded at every possible point, and
loved as the very apple of his eye. His feelings toward the
perpetrators of this gruesome sport were such that he
dared not think about them yet. No punishment seemed
too great for such. And she, his little Starr, had looked
upon that shameful scene; had seen the man she was expecting to marry lying as one dead! It was too awful! And
what had it done to her? Had it killed her? Had the shock
unsettled her mind? The journey to his home seemed
longer than his whole ocean voyage. Oh, why had he not
left business to go to the winds and come back long ago to
shield his little girl!

Meantime, Michael, his precious burden in his arms,
had stepped into the waiting car, motioning Morton to follow and sit in the opposite seat. The delicate Paris frock
trailed unnoticed under foot, and the rare lace of the veil
fell back from the white face, but neither Michael nor the

nurse thought of satin and lace now, as they bent anxiously above the girl to see if she still breathed.

All the way to her home Michael held the lovely little bride in his arms, feeling her weight no more than a feather, fervently thankful that he might bear her thus for the moment, away from the danger that had threatened her life. He wished with all his heart he might carry her so to the ends of the earth and never stop until he had her safe from all harm that earth could bring. His heart thrilled wildly with the touch of her frail sweetness, even while his anxious face bent over her to watch for signs of returning consciousness.

But she did not become conscious before she reached the house. His strong arms held her as gently as though she had been a baby as he stepped carefully out and carried her to her own room, laying her upon the white bed, where but two hours before the delicate wedding garments had been spread ready for her to put on. Then he stood back, reverently looked upon her dear face, and turned away. It was in the hall that he met her mother, and her face was fairly disfigured with her sudden recognition of him.

"What! Is it you have dared come into this house? The impertinence! I shall report all your doings to my husband. He will be very angry. I believe that you are at the bottom of this whole business! You shall certainly be dealt with as you deserve!"

She hissed the words after him as Michael descended the stairs with bowed head and closed lips. It mattered not now what she said or thought of him. Starr was saved!

He was about to pass out into the world again, away from her, away even from the knowledge of how she came out of her swoon. He had no further right there now. His duty was done. He had been allowed to save her when she needed him!

But just as he reached it the door opened and Mr. Endicott hurried in.

He paused for an instant.

"Son!" said he, "it was you who brought her home!" It was as if that conviction had but just been revealed to his perturbed mind. "Son, I'm obliged. Sit here till I come. I want to speak with you."

The doctor came with a nurse, and Michael sat and listened to the distant voices in her room. He gathered from the sounds by and by that Starr was conscious, was better.

Until then no one had thought of the wedding or of the waiting guests that would be gathering. Something must be done. And so it came about that as the great organ sounded forth the notes of the wedding march—for by some blunder the bride's signal had been given to the organist when the Endicott car drew up at the church—that Michael, bareheaded, with his hat in his hand, walked gravely up the aisle, unconscious of the battery of eyes, and astonished whispers of "Who is he? Isn't he magnificent? What does it mean? I thought the ushers were to come first?" until he stood calmly in the chancel and faced the wondering audience.

If an angel had come straight down from heaven and interfered with their wedding they could not have been more astonished. For, as he stood beneath the many soft lights in front of the wall of living green and blossoms, with his white face and grave sweet dignity, they forgot for once to study the fashion of his coat, and sat awed before his beautiful face; for Michael wore tonight the look of transport with chin uplifted, glowing eyes, and countenance that showed the spirit shining through.

The organist looked down, and instinctively hushed his music. Had he made some mistake? Then Michael spoke. Doubtless he should have gone to the minister who was to perform the ceremony, and given him the message, but Michael little knew the ways of weddings. It was the first one he had ever attended, and he went straight to the point.

"On account of the sudden and serious illness of the groom," he said, "it will be impossible for the ceremony to go on at this time. The bride's family ask that you will kindly excuse them from further intrusion or explanation this evening."

With a slight inclination of his head to the breathless audience Michael passed swiftly down the aisle and out into the night, and the organist, by tremendous self-control, kept on playing softly until the excited people who had drifted usherless into the church got themselves out into their carriages once more.

Michael walked out into the night, bareheaded still, his eyes lifted to the stars shining so far away above the city, and said softly, with wondering, reverent voice: "O, God! O, God!"

Chapter 24

Following hard upon the interrupted wedding came other events that not only helped to hush matters up, but gave the world a plausible reason why the ceremony did not come off as soon as the groom was convalescent from what was reported in the papers to be an attack of acute indigestion, easily accounted for by the round of banquets and entertainments which usually precede a society wedding.

During that eventful night while Starr still lay like a crushed lily torn rudely from its stem, her mother, after a stormy scene with her husband, in which he made it plain to her just what kind of a man she was wanting her daughter to marry, and during which she saw the fall of her greatest social ambitions, was suddenly felled by a stroke.

The papers next morning told the news as sympathetically as a paper can tell one's innermost secrets. It praised the wonderful ability of the woman who had so successfully completed all the unique arrangements for what had promised to be the greatest wedding of the season, if not of all seasons, and upon whose overtaxed strength the last straw had been laid in the illness of the bridegroom. It stated that now of course the wedding would be put off indefinitely, as nothing could be thought of while the bride's mother lay in so critical a state.

For a week there were daily bulletins of her condition published always in more and more remote corners of the paper, until the little ripple that had been made in the stream of life passed, and no further mention was made of the matter save occasionally when they sent for some famous specialist; when they took her to the shore to try what sea air might do; or when they brought her home again.

But all the time the woman lay locked in rigid silence. Only her cold eyes followed whoever came into her room. She gave no sign of knowing what they said, or of caring who came near her. Her husband's earnest pleas, Starr's tears, drew from her no faintest expression that might have been even imagined from a fluttering eyelash. There was nothing but that stony stare, that almost unseeing gaze, that yet followed, followed wherever one would move. It was a living death.

And when one day the release came and the eyes were closed forever from the scenes of this world, it was a sad relief to both husband and daughter. Starr and her father stole away to an old New England farmhouse where Mr. Endicott's elderly maiden sister still lived in the old family homestead; a mild-eyed, low-voiced woman with plain gray frocks and soft white laces at wrists and neck and ruched about her sweet old face above the silver of her hair.

Starr had not been there since she was a little child, and her sad heart found her aunt's home most restful. She stayed there through the fall and until after the first of the year; while her father came and went as business dictated, and the Endicott home on Madison Avenue remained closed except for the caretakers.

Meanwhile young Carter had discreetly escorted his mother to Europe, and was supposed by the papers to be going to return almost immediately. Not a breath of gossip, strange to say, stole forth. Everything seemed arranged to quiet any suspicion that might arise.

Early in the fall he returned to town but Starr was still in New England. No one knew of the estrangement between them. Their immediate friends were away from town still, and everything seemed perfectly natural in the order of decency. Of course people could not be married at once when there had been a death in the family.

No one but the two families knew of Carter's repeated attempts to be reconciled to Starr; of his feeble endeavor at explanation; of her continued refusal even to see him; and the decided letter she wrote him after he had written her the most abject apology he knew how to frame; nor of her father's interview with the young man wherein he was told some facts about himself more plainly than anyone, even in his boyhood, had ever dared to tell him. Mr. Endicott agreed to keep silence for Starr's sake, provided the young man would do nothing to create any gossip about the matter, until the intended wedding had been forgotten, and other events should have taken the minds of society from their particular case. Carter, for his own sake, had not cared to have the story get abroad and had sullenly acceded to the command. He had not, however, thought it necessary to make himself entirely miserable while abroad, and there were those who more than once spoke his name in company with that of a young and dashing divorcée. Some even thought he returned to America sooner than he intended in order to travel on the same steamer that she was to take. However, those whispers had not as yet crossed the water, and even if they had, such things were too common to cause much comment.

Then, one Monday morning, the papers were filled with horror over an unusally terrible automobile accident, in which a party of seven, of whom the young divorcée was one and Stuyvesant Carter was another, went over an embankment sixty feet in height, the car landing upside down on the rocks below, and killing every member of the party. The paper also stated that Mr. Theodore Brooks, intimate friend of Carter's, who was to have been best man at the wedding some months previous, which was postponed on account of the sudden illness and death of the bride's mother, was of the party.

Thus ended the career of Stuyvesant Carter, and thus the world never knew exactly why Starr Endicott did not become Mrs. Carter.

Michael, from the moment that he went forth from delivering his message in the church, saw no more of the Endicotts. He longed inexpressibly to call and inquire for Starr; to get some word of reconciliation from her father; to ask if there was not some little thing that he might be trusted to do for them; but he knew that his place was not there, and his company was not desired. Neither would he write, for even a note from him could not seem to Starr a reminder of the terrible things of which he had been witness, that is if anybody had ever told her it was he that brought her home.

One solace alone he allowed himself. Night after night as he went home late he would walk far out of his way to pass the house and look up at her window; and always it comforted him a little to see the dim radiance of her soft night light; behind the draperies of whose windows, somewhere, safe, she lay asleep, the dear little white-faced girl that he had been permitted to carry to her home and safety, when she had almost reached the brink of destruction.

About a week after the fateful wedding day Michael received a brief note from Starr.

> My dear Mr. Endicott:
>   I wish to thank you for your trouble in bringing me home last week. I cannot understand how you came to be there at that time. Also I am deeply grateful for your kindness in making the announcement at the church. Very sincerely, S. D. E.

Michael felt the covert question in that phrase: "I cannot understand how you came to be there at that time." She thought, perhaps, that to carry his point and stop the marriage he had had a hand in that miserable business! Well, let her think it. It was not his place to explain, and really of course it could make little difference to her what she believed about him. As well to let it rest. He belonged out of her world, and never would he try to force his way into it.

And so with the whiteness of his face still lingering from the hard days of tension, Michael went on, straining every nerve in his work; keeping the alley room open nightly even during hot weather, and in constant touch with the farm which was now fairly on its feet and almost beginning to earn its own living; though the contributions still kept coming to him quietly, here and there, and helped in the many new plans that grew out of the many new necessities.

The carpenter had built and built, until there were pretty little bungalows of one or two and three rooms dotted all about the farm to be rented at a low price to the workers. It had come to be a little community by itself, spoken of as "Old Orchard Farms," and well respected in the neighborhood, for in truth the motley company that Michael and Sam gathered there had done far better in the way of law and orderliness than either had hoped. They seemed to have a pride that nothing that could hurt "the boss's" reputation as a landowner should be laid to their charge. If by chance there came into their midst any sordid being who could not see matters in that light the rest promptly taught him better, or else put him out.

And now the whole front yard was aflame with brilliant flowers in their season. The orchard had been pruned and trimmed and grafted, and in the spring presented a foreground of wonderful pink and white splendor, and at all seasons of the year the grassy drive wound its way up to the old house, through a vista of branches, green or brown.

It had long been in Michael's heart to build over the old house—for what he did not know. Certainly he had no hope of ever using it himself except as a transitory dwelling, yet it pleased his fancy to have it as he dreamed it out. Perhaps someday it might be needed for some supreme reason, and now was the time to get it ready. So one day he took a great and simple-hearted architect down to the place to stay overnight and get an idea of the surroundings, and a few weeks later he was in possession of a plan that showed how the old house could be made into a beautiful new house, and yet keep all the original outlines. The carpenter, pleased with the prospect of doing something really fine, had undertaken the work and it was going forward rapidly.

The main walls were to be built around with stone, old stone bought from the ruins of a desolated barn of forgotten years, stone that was rusty and golden and green in lovely mellow tones; stone that was gray with age and mossy in places; now and then a stone that was dead black to give strength to the coloring of the whole. There were to be windows, everywhere, wide, low windows, that would let the sunlight in, and windows that nestled in the slopping, rambling roofs that were to be stained green like the moss that would grow on them someday. There was to be a piazza across the entire front with rough stone pillars, and a stone-paved floor up to which the orchard grass would grow in a gentle terrace. Even now Sam and his helpers were at work

starting rose vines of all varieties, to train about the trellises
and twine about the pillars. Sam had elected that it should
be called "Rose Cottage." Who would have ever suspected
Sam of having any poetry in his nature?

The great stone fireplace with its ancient crane and
place to sit inside was to be retained, and built about with
more stone, and the partitions between the original sitting
room and dining room and hall were to be torn down, to
make one splendid living room of which the old fireplace
should be the center, with a great window at one side looking toward the sea, and a deep seat with bookcases in the
corner. Heavy beams were somehow to be put in the ceiling
to support it, and fine wood used in the wainscoting and
paneling, with rough soft-toned plaster between and above.
The floors were to be smooth, wide boards of hard wood
well fitted.

A little gable was to be added on the morning side of
the house for a dining room, all windows, with a view of the
sea on one side and the river on the other. Upstairs there
would be four bedrooms and a bathroom, all according to
the plan to be white wainscoting halfway up and delicately
vined or tinted papers above.

Michael took great pleasure in going down to look at
the house, and watching the progress that was made with it,
as indeed the whole colony did. They called it "The Boss's
Cottage," and when they laid off work at night always took a
trip to see what had been done during the day, men,
women, and children. It was a sort of sacred pilgrimage,
wherein they saw their own highest dreams coming true for
the man they loved because he had helped them to a future
of possibilities. Not a man of them but wistfully wondered if
he would ever get to the place where he could build him a
house like that, and resolved secretly to try for it, and always
the work went better the next day for the visit to the shrine.

But after all, Michael would turn from his house with
an empty ache in his heart. What was it for? Not for him. It
was not likely he would ever spend happy hours there. He
was not like other men. He must take his happiness in making others happy.

But one day a new thought came to him as he watched
the laborers working out the plan, and bringing it ever

nearer and nearer to the perfect whole. A great desire came
to him to have Starr see it someday, to know what she would
think about it, and if she would like it. The thought occurred to him that perhaps, sometime, in the changing of
the world, she might chance near that way, and he have
opportunity to show her the house that he had built—for
her! Not that he would ever tell her the last. She must never
know of course that she was the only one in all the world he
could ever care for. That would seem a great presumption
in her eyes. He must keep that to himself. But there would
be no harm in showing her the house, and he would make it
now as beautiful as if she were to occupy it. He would take
his joy in making all things fair, with the hope that she
might one day see and approve it.

So, as the work drew near its completion he watched it
more and more carefully, matching tints in rooms, and always bringing down some new idea, or finding some particular bit of furniture that would someday fit into a certain
niche. In that way he cheated the loney ache in his heart,
and made believe he was happy.

And another winter drew its white mantle about its
shoulders and prepared to face the blast.

It bade fair to be a bitter winter for the poor, for everything was high, and unskilled labor was poorly paid. Sickness and death were abroad, and lurked in the milk supply,
the food supply, the unsanitary tenements about the alley,
which, because it had not been so bad as some other districts had been left uncondemned. Yet it was bad enough,
and Michael's hands were full to keep his people alive, and
try to keep some of them from sinning. For always where
there is misery, there is the more sinning.

Old Sal sat on her doorstep shivering with her tattered
shawl about her shoulders, or when it grew too cold peered
from her little muslin curtained window behind the geranium, to see the dirty white hearse with its pink-winged
angel atop, pass slowly in and out with some little fragment
of humanity, and knew that one day her turn would come
to leave it all and go! Then she turned back to her little
room which had become the only heaven she knew, and
solaced herself with the contents of a black bottle!

Chapter 25

During the years of his work in the alley Michael had become known more and more among workers for the poor, and he found strength in their brotherhood, though he kept mainly to his own little corner, and had little time to go out into other fields. But he had formed some very pleasant distant friendships among workers, and had met prominent men who were interested in reforms of all sorts.

He was hurrying back to his boarding place one evening late in January with his mind full of the old problem of how to reach the mass of humanity and help them to live in decency so that they might stand some little chance of being good as well as being alive.

At the crossing of another avenue he met a man whose eloquence as a public speaker was only equalled by his indefatigable tirelessness as a worker among men.

"Good evening, Endicott," he said cordially, halting in his rapid walk, "I wonder if you're not the very man I want? Will you do me a favor? I'm in great straits and no time to hunt up anybody."

"Anything I can do, Doctor, I am at your service," said Michael.

"Good! Thank you!" said the great man. "Are you free this evening for an hour?"

"I can be," said Michael smiling. The other man's hearty greeting and warm "thank you" cheered his lonely heart.

"Well, then you'll take my place at Madison Square Garden tonight, won't you? I've just had a telegram that my mother is very ill, perhaps dying, and I feel that I must go at once. I'm on my way to the station now. I thought Patton would be at his rooms perhaps and he might help me out, but they tell me he is out of town on a lecture tour."

"Take your place?" said Michael aghast. "That I'm sure I could never do, Doctor. What were you going to do?

"Why, there's a mass meeting at Madison Square Garden. We're trying to get more playgrounds and roof gardens for poor children, you know. I was to speak about the tenement district, give people a general idea of what the need is, you know. I'm sure you're well acquainted with the subject. They're expecting some big men there who can be big givers if they're touched in the right way. You're very good to help me out. You'll excuse me if I hurry on, it's almost train time. I want to catch the six o'clock express west."

"But, Doctor," said Michael in dismay, striding along by his side down the street, "I really couldn't do that. I'm not a public speaker, you know—I never addressed a big audience in my life! Isn't there someone else I could get for you?"

It was odd that while he was saying it the vision of the church filled with the fashionable world, waiting for a wedding which did not materialize, came to his thoughts.

"Oh, that doesn't make the slightest difference in the world!" said the worried man. "You know the subject from *a* to *z*, and I don't know another available soul tonight who does. Just tell them what you know, you needn't talk long; it'll be all right anyway. Just smile your smile and they'll give all right. Good night, and thank you from my heart! I must take this cab," and he hailed a passing cab and sprang inside, calling out above the city's din, "Eight o'clock the meeting is. Don't worry! You'll come out all right. It'll be good practice for your business."

Michael stood still in the middle of the crowded pavement and looked after the departing cab in dismay. Never in all his life had he come to a spot where he felt so utterly inadequate to fill a situation. Frantically he tried as he started down the street again, to think of someone else to ask. There seemed to be no one at all who was used to speaking that knew the subject. The few who knew were either out of town or at a great distance. He did not know how to reach them in time. Besides, there was something about Michael that just would not let him shirk a situation no matter how trying it was to him. It was one of the first principles he had been taught with football, and before he reached his boarding place, his chin was up, and his lips firmly set. Anyone who knew him well would have felt sure Michael was going into a scrimmage and expected the fighting to be hard.

It was Will French who dug it out of him after dinner, and laughed and slapped him gleefully on the shoulder. Will was engaged to Hester now and he was outrageously happy.

"Good work, old fellow! You've got your chance, now give it to 'em! I don't know anybody can do it better. I'd like to bring a millionaire or two to hear you. You've been there, now tell 'em! don't frown like that, old fellow, I tell you you've got the chance of your life. Why don't you tell 'em about the tenement in the alley?

Michael's face cleared.

"I hadn't thought of it, Will. Do you think I could? It isn't exactly on the subject. I understood from him I was to speak of the tenement in relation to the playground."

"The very thing," said Will. "Didn't he tell you to say what you knew? Well, give it to 'em straight, and you'll see those rich old fellows open their eyes. Some of 'em own some of those old rickety shacks, and probably don't know what they own. Tell 'em. Perhaps the old man who owns our tenement will be there! Who knows?"

"By the way," said Michael, his face all alight, "did I tell you that Milborn told me the other day that they think they're on track of the real owner of our tenement? The agent let out something the last time they talked with him and they think they may discover who he is, though he's hidden himself well behind agents for years. If we can find out who he is we may be able to help him understand what great need there is for him to make a few changes."

"Yes, a few changes!" sneered Will. "Tear down the whole rotten death trap and build a new one with light and air and a chance for human beings to live! Give it to 'em, old man! He may be there tonight."

"I believe I will," said Michael thoughtfully, the look of winning beginning to dawn on his speaking face, and he went up to his room and locked the door.

When he came out again, Will, who was waiting to accompany him to the meeting saw in his eyes the look of the dreamer, the man who sees into the future and prophesies. He knew that Michael would not fail in his speech that night. He gave a knowing look to Hester as she came out to go with him and Hester understood. They walked behind him quietly for the most part, or speaking in low tones. They felt the pride and anxiety of the moment as much as if they had been going to make the speech themselves. The angel in the man had dominated them also.

Now it happened that Starr had come down with her father for a week's shopping the last time he ran up to his sister's and on this particular evening she had claimed her father's society.

"Can't you stay at home, Daddy dear?" she asked wistfully. "I don't want to go to Aunt Frances's 'quiet little evening' one bit. I told her you needed me tonight as we've only a day or two more left before I go back."

Aunt Frances was Starr's mother's sister, and as the servants of the two families agreed mutually, "Just like her, only more so." Starr had never been quite happy in her company.

"Come with me for a little while, daughter. I'm sorry I can't stay at home all the evening, but I rather promised I'd drop into a charitable meeting at at Madison Square for a few minutes this evening. They're counting on my name, I believe. We won't need to stay long, and if you're with me it will be easier to get away."

"Agreed!" said Starr eagerly, and got herself ready in a twinkling. And so it came about that as the roll of martial music poured forth from the fine instruments secured for the occasion, and the leaders and speakers of the evening, together with the presidents of this society, and that army, or settlement, or organization for the relief and benefit of the poor, filed on to the great platform, that Starr and her father occupied prominent seats in the vast audience, and joined in the enthusiasm that spread like a wave before the great American flag that burst out in brilliant electric lights of red and white and blue, a signal that the hour and the movement was come.

Michael came in with the others, as calmly as though

he had spent his life preparing for the public platform.
There was fire in his eyes, the fire of passion for the people
of the slums who were his kin. He looked over the audience
with a throb of joy to think he had so mighty an opportunity. His pulses were not stirred, because he had no consciousness of self in this whole performance. His subject
was to live before the people, he himself was nothing at all.
He had no fear but he could tell them, if that was all they
wanted. Burning sentences hot with the blood of souls had
been pouring through his mind ever since he had decided
to talk of his people. He was only in a hurry to begin lest
they would not give him time to tell all he knew! All he
knew! Could it ever be told? It was endless as eternity.

With a strange stirring of her heart Starr recognized
him. She felt the color stealing into her face. She thought
her father must notice it, and cast a furtive glance at him,
but he was deep in conversation about some banking business, so she sat and watched Michael during the opening
exercises and wondered how he came to be there and what
was his office in this thing. Did lawyers get paid for doing
something to help along charitable institutions? She supposed so. He was probably given a seat on the platform for
his pains. Yet she could not help thinking how fine he
looked sitting there in the center, the place of honor it
would seem. How came he there? He was taller than all the
others, whether sitting or standing, and his fine form and
bearing made him exceedingly noticeable. Starr could hear
women about her whispering to their escorts: "Who is he?"
and her heart gave strange little throbs to think that she
knew. It seemed odd to her that she should be taken back
by the sight of him now through all the years to that morning in Florida when she had kissed him in the chapel.
Somehow there seemed something sweet and tender in the
memory and she dwelt upon it, while she watched him looking calmly over the audience, rising and moving to let another pass him, bowing and smiling to a noted judge who
leaned over to grasp his hand. Did young lawyers like that
get to know noted judges? And wherever did he get his
grace? There was rhythm and beauty in his every motion.
Starr had never had such a splendid opportunity to look at

him before, for in all the sea of faces she knew hers would be lost to him, and she might watch him at her will.

"Daddy, did you know that Michael was up there?" she asked after awhile when her father's friend went back to his seat.

"Michael? No, where? On the platform? I wonder what in the world he is doing there? He must be mixed up in this thing somehow. I understand he's stuck at his mission work. I tried to stop him several years ago. Told him it would ruin his prospects, but he was too stubborn to give up. So he's here!"

And Mr. Endicott searched out Michael and studied the beautiful face keenly, looking in vain for any marks of degradation or fast living. The head was lifted with its conquering look; the eyes shone forth like jewels. Michael was a man, a son—to be proud of, he told himself, and breathed a heavy sigh. That was one time when his stubbornness had not conquered, and he found himself glad in spite of himself that it had not.

The opening exercises were mere preliminary speeches and resolutions, mixed with music, and interspersed by the introduction of the mayor of the city and one or two other notables who said a few apathetic words of commendation for the work in hand and retired on their laurels.

"I understand this Dr. Glidden who is to speak is quite an eloquent fellow," said Starr's father as the president got up to introduce the speaker of the evening whom all had come to hear. "The man who was just talking with me says he is really worth hearing. If he grows tiresome we will slip out. I wonder which one he is? He must be the man with the iron-gray hair over there."

"Oh, I don't want to go out," said Starr. "I like it. I never was in a great meeting like this. I like to hear them cheer."

Her cheeks were rosy, for in her heart she was finding out that she had a great longing to stay there and watch Michael a little longer.

"I am sorry to have to tell you that our friend and advertised speaker for the evening was called away by the sudden and serious illness of his mother, and left for the West on the six o'clock express," said the chairman in his inadequate little voice that seemed always straining beyond its height and never accomplishing anything in the way of being heard.

A sign of disappointment swept over the part of the audience near enough to the platform to hear, and some men reached for their hats.

"Well, now that's a pity," whispered Endicott. "I guess we better go before they slip in any dry old substitutes. I've been seen here, that's enough."

But Starr laid a detaining hand on her father's arm.

"Wait a little, Daddy," she said softly.

"But he has sent a substitute," went on the chairman, "a man whom he says is a hundred percent better able to talk on the subject than himself. He spoke to me from the station phone just before he left and told me that he felt that you would all agree he had done well to go when you had heard the man whom he has sent in his place. I have the pleasure to introduce to you Mr. Michael Endicott who will speak to you this evening on the needs of the tenement dwellers—Mr. Endicott."

Amid the silence that ensued after the feebly polite applause Michael rose. For just an instant he stood, looking over the audience and a strange subtle thrill ran over the vast assemblage.

Then Michael, insensibly measuring the spacious hall, flung his clear, beautiful voice out into it, and reached the uttermost bounds of the room.

"Did you know that there are in this city now seventy-one thousand eight hundred and seventy-seven totally dark rooms; some of them connected with an air shaft twenty-eight inches wide and seventy feet deep; many of them absolutely without access to even a dark shaft, and that these rooms are the only place in the whole wide, beautiful world for thousands of little children, unless they stay in the street?"

The sentence shot through the audience like a great deliberate bolt of lightning that crashed through the hearts of the hearers and tore away every vestige of their complacency. The people sat up and took notice. Starr thrilled and trembled, she knew not why.

"There is a tenement with rooms like this, a dumbbell tenement, it is called, in the alley where, for aught I know, I was born."

"Oh!" The sound swept over the listeners in a great wave like a sob of protest. Men and women raised their opera glasses and looked at the speaker again. They asked one another: "Who is he?" and settled quiet to hear what more he had to say.

Then Michael went on to tell of three dark little rooms in "his" tenement where a family of eight, accustomed to better things, had been forced by circumstances to make their home, and where in the dark the germs of tuberculosis had been silently growing, until the whole family were infected. He spoke of a little ten-year-old girl, living in one of these little dark rooms, pushed down on the street by a playmate, an accident that would have been thought nothing of in a healthy child, but in this little one it produced tubercular meningitis and after two days of agony the child died. He told of a delicate girl, who with her brother were the sole wage earners of the family, working all day, and sewing far into the night to make clothes for the little brothers and sisters, who had fallen prey to the white plague.

He told instance after instance of sickness and death all resulting from the terrible conditions in this one tenement, until a delicate, refined-looking woman down in the audience who had dropped in with her husband for a few minutes on the way to some other gathering, drew her soft mantle about her shoulders with a shiver and whispered: "Really, Charles, it can't be healthy to have such a terrible state of things in the city where we live. I should think germs would get out and float around to us. Something ought to be done to clean such low creatures out of a decent community. Do let's go now. I don't feel as if I could listen to another word. I shan't be able to enjoy the reception."

But the husband sat frowing and listening to the end of the speech, vouchsafing to her whisper only the single growl:

"Don't be a fool, Selina!"

On and on Michael went, literally taking his audience with him, through room after room of "his" tenement, showing them horrors they had never dreamed; giving them now and again a glimmer of light when he told of a curtained window with fifteen minutes of sun every morning, where a little cripple sat to watch for her sunbeam, and push her pot of geraniums along the sill that it might have the entire benefit of its brief shining. He put the audience into peals of laughter over the wit of some poor creatures in certain trying situations, showing that a sense of humor is not lacking in "the other half"; and then set them weeping over a little baby's funeral.

He told them forcibly how hard the workers were trying to clean out and improve this terrible state of things. How cruelly slow the owner of this particular tenement was even to cut windows into dark air shafts; how so far it had been impossible to discover the name of the true owner of the building, because he had for years successfully hidden behind agents who held the building in trust.

The speech closed in a mighty appeal to the people of New York to rise up in a mass and wipe out this curse of the tenements, and build in their places light, airy, clean, wholesome dwellings, where people might live and work and learn the lessons of life aright, and where sin could find no dark hole in which to hatch her loathsome offspring.

As Michael sat down amid a burst of applause such as is given to few speakers, another man stepped to the front of the platform; and the cheers of commendation were hushed somewhat, only to swell and break forth again; for this man was one of the city's great minds, and always welcome on any platform. He had been asked to make the final appeal for funds for the playgrounds. It had been considered a great stroke of luck on the part of the committee to secure him.

"My friends," said he when the hush came at last and he could be heard, "I appreciate your feelings. I would like to spend the remainder of the night in applauding the man who has just finished speaking."

The clamor showed signs of breaking forth again:

"This man has spoken well because he has spoken from his heart. And he has told us that he knows whereof he speaks, for he has lived in those tenement rooms himself, one of the little children like those for whom he pleads. I am told that he has given almost every evening for four years out of a busy life which is just opening into great promise, to help these people of his. I am reminded as I have been listening to him of Lanier's wonderful poem, 'The Marshes of Glynn.' Do you recall it?

"'Ye spread and span like the catholic man who
        hath mightily won
God out of knowledge, and good out of infinite
        pain,
and sight out of blindness, and purity out of a
        stain.'

"Let us get to work at once and do our duty. I see you do not need urging. My friends, if such a man as this, a prince among men, can come out of the slums, then the slums are surely worth redeeming."

The audience thundered and clamored and thundered again; women sobbed openly, while the ushers hurried about collecting the eager offerings of the people, for Michael had won the day and everybody was ready to give. It sort of helped to get the burden of such a state of things off their consciences.

Starr had sat through the whole speech with glowing cheeks and lashes wet. Her heart throbbed with wonder and a kind of personal pride in Michael. Somehow all the years that had passed between seemed to have dropped away and she saw before her the boy who had told her of the Florida sunset, and filled her with childish admiration over his beautiful thoughts. His story appealed to her. The lives of the little ones about whom he had been telling were like his poor neglected existence before her father took him up; the little lonely life that had been freely offered to save her own.

She forgot now all that had passed between, her anger at his not coming to ride; and after her return from abroad, not coming to call; nor accepting her invitations; her rage at his interference in her affairs. Her persistence in her own folly seemed now unspeakable. She was ashamed of herself. The tears were streaming down her cheeks, but of this she was quiet unaware.

When the speeches were over and the uproar of applause had somewhat subsided, Starr turned to her father her face aglow, her lashes still dewy with tears. Her father had been silent and absorbed. His face was inscrutable now. He had a way of masking his emotions even to those who knew him best.

"Daddy, dear," whispered Starr, "couldn't we buy that tenement and build it over? I should so love to give those little children happy homes."

Endicott turned and looked at his treasured child, her lovely face all eagerness now. She had infinite faith in her father's ability to purchase anything she wanted. The father himself had been deeply stirred. He looked at her searchingly at first; then yearningly, tenderly, but his voice was almost gruff as he said:

"H'm! I'll see about it!"

"Couldn't you let Michael know now, Daddy? I think it would be such a help to him to know that his speech has done some good." The voice was very sweet and appealing. "Couldn't you send him word by one of the ushers?"

"H'm! I suppose I could." Endicott took out his fountain pen and a business card, and began to write.

"You don't suppose, Daddy, that the owner will object to selling? There won't be any trouble about it that way, will there?"

"No, I don't think there'll be any trouble."

Endicott slipped the card into an envelope he found in his pocket and calling an usher asked him to take it to the platform to Michael. What he had written was this:

> I suppose you have been talking about my property. Pull the tenement down if you like and build a model one. I'll foot the bills.   D. E.

When Michael, surprised at receiving a communication on the platform, tore the envelope open and read, his face fairly blazed with glory. Starr was watching him, and her heart gave a queer little throb of pleasure at the light in his eyes. The next instant he was on his feet, and with a whispered word to the chairman, came to the front of the platform. His raised hand brought instant silence.

"I have good news. May I share it with you? The owner of the tenement is in this house, and has sent me word that he will tear it down and build a model one in its place!"

The ring in Michael's voice, and the light on his face was equivalent to a dozen votes of thanks. The audience rose to its feet and cheered.

"Daddy! Oh, Daddy! Are you the owner?" There was astonishment, reproof, excuse, and forgiveness all mingled in Starr's voice.

"Come, Starr," said her father abruptly, "we'd better go home. This is a hot noisy place and I'm tired."

"Daddy dear! Of course you didn't now how things were!" said Starr sweetly. "You didn't, did you, Daddy?"

"No, I didn't know," said Endicott evasively, "that Michael has a great gift of gab! Would you like to stop and have an ice somewhere, daughter?"

"No, Daddy, I'd rather go home and plan how to make over that tenement. I don't believe I'd enjoy an ice after what I've heard tonight. Why is it some people have so much more than others to start with?"

"H'm! Deep question, child, better not trouble your brains with it," and Starr saw that her father, though deeply moved, did not wish to discuss the matter.

The next day Michael called at Endicott's office but did not find him in, and wrote a letter out of the overwhelming joy of his heart, asking permission to call and thank his benefactor and talk over plans. The following day he received the curt reply:

Son—Make your plans to suit yourself. Don't spare expense within reason. No thanks needed. I did it for Starr. You made a good speech.

Michael choked down his disappointment over this rebuff, and tried to take all the joy of it. He was not forgiven yet. He might not enter the sacred precincts of intercourse again, but he was beloved. He could not help feeling that, because of that "Son" with which the communication began. And the grudging praise his speech received was more to Michael than all the adulation that people had been showering upon him since the night of the mass meeting. But Starr! Starr knew about it. He did it for Starr! She had wanted it! She had perhaps been there! She must have been there, or how else would she have known? The thought thrilled him, and thrilled him anew! Oh, if he might have seen her before him! But then perhaps he would not have been able to tell his story, and so it was just as well. But Starr was interested in his work, his plans! What a wonderful thing to have her work with him even in this indirect way. Oh, if some day! If—!

But right here Michael shut down his thoughts and went to work.

Chapter 26

Late in January Michael was taking his nightly walk homeward by way of the Endicott home. He was convinced that Starr was still away from home, for he had seen no lights now for several weeks in the room that he knew was her own, but there was always the chance that she might have returned.

He was nearing the house when he saw from the opposite direction a man turn the corner and with halting gait come slowly toward the house and pause before the steps uncertainly. Something familiar in the man's attitude caused Michael to hasten his steps, and coming closer he found that it was Mr. Endicott himself, and that he stood looking up the steps of his home as though they had been a difficult hill which he must climb.

Michael stopped beside him, saying good evening, the thrill of his voice conveying his own joy in the meeting in addition to a common greeting.

"Is that you, son?" asked the older man swaying slightly toward him. "I'm glad you came. I feel strangely dizzy. I wish you'd help me in."

Michael's arm was about the other's shoulders at once and his ready strength almost lifted his benefactor up the steps. His steady hand with the key made short work of the night latch, and without waiting to call a servant he helped Mr. Endicott up to his room and to his bed.

The man sank back wearily with a sigh and closed his eyes, then suddenly roused himself.

"Thank you, son, and will you send a message to Starr that I am not able to come on tonight as I promised? Tell her I'll likely be all right tomorrow and will try to come then. You'll find the address at the head of the telephone list in the hall there. I guess you'll have to phone for the doctor. I don't seem to feel like myself. There must be something the matter. I think I've taken a heavy cold."

Michael hurried to the phone and called up the physician begging him to come at once, for he could see that Mr. Endicott was very ill. His voice trembled as he gave the message to the Western Union over the phone. It seemed almost like talking to Starr, though he sent the telegram in her father's name.

The message sent, he hurried back to the sick man, who seemed to have fallen in a sort of stupor. His face was flushed and hot, the veins in his temples and neck were throbbing rapidly. In all his healthy life Michael had seen little of illness, but he recognized it now and knew it must be a violent attack. If only he knew something to do until teh doctor should arrive!

Hot water used to be the universal remedy for all diseases at college. The matron always had someone bring hot water when anyone was ill. Michael went downstairs to find a servant, but they must all be asleep, for he had been unusually late in leaving the alley that night.

However, he found that the bathroom would supply plenty of hot water, so he set to work to undress his patient, wrap him in a blanket and soak his feet in hot water. But the patient showed signs of faintness, and was unable to sit up. A footbath under such conditions was difficult to administer. The unaccustomed nurse got his patient into bed again with arduous labor, and was just wondering what to do next when the doctor arrived.

Michael watched the grave face of the old doctor as he examined the sick man, and knew that his intuitions had been right. Mr. Endicott was very seriously ill. The doctor examined his patient with deliberation, his face growing more and more serious. At last he stepped out of the room and motioned Michael to follow him.

"Are you a relative, young man?" he asked looking at Michael keenly.

"No, only one who is very much indebted to him."

"Well, it's lucky for him if you feel that indebtedness now. Do you know what is the matter with him?"

"No," said Michael. "He looks pretty sick to me. What is it?"

"Smallpox!" said the doctor laconically, "and a tough case at that." Then he looked keenly at the fine specimen of manhood before him, noting with alert eye that there had been no blanching of panic in the beautiful face, no slightest movement as if to get out of the room. The young man was not a coward, anyway.

"How long have you been with him?" he asked abruptly.

"Since I telephoned you," said Michael, "I happened to be passing the house and saw him trying to get up the steps alone. He was dizzy, he said, and seemed glad to have me come to his help."

"Have you ever been vaccinated?"

"No," said Michael indifferently.

"The wisest thing for you to do would be to get out of the room at once and let me vaccinate you. I'll try to send a nurse to look after him as soon as possible. Where are the family? Not at home? And the servants will probably scatter as soon as they learn what's the matter. A pity he hadn't been taken to the hospital, but it's hardly safe to move him now. The fact is he is a very sick man, and there's only one chance in a hundred of saving him. You've run some big risks, taking care of him this way."

"Any bigger than you are running, doctor?" Michael smiled gravely.

"H'm! Well, it's my business, and I don't suppose it is

yours. There are people who are paid for those things. Come get out of this room or I won't answer for the consequences."

"The consequences will have to answer for themselves, Doctor. I'm going to stay here till somebody better comes to nurse him."

Michael's eyes did not flinch as he said this.

"Suppose you take the disease?"

Michael smiled, one of his brilliant smiles that you could almost hear it was so bright.

"Why, then I will," said Michael, "but I'll stay well long enough to take care of him until the nurse comes anyway."

"You might die!"

"Of course." In a tone with not a ruffle in the calm purpose.

"Well, it's my duty to tell you that you'd probably be throwing your life away, for there's only a chance that he won't die."

"Not throwing it away if I made him suffer a little less. And you said there was a chance. If I didn't stay he might miss that chance, mightn't he?"

"Probably."

"Can I do anything to help or ease him?"

"Yes."

"Then I stay. I should stay anyway until someone came. I couldn't leave him so."

"Very well, then. I'm proud to know a man like you. There's plenty to be done. Let's get to work."

The hour that followed was filled with instructions and labor. Michael had no time to think what would become of his work, or anything. He only knew that this was the present duty and he went forward in it step by step. Before the doctor left he vaccinated Michael, and gave him careful directions how to take all necessary precautions for his own safety; but he knew from the lofty look in the young man's face, that these were mere secondary considerations with him. If the need came for the sake of the patient, all precautions would be flung aside as not mattering one whit.

The doctor roused the servants and told them what had happened, and tried to persuade them to stay quietly in their places, and he would see that they ran no risks if

they obeyed his directions. But to a man and a woman they
were panic-stricken; gathering their effects, they, like the
Arabs of old, folded their tents and silently stole away in the
night. Before morning dawned Michael and his patient
were in sole possession of the house.

Early in the morning there came a call from the doctor.
He had not been able to secure the nurse he hoped to get.
Could Michael hold the fort a few hours longer? He would
relieve him sooner if possible, but experienced nurses for
contagious cases were hard to get just now. There was a
great deal of sickness. He might be able to get one this
morning, but it was doubtful. He had telephoned everywhere.

Of course Michael would hold the fort.

The doctor gave explicit directions, asked a number of
questions, and promised to call as soon as possible.

Michael, alone in the great silence that the occasional
babble of a delirious person emphasizes in an otherwise
empty house, began to think of things that must be done.
Fortunately there was a telephone in the room. He would
not have to leave his patient alone. He called up Will French
and told him in a few words what had happened; laughed
pleasantly at Will's fears for him; asked him to look after the
alley work and to attend to one or two little matters connected with the office work which could not be put off.
Then he called up Sam at the farm, for Michael had long
ago found it necessary to have a telephone put in at Old
Orchard.

The sound of Sam's voice cheered his heart, when,
after Michael's brief simple explanation of his present position as trained nurse for the head of the house of Endicott
who lay sick of smallpox, Sam responded with a dismayed
"Fer de lub o' Mike!"

When Michael had finished all his directions to Sam,
and received his partner's promise to do everything just as
Michael would have done it, Sam broke out with:

"Say, does dat guy know what he's takin' off'n you?"

"Who? Mr. Endicott? No, Sam, he doesn't know anything. He's delirious."

"Ummm!" grunted Sam deeply troubled. "Well, he better fin' out wen he gets hisself agin er there'll be sompin'
comin' to him."

"He's done a great deal for me, Sam."

"Ummm! Well, you're gettin' it back on him sure thing now, all right. Say, you t' care o' yer'se'f, Mikky! We-all can't do nothin' w'th'ut yer. You lemme know every day how you be."

"Sure Sam!" responded Michael deeply touched by the choking sound of Sam's voice. "Don't you worry. I'm sound as a nut. Nothing'll happen to me. The doctor vaccinated me, and I'll not catch it. You look after things for me and I'll be on deck again someday all the better for the rest."

Michael sat back in the chair after hanging up the receiver, his eyes glistening with moisture. To think the day had come when Sam should care like that! It was a miracle.

Michael went back again to the bed to look after his patient, and after he had done everything that the doctor had said, he decided to reconnoiter for some breakfast. There must be something in the house to eat even if the servants had all departed, and he ought to eat so that his strength should be equal to his task.

It was late in the morning, nearly half-past ten. The young man hurried downstairs and began to ransack the pantry. He did not want to be long away from the upper room. Once, as he was stooping to search the refrigerator for butter and milk he paused in his work and thought he heard a sound at the front door, but then all seemed still, and he hurriedly put a few things on a tray and carried them upstairs. He might not be able to come down again for several hours. But when he reached the top of the stairs he heard a voice, not his patient's, but a woman's voice, sweet and clear and troubled:

"Daddy! Oh, Daddy dear! Why don't you speak to your little girl? What is the matter? Can't you understand me? Your face and your poor hands are so hot, they burn me. Daddy, Daddy dear!"

It was Starr's voice and Michael's heart stood still with the thrill of it, and the instant horror of it. Starr was in there in the room of death with her father. She was exposed to the terrible contagion; she, the beautiful, frail treasure of his heart!

He set the tray down quickly on the hall table and went swiftly to the door.

She sat on the side of the bed, her arms about her father's unconscious form and her head buried in his neck, sobbing.

For an instant Michael was frozen to the spot with horror at her dangerous situation. If she had wanted to take the disease she could not have found a more sure way of exposing herself.

The next instant Michael's senses came back and without stopping to think he sprang forward and caught her up in his arms, bearing her from the room and setting her down at the bathroom door.

"Oh, Starr! What have you done!" he said, a catch in his voice like a sob, for he did not know what he was saying.

Starr, frightened, struggling, sobbing, turned and looked at him.

"Michael! How did you come to be here? Oh, what is the matter with my father?"

"Go wash your hands and face quickly with this antiseptic soap," he commanded, all on the alert now, and dealing out the things the doctor had given for his own safety, "and here! Rinse your mouth with this quickly, and gargle your throat! Then go and change your things as quick as you can. Your father has the smallpox and you have been in there close to him."

"The smallpox!"

"Hurry!" commanded Michael, handing her the soap and turning on the hot water.

Starr obeyed him because when Michael spoke in that tone people always did obey, but her frightened eyes kept seeking his face for some reassurance.

"The smallpox! Oh, Michael! How dreadful! But how do you know? Has the doctor been here? And how did you happen to be here?"

"I was passing last night when your father came home and he asked me to help him in. Yes, the doctor was here, and will soon come again and bring a nurse. Now hurry! You must get away from the vicinity of this room!"

"But I'm not going away!" said Starr stubbornly. "I'm going to stay by my father. He'll want me."

"Your father would be distressed beyond measure if he knew that you were exposed to such a terrible danger. I know that he would far rather have you go away at once. Besides, he is delirious, and your presence cannot do him any good now. You must take care of yourself, so that when he gets well you will be well too, and able to help him get back into health again."

"But you are staying."

"It does not matter about me," said Michael, "there is no one to care. Besides, I am a man, and perfectly strong. I do not think I will take the disease. Now please take off those things you wore in there and get something clean that has not been in the room and go away from here as quickly as you can."

Michael had barely persuaded her to take precautions when the doctor arrived with a nurse and the promise of another before night.

He scolded Starr thoroughly for her foolhardiness in going into her father's room. He had been the family physician ever since she was born, knew her well, and took the privilege of scolding when he liked. Starr meekly succumbed. There was just one thing she would not do, and that was to go away out of the house while her father remained in so critical a condition. The doctor frowned and scolded, but finally agreed to let her stay. And indeed it seemed as if perhaps it was the only thing that could be done, for she had undoubtedly been exposed to the disease, and was subject to quarantine. There seemed to be no place to which she could safely go, where she could be comfortable, and the house was amply large enough for two or three parties to remain in quarantine in several detachments.

There was another question to be considered. The nurses would have their hands full with their patient. Someone must stay in the house and look after things, see that they needed nothing, and get some kind of meals. Starr, of course, knew absolutely nothing about cooking, and Michael's experience was limited to roasting sweet potatoes around a bonfire at college, and cooking eggs and coffee at the fireplace on the farm. But a good cook to stay in a plague-stricken dwelling would be a thing of time, if procurable at all, so the doctor decided to attempt the willing services of these two. Starr was established in her own room upstairs, which could be shut away from the front part of the house by a short passageway and two doors, with access to the lower floor by means of the back stairs; and Michael made a bed of the soft couch in the tiny reception room where he had twice passed through trying experiences. Great curtains kept constantly wet with antiseptics shut away the sick room and adjoining apartments from the rest of the house.

It was arranged that Michael should place such supplies as were needed at the head of the stairs, just outside the guarding curtains, and the nurses would pass all dishes through an antiseptic bath before sending them downstairs again. The electric bells and telephones with which the house was well supplied made it possible for them to communicate with one another without danger of infection.

Starr was at once vaccinated and the two young people received many precautions, and injunctions, with medicine and a strict regime, and even then the old doctor shook his head dubiously. If those two beautiful faces should have to pass through the ordeal of that dread disease his old heart would be quite broken. All that skill and science could do to prevent it should be done.

So the house settled down to the quiet of a daily routine; the busy city humming and thundering outside, but no more a part of them than if they had been living in a tomb. The card of warning on the door sent all the neighbors in the block scurrying off in a panic to Palm Beach or Europe; and even the strangers passed by on the other side. The grocery boy and the milkman left their orders hurriedly on the front steps and Michael and Starr might almost have used the street for an exercise ground if they had chosen, so deserted had it become.

But there was no need for them to go farther than the door in front, for there was a lovely side and back yard, screened from the street by a high wall, where they might walk at will when they were not too busy with their work; which for their unskilled hands was hard and laborious. Nevertheless, the orders were strict, and every day they were out for a couple of hours at least. To keep from getting chilled, Michael invented all sorts of games when they grew tired of walking, and twice after a new fall of snow they

went out and had a game of snowballing, coming in with
glowing faces and shining eyes, to change wet garments and
hurry back to their kitchen work. But this was after the first
few serious days were passed, and the doctor had given
them hope that if all went well there was a good chance of
the patient pulling through.

They settled into their new life like two children who
had known each other a long time. All the years between
were as if they had not been. They made their blunders,
were merry over their work, and grew into each other's
companionship charmingly. Their ideas of cooking were
most primitive and had it not been possible to order things
sent in from caterers they and the nurses might have been
in danger of starving to death. But as it was, what with telephoning to the nurses for directions, and what with studying the recipes on the outside of boxes of cornstarch and
farina and oatmeal and the like that they found in the pantry, they were learning day by day to do a little more.

And then, one blessed day, the dear nurse Morton
walked in and took off her things and stayed. Morton had
been on a long-delayed visit to her old father in Scotland
that winter, but when she saw in the papers the notice of the
calamity that had befallen the house of her old employer,
she packed her trunk and took the first steamer back to
America. Her baby, and her baby's father needed her, and
nothing could keep Morton away after that.

Her coming relieved this situation very materially, for
though she had never been a fancy cook, she knew all about
good old-fashioned Scottish dishes, and from the first hour
took up her station in the kitchen. Immediately comfort
and orderliness began to reign, and Starr and Michael had
time on their hands that was not spent in either eating,
sleeping, working, or exercise.

It was then that they began to read together, for the
library was filled with all the treasures of literature, to many
of which Michael had never had access save through the
public libraries, which of course was not as satisfactory as
having books at hand when one had a bit of leisure in a
busy life. Starr had been reading more than ever before this
winter while with her aunt, and entered into the pleasant
companionship of a book together with zest.

Then there were hours when Starr played softly, and sang, for the piano was far from the sick room and could not be heard upstairs. Indeed, if it had not been for the anxious struggle going on upstairs, these two would have been having a beautiful time.

For all unknowing to themselves they were growing daily into a dear delight in the mere presence of one another. Even Michael, who had long ago laid down the lines between which he must walk through life, and never expected to be more to Starr than a friend and protector, did not realize whither this intimate companionship was tending. When he thought of it at all he thought that it was a precious solace for his years of loneliness; a time that must be enjoyed to the full, and treasured in memory for the days of barrenness that must surely follow.

Upstairs the fight went on day after day, until at last one morning the doctor told them that it had been won, that the patient, though very much enfeebled, would live and slowly get back his strength.

That was a happy morning. The two caught each other's hands and whirled joyously round the dining room when they heard it, and Morton came in with her sleeves rolled up, and her eyes like two blue lakes all blurred with raindrops in the sunlight. Her face seemed like a rainbow.

The next morning the doctor looked the two over before he went upstairs and set a limit to their quarantine. If they kept on doing well they would be reasonably safe from taking the disease. It would be a miracle, almost, if neither of them took it, but it began to look as if they were going to be all right.

Now these two had been so absorbed in one another that they had thought very little about the danger of their taking the disease themselves. If either had been alone in the house with nothing to do but brood it would have probably been the sole topic of thought, but their healthy busy hours had helped the good work on, and so they were coming safely out from under the danger.

It was one bright morning when they were waiting for the doctor to come that Michael was glancing over the morning paper, and Starr trying a new song she had sent for that had just come in the mail the evening before. She wanted to be able to play it for Michael to sing.

Suddenly Michael gave a little exclamation of dismay, and Starr, turning on the piano stool, saw that his face was white and he was staring out the window with a drawn, sad look about his mouth and eyes.

"What is it?" she asked in quick, eager tones of sympathy, and Michael turning to look at her vivid beauty, his heart thrilling with the sound of her voice, suddenly felt the wide gulf that had always been between them, for what he had read in the paper had shaken him from his happy dream and brought him back to a sudden realization of what he was.

The item in the paper that had brought about the rude awakening was an account of how Buck had broken jail and escaped. Michael's great heart was filled with trouble about Buck, and instantly he rememered that he belonged to the same class with Buck and not at all in the charmed circle where Starr moved.

He looked at the girl with grave, tender eyes, that yet seemed to be less intimate than they had been all these weeks. Her sensitive nature felt the difference at once.

He let her read the little item.

Starr's face softened with ready sympathy, and a mingling of indignation. "He was one of those people in your tenements you have been trying to help?" she questioned, trying to understand his look. "He ought to have been ashamed to get into jail after you had been helping him. Wasn't he a sort of a worthless fellow?"

"No," said Michael in quick defense, "he never had a chance. And he was not just one of those people, he was *the* one. He was the boy who took care of me when I was a little fellow, and who shared everything he had, hard crust or warm cellar door, with me. I think he loved me—"

There was something in Michael's face and voice that warned Starr these were sacred precincts, where she must tread lightly if she did not wish to desecrate.

"Tell me about him," she breathed softly.

So Michael, his eyes tender, his voice gentle, because she had cared to know, told her eloquently of Buck, till

when he had finished her eyes were wet with tears, and she
looked so sweet that he had to turn his own eyes away to
keep from taking the lovely vision into his arms and kissing
her. It was a strange wild impulse he had to do this, and it
frightened him. Suppose someday he should forget himself, and let her see how he had dared to love her? That
must never be. He must put a watch upon himself. This
sweet friendship she had vouchsafed him must never be
broken by word, look, or action of his.

And from that morning there came upon his manner a
change, subtle, intangible—but a change.

They read and talked together, and Michael opened
his heart to her as he had not yet done, about his work in
the alley, his farm colony, and his hopes for his people;
Starr listened and entered eagerly into his plans, yet felt the
change that had come upon him, and her troubled spirit
knew not what it was.

Chapter 27

All this while Michael had been in daily communication
with Sam, as well as with Will French, who with Hester's
help had kept the rooms in the alley going, though they
reported that the head had been sorely missed.

Sam had reported daily progress with the house and
about two weeks before Michael's release from quarantine
announced that everything was done, even to the papering
of the walls and oiling of the floors.

A fire had been burning in the furnace and fireplaces
for several weeks, so the plaster was thoroughly dry, and it
was Michael's plan that Starr and her father were to go
straight down to the farm as soon as they were free to leave
the house.

To this end Hester and Will had been given daily com-
missions to purchase this and that needful article of fur-

niture, until now at last Michael felt that the house would be habitable for Starr and her precious invalid.

During the entire winter Michael had pleased himself in purchasing rugs here and there, and charming, fitting, furniture for the house he was building. A great many things—the important things—had already been selected, and Michael knew he could trust Hester's taste for the rest. For some reason he had never said much to Starr about either Hester or Will, perhaps because they had always seemed to him to belong to one another, and thus were somewhat set apart from his own life.

But one morning, Starr, coming into the library where Michael was telephoning Hester about some last purchases she was making, overheard these words: "All right, Hester, you'll know best of course, but I think you better make it a dozen instead of a half. It's better to have too many than too few, and we might have company, you know."

Now, of course, Starr couldn't possibly be supposed to know that it was a question of dishes that was being discussed so intimately. In fact, she did not stop to think what they were talking about; she only knew that he had called this other girl "Hester"; and she suddenly became aware that during all these weeks of pleasant intercourse, although she had addressed him as Michael, he had carefully avoided using any name at all for her, except on one or two occasions, substituting pronouns wherever possible. She had not noticed this before, but when she heard that "Hester" in his pleasant tones, her heart brought the fact before her at once for invoice. Who was this girl Hester? And why was she Hestered so carelessly as though he had a right? Could it be possible that Michael was engaged to her? Why had she never thought of it before? Of course it would be perfectly natural. This other girl had been down in his dear alley, working shoulder to shoulder with him all these years, and it was a matter of course that he must love her. Starr's bright morning that but a moment before had been filled with so much sunshine seemed suddenly to cloud over with a blackness that blotted out all the joy, and though she strove to hide it even from herself, her spirit was heavy with something she did not understand.

That evening Michael came into the library unexpectedly. He had been out in the kitchen helping Morton to open a box that was stuck. He found the room entirely dark, and thought he heard a soft sound like sobbing in one corner of the room.

"Starr!" he said. "Starr, is that you?" nor knew that he had called her by her name, though she knew it very well indeed. She kept quite still for an instant, and then she rose from the little crumpled heap in the corner of the leather couch where she had dropped for a minute in the dark to cry out the strange ache of her heart when she thought Michael was safely in the kitchen for a while.

"Why, yes, Michael!" she said, and her voice sounded choky, though she was struggling to make it natural.

Michael stepped to the doorway and turned on the hall lights so that he could dimly see her little figure standing in the shadow. Then he came over toward her, his whole heart yearning over her, but a mighty control set upon himself.

"What is the matter—dear?" He breathed the last word almost under his breath. He actually did not realize that he had spoken it aloud. It seemed to envelope her with a deep tenderness. It broke her partial self-control entirely and she sobbed again for a minute before she could speak.

Oh, if he but dared to take that dear form into his arms and comfort her! If he but dared! But he had no right!

Michael stood still and struggled with his heart, standing quite near her, yet not touching her.

"Oh, my dear!" he breathed to himself, in an agony of love and self-restraint. But she did not hear the breath. She was engaged in a struggle of her own, and she seemed to remember that Hester girl, and know her duty. She must not let him see how she felt, not for anything in the world. He was kind and tender. He had always been. He had denied himself and come here to stay with them in their need because of his gratitude toward her father for all he had done for him, and he had breathed that "dear" as he would have done to any little child of the tenement whom he found in trouble. Oh, she understood, even while she let the word comfort her lonely heart. Why, oh why had she been left to trifle with a handsome scoundrel? Why hadn't she been worthy to have won the love of a great man like this one?

These thoughts rushed through her brain so rapidly that they were not formulated at all. Not until hours afterward did she know they had been thought, but afterwards she sorted them out and put them in array before her troubled heart.

A minute she struggled with her tears, and then in a sweet little voice, like a tired, naughty child she broke out:

"Oh, Michael, you've been so good to me—to us, I mean—staying here all these weeks and not showing a bit of impatience when you had all the great work in the world to do—and I've just been thinking how perfectly horrid I was to you last winter—the things I said and wrote to you—and how I treated you when you were trying to save me from an awful fate! I'm so ashamed, and so thankful! It all came over me tonight what I owed you, and I can't ever thank you. Can you forgive me for the horrid way I acted, and for passing you on the street that Sunday without speaking to you—I'm so ashamed! Will you forgive me?"

She put out her little hands with a pathetic motion toward him in the half light of the room, and he took them in both his great warm ones and held them in his firm grasp, his whole frame thrilling with her sweet touch. "Forgive you, little Starr!" he breathed—"I never blamed you—" And there is no telling what might not have happened if the doctor had not just then unexpectedly arrived to perfect the arrangements for their going to the farm.

When Michael returned from letting the doctor out, Starr had fled upstairs to her room; when they met the next morning it was with the bustle of preparation upon them; and each cast shy smiling glances toward the other. Starr knew that she was forgiven, but she also knew that there was a wall reared between them that had not been there before, and her heart ached with the knowledge. Nevertheless, it was a happy morning, and one could not be absolutely miserable in the company of Michael, with a father who was recovering rapidly, and the prospects of seeing him and going with him into the beautiful out-of-doors within a few hours.

Michael went about the work of preparing to go with a look of solemn joy. Solemn because he felt that the wonderful companionship he had had alone with Starr was so soon to end. Joyful because he could be with her still and know she had passed through the danger of the terrible disease and come safely out of the shadow with her beauty as vivid as ever. Besides, he might always serve her, and they were friends now, not enemies—that was a great deal!

The little world of Old Orchard stood on tiptoe that lovely spring morning when the party came down. The winding road that led to the cottage was arched all over with bursting bloom, for the apple trees had done their best at decorating for the occasion and made a wondrous canopy of pink and white for Starr to see as she passed under.

Not a soul was in sight as they drove up to the cottage save Sam, standing respectfully to receive them in front of the piazza, and Lizzie, vanishing around the corner of the cottage with her pretty boy toddling after—for Lizzie had come down to be a waitress at Rose Cottage for the summer—but every soul on the farm was watching at a safe distance. For Sam, without breathing a word, had managed to convey to them all the knowledge that those who were coming as their guests were beloved of Michael, their angel-hearted man. As though it had been a great ceremony they stood in silent, adoring groups behind a row of thick hedges and watched them arrive, each one glorying in the beauty of her whom in their hearts they called "the boss's girl."

The room stood wide and inviting to receive them. There was a fire of logs on the great hearth, and a deep leather chair up before it, with a smaller rocker at one side, and a sumptuous leather couch for the invalid just to the side of the fireplace, where the light of the flames would not strike the eyes, yet the warmth would reach him. Soft greens and browns were blended in the silk pillows that were piled on the couch and on the seats that appeared here and there about the walls as if they grew by nature. The bookcase was filled with Michael's favorites, Will French had seen to this, and a few were scattered on the big table where a green shaded lamp of unique design, a freshly cut magazine, and a chair drawn at just the right angle suggested a pleasant hour in the evening. There were two or three pictures—these Michael had selected at intervals as he learned to know more about art from his study at the exhibitions.

"Oh!" breathed Starr. "How lovely! It is a real home!" and the thought struck her that it would probably be Michael's and Hester's someday. However, she would not let shadows come spoiling her good time now, for it *was* her good time and she had a right to it, and she too was happy in the thought that she and Michael were friends, the kind of friends that can never be enemies again.

The invalid sank into the the cushions of the couch with a pleased light in his eyes and said: "Son, this is all right. I'm glad you bought the farm," and Michael turned with a look of love to the man who had been the only father he had ever known. It was good, *good* to be reconciled with him, and to know that he was on the road to health once more.

The doctor who had come down with them looked about with satisfaction.

"I don't see but you are fixed," he said to Endicott. "I wouldn't mind being in your shoes myself. Wish I could stay and help you enjoy yourself. If I had a pair of children like those I'd give up work and come buy a farm alongside, and settle down for life."

The days at the farm passed in a sort of charmed existence for Starr and her father. Everything they needed seemed to come as if by magic. Every wish of Starr's was anticipated, and she was waited upon devotedly by Lizzie, who never by so much as a look tried to win recognition. Starr, however, always keen in her remembrances, knew and appreciated this.

After the first two days Michael was back and forth in the city. His business, which had been steadily growing before his temporary retirement from the world, had piled up and was awaiting his attention. His work in the alley called loudly for him every night, yet he managed to come down to the farm often and spent all his Sundays there.

It was one Saturday evening about three weeks after their arrival at the farm, when they were all seated cozily in the living room of the cottage, the invalid resting on the couch in the shadow, Starr seated close beside him, the fire-

light glowing on her face, her hand in her father's; and
Michael by the table with a fresh magazine which he was
about to read to them, that a knock came at the door.

Opening the door, Michael found Sam standing on the
piazza, and another dark form huddled behind him.

"Come out here, can't yer, Buck's here!" whispered
Sam.

"Buck!" Michael spoke the word with a joyful ring that
thrilled Starr's heart with sympathy as she sat listening, her
ears alert with interest.

"I'm so glad! So glad!" said Michael's voice again,
vibrant with real welcome. "Come in, Buck, I've a friend in
here who knows all about you. No, don't be afraid. You're
perfectly safe. What? Through the windows? Well, we'll
turn the light out and sit in the firelight. You can go over in
that corner by the fireplace. No one will see you. The
shades are down."

Michael's voice was low, and he stood within the doorway, but Starr, because she understood the need, heard
every word.

There was dissent in a low whisper outside, and then
Sam's voice growled, "Go on in, Buck, ef he says so," and
Buck reluctantly entered, followed by Sam.

Buck was respectably dressed in an old suit of Sam's,
with his hands and face carefully washed and his hair
combed. Sam had imbibed ideas and was not slow to impart
them. But Buck stood dark and frowning against the closed
door, his hunted eyes like black coals in a setting of snow,
went furtively around the room in restless vigilance. His
body wore the habitual air of crouching alertness. He
started slightly when anyone moved or spoke to him.

Michael went quickly over to the table and turned
down the lamp.

"You won't mind sitting in the firelight, will you?" he
said to Starr in a low tone, and her eyes told him that she
understood.

"Come over here, Buck," said Michael motioning toward the sheltered corner of the other side of the fireplace
from where Starr was sitting. "This is one of my friends,
Miss Endicott, Mr. Endicott. Will you excuse us if we sit

here and talk a few minutes? Miss Endicott, you remember me telling you of Buck?"

Starr with sudden inspiration born of the moment, got up and went over to where the dark-browned Buck stood frowning and embarrassed in the chimney corner and put out her little roseleaf of a hand to him. Buck looked at it in dismay and did not stir.

"Why don't yer shake?" whispered Sam.

Then with a grunt of astonishment Buck put out his rough hand and underwent the unique experience of holding a lady's hand in his. The hunted eyes looked up startled to Starr's and like a flash he saw a thought. It was as if her eyes knew Browning's poem and could express his thought to Buck in language he could understand:

"All I could never be,
All men ignored in me,
This, I was worth to God, whose wheel the
pitcher shaped."

Somehow, Starr, with her smile and her eyes, and her gentle manner, unknowingly conveyed that thought to Buck! Poor, neglected, sinful Buck! And Michael, looking on, knew what she had done, and blessed her in his heart.

Buck sat down in the chimney corner, half in shadow with the lights from the great log flaring over his face. The shades were all drawn down, the doors were closed. He was surrounded by friendly faces. For a few minutes the hunted eyes ceased their roving round the room, and rested on Starr's sweet face as she sat quietly, holding her father's hand. It was a sight such as poor Buck's eyes had never rested upon in the whole of his checkered existence, and for the moment he let the sweet wonder of it filter into his dark, scarred soul, with blessed healing. Then he looked from Starr to Michael's fine face nearby, tender with the joy of Buck's coming, anxious with what might be the outcome, and for a moment the heavy lines in forehead and brow that Buck had worn since babyhood softened with a tender look. Perhaps 'tis given once to even the dullest soul to see, no matter how low fallen, just what he might have been.

They had been sitting thus for about fifteen minutes, quietly talking. Michael intended to take Buck upstairs soon and question him, but first he wanted time to think what he must do. Then suddenly a loud knock startled them all, and as Michael rose to go to the door there followed him the resounding clatter of the tongs falling on the hearth.

A voice with a knife edge to it cut through the room and made them all shiver.

"Good evening, Mr. Endicott!" it said. "I'm sorry to trouble you, but I've come on a most unpleasant errand. We're after an escaped criminal, and he was seen to enter your door a few minutes ago. Of course I know your goodness of heart. You take 'em all in, but this one is a jailbird! You'll excuse me if I take him off your hands. I'll try to do it as quietly and neatly as possible."

The big, blustery voice ceased and Michael, looking at the sinister gleam of dull metal in the hands of the men who accompanied the county sheriff, knew that the crisis was upon him. The man, impatient, was already pushing past him into the room. It was of no sort of use to resist. He flung the door wide and turned with the saddest look Starr thought she ever had seen on the face of a man.

"I know," he said, and his voice was filled with sorrow, "I know—but—he was one whom I loved!"

"Wasted love! Mr. Endicott. Wasted love. Not one of 'em worth it!" blustered the big man walking in.

Then Michael turned and faced the group around the fireplace and looking from one to another turned white with amazement, for Buck was not among them!

Starr sat beside her father in just the same attitude she had held throughout the last fifteen minutes, his hand in hers, her face turned, startled, toward the door, and something inscrutable in her eyes. Sam stood close beside the fireplace, the tongs which he had just picked up in his hands, and the look of sullen rage upon his face. Nowhere in the whole wide room was there a sign of Buck, and there seemed no spot where he could hide. The door into the dining room was on the opposite wall, and behind it the cheerful clatter of the clearing off of the table could be plainly heard. If Buck had escaped that way there would have been an outcry from Morton or the maid. Every window had its shade closely drawn.

The sheriff looked suspiciously at Michael whose blank face plainly showed he had no part in making way with the outlaw. The man behind him looked sharply round and finished with a curious gaze at Starr. Starr, rightly interpreting the scene, rose to the occasion.

"Would they like to look behind this couch?" she said moving quickly to the other side of the fireplace over toward the window, with a warning glance toward Sam.

Then while the men began a fruitless search around the room, looking in the chimney closet, and behind the furniture, she took up her stand beside the corner window.

It had been Michael's thoughtfulness that had arranged that all the windows should have springs worked by the pressing of a button like some car windows, so that a touch would send them up at will.

Only Sam saw Starr's hand slide under the curtain a second, and unfasten the catch at the top; then quickly down and touch the button in the windowsill. The window went up without a noise, and in a moment more the curtain was moving out gently puffed by the soft sparing breeze, and Starr had gone back to her father's side. "I cannot understand it," said Michael, "he was here a moment ago!"

The sheriff who had been nosing about the fireplace turned and came over to the window, sliding up the shade with a motion and looking out into the dark orchard.

"H'm! That's where he went, boys," he said. "After him quick! We ought to have had a watch at each window as well as at the back. Thank you, Mr. Endicott! Sorry to have troubled you. Good night!" and the sheriff clattered after his men.

Sam quickly pulled down the window, fastening it, and turned a look of almost worshipful understanding on Starr.

"Isn't that fire getting pretty hot for such a warm night?" said Starr pushing back the hair from her forehead and bright cheeks. "Sam, suppose you get a little water and pour over the log. I think we will not need anymore fire tonight anyway."

And Sam, quickly hastened to obey, his mouth stretching in a broad grin as he went out the door.

"She'd make a peach of a burglar," he remarked to himself as he filled a bucket with water and hurried back with it to the fire.

Michael, in his strait betwixt law and love, was deeply troubled and had followed the men out into the dark orchard.

"Daddy, I think you'd better get up to your room. This excitement has been too much for you," said Starr decidedly.

But Mr. Endicott demurred. He had been interested in the little drama that had been enacted before him, and he wanted to sit up and see the end of it. He was inclined to blame Michael for bringing such a fellow into Starr's presence.

But Starr laughingly bundled him off to bed and sat for an hour reading to him, her heart all the time in a flutter to know how things came out, wondering if Sam surely understood, and put out the fire, and if it would be safe for her to give him any broader hint.

At midnight, Michael lay broad awake with troubled spirit, wondering over and over if there was anything he might have done for Buck if he had only done it in time—anything that would have been right to do.

Softly, cautiously a man stole out of the darkness of the orchard until he came and stood close to the old chimney, and then, softly stealing on the midnight summer air there came a peculiar sibilant sound, clear, piercing, yet blending with the night, and leaving no trace behind of its origin. One couldn't tell from whence it came. But Michael, keeping vigil, heard, and rose upon his elbow, alert, listening. Was that Buck calling him? It came again, softer this time, but distinct. Michael sprang from his bed and began hastily throwing on his garments. That call should never go unanswered!

Stealthily, in the light of the low, late moon, a dark figure stole forth from the old chimney top, climbed down on the ladder that had been silently tilted against it, helped to lay the ladder back innocently in the deep grass again, and joining the figure on the ground crept away toward the river where waited a boat.

Buck lay down in the bottom of the boat, covered with a

piece of sacking, and Sam took up the oars, when a long, sibilant whistle like a night bird floated keenly through the air. Buck started up and turned suspicious eyes on Sam:

"What's that?"

"It's Mikky, I reckon," said Sam softly, reverently. "He couldn't sleep. He's huntin' yer!"

Buck lay down with a sound that was almost a moan and the boat took up its silent glide toward safety.

"It's fierce ter leave him this 'a'way!" muttered Buck. "Youse tell him, won't yer, an' her—she's a ly-dy, she is. She's all white! Tell her Buck'll do ez much fer her someday ef he ever gits the chanct."

"In doin' fer her you'd be doin' fer him, I spekullate," said Sam after a long pause.

"So?" said Buck.

"So," answered Sam. And that was the way Sam told Buck of the identity of Starr.

Now Starr, from her darkened window beside the great chimney, had watched the whole thing. She waited until she saw Michael come slowly, sadly back from his fruitless search through the mist before the dawning, alone, with bowed head, and her heart ached for the problem that was filling him with sorrow.

Chapter 28

Starr was coming up to the city for a little shopping on the early morning train with Michael. The summer was almost upon her and she had not prepared her apparel. Besides, she was going away in a few days to be bridesmaid at the wedding of an old school friend who lived away out West, and secretly she told herself she wanted the pleasure of this little trip to town with Michael.

She was treasuring every one of these beautiful days filled with precious experiences, like jewels to be strung on memory's chain, with a vague unrest lest some close-drawing future was to snatch them from her forever. She wished with all her heart that she had given a decided refusal to her friend's pleading, but the friend had put off the wedding on her account to wait until she could leave her father, and her father had joined his insistence that she should go away and have the rest and change after the ordeal of the winter. So Starr seemed to have to go, much as she would rather have remained. She had made a secret vow to herself that she would return at once after the wedding in spite of all urgings to remain with the family who had invited her to stay all summer with them. Starr had a feeling that the days of her companionship with Michael might be short. She must make the most of them. It might never be the same again after her going away. She was not sure even that her father would consent to remain all summer at the farm as Michael urged.

And on this lovely morning she was very happy at the thought of going with Michael. The sea seemed sparkling with a thousand gems as the train swept along its shore, and Michael told her of his first coming down to see the farm, called her attention to the flowers along the way, and she assured him Old Orchard was far prettier than any of them, now that the roses were all beginning to bud. It would soon be Rose Cottage indeed!

Then the talk fell on Buck and his brief passing.

"I wonder where he can be and what he is doing," sighed Michael. "If he only could have stayed long enough for me to have a talk with him. I believe I could have persuaded him to a better way. It is the greatest mystery in the world how he got away with those men watching the house. I cannot understand it."

Starr, her cheeks rosy, her eyes shining mischievously, looked up at him.

"Haven't you the least suspicion where he was hiding?" she asked.

Michael looked down at her with a sudden start, and smiled into her lovely eyes.

"Why, no. Have you?" he said, and could not keep the worship from his gaze.

"Of course. I knew all the time. Do you think it was

very dreadful for me not to tell? I couldn't bear to have him caught that way before you'd had a chance to help him, and when he used to be so good to you as a little boy; besides, I saw his face, that terrible, hunted look; there wasn't anything really wrong in my opening that window and throwing them off the track, was there?"

"Did you open the window?"

Starr nodded saucily. "Yes, and Sam saw me do it. Sam knew all about it. Buck went up the chimney right through that hot fire. Didn't you hear the tongs fall down? He went like a flash before you opened the door, and one foot was still in sight when that sheriff came in. I was so afraid he'd see it. Was it wrong?"

"I suppose it was," he said sadly. "The law must be maintained. It can't be set aside for one fellow who has touched one's heart by some childhood's action. But right or wrong I can't help being glad that you cared to do something for poor Buck."

"I think I did it mostly for—you," she said softly, her eyes still down.

For answer, Michael reached out his hand and took her little gloved one that lay in her lap in a close pressure for just an instant. Then, as if a mighty power were forcing him, he laid it gently down again and drew his hand away.

Starr felt the pressure of that strong hand and the message that it gave through long days afterward, and more than once it gave her strength and courage and good cheer. Come what might, she had a friend—a friend strong and true as an angel.

The spoke no more till the train swept into the station and they had hurried through the crowd and were standing on the front of the ferryboat, with the water sparkling before their onward gliding and the whole, great, wicked, stirring city spread before their gaze, the light from the cross on Trinity Church steeple flinging its glory in their faces.

"Look!" said Michael pointing. "Do you remember the poem we were reading the other night: Wordsworth's 'Upon Westminster Bridge.' Doesn't it fit this scene perfectly? I've often thought of it when I was coming across in the mornings. To look over there at the beauty one would never dream of all the horror and wickedness and suffering that lies within those streets. It is beautiful now. Listen! Do you remember it?"

> "'Earth has not anything to show more fair:
>   Dull would he be of soul who could pass by
>   A sight so touching in its majesty:
> This City now doth like a garment wear
> The beauty of the morning; silent, bare,
>   Ships, towers, domes, theatres, and temples lie
>   Open unto the fields, and to the sky;
> All bright and glittering in the smokeless air.
> Never did sun more beautifully steep
>   In his first splendour valley, rock, or hill;
> Ne'er saw I, never felt, a calm so deep!
>   The river glideth at its own sweet will:
> Dear God! the very houses seem asleep;
>   And all that mighty heart is lying still!'"

Starr looked long at the picture before her, and then at the face of her companion speaking the beautiful lines word by word as one draws in the outlines of a well-loved picture.

Michael's hat was off and the beauty of the morning lay in sunlight on his hair and cheek and brow. Her heart swelled within her as she looked and great tears filled her eyes. She dared not look longer lest she show her deep emotion. The look of him, the words he spoke, and the whole wonderful scene would linger in her memory as long as life should last.

Two days later Starr started west, and life seemed empty for Michael. She was gone from him, but still she would come back. Or, would she come back after all? How long could he hope to keep her if she did? Sad foreboding filled him and he went about his work with set, strained nerves, for now he knew that right or wrong she was heart of his heart, part of his consciousness. He loved her better than himself, and he saw no hope for himself at all in trying to forget. Yet, never, never, would he ask her to share the dishonor of his heritage.

The day before Starr was expected to come back to Old

Orchard Michael took up the morning paper and with rising horror read:

BANDIT WOUNDED AS FOUR HOLD UP TRAIN

Express Messenger Protects Cash During Desperate Revolver Duel in Car.

Fort Smith, Ark.—Four bandits bungled the holdup of a Kansas City passenger train, between Hatfield and Mena, Ark., early today. One was probably fatally wounded and captured and the others escaped after a battle with the express messenger in which the messenger exhausted his ammunition and was badly beaten.

When the other robbers escaped the wounded bandit eluded the conductor, and made his way into the sleeper, where he climbed into an empty berth. But he was soon traced by the drops of blood from his wound. The conductor and a brakeman hauled him out and battled with him in the aisle amid the screams of passengers.

The bandit aimed his revolver at the conductor and fired, but a sudden unsteady turn of his wrist sent the bullet into himself instead of the conductor. The wounded bandit received the bullet in his left breast near the heart and will probably die. The express messenger is in the hospital at Mena and may recover.

Had the bullet of the bandit gone as intended it would more than likely have wounded one or two women passengers, who at the sound of trouble had jumped from their berths into the aisle and were directly in the path of the bullet.

There is some likelihood that the captured bandit may prove to be the escaped convict, named Buck, who was serving a long sentence in the state penitentiary, and for whom the police have been searching in vain for the last three months.

Michael was white and trembling when he had finished reading this account. And was this then the end of Buck? Must he die a death like that? Disgrace and sin and death, and no chance to make good? Michael groaned aloud and bowed his head upon the table before him, his heart too heavy even to try to think it out.

That evening a telegram reached him from Arkansas. "A man named Buck is dying here, and calls incessantly for you. If you wish to see him alive come at once."

Michael took the midnight train. Starr had telegraphed her father she would reach Old Orchard in the morning. It was hard to have to go when she was just returning. Michael wondered if it would always be so now.

Buck roused at Michael's coming and smiled feebly.

"Mikky! I knowed you'd come!" he answered feebly. "I'm done for, pardner. I ain't long fer here, but I couldn't go 'thout you knowin'. I'd meant to git jes' this one haul an' git away to some other country where it was safe, 'nen I was goin' to try'n keep straight like you would want. I would a'got trough all right, but I seen her—the pretty lady—your girl—standing in the aisle right ahin' the c'ndct'r, jes' es I wuz pullin' the trigger. I knowed her right off, 'ith her eyes shinin' like two stars; an' I couldn't run no resks. I ain't never bin no bungler at my trade, but I had to bungle this time 'cause I couldn't shoot your girl! So I turned it jes' in time an' took it mese'f. She seen how 'twas 'ith me that time at your house, an' she he'ped me git away. I sent her word I'd do the same for her someday, bless her—an' now—you tell her we're square! I done the bunglin' fer her sake, but I done it fer you too, pard—little pard—Mikky!"

"Oh, Buck!" Michael knelt beside the poor bed and buried his face in the coverlet. "Oh, Buck! If you'd only had my chance!" he moaned.

"Never you mind, Mikky! I ain't squealin'. I knows how to take my dose. An' mebbe, they'll be some kind of a collidge whar I'm goin', at I kin get a try at yet—don't you fret, little pard—ef I git my chancet I'll take it fer your sake!"

The life breath seemed to be spent with the effort and Buck sank slowly into unconsciousness and so passed out of a life that had been all against him.

Michael after doing all the last little things that were permitted him, sadly took his way home again.

He reached the city in the morning and spent several hours putting to rights his business affairs, but by noon he found himself so unutterably weary that he took the two o'clock train down to the farm. Sam met him at the station. Sam somehow seemed to have an intuition when to meet him, and the two gripped hands and walked home together across the salt grass, Michael telling in low, halting tones all that Buck had said. Sam kept his face turned the other way, but once Michael got a view of it and he was sure there were tears on his cheeks. To think of Sam having tears for anything!

Arriving at the cottage Sam told him he thought that Mr. Endicott was taking his afternoon nap upstairs, and that Miss Endicott had gone to ride with some kind of a fancy woman in an auto who had called to see her.

Being very weary and yet unwilling to run the risk of waking Mr. Endicott by going upstairs, Michael asked Sam to bolt the dining room door and give orders that he should not be disturbed for an hour; then he lay down on the leather couch in the living room.

The windows were open all around and the sweet breath of the opening roses stole in with the summer breeze, while the drone of bees and the pure notes of the song sparrow lulled him to sleep.

Chapter 29

Michael had slept perhaps an hour when he was roused by the sound of voices, a sharp, hateful one with an unpleasant memory in it, and a sweet, clear one that went to his very soul.

"Sit down here, Aunt Frances. There is no one about. Papa is asleep and Michael has not yet returned from a trip out West. You can talk without fear of being heard."

"Michael, Michael!" sniffed the voice. "Well, that's what I came to talk to you about. I didn't want to say anything out there where the chauffeur could hear; he is altogether too curious and might talk with the servants about it. I wouldn't have it get out for the world. Your mother would have been mortified to death about all this, and I can't see what your father is thinking about. He never did seem to have much sense where you were concerned!"

"Aunt Frances!"

"Well, I can't help it. He doesn't. Now take this matter of your being down here, and the very thought of your calling that fellow Michael—as if he were a cousin or something! Why, it's simply disgusting! I hoped you were going to stay out West until your father was well enough to go away somewhere with you, but now that you have come back I think you ought to leave here at once. People will begin to talk, and I don't like it. Why, the fellow will be presuming on it to be intimate with you—"

Michael was suddenly roused to the fact that he was listening to a conversation not intended for his ears, and yet he had no way of getting out of hearing without passing the door in the front of which the two women were seated. Both the dining-room door and the stairs were on the other side of the room from him and he would have to run the risk of being seen by either or both of them if he attempted to cross to them. The windows were screened by wire nailed over the whole length, so he could not hope to get successfully out of any of them. There was nothing for it but to lie still, and pretend to be asleep if they discovered him afterwards. It was an embarrassing situation but it was none of his choosing.

There was a slight stir outside. Starr had risen and was standing with her back to the doorway.

"Aunt Frances! What do you mean? Michael is our honored and respected friend, our protector—our—host. Think what he did for Papa! Risked his life!"

"Stuff and nonsense! Risked his life. He took the risk for perfectly good reasons. He knew how to worm himself into the family again."

"Aunt Frances! I will not hear you say such dreadful things. Michael is a gentleman, well educated, with the highest ideals and principles. If you knew how self-sacrificing and kind he is!"

"Kind, yes kind!" sniffed the aunt, "and what will you think about it when he asks you to marry him? Will you think he is kind to offer you a share in the inheritance of a nobody—a charity—dependent—a child of the slums? If you persist in your foolishness of staying here you will presently have all New York gossiping about you, and then when you are in disgrace—I suppose you will turn to me to help you out of it."

"Stop!" cried Starr. "I will not listen to another word. What do you mean by disgrace? There could be no disgrace in marrying Michael. The girl who marries him will be the happiest woman in the whole world. He is good and true and unselfish to the heart's core. There isn't the slightest danger of his ever asking me to marry him, Aunt Frances, because I am very sure he loves another girl and is engaged to marry her, and she is a nice girl too. But if it were different, if he were free and asked me to marry him I would feel as proud and glad as if a prince of the highest realm had asked me to share his throne with him. I would rather marry Michael than any man I ever met, and I don't care in the least whether he is a child of the slums or a child of a king. I know what he is, and he is a prince among men."

"Oh, really! Has it come to this? Then you are in love with him already and my warning comes too late, does it? Answer me! Do you fancy yourself in love with him."

"Aunt Frances, you have no right to ask me that question," said Starr steadily, her cheeks very red and her eyes very bright.

Michael was sitting bolt upright on the couch now, utterly forgetful of the dishonor of eavesdropping, fairly holding his breath to listen and straining his ears that he might lose no slightest word. He was devouring the dear, straight, little form in the doorway with his eyes, and her every word fell on his tired heart like raindrops in a thirsty land, making the flowers of hope spring forth and burst into lovely bloom.

"Well, I do ask it!" snapped the aunt hatefully. "Come, answer me, do you love him?"

"That, Aunt Frances, I shall never answer to anybody but Michael. I must refuse to hear another word on this subject."

"Oh, very well, good-bye. I'll leave you to your silly fate, but don't expect me to help you out of trouble if you get into it. I've warned you and I wash my hands of you," and the angry woman flounced out to her waiting car, but the girl stood still in the doorway and said with dignity:

"Good afternoon, Aunt Frances. I shall never ask your help in any way."

Starr watched the car out of sight, great tears welling into her eyes and rolling down her cheeks. Michael sat breathless on the couch and tried to think what he ought to do, while his very being was rippling with the joy of the words she had spoken.

Then she turned and saw him, and he stood up and held out his arms.

"Starr, my little Starr! My darling! Did you mean all you said? Would you really marry me? I've loved you always, Starr, since first I saw you a tiny little child. I've loved your soft baby kisses and those others you gave me later when you were a little girl and I an awkward boy. You never knew how dear they were, nor how I used to go to sleep at night dreaming over and over again those kisses on my face. Oh, Starr! Answer me? Did you mean it all? And could you ever love me? You said you would answer that question to no one else but me. Will you answer it now, darling?"

For answer she came and stood within his arms, her eyes downdrooped, her face all tears and smiles, and he folded her within his strong clasp and stooping, whispered softly:

"Starr, little darling—my life—my love—my—*wife!*"

And then he laid his lips against her and held her close.

Three weeks later when the roses were all aburst of bloom over the porch at Rose Cottage and June was everywhere with her richness and perfection of beauty, Starr and Michael were married on the piazza under an arch of roses, and a favored few of society's cream motored down to Old Orchard to witness the ceremony. In spite of all her disagreeable predictions and ugly threats Aunt Frances was among them, smiling and dominating.

"Yes, so sensible of her not to make a fuss with her wedding just now, when her father is getting his strength back again. Of course she could have come to my house and been married. I begged her to—naturally she shrank from another wedding in connection with the old home you know—but her father seemed to dread coming into town and so I advised her to go ahead and be married here. Isn't it a charming place? So rustic you know, and quite simple and artistic too in its way. Michael had done it all, planned the house and everything, of course with Starr's help. You know it's quite a large estate, belonging to Michael's great-grandfather once, several hundred acres, and he has used part of it for charitable purposes; has a farm school or something for poor slum people, and is really teaching them to be quite decent. I'm sure I hope they'll be duly grateful. See those roses? Aren't they perfectly *dear?*"

It was so she chattered to those in the car with her all the way down to the farm; and to see her going about among the guests and smiling and posing to Michael when he happened to come near her, you would have thought the match all of her making, and never have dreamed that it was only because Michael's great forgiving heart had said: "Oh, forgive her and ask her down. She is your mother's sister, you know, and you'll be glad you did it afterwards. Never mind what she says. She can't help her notions. It was her unfortunate upbringing, and she's as much to be pitied as I for my slum education."

The pretty ceremony under the roses was over, and Starr had gone upstairs to change the simple embroidered muslin for her traveling frock and motor coat, for Michael and Starr were to take their honeymoon in their own new car, a wedding gift from their father, and Endicott himself was to go to his sister's by rail in the company of Will French, to stay during their absence and be picked up by them on their homeward route.

Michael stood among his friends on the piazza giving last directions to French who was to look after his law business also during his absence, and who was eager to tell his friend how he and Hester had planned to be married early in the fall and were to go to housekeeping in a five-roomed flat that might have been a palace from the light in Will's eyes. Hester was talking with Lizzie who had edged near the porch with her pretty boy hiding shyly behind her, but the smile that Hester threw in Will's direction now and then showed she well knew what was his subject of conversation.

All the little colony had been gathered in the orchard

in front of the rose arch, to watch the wedding ceremony, and many of them still lingered there to see the departure of the beloved bride and groom. Aunt Frances leveled her lorgnette at them with all the airs of her departed sister, and exclaimed "Aren't they picturesque? It's quite like the old country to have so many servants and retainers gathered about adoring, now isn't it!" And a young and eager debutante who was a distant cousin of Starr's replied:

"I think it's perfectly peachy, Aunt Frances."

Suddenly in one of Will's eager perorations about the flat and its outlook Michael noticed the shy, eager look of Sam's face as he waited hungrily for notice.

"Excuse me, Will, I must see Sam a minute," said Michael hurring over to where the man stood.

"Say, Mikky," said Sam shyly, grasping Michael's hand convulsively, "me an' Lizzie sort o' made it up as how we'd get tied, an' we thought we'd do it now whiles everybody's at it, an' things is all fixed. Lizzie she wanted me to ask you ef you 'sposed *she'd* mind, ef we'uns stood thur on the verandy whur yous did, arter you was gone?" Sam looked at him anxiously as though he had asked the half of Michael's kingdom and scarcely expected to get it, but Michael's face was filled with glory as he clasped the small hard hand on his comrade and gripped it with his mighty hearty grip.

"Mind! She'd be delighted, Sam! Go ahead. I'm sorry we didn't know it before. We'd have liked to give you a present, but I'll send you the deed of the little white cottage at the head of the lane, the one that looks toward the river and the sunset, you know. Will you two like to live there?"

Sam's eyes grew large with happiness, and a mist came over them as he held tight to the great hand that enclosed his own, and choked and tried to answer.

Amid a shower of roses and cheers Michael and Starr rode into the sweet June afternoon, alone together at last. And when they had gone beyond the little town, and were on a stretch of quiet woodsy road, Michael stopped the car and took his bride into his arms.

"Dear," he said as he tenderly kissed her, "I've just been realizing what might have happened if Buck hadn't seen you in time and taken the shot himself that I might not have you, my life, my dear, precious wife!"

Then Starr looked up with her eyes all dewy with tears and said, "Michael, we must try to save a lot of others for his sake." And Michael smiled and pressed his lips to hers again, with deep, sweet understanding.

Then, when they were riding along again Michael told her of what Sam had asked, and how another wedding was to follow theirs.

"Oh, Michael!" said Starr, all eagerness at once. "Why didn't you tell me sooner! I would have liked to stay and see them married. Couldn't we turn around now and get there in time if you put on high speed?"

"We'll try," said Michael reversing the car, and in an instant more it was shooting back to Old Orchard, arriving on the scene just as Sam and Lizzie were shyly taking their place, hand in hand, under the roses, in as near imitation of Michael and Starr as their unaccustomedness could compass.

It was Jim who discovered the car coming up the orchard lane.

"For de lub o' Mike!" he exclaimed aloud. "Ef here don't come Mikky hisse'f, and *her!* Hold up dar, mister preacher. Don't tie de knot till dey gits here!"

And a cheer arose loud and long and echoed through the trees and over the river to the sea. Three cheers for the love of Michael!

Sam and Lizzie bloomed forth with smiles, and the ceremony went forward with alacrity now that the real audience was present.

An hour later, having done their part to make the wedding festivities as joyous as their own had been, Michael and Starr started out again into the waning day, a light on their faces and joy in their hearts.

Starr, her heart very full, laid her hand upon Michael's and said with shining eyes:

"Michael, do you know, I found a name for you. Listen: 'And at that time shall Michael stand up, the great prince which standeth for the children of thy people: and at that time thy people shall be delivered, every one that shall be found written in the book.' Michael, you are *my prince!*"

And Michael as he stooped and kissed her, murmured, "My Starr."

Novels of Enduring Romance and Inspiration by

GRACE LIVINGSTON HILL